ALEXANDRA RIPLEY

THE TIME RETURNS

AVON
PUBLISHERS OF BARD, CAMELOT, DISCUS AND FLARE BOOKS

This book is dedicated to
Elizabeth and Merrill
with my love
Attenti alle meduse

AVON BOOKS
A division of
The Hearst Corporation
1790 Broadway
New York, New York 10019

The Doubleday edition contains the following Library of Congress Cataloging
in Publication Data:

Ripley, Alexandra.
   The time returns.

   1. Florence (Italy)—History—1421–1737—Fiction.   2. Medici, Lorenzo
de', 1449–1492—Fiction.   3. Pazzi family—Fiction.   I. Title.
PS3568.I597T5 1985   813'.54   85-4613

First Avon Printing: January 1987

CONTENTS

NOTE TO THE READER

The names of the characters in this story are Italian, because the people are Italian. Some names may look strange to you at first. In Italian, the sound that is spelled *J* in English is written *GIU*. So Julia becomes Giulia. I'm sure this will cause no trouble after the first few pages. I could not call Giulio and Giuliano anything else. They were real people, and those were their names.

BOOK ONE

Lorenzo
1469–1478

Chapter One

Lorenzo opened his eyes and sat up, fully awake. It was one of his many blessings that he always woke instantly, without the cloudy interval between sleep and alertness that slowed the lives of so many men.

The room was dark, the high windows only slightly paler than the walls. It was not yet day. He had to light a candle before he could see to dress.

He put on parti-colored hose, one leg red, the other white, an ivory silk shirt and a padded doublet made of gold-embroidered red silk brocade. Today was his birthday, and he wanted to look as gala as he felt. He strapped a jeweled dagger to his calf instead of the plain steel one he usually wore and transferred his sword to an incised gold and silver scabbard suspended from a belt studded with rubies. He pulled on a fur-lined brown velvet surcoat before he buckled on his sword and stamped his feet into brown suede boots. It was cold in his bedroom and would be even colder on the stone streets of Florence. It was the first day of January in the year of our Lord fourteen hundred and sixty-nine.

Lorenzo's bedroom was on the ground floor of the Medici palace; it opened onto the columned arcade around the central courtyard. He blew out his candle and stepped quietly through the door into the dim torch-lit center of the great house. The guards inside the immense entry doors were sleeping. Lorenzo smiled. He remembered a time when the household was on alert day and night, when his father narrowly escaped assassination. In those days, it was dangerous to be the chief Medici, the recognized head of the Florentine Republic.

But that was almost five years ago. Now the guards could sleep.

He hurried through the courtyard and the frost-rimmed garden behind it. The small gate in the garden wall opened easily and closed quietly after him.

The false pre-dawn light made the sky seem low and gray; its reflection glowed in the damp mist that clung to the stone street and the stone buildings that lined it. Lorenzo did not need light to guide his steps; he knew the way he was taking as well as he knew the sinews of his own arm. He ran with an athlete's economical, easy movement, making no sound, his footsteps silenced by the soft suede boots and the mist that they disturbed.

He slowed when he came near the city walls and the gate in them. The guards at the Porta San Gallo would not be asleep, and it was against the law to be abroad in the city streets in darkness. He did not want to alarm them.

"Sentinels," he called, "here is Lorenzo de' Medici. I am come to help you open the gates."

His voice was distinctive: sharp and oddly high-pitched for such a strong, muscular young man. The guards called out a friendly greeting. Lorenzo walked into the circle of light around the fire outside the guard-house.

The sleepy eyes of the two guards popped open wide at the glitter of Lorenzo's jewels. "The peacock's tail is spread," said one. "What do you hope to find outside the gate, Lorenzo?" He elbowed the younger guard next to him and rolled his eyes, leering.

Lorenzo smiled. "It may be that you need to wear finery to catch a female eye, Sebastiano," he drawled. "As for me, I impress them most when I shed my clothing." He winked at the younger man.

Sebastiano would not admit defeat. "Well said, but no answer to my question. The world knows that you practice your impressions freely on your farms. Which milkmaid brought you out to meet her?"

The road that led from the Porta San Gallo into the countryside wound through the hills to the region known as the Mugello, an area of rich farms where the Medici family had its beginning and still owned property. Lorenzo often traveled there and frequently enjoyed the favors available from the daughters or wives of the farmers. He was, like the other young men of the time, openly and happily libertine.

He grinned at Sebastiano. "Open the passportal for me, and you can see for yourself. Perhaps she'll have her sister with her."

The guard lifted the iron bar that crossed a small door in the huge wooden gate and opened it slightly. Before Lorenzo edged through, he grabbed a burning branch from the fire for a torch. Outside the gate he leapt up on one of the massive stone buttresses. His movement was lithe and effortless.

Other torches lit the crowd of men and women and children and animals outside the gate. They were farmers and artisans who had come to sell their produce or crafts in Florence's busy marketplace. Some of them had traveled half the night to be first through the gates when they opened at sunrise. Lorenzo was greeted with shouts of "see these fine sheep, Excellency," and ". . . eggs still warm from the hen . . . cheese . . . oil from the fattest olives . . . grappa to warm you this bitter morning . . . a horse worthy of a king . . . prosciutto sweet as the kiss of a virgin . . ."

Lorenzo held his torch higher so that everyone could see his head shaking a refusal. The light cast deep shadows in the hollows of his cheeks and under his sharp jawline; it emphasized his long nose, flattened at the bridge. He was an ugly young man and several of the people nearest him shrank away from his menacing appearance.

But others recognized him and began to shout "Lorenzo, Lorenzo."

He smiled, and the harsh planes of his face shifted, revealing his youth and his contagious joy in living. "Friends," he shouted, "I want you all to be my guests. Today I celebrate my twentieth birthday. At the Medici palace on the Via Larga, there will be wine and food and music the day long. Will you share my coming of age?"

The roar of approval made his smile broaden, his eyes shine. He waved a salute and jumped down. Looking over his shoulder to make sure the guards were watching, he put his arm around the black-shawled shoulders of an old woman who was struggling with a bucking leashed goat. "Let me help you, *donna*," Lorenzo said. He took the rope from her hand. "We'll go together, and you'll take your choice of spaces in the Mercato." He spoke quietly and gently to her, using the peasant dialect in which he had addressed the crowd.

The woman rubbed her bruised hands on her dusty black skirt. "But it is dark yet, Excellency. No one can enter."

"You can enter with me. I am Lorenzo, and it is my birthday. The guard cannot say 'no' to me today. It would ruin my happiness. Come, donna. See, the sun will soon top the mountains. We must hurry if we are to beat the others."

"God bless you, Lorenzo," the old woman said. She gave him a toothless smile.

Lorenzo kissed her weathered cheek, pulled the goat firmly to his side and led them to the portal. "Open wider, Sebastiano," he laughed. "My sweetheart and I want to enter. I'm sorry to disappoint you, but the goat is not a nanny. You'll have to find amusement elsewhere."

As they passed through the door, the crowd outside cheered. "Lorenzo, Lorenzo. *Auguri*, Lorenzo." "Good omens" they wished him.

When Lorenzo left the old woman, she, too, wished him auguri. Lorenzo thanked her seriously. He knew that he would need the help of the stars and the fates in his future, as well as the help of God. His could never be an ordinary life.

The sun had shown itself while Lorenzo was walking the woman and her goat to the marketplace. It was greeted, as it was every day, by the great bell in the tower of the government palace. At that signal, the eleven gates of the city opened and the waiting people streamed in, halted to pay taxes on their produce and to argue about the amount, then rushed through the growing rose light to the Mercato. The bustle of tents and umbrellas being raised and the shouted greetings of the vendors almost drowned out the sounds of the church bells ringing all across the stone city.

Lorenzo was tempted to stay in the market. He loved the activity and the noises and the smells. A man could find anything there. There were stalls selling everything from old clothes to the finest pearls imported from Persia. Already, with dawn still staining the sky, four separate grills were cooking fat birds brought by hunters and succulent pork livers basted with Tuscany's world-famous olive oil. Three women held out coins in gloved hands to buy a spit-roasted pigeon. They were prostitutes, the gloves worn as a badge of their profession, required by law.

"How handsome you look, Lorenzo," said one. "Will you share my breakfast?"

"Thank you, Anna, but I cannot. I have a busy day today. Let me buy you a second bird, though." Lorenzo took a coin from the pouch on his belt and flipped it to the cook's deft receiving hand.

The young whore smiled gratefully. "Perhaps tomorrow," she said, "I could do a favor for you."

"Perhaps. Eat well." Lorenzo kissed his fingers toward her and pushed his way through the thickening crowd. So many people spoke to him that his progress was slow, but he did not mind. He liked to be recognized, to be called by name, to be regarded with affection by the citizens of Florence. He invited them all to his birthday celebration.

He was laughing with a group of University students when the church bells stopped ringing. "I'll be late," Lorenzo said. "Goodbye." He set off at a run. Like all Florentines, he went to mass every day. Today he wanted to attend the earliest mass, to begin his twenty-first year by thanking God for his great good fortune and his happiness.

The sun was well up now. It warmed his shoulders and turned the grayish-brown stone of the streets to gold. The sky was a pure beautiful blue, cloudless. Lorenzo, eager for the future, welcomed the good omen on his birthday.

"Curses on Lorenzo! I refuse to waste the morning by going to his vulgar birthday celebration."

"Francesco, be quiet. Bianca will hear you."

"Don't bellow at me to be quiet. And let Bianca hear anything she pleases. I'll tell her myself. It is no secret that I do not like her ugly brother."

The quarrelers were Guglielmo—called Elmo—and Francesco de' Pazzi. It was no novelty for them to shout angrily at each other. They were brothers; they were very different in temperament; and the family they came from was notorious for its ill temper.

The Pazzi were one of Florence's oldest and noblest families. That nobility had cost them dearly. Almost two centuries earlier, when Florence became a Republic, nobility had been declared virtually a crime. While common tradesmen and workers could vote and hold government office, nobles could have no part in running the State. Most titled families changed their names, declared themselves commoners and reentered the intricate game of political maneuvering. The Pazzi did not. Instead, they nursed their grievances and flaunted their conviction of superiority while they increased the immense fortune they were making in the family banking enterprise.

There were dozens of family-owned banks in Italy. The Pazzi bank was the richest. But the bank owned by the Medici was the biggest and most respected. It was no wonder that Francesco de' Pazzi railed at the prospect of having to honor Lorenzo de' Medici on his birthday. He despised the Medici for their lowly origins; he resented their business success; he was frustrated by the invisible control that the Medici held over the Florentine government. Most of all, he was bitterly aware of everyone's admiration and affection for Lorenzo. Francesco knew that people made fun of his own short stature and exaggerated refinement of dress and manner. And of the half-dozen beautiful young pages who were a pampered addition to the regular staff of servants in his household.

He glowered now at his older brother. Elmo was tall. And still handsome despite his thirty-one self-indulgent years. His flesh was getting soft, Francesco noted with satisfaction. Good. He'd show what he was. Soft. Soft, to allow the Medici to buy his allegiance by making him a petty ambassador for their affairs of state and arranging for the Pazzi to be returned to full citizenship. Soft, to act as older friend and advisor to Lorenzo. Soft, to be deluded into loyalty to the Medici interests when the old fox Cosimo de' Medici arranged a marriage between Elmo and Cosimo's granddaughter Bianca.

Francesco loathed Bianca because she was a Medici and because she was so relentlessly, eternally female. She bustled around the great Pazzi palace, making a constant stir of supervising the cleaning and cooking and complicated arrangements for the care of her brood of children. She always smelled of milk and babies, because she was always pregnant or nursing or both. In nine years of marriage, she had given Elmo seven children, four still living. Francesco admitted that Bianca was doing what was expected of a wife, but her fecundity offended his fastidious nature. Such breeding was, he thought, suitable only to peasants.

Peasants, the Medici. It galled him that commoners should be in control of Florence while nobles like the Pazzi accepted crumbs from their table in the form of appointments to small offices.

"Typical Medici vulgarity," he sneered, "to feed the entire city for their precious son's coming of age. I don't propose to share in their vote-buying bread and circus."

"Well then, don't go," Elmo roared. "You won't be missed."

Preceded by three yapping tiny dogs and an enormous end-of-term belly covered in richly embroidered brocade, Bianca de' Medici de' Pazzi entered the room while her husband's loud voice still echoed from the stone walls.

"Such a racket you two make," she said placidly. It had been years since she had bothered to listen to the arguments between the men in the family. The sun slanted through the tall windows and glowed in the looped golden braids of her hair. Even in her swollen condition, Bianca was a lovely young woman. Her fair, smooth skin and wide blue eyes made her look like a girl, although she was twenty-five.

"Elmo, I am extremely upset," she said. Her calm voice belied her words, but bright streaks of color in her cheeks confirmed them.

Elmo led her to a bench. "Sit here and tell me what's wrong," he said.

"We cannot go to Lorenzo's birthday," Bianca said quietly. Then her lips quivered; tears gushed from her eyes and over her red face.

"Good," Francesco grunted. He grinned and hurried from the room, leaving his brother to calm the storm.

Chapter Two

When the mass was completed, Lorenzo left the church with a group of friends, but he stopped in the piazza outside. "Go on to my house," he said to them. "Tell my mother that I'll be there in ten minutes. There's something I have to do first."

The friends laughed and left him. They were sure that Lorenzo planned to visit his beautiful mistress. "What better way to celebrate the official day one becomes a man?" said one.

Lorenzo guessed what they were laughing about, but he did not correct them. What he was going to do was too private to share with even his closest companions. When they turned a corner and were out of sight, he reentered the church.

It was dim and quiet inside. Lorenzo walked slowly past the beautiful gray stone arches, through the lingering thin odors of incense, candle wax and women's perfumes. His footsteps reverberated in whispers. When he reached the nave, he halted. He spoke, and his voice, too, was a whisper.

"I promised you that I would come to you on this day. Here I am."

In front of Lorenzo's feet, a plain marble rectangle set level into the floor was incised with two words: PATER PATRIAE. "Father of the State." The greatest epitaph ever awarded a citizen of the Florentine Republic.

It marked the burial place of his grandfather, Cosimo de' Medici, Lorenzo's hero and his measure of all that a man could be.

A thin, quiet, unprepossessing man, Cosimo had used

11

his brilliant mind and finely honed understanding of human nature to lead Florence from internecine warfare to the longest period of peace she had ever known. Simultaneously he made the city a great center of learning and art, added to its beauty, multiplied the Medici fortune a thousandfold and established the family as acknowledged untitled rulers of the Republic. He had died less than five years earlier, when Lorenzo was fifteen.

Lorenzo knelt and traced the letters cut into the marble with his finger. "Grandfather," he said softly, "I miss you every hour of the day. All Florence misses you. My father is a good man, but he is no Cosimo.

"As you bade me, I obey him in all things, and I do all in my power to aid him. I have been on two diplomatic missions and represented our family and our Republic with honor. I am betrothed to a woman of the Roman Orsini family, a union that will strengthen our influence in the circle of power near the Pope. I continue my studies and my devotions. I believe that I will be worthy when I become head of the family and the State."

He bent lower so that his lips were near the title of tribute. They were tilted up at the corners in a smile, and his eyes were sparkling. "Grandfather," he murmured, "I will tell you a secret, just as I used to do. You always were the one to whom I could open my heart. I intend to do all that you asked of me. I will guard our Republic and our family. And then, Grandfather, I intend to do more. I will surpass you. I don't know how, by what road I will go. But I will do it."

Lorenzo stood, still smiling. "You told me to come to you on the day I reached manhood, to remember the charge you placed on me, to swear to you that I had not forgotten, that I would live my life to honor you and our family. If you can hear me, then hear my pledge. I have done all that you asked; I will do all that you wished. Then I will do so much more that the name of Medici will never be forgotten in Florence or in the world. I am a man, and I can do the work of twenty men. This I swear to you."

His smile widened.

"And I will have joy of it, Grandfather. This I am that you were not. I am a poet and a musician. My duties will be dressed in song and gaiety. I will make you proud. I will make our people proud. And merry."

He bowed to his grandfather's memory. "Be with God, Cosimo. My love and respect are with you."

Shoulders and head high, Lorenzo turned and left his boyhood behind him.

Lorenzo's friends had not lingered in the street after they left him. The air was biting, in spite of the sunshine. They hastened to the Medici palace, only a block away, and pushed through the crowd that had already gathered outside.

Huge braziers were set on both sides of the streets that bordered the palazzo to warm the people eating the steaming meat pies that pages in Medici livery were distributing from huge trays. In the *loggia*, an open columned room on the corner of the palace, more pages poured wine into wooden cups for all comers. Jugglers entertained the lines of people waiting to enter the loggia, and a group of singers passed through the crowds in the streets, delighting them with the bawdiest of the popular street songs.

Inside the palazzo it was quiet. The yard-thick stone walls kept out the noise. Lorenzo's friends ran up the stairs from the courtyard and greeted Lorenzo's mother in the hall above.

"Madonna Lucrezia," said the one in the lead, "there is already such a horde in the street that I'm afraid there will be no food left for my starving artist's belly." He kissed her on both cheeks. Sandro Botticelli had lived in the Medici palace for ten years, from the time he was fifteen until the previous year when he was successful enough to buy a house and studio nearby. He was like one of the family.

Lucrezia de' Medici smiled at Sandro's complaint. It was a long-standing joke that the handsome blond man ate enough for five and never showed an ounce of fat. She welcomed the other guests and directed them to the *grand salone* where a fire was roaring in the great chimney. They, too, were painters, but not yet as prosperous as Botticelli. Their cloaks were thin, as were their faces. They could use a warming fire and the hot meal that was to come.

Inside the great room everything was ready for the festivities. A number of guests were already there, in groups by the fire or by the tall windows, looking down at the boisterous activity in the street. Lorenzo's younger brother Giuliano acted as substitute host for him, making sure that everyone had a glass of wine and a small hot pie to stave off hunger until the meal was served.

Giuliano was sixteen. Already taller than his brother, he had inherited the family's good looks, a heritage that had bypassed Lorenzo. Sandro Botticelli looked at him with the appraising eye of an artist. It would soon be time, he decided, for another portrait. Giuliano was at the interesting stage of life when shifts in posture and light showed the man about to emerge from the boy. They embraced each other, and Sandro introduced his companions. He left them in Giuliano's capable care and went to talk to the other members of his adopted family. Lorenzo and Giuliano had three sisters. Sandro saw that only Nannina and Maria were in the room. Bianca must be delivering her latest baby, he thought. Nothing else would keep her from being the first arrival at Lorenzo's coming of age.

Bianca's mother was thinking the same thing. Lucrezia whispered to a page during an interval between welcoming guests; he ran to inquire at the Pazzi palace.

More and more guests arrived. Lucrezia was so busy that she did not realize that Lorenzo was home until she felt his hand on her shoulder and saw the pleasure on the face of the man in front of her as he looked beyond her.

"Lorenzo," the man said. "Auguri."

Lucrezia turned her head and smiled at her beloved tardy boy. "Auguri, my son."

The party was going well, Lucrezia saw. She stood just inside the door to the grand salone, ready to step back into the hall to welcome any late-arriving guests.

And to intercept the page she had sent for news of Bianca.

Inside the enormous salone, the noises of talk and laughter nearly drowned out the musicians on the gallery that thrust out from one soaring wall. The fire added its crackling to the festive din. Sun poured in through the tall windows; it made the bright silks and satins of the guests' clothing glow like jewels; it made their jewels glitter and flash. The long linen-draped tables were ready for the meal. So, Lucrezia was sure, were the guests. She nodded to the head steward, and he signaled to the servants waiting in the service hall at the end of the salone. Immediately trios of pages began to circulate among the people in the room. One held a silver bowl beneath a guest's hands while the second poured perfumed water over them from a silver pitcher. The third offered a linen towel to dry them. It was the traditional beginning for a meal and announcement that everyone should take a place at one of the tables.

It was time to call her husband. Two small furrows creased the smooth skin between Lucrezia's brows. He would notice Bianca's absence and ask the reason. Lucrezia made her way to a window to look for the page she had sent to the Pazzi palace. Instead she saw Bianca. The sight made her laugh softly.

Bianca was wrapped in a fur-lined cloak of bright red velvet. It accentuated her bulk. She looked like a brightly painted barge pushing through a river of people. But her size did not slow her down. Her husband, her maid, the nursemaids and the children were well behind her, all but lost in the crowd. Lucrezia hurried to her husband's room. There would be no worries for him now.

Piero de' Medici was a cripple. He suffered from a bone and joint disease that the Florentines called "gout." His father Cosimo had died from it when he was seventy-five, but it had not caused him real pain until the last months of his life. Piero was not so fortunate. His symptoms began in his childhood. By the time he was a young man he had attacks so severe that he could not move without agony. From the time he was forty, he had to be carried everywhere, in a chair on his good days, lying flat in a litter when the pain was too great for him to sit up. He was fifty-two years old now, his head and face still extremely handsome, his body a tormented bundle of grotesquely swollen joints and twisted limbs.

He was lying on his bed when Lucrezia entered his room. She stopped short, afraid that he was too ill to be disturbed. He had wanted so much to take part in his son's coming of age. Tears clogged her throat. Then Piero raised his head and smiled. "I was storing up strength," he said. "Is it time?"

Lucrezia pulled the bell rope to call Piero's manservants. "Perfect timing, my dear."

"Good. I'll join you shortly. Go now." Lucrezia obeyed at once. Her husband hated to have her see the indignity of his dependence on the servants who cared for his body.

Bianca reached the hall at the same moment as her mother. "I'm so sorry to be late," Bianca panted. "Have you begun the party?"

"Not yet. You're just in time. Are you feeling all right?" Her daughter's face was bright red and damp with perspiration.

"Quite all right, Mama. I had to hurry, that's all. We were delayed, and I was frantic. At dawn, mind you, before I was even properly dressed, a completely foreign page appeared at the house announcing that visitors were arriving any minute. I wasn't expecting anybody. I didn't know what to do. I thought I'd just have to wait for them, probably miss the party. You know what 'arriving any minute' means. Sometimes it's all day."

Bianca fanned herself with a corner of her cloak. "It's hot in here." She untied the laces at her throat and dropped the rich fur on a stool. Lucrezia clucked disapproval, picked up the cloak and folded it neatly while Bianca chattered on. "As it turned out, they did arrive in under an hour. An enormous troupe, very gaudy. They had spent the night outside the gates because it was dark when they got there. I saw the guards and all the horses, and my heart sank. It looked like the King of France or something. But it was no one at all impor-

tant. Just a child, the granddaughter of Elmo's uncle
Antonio. You remember, Antonio's daughter married a
Count of Burgundy. Then she died giving birth. This is
her little girl, Ginevra. She's a dreadful child, plain as
mud, and all tricked out in the outlandish clothes the
Burgundians wear. I was ashamed to be seen in the street
with her.''

"You brought her here?"

"Of course. I just shoved her in with my children and
their nurses. They'll have to entertain her. I can't be
expected to be hostess to a child. Besides, my French
is too weak to talk to her. She speaks impossible Italian,
learned it from one of her mother's servants, I suppose
. . . Here they come. And Elmo. And Francesco and
their uncle Jacopo.''

Lucrezia embraced her son-in-law. She offered her
hand to Jacopo, the head of the Pazzi family. He bowed
and kissed it with such dignity that only the breath from
his lips actually touched Lucrezia. "Honored, Madonna
Lucrezia.''

"You honor my son by your presence, Jacopo. Francesco, I am happy to welcome you." Lucrezia's practiced courtesy abandoned her suddenly when Bianca's
older children swarmed around her, tugging at her skirts
and demanding kisses. "Monsters," she said affection-
ately, bending to grant their demands. Then behind them
she saw the visitor from Burgundy; Lucrezia was
stunned.

Ginevra was a small child, pale and frightened-look-
ing. She was dressed in a miniature version of adult
clothing, as all children of the time were. But the Burgundian fashions were so extravagant that Lucrezia
gaped. The little girl's cloak was made of blue brocade,
sewn all over with gold thread and large pearls. It was
lined and bordered with black and white fur in alternat-
ing stripes and it had a long train that had gathered half
the dust of Florence's streets. She wore a headdress also
made of gold-and-pearl-embroidered brocade. It was a
tall, pointed cone, almost as tall as she was, and draped
in gold silk gauze. Yards of gold fabric hung from the
tip of the headdress, extending even longer and more

bedraggled than the train. The weight of it pulled the child's head back; the silk cord that held it on her head rubbed deep into her soft young throat. Lucrezia felt like weeping with pity. She opened her arms to the little girl. "Come to me, Ginevra," she said.

But the child did not notice Lucrezia. She was looking through the door into the salone, her eyes wide, staring at Lorenzo. He was laughing, surrounded by friends, his face illuminated by the light from the window near him.

That's the same man, the little girl said to herself. The one that was there this morning at the gate where we had to wait. Her heart pounded with hope. She was unbearably confused and frightened; she had tried to ask questions, to talk to Bianca, but she could not make herself understood, nor understand what was said to her. Lorenzo's speech at the Porta San Gallo had been in the dialect that was all she knew of Italian. Maybe he would talk with her, listen to her. If she could find the courage to ask his help.

She felt a hand on her shoulder. It was Bianca, pushing her toward the children, who were being taken away, saying something in a hurried, irritated voice. "No," Ginevra cried. She grabbed hold of her towering unsteady hat with her small hands and ran to Lorenzo.

"Help me," she begged. She clutched his sleeve and spoke with frantic speed, stumbling over her words.

Lorenzo stared at the apparition that had attached itself to him. Then the jumbled, desperate words took on meaning. He dropped to one knee and put an arm around the child. "Gently, little one," he said in the language of the *contado*, "there is no need to hurry. Lorenzo will help you." He raised his hand to ward off Bianca's angry approach.

The noise of the party lessened, then stopped. Everyone watched the unlikely pair talking intensely by the window. After a few minutes Lorenzo gently loosened the ties of Ginevra's hat, removed it from her head and sat it on the floor. Then he kissed her forehead, stood and lifted her in his arms to sit on his broad shoulder.

"Friends," he said smiling, "I want to present to you

this lady. Her name is Ginevra, and she is six years old today. We share the same stars. I have invited her to share the celebration of them. Let the party begin.''

Lorenzo's party was a feast for the Florentines. Not the food; food was available everywhere. The party gave them something much more to their taste, something infinitely more delicious than the tenderest sweet. It gave them a banquet of gossip. In the old walled city, everyone knew everyone else, and their chief entertainment came from talking about each other. Almost every prominent Florentine had been at the party, seen the same things. They could compare their impressions endlessly, with relish. And they did. They talked about the magnitude of feeding the multitude in the streets, about Piero's physical deterioration since his previous public appearances, about Bianca's hasty departure when the sweetmeats were served, about the baby that was born only two hours later. Most of all they gossiped about Ginevra.

It was unheard of to include a child in a party of adults. Granted, it was Lorenzo's party and he could do as he pleased, but it was nonetheless shocking behavior on his part.

Most people correctly attributed it to the circumstance of the child's having the same birthday. A shared birthday was rare and must have great meaning. Astrology was an accepted and respected science; no important venture was begun without a horoscope reading. A few young women insisted, with tear-filled eyes, that Lorenzo was simply showing his deepest, sweetest nature, that he would be a loving father one day and that it was shameful that he was going to marry a foreign woman when Florence had plenty of girls worthy of him.

Soon after the party, more news about Ginevra leaked out, and the gossip intensified. The little girl's grandfather was not pleased by her visit, it was said.

Antonio de' Pazzi was a proud, reclusive man who lived the year round at his country house, an unpretentious villa a mile south of Florence. The Pazzi servants whispered to other servants that Antonio roared like a

bull when he answered his brother's summons to come
to the city. When the child was brought to him, he questioned her, was offended by her accent and insisted that
she be taught to speak Florentine Italian before he saw
her again. The servants repeated the tale to their masters
and the story spread all over the city. Within hours,
everyone was laughing.

A few days later the gossip changed from amused to
excited. It was learned that Ginevra had not come on a
visit. Her father had sent her back to her mother's family permanently; he had recently married again and his
new wife would not have her in the house. It was an
insult to the Pazzi, allowable only because the mother's
dowry had been returned with her daughter. Not only
returned, but doubled, as the Burgundian count's contribution to his own daughter's dowry. The plain, ill-
mannered, oddly dressed little girl was a great heiress.
In houses all over the city hasty conferences were called
to plot the promotion of one or more male children as
suitable prospective husbands.

The Medici palace was no exception. Piero had only
one close cousin, Pierfrancesco. They had quarreled bitterly about the division of Cosimo's estate and for five
years Pierfrancesco had not spoken to Piero or replied
to Piero's letters urging reconciliation. Pierfrancesco had
two sons, the elder only a few months younger than
Ginevra.

"If you can arrange a betrothal, Piero, the breach will
be healed." Lucrezia de' Medici held her husband's
gnarled hand between her two smooth strong ones. She
knew that Piero feared the idea of dying without being
at peace with his family. "You are the head of the family, my dear. Pierfrancesco cannot do it on his own.
Jacopo will decide for the Pazzi. Shall I write to him
over your seal? It's too delicate a matter to trust to a
secretary."

Piero thought, then shook his head. "Jacopo will want
something extraordinary in exchange for his heiress. She
could stay uncommitted for years while he laughs at
everyone seeking the prize. We must find a way to per-

suade him, a soft spot in his hide. There's no hurry. He will not agree to any offers for a long time.''

But there is a hurry, my dearest, Lucrezia thought. You are getting weaker every day.

Chapter Three

In mid-January, gossip about Lorenzo's tournament replaced gossip about his birthday party. The tournament was scheduled for February seventh, and it promised to be the most dazzling spectacle ever seen in Florence, a city world-famous for its extravagant festivals and celebrations.

Jousting was an anachronism. Battles were fought by hired professional soldiers now, and a young man could win renown and fair maidens more readily by success in finance than by unhorsing an opponent. But the tradition was far from dead. Many towns in Italy held tournaments open to all comers, with fat purses for the winner, and the itinerant "knight" with a good horse could earn a rich living with his sharp, skilled lance.

Republican Florence disdained the implications of knighthood. They were too linked with aristocracy. But the drama of competition, the excitement of danger and the opportunity for pageantry all combined in one event when there was a tournament. Everyone agreed that Lorenzo was a genius to have thought of staging one.

The circumstances also provided titillating speculation. It was publicly announced that the tournament was to be given to celebrate his approaching marriage. And yet it was common knowledge that the Queen of the Tournament would be Lucrezia Donati, Lorenzo's mistress. Was Lorenzo spending a fortune on the spectacle just so that Lucrezia could be publicly honored by him? Had she demanded it? Did his future wife know about the tournament? About Lucrezia? The gossip was almost as fascinating as the question of what to do about or-

dering new clothes that would put every other partici-
pant's new costume to shame.

The only people in Florence who did not get caught
up in the gossip or the fashion competition were Lorenzo de' Medici and Lucrezia Donati. He had designed
and ordered their clothing when he planned the tournament, months before it was announced. And Lucrezia
never asked him why he did what he did. She understood the limits of her position better than Lorenzo did.

He had fallen in love with her when he was sixteen
and she only eleven. It was then that her beauty had
emerged from the anonymity of childhood. He had written his first love poetry for her and burned it because it
wasn't good enough for a goddess. He thought of her
as Venus come to life and of himself as a clumsy mortal
unaccountably granted the gift of her notice when she
felt his stare at mass and smiled at him.

The Donati were a family of the old nobility, still
living in the cramped centuries-old tower on the tiny
piazza that bore their name. Lorenzo haunted the opposite street, dreaming of the fair maiden inside, hoping
for a glimpse of her in one of the narrow windows high
above him. He was intoxicated with the romance of his
adoration. He wanted to marry her and build her a tem-
ple and bring her offerings of flowers and combs of
honey.

His father reminded him of his obligation to his family, and Lorenzo was sent on his first diplomatic mission. When he returned, all the arrangements had been
made. The Donati were no longer powerful; marriage
would not be advantageous. But if he still loved Lucrezia when she reached the age for love between a man and
a woman, and if she accepted his love, there would be
no obstacles.

Three years later Lucrezia was married in name to
Niccolo Ardinghelli. The next day he started his voyage
to Portugal as a representative of Florence, and Lucrezia
moved into a house bought for her in the Via de' Pucci,
a short block from the Medici palace. Lorenzo was waiting for her there. He gave her flowers and honey and a
poem:

Was the sky bright or clouded when we met?
No matter. Summer dwells beneath those eyes
And that fair face creates a paradise.

She gave him her body to worship.

Almost a year had passed since then; Lorenzo was still awed by the realization of his youthful dreams. He visited Lucrezia nearly every day, usually bringing flowers, always offering her a new poem he had written to her beauty. She was always waiting for him, scented and robed in soft colors. And she always initiated their lovemaking, touching his lips with her fingers, saying, "Hush. We need no words. Take me to bed." Then Lorenzo undressed her slowly, marveling always at the whiteness of her skin, the perfection of her body and her face. He ran his hands over her body when she stood naked before him. His swarthy coloring looked dark on her skin. She was like pure marble, but warm and silken. He lifted her in his arms and she molded herself to him, resting her head in the hollow of his shoulder. Lorenzo's rapid breathing was the only sound in the house.

She weighs nothing at all, Lorenzo always thought, astonished by Lucrezia's delicacy. He carried her to her bed and laid her gently on the rose-pink silk coverlet. Then he took the ivory pins from her coronet of golden braids and slowly loosened her hair. When it was spread in a fan around her small head, he stepped back to look at her. Lucrezia opened her blue eyes. She smiled slowly.

Lorenzo's heart thudded painfully, his erection straining against its cup. But he did not move. The possession of Lucrezia with his eyes was the most exciting part of lovemaking for him. He prolonged it to the limit of his endurance. When he could wait no longer, he threw off his clothes and pulled a sheath over his aching penis. Lucrezia opened her legs for him and he thrust into her with a bacchanalian cry of triumph and possession and release.

Later he held her in his arms and inhaled the scent of her hair and spoke of his love until his throat was raspy. Then he closed his eyes and was immediately asleep.

Lucrezia slipped out of his arms. She gathered up his clothes and folded them on the foot of the bed, then went into the salone for hers. Lorenzo would sleep for ten or fifteen minutes and then come fully awake, his energy renewed. It was his way to cheat the limits of time. He could sleep anywhere, on horseback, on the floor, sitting upright in a chair, and wake with his mind and body refreshed. By napping when ten minutes were available, he could do without the hours of sleep at night that most people needed. The guards that patrolled the dark night streets of Florence were accustomed to the single lit window in the Medici palace where Lorenzo was working or reading or writing or composing. He used every minute he could wrest from every day, and still there were not enough. There was so much he wanted to do, so many pleasures to taste, so many things to learn, to try, to see.

When he woke, he dressed rapidly and joined Lucrezia in the salone. He poured wine for both of them, sat opposite her and said, "Tell me the news of the city."

A true Florentine, Lucrezia loved gossip. She chattered happily while Lorenzo sipped his wine, telling him about the new cook that her cousin had found, the design of a robe she had ordered, the latest scandal when the archbishop visited the fashionable convent where the nuns all had lovers, the price of bread at the baker's shop that had just opened, the rumor that Maria Rasponi was pawning her jewels to pay her husband's gambling debts.

Lorenzo nodded, smiled, encouraged her. He never tired of the graceful gestures her hands made and the exquisite changing outline of her lips. When it was time for him to go he held her face in his hands and looked deep into her wide eyes. "Happy, my love?"

"Yes, so very happy." Lorenzo kissed her and left. She did not ask when she would see him again. He would send a page to tell her that he was coming. She would be waiting.

When Lucrezia assured Lorenzo that she was happy, she was totally sincere. She loved the life that he gave her: her own house, furnished with soft cushions and beautiful objects; her own servants, dedicated to satisfying her needs and her whims; her clothing, her jewels, her perfumes and oils. Lucrezia had grown up in a household with memories of riches amid daily dignified shabbiness. She was constantly delighted by the comfort and pleasure that wealth could provide.

She remembered that her father had wept after he returned from his conference with Piero de' Medici. Lucrezia had been too young to understand why. Now she was four years older, and she knew that her father's heart was broken because his daughter was desired as a mistress, not as a wife. Lucrezia thought he was very silly.

Her older sisters were married. So, too, were friends and cousins the same age as she. A wife's lot, in her view, was infinitely less desirable. She was expected to have babies, to worry about her household, to make sure that her husband's every wish was satisfied. Whereas, for Lucrezia everything was reversed. Lorenzo fretted about her wants, showered her with gifts and poems and thoughtfulness.

Under his protection, and with the long proud history of the Donati family, Lucrezia was treated with respect by everyone. Her convenient marriage, and the even more convenient absence of her husband, made it possible for her to be invited and welcomed everywhere that a young conventionally married woman would go. She was, she believed, envied by everyone.

It was all, she knew, because of her beauty. Lucrezia knew that she was beautiful. She saw it in her mirrors and in the eyes of everyone around her. Beauty was worshiped in Florence. The entire city was intoxicated by art and the ideal of beauty. Lucrezia was recognized, acknowledged, adored as the greatest living beauty in the city. The tributes came from everywhere, took every form. She received dozens of poems and songs every day, masses of flowers, boxes of sweetmeats, ribbons, gilded combs and fans.

Lorenzo did not object to the adulation. It was the

custom in Florence and implied no familiarity. Just so did people leave flowers and poetry in front of Florence's other works of art, the sculpture of Donatello, the paintings of Masaccio and Giotto.

Lucrezia reveled in her glory. In her prayers she sometimes offered up her thanks to Heaven. She felt like a queen. At the tournament, she would sit on a throne. It seemed exactly right to her.

She never wondered if it might end one day. She was fifteen years old and believed it would last forever.

Lucrezia's procession to her tournament throne was announced by trumpeters and heralds. When she walked into the piazza in front of the church of Santa Croce, the cheers of the crowds around the square were as loud as cannon fire. She turned her head from side to side, accepting the welcome from the tightly packed crowds on all four sides of the piazza. Her golden braids were coiled and looped and wound with ropes of pearls the color of her skin and with chains of pale sapphires the color of her eyes and her gown and the enameled-porcelain-like bowl of sky overhead.

She seated herself on the velvet panoplied throne that was placed in the front center of the stands built for the judges and favored citizens. Then she nodded regally, and the tournament began.

It delivered everything Lorenzo had promised: spectacle, drama, surprise, danger, excitement. There were twenty competitors, dubbed "knights" for the occasion. One was a famous free-lance professional. Eighteen came from the great families of Florence. And there was Lorenzo.

The knights entered the piazza one by one, preceded by liveried servants carrying standards with the knight's coat of arms and pages carrying a painted silk banner with an allegorical depiction of the knight's lady. The pageantry was a feast for the eye, with the gilded standards dazzling in the sunlight and the huge bright banners rippling their colors and beautiful maidens in the breeze.

Even the illiterate could understand the broad mean-

ings of the banners. They had always learned by symbols and pictures, in their commercial reckonings and in
the tremendous cycles of the stories of the Bible and the
saints that decorated the churches. They applauded the
nymph in chaste white robes who broke Cupid's arrows,
the goddess who brought life to dead wheat with the
touch of her hand, the maid stroking the mane of a un-
icorn.

The more sophisticated recognized puns and refer-
ences to the history or character of the knight and his
lady. They applauded the wit as well as the skill of the
painter.

The knights were brilliantly garbed and jeweled; their
horses caparisoned in velvets and brocades. Each man
was greeted with shouts of admiration and cheers of
approval.

The last to enter was Lorenzo. He was welcomed
with a roar that filled the air of the great square. It was
magnified by the stone walls of the church and the
houses on all sides of the piazza until people clapped
their hands over their ears while they continued to cheer.
The windows and balconies and roofs were all packed
with spectators. They pushed and craned to see and
nearly fell, shouting as they risked their lives: "Lorenzo! Lorenzo! Lorenzo!"

He was a magnificent sight. Astride a huge white
horse, a gift from the famous stables of the King of
Naples. The horse moved as if it were conscious of its
royalty, head arrogantly raised, legs lifting high in parade dressage. Its fittings and saddle were of gold-tooled
red leather, with bit and stirrups made of gold.

Lorenzo's spurs were gold, and gold embroidery covered his red and white surcoat. A tall, jeweled gold
feather pierced his diamond-and-pearl-decorated black
velvet cap. From his shoulders a wide, heavy white silk
scarf stretched to the gold ribbon-braided tail of his
horse. The scarf was embroidered with roses, some
withered, others full-blown. A motto was worked in
pearls. It read, in French, "The time returns."

Whispers raced through the crowds, asking and receiving a translation. Everyone believed he understood the meaning:

The Republic of Florence is the rebirth of the great days of freedom and power when Republican Rome ruled the world.

The learning and art of Florence are a rebirth of the glories of ancient Athens.

Only Lorenzo knew that the meaning was all of these things and more. It was his promise to the people of Florence. All of them here today. The powerful in the stands. The artisans and workingmen on the streets. Their wives and children on the roofs and in the windows. He loved them all, even the cutpurses working busily through the crowds, the prostitutes soliciting later business, the vendors of watered wine and spoiled cheese who pocketed their profits and got away before the buyers could taste their wares. These were the Florentines, and he would bring them even greater things than this day's spectacle. Someday he would be the Medici who ruled, and he would bring back the glory of his grandfather's years. And then increase it. It was his promise to the crowds, his pledge to Cosimo.

When the tournament ended, the extravagant finery of horses and riders was tattered and grimy, with bloodstains on many sleeves and legs. The judges conferred briefly and awarded Lorenzo the prize, a silver helmet with a sculpted figure of Mars as the crest. Lorenzo held it high and trotted his horse around the sides of the piazza to give the spectators a closer look at the beautiful object. He grinned at the cheering and shouts of congratulation. He knew, and the people knew, that it was not his skill at fighting that had made him the winner. He was being rewarded for his talents at planning and staging. Most of all he was given the trophy because he had paid for it, together with all the other helmets, the banners, the heralds, pages, musicians, decorated armor, lances, attendants, the judges' benches and Lucrezia's throne. The tournament was his gift to the city.

Still, even with the undercurrent of cynicism the

cheering was real, and Lorenzo knew that, too. He had heard it many times before in just this way, magnified by the walls of just these houses. *Calcio* was played on the Piazza Santa Croce. Calcio, the wild, battering, no-holds-barred football that tested a man's strength and nerve in a way that no other combat could do. Any boy or man in Florence could play—if he had enough reckless courage. There were no distinctions made because of wealth or power. Lorenzo had joined the fray almost as soon as he could run. He had been bloodied, bruised, shouted at, shamed. But he had kept playing. Over the years, as his body matured, he had become one of the best players in the city. He was a hero, and he had done it alone. He was Lorenzo the man, not Lorenzo the Medici, on the football field. So he stood in his golden stirrups and rode past the adoring crowds and accepted the cheers as his due.

Lucrezia Donati watched him from her throne and loved him. He was like a king, and she was his queen.

Above her in the stands an older Lucrezia watched, Lorenzo's mother, Lucrezia de' Medici. Her lovely face was soft and glowing with pride and love. It seemed natural to everyone around her that her eyes were luminous with unshed tears. They could not know what she was thinking . . . Drink deep of this triumph, my son, this happy freedom, this joy. Soon, too soon, it will all be over. When you become the Medici, when every smiling face may mask an enemy, when Florence demands more—so much more—of you than a day of festivity in the sunlight. I wish you could remain forever as you are today, youthful and trusting and happy. And yet, it is what I fear most: that your nature will cause your destruction.

Forgive me my thoughts, Holy Mother, she prayed silently. My children are my greatest blessings, and I am grateful for them. But they are so much more fragile than they know, and fear for them is a sword in my heart.

At Lucrezia's side, Giuliano cheered for his brother until he was hoarse. Nearby his sisters clapped and held their heads high, basking in Lorenzo's reflected glory.

Shadowed by Bianca's older children, little Ginevra crouched down to see between the legs of the tallest boy. Her eyes were staring, her thin body trembling with emotion. This Lorenzo, this heroic figure, had held her on his shoulder, had shared his plate with her, had called her his star-sister. She thought he was like a god, and she worshiped.

Chapter Four

"Stand up straight. Don't hang your head down like that. Look at me. Let me look at you." Bianca stepped back a few paces and scrutinized her husband's little cousin.

Ginevra bore little resemblance now to the ornately dressed child who had come from her father's castle in Burgundy. Except for her difficulty with the language she might have been any young girl of good family in Florence. And even the difficulty was fast vanishing, thanks to the tutor Bianca had engaged. She was pleased with what she had accomplished in only a few months. Ginevra looked respectable. Bianca had refashioned her.

Florentine women and girls all wore the same basic garments: a thin, usually white, long chemise with a round neck and long sleeves under a dress, called a *gamurra*, topped by a *cioppa*, a long lined coat, often sleeveless and open in the front. The gamurra was the test of the tailor's skill. It had a round neck, cut somewhat lower than that of the chemise, and long tight sleeves. It laced up the back and hung straight from the shoulders to a slightly widened hem. Cut by a master, it could be immensely flattering to any body shape. On a woman with a good figure, it emphasized the curves of bust and waist and hips without ever losing its simplicity.

The cioppa could be as plain or as elaborate as its owner's taste and purse allowed.

Florence was the world's center for the manufacture, processing and dying of wool; its workshops also produced linens, velvets, silks, brocades and embroideries of unsurpassable richness. The varieties of fundamentally simple clothing were limitless.

Bianca had chosen well for Ginevra. The child had two white linen chemises and two gamurre of good Florentine wool, one brown and one dark green. The hems of the skirt and sleeves were deep; the overlap under the back lacing was wide. The dresses could be lengthened and widened for years as she grew. Her cioppa was of wool, too, brown lined with green and again deeply hemmed. The clothing would serve until Ginevra was full grown, because the wool made in Florence never wore out. For summer wear, the three warm woolen garments could be replaced by the same in a lighter weight wool and paler colors. The linen chemises were suitable year-round.

It was the same wardrobe that Bianca had bought for her own daughters. Like all Florentines, Bianca was practical and thrifty.

Now she squinted at the little girl and was almost satisfied. It was a shame Ginevra's hair was brown instead of the blond prevalent and preferred in Florence, but there was nothing Bianca could do about that. If only her language passed examination, Ginevra would probably be taken off her hands in a few days.

"Now say it again," Bianca commanded, "and hold your head up and don't slur your words. 'Good morning, honored Grandfather.' Speak up." Antonio de' Pazzi, Ginevra's grandfather, was coming into the city.

The occasion was the ceremony in which Jacopo de' Pazzi would become leader of the government of the Republic. *Gonfaloniere*.

The politics of Florence were an intricate amalgam of tradition, theater and invisible maneuvering. Every citizen was proud of the Republican government, even those who knew that the strings were pulled from behind the scenes. Every other city-state in Italy was ruled by a despot. It was only in Florence that all men had an equal opportunity to become a ruler.

The visible government was the group of nine men known as the Signoria. The head of the Signoria was the Gonfaloniere. They were chosen by a complicated lottery-type system of drawing names from large leather bags, and their term of office was two months.

During that time they lived in superlative luxury in the ancient government building, the Palazzo della Signoria. They wore sumptuous robes of office, ate meals prepared by the finest chefs in Florence, were pampered by a large staff of green-liveried servants, protected by a specially uniformed troop of guards, entertained by a court jester, soothed by musicians.

They were the most honored men in the city, and the honor was permanent. For the rest of his life, a man would be known as a former prior or Gonfaloniere.

No official decision could be made without them. The Signoria was the legislative body of the State.

The less visible, but still important, government was an enormous bureaucracy of committees that governed the operation of the State and the implementation of the Signoria's decisions and laws.

The most important government figure had no title and no badge of office. He was the head of the Medici family. His suggestions and recommendations determined appointments to committees and the names that were put into the leather bags for the public drawing of the Signoria. It had been like this for thirty-five years, ever since Cosimo de' Medici had studied the way the government functioned and made a few shrewd adjustments that caused no outward changes but delivered the real power to him.

He brought order out of chaos. The Florentines named him Pater Patriae and turned to his son for leadership when he was gone.

Piero de' Medici arranged in March for Jacopo de' Pazzi to be elected Gonfaloniere. "This will buy the heiress for Pierfrancesco's boy," he said with confidence.

Lucrezia agreed. "Jacopo values public honor above all else. You've touched his weak spot. He won't turn the office down, even though he knows it puts him in debt to you morally.''

The introductions of the new Signoria to the city was always a holiday. On this beautiful spring day, it was a double holiday. It was March 25, the Feast of the Annunciation, the day Florentines celebrated as the beginning of the New Year. The crowds in the Piazza Santa Croce were the largest since Lorenzo's tournament. They were all in high good spirits, enjoying the balmy weather and the work-free day.

Jacopo was warmed by their applause when he appeared at the door of the church in his ceremonial robe of office. All the priors wore crimson coats lined in ermine, with ermine collars and cuffs. The robe of the Gonfaloniere was also embroidered all over with gold stars.

Jacopo raised his arm in response to the crowd's salute. Then he accepted the silk standard of the Republic from the outgoing Gonfaloniere. The red lily on a white field was the symbol of Florence, the identity of the State. For the next two months, no one could touch it except Jacopo. The Republic was in his custody.

He walked proudly down the steps, holding the bright standard high, and began the stately procession to the Palazzo della Signoria. The priors fell into step behind him. Jacopo was so filled with pride that he was almost deaf to the sounds of cheering from the people lining the route of the procession. His feet crushed the flowers thrown into his path with the carelessness of an emperor.

"He could have nodded at least," said Bianca. Jacopo had not even noticed his family's presence in the church, but there was no irritation in her voice. She was too pleased by Jacopo's appointment. During the two months that he would be living in the Palazzo della Signoria, she would have uncontested sway over the Pazzi palace. At last she could order a good cleaning of the rooms. Perhaps she would have new curtains made, too. Her mind churned with plans.

Elmo nudged her arm. "Things seem to be going well with the little visitor," he murmured.

"What?" Bianca's eyes followed the direction of Elmo's gesture.

Antonio de' Pazzi was leaning down, his head level with his granddaughter's. They were talking together.

Jacopo's election brought major changes to Ginevra's life. The day following the ceremony, she went to live with her grandfather at his Villa La Vacchia.

And the week following the end of Jacopo's reign, he sent a message to Piero de' Medici. The letter said nothing more than that Jacopo would like to call on Piero at his convenience. Both men knew that it was the opening move in the negotiation for Ginevra's betrothal to Piero's young cousin.

Both also knew that Jacopo could hardly have chosen a more inconvenient time to indicate his willingness to discuss the matter. Lorenzo's wedding was only a week away and the Medici palace was a turmoil of preparation.

Piero sent a page to bring his wife and Lorenzo to him. Before a response went to Jacopo, the family must meet and discuss the details of the potential betrothal. As head of the Medici, Piero's was the final decision. But every family discussed a major move before it was taken. It was each man's right to have his opinions heard. Any action taken by any one member of a family affected every other member. The family was more than simply a group of people related by blood. It was a unit, the only consistently dependable alliance in uncertain times. It was an unwritten law that each family member would aid another when necessary. With shelter, with goods, with money, with his life if need be in a battle. So strong was this tradition that it was recognized in the laws of the Republic. Every man in a family could be held responsible for a crime committed by any other man bearing the same family name, even a cousin many times removed.

The meeting at the Medici palace was unlike most

family meetings in two important respects: there were only three people there and one of them was a woman.

Only males who had reached the age of manhood were normally considered capable of decision-making. But Lucrezia de' Medici was not an average woman. Cosimo himself had respected her judgment and included her in his talks with Piero about the delicate art of governing Florence. She had been Piero's closest advisor throughout his time as head of the family and the State.

And Lorenzo had been regarded as a man, included in decisions, for years before he came of age.

Still, a group of three, no matter how wise or experienced, was hardly enough to constitute a family as Florentines understood the word. Piero was flushed with excitement when Lucrezia and Lorenzo came to his study. "Jacopo de' Pazzi wants to see me," he said. "We may bring Pierfrancesco back to us soon."

"What good news," Lucrezia sighed.

Lorenzo laughed. "I told you the little *contadina* Ginevra would bring us luck. When Bianca brought her in, and it was also her birthday, I believed it was a good omen. Then Bianca's son was born on the same day, making three, and I knew I was right. How shall we send the news to Pierfrancesco?"

Piero smiled. "You go, my son. Pierfrancesco's son is your namesake, so your interest is natural. Go now. There is still time for Pierfrancesco to take part in your wedding celebrations."

Lucrezia noticed Lorenzo's sudden involuntary intake of breath. Poor lamb, she thought. He's terrified about becoming a husband.

Chapter Five

For one of the few times in her life Lucrezia was wrong in her intuition about her son. Lorenzo had gasped when he remembered that he had promised to meet some friends in the Piazza Santa Croce. There would be time for a visit to Lucrezia Donati before he joined them. They were going to play football and then go to the Medici villa in Fiesole to begin training a new falcon.

He seldom thought about his approaching marriage; it would make no real changes in his life. There would still be time for football and falcons and friends. And Lucrezia. He knew what was expected of him as a husband. Monogamy was not part of it. The structures and protocols of marriage were clearly spelled out by law and by custom. He knew them; so did Clarice Orsini, his future wife.

He would be responsible for protecting, housing, clothing and maintaining her and later his children. He would always treat her with the respect due her and her family. And in all things he would be her ruler.

He would visit her bed regularly. They were expected to have children, as many as possible, both because it was God's purpose and because it was through the marriages of his children that the family would make alliances in the future. He wasn't worried about his ability to father children; although he guarded against producing bastards, he had been proving his virility for years.

Clarice might have some difficulty. Marriage would change her life enormously because it meant moving from Rome to Florence. She'd have to adjust to the different style of life. But that wasn't Lorenzo's responsibility. His mother would take care of it.

Like all big houses, the Medici palace had an interior world for the women of the household. Their bedrooms and sitting rooms were clustered conveniently close to the kitchens and pantries and laundry and sewing rooms so that they could supervise the servants and the business of the home. In the city Clarice would be near Lucrezia and Lorenzo's grandmother, Contessina, the widow of Cosimo.

Lucrezia had gone to Rome as Piero's representative, and she had accepted Clarice. Lorenzo trusted her judgment. She was so careful in describing Clarice's attributes as modesty, obedience and good health that Lorenzo wondered from time to time if his bride would be fantastically ugly. It wasn't important, but it would be more agreeable if she were reasonably pretty.

He'd find out soon enough. Clarice and her attendants were en route from Rome. Giuliano and a troop of Medici horsemen were their escorts. By custom, wedding celebrations took place at the home of the groom's family.

Lorenzo's wedding lived up to the expectations of everyone. The feasting and entertainment went on for three days and three nights in the Medici palace and in the streets of the city. The weather was perfect; the bride and her fifty maids of honor were lavishly gowned; the fountains spouted wine instead of water. Every guest at the six banquets in the palace was given a silver box filled with sugared almonds. Every citizen in the streets received a silver-colored wooden one. *Confetti* the Florentines called the sweetmeats. They were distributed as souvenirs at every important family celebration as a token of happiness shared.

Sandro Botticelli was the last Florentine to receive his confetti. "Auguri, Lorenzo," he said, while Lorenzo pushed him through the doorway from the grand salone.

"Thank you, Sandro." Lorenzo took the single remaining silver box from the table in the hall and pressed it into Botticelli's hand. "Please accept this small token, and take it home with you." Lorenzo was laughing.

Sandro grinned. He looked at Clarice, then at Lorenzo. "I have an idea you want me to go," he said. Then he winked lewdly and ran down the stairs.

Lucrezia sighed heavily. "Trust Sandro to be the last to leave. There is probably not a scrap of food remaining in this house . . . Goodnight, children. I am taking these exhausted bones of mine to a well-earned rest." She kissed Lorenzo, then Clarice.

"My dear daughter," she said gently, "you have made me proud. I'm sure that all Florence envies me my good fortune to have you in my family."

"Thank you, Madonna Lucrezia." Clarice's words were almost inaudible. She was a tall slim girl, with no real beauty, but a pleasant face, marred only by narrow, prim lips.

Lorenzo took his new wife's hand. "She is right, Clarice. You have been very strong and brave these three busy days. We are all proud of you." He had noticed Clarice's frightening pallor. She was so tired that her skin and lips and fingernails were gray.

"You need have no worries, Lorenzo," she said. "I know what my duty is, and I will always do it." For the first time Clarice's voice was firm and loud. Lorenzo was greatly relieved; he had thought she could only whisper. The tone was very close to hostile, but he could understand that and forgive it. She must be frightened. She was far from her home and her family, surrounded by strangers, worn out by strenuous celebrations. And it was now the time for the marriage to be consummated. She could not have missed the meaning of Sandro's lascivious wink. A woman with gentle upbringing did not lose her virginity without fear. Lorenzo remembered the frightened trembling of his mistress when they first loved. Clarice was sixteen and had certainly never been alone with a man before this moment.

Lorenzo thought quickly. Which would be easier for Clarice? To bed her now and let her learn there was nothing to be afraid of? Or to wait until her fatigue was washed away by a long sleep?

Her hand was still resting limply in his. Despite the warmth of the June evening, it was chilled and clammy. He would wait.

"I'll see you to your room," he said gently, "and leave you tonight. We both need rest."

The next morning Lorenzo was gone before the rest of the family woke. He had things to do. Florence's annual carnival was less than three weeks away, and he was organizing one of the floats.

Giuliano told the others. Lorenzo had left a message for his brother to meet him at the hidden workshop where the float was being constructed. "So you see, Mamina, I cannot stop to eat." He grabbed a piece of cheese and broke an end off a loaf of bread. "Good morning, Clarice. Goodbye." He kissed his mother and his grandmother on the top of the head and ran.

Lucrezia laughed. "We're back to normal. Sit here by me, Clarice. We can have a leisurely breakfast." The family dining room was a smaller chamber next to the grand salone. When there were no guests, the Medici took their meals there, together at one table with chairs for each of them instead of the more usual arrangement of benches for all except the head of the house.

Clarice sat stiffly on the edge of her chair and smiled at Lucrezia and Piero's mother. Contessina was a hugely fat, good-natured old woman. Her hearing was gone, but she had not lost a tooth. It was a point of great pride for her; she delighted in showing people her gleaming intact molars. It was also a source of great pleasure. She loved food. She nodded cheerfully at Clarice then resumed eating.

The meal was plentiful but simple, as were all the family meals in the palace. Clarice looked at the bowls of oranges, platters of bread, cheese and sausage and wondered when the servants would bring the main courses. In Rome every great household employed several chefs who competed with each other in preparing elaborate, complicated dishes.

"We have good wells," Lucrezia said. "You can be sure of the water here, but never drink from the city fountains." She placed pitchers of wine and water in front of her new daughter after she poured herself a cup of watered wine to show Clarice the custom in Florence. Rome was notorious as a city of debauchery, but the Florentines abhorred excess.

Clarice filled her cup with water. "In my family the women drink wine only at communion, Madonna Lucrezia. I am accustomed to the juice of a lemon with honey and water."

Good, thought Lucrezia, the girl can speak up for herself. We'll have no trouble understanding each other. "I'll have some prepared for you at once," she said, signaling the steward. Then she lifted her fork and speared a bit of sausage. Forks, she knew, were as yet unknown outside of Florence. "I was so pleased when people started using these," she said. "It saves so much on linen when the hands don't get greasy."

Clarice followed her lead.

"After breakfast I'll begin introducing you to the house, Clarice. It won't take long for it to begin to feel like home. Then we'll go to mass. Would you prefer San Lorenzo, our family church, or the cathedral? We're very proud of it in Florence. The dome is one of the wonders of the modern world."

"I should like very much to see it."

Lucrezia was pleased.

Lorenzo was pleased with the work done so far on the float. The big cart was built. Its twelve wheels were as tall as he was; it would be easy for the people in the street to see the short play that would be acted on it.

"There's never been one so fine," he said. "Are you sure no one has seen it, Andrea?"

"No one except all my apprentices who have had to stop all other work, Lorenzo. You will bankrupt me."

Lorenzo made a rude noise. Andrea del Verrocchio had the most profitable studio in all Florence. He and his apprenticed artists carried out commissioned work in all the arts: painting in fresco or on panels, sculpting in bronze or marble, pottery, woodworking, goldsmithing. They made jewelry and armor, fountains and musical instruments, swords and decorated parchment fans. There was nothing Verrocchio could not do. If he were sufficiently well paid.

Lorenzo admired the older man and was proud to call him his friend. Andrea, in turn, appreciated Lorenzo's talents as a poet, musician, philosopher and athlete.

"I have designed a magnificent lute for the accompaniment," said Andrea with a wicked look. "Have you written the poem yet?"

"I've been too busy," Lorenzo complained. "Besides, I think Gigi will write a better one than I could."

"Hear, hear," shouted Luigi Pulci, nicknamed Gigi. He was one of Lorenzo's favorite companions. Son of a farmer in the Mugello, he loved the city and lived there, earning his living by his wit. He invented poems on any subject demanded by other patrons of Florence's taverns, creating such impromptu masterpieces of comedy, puns and vulgarity that everyone listening threw money into the bowl on the table near him.

"Considering the subject, I suppose you're right," said Andrea. The song would tell the story of an old man cuckolded by his young wife. It was a perennial favorite theme for the carnival crowds. Variations and embellishments were the tests of the sponsor's wit and skill.

Giuliano had to shout to be heard over the laughter in the workshop. "Let me in and tell me the joke." Verrocchio unbolted the door. Surprise was an essential element for carnival floats, and security was vital.

"Come in quickly. Were you followed?"

"No, I was careful. That's why it took me so long. What is so funny?"

Andrea began to laugh again. "A new husband buying a play about an unfaithful wife. It will make everyone laugh. Is your brother worried or is he bragging that he isn't worried?"

Giuliano's handsome face grew ugly with anger. Lorenzo was his idol, and Giuliano resented any suggestion that he was less than perfect. But then he heard Lorenzo laughing. The younger brother tried to smile.

"Look at this, Giuliano," Lorenzo shouted. He threw something at the boy.

Giuliano caught it neatly. Then he, too, began to laugh. It was a lute, not yet strung, beautifully crafted of a variety of woods. It was in the shape of a giant phallus.

The Florentines enjoyed earthy humor. A hundred years earlier Giovanni Boccaccio had captured their spirit in his tales *The Decameron*. Everyone in Florence who could read still laughed at themselves and at human nature in Boccaccio's stories.

"Bravo, Andrea," Lorenzo said. "That's something new. Why not make it the theme of the decorations? Instead of the gildings on the sides of the wagon, we could get della Robbia to make enamel plaques of the suitor serenading. Only the lute much bigger, weighing him down."

"No, no, Lorenzo," said Gigi, "the suitor beating the husband with the lute."

"Or breaking down the door of the house," Lorenzo added.

Before Gigi Pulci could suggest a further variation, Verrocchio held up his hand to stop them. "Save your brilliance, my friends. None of the della Robbias are available. Old Antonio de' Pazzi has hired the whole studio to make a series of decorations for his villa."

"They can put him off," Pulci insisted.

"Not a Pazzi," said Andrea. "The family has been patrons of the della Robbia since Luca first began to work. He won't disappoint Antonio."

Lorenzo shrugged. "They would probably have said no to us anyhow. Luca has no sense of humor and his nephews very little . . . But what work they do. Angels sit on their shoulders when they mix their colors."

Verrocchio nodded. "Luca tells me the work they're doing for old Pazzi is the finest they've ever done. He will tell me when they mount the enamels on the villa's walls. Then we'll go see them."

"A good plan," said Lorenzo. "I'd like to see how

the little contadina is doing, too.'' He saw Pulci's eyes
flash. ''No, no, Gigi, not a delectable brown-skinned
girl from the fields for you to deflower. I'm talking about
Antonio's granddaughter. I call her contadina as a pet
name.'' He recounted the history of Ginevra's burst into
his birthday celebration speaking peasant dialect. But he
said nothing about the negotiations taking place with
Jacopo de' Pazzi. ''She's good luck for me,'' he said
instead.

Verrocchio chuckled. ''Don't tell Andrea della Robbia that child is good luck. She's driven him half crazy.
Antonio lets her run wild once her lessons are over; she
followed Andrea everywhere when he was planning and
measuring. Even up the ladders. And always asking
questions.''

Lorenzo's expression did not change, but his mind
was racing. It wouldn't do at all for Pierfrancesco to
hear that Piero was arranging a betrothal with an ill-
trained girl. He might regard it as another injury and
break with the family again.

''Let me know when you hear from Luca,'' Lorenzo
said. ''I want to see the enamels as soon as we can.''
And I will have a few words with Antonio de' Pazzi,
he promised silently. He must not allow anything that
approaches ''running wild.''

He walked around the wagon again, squinting as he
visualized different effects. ''Let's talk some more about
the decorations,'' he said. ''If not enamels, what about
paintings?''

It was two hours before they settled on painted
wooden bas-reliefs.

''I've got to go,'' Lorenzo said suddenly.

''Ah, these new husbands,'' groaned Pulci. ''They
cease being good companions the instant they marry.''

Lorenzo thumbed his nose at his friends and left.

It was true that he was leaving them to go to Clarice.
He wanted to be attentive, to make her adjustment to
her new life easy.

In his innermost heart he hoped that perhaps they
would be able to create the same kind of marriage that
his parents had. The same closeness and caring and

shared plans and laughter and happiness. But he did not confess his hopes even to himself. Piero and Lucrezia were a rare couple, possibly unique.

So he told himself that it was only decent to spend time with his wife instead of amusing himself with his friends. It was necessary to get to know each other, to talk, to touch and to make love.

He did admit to himself that he was glad Clarice was not ugly. In fact, her long, slim, white neck was really quite lovely.

Chapter Six

Lorenzo headed for his bedroom to change out of his dusty clothes before he saw Clarice and his mother. His hand was on the door latch before he remembered that he had more luxurious quarters now on the floor above. He raced up the small circular servants' stairs, washed hurriedly, dressed and ran to the dining room.

"My belly is clinging to my backbone," he cried when he entered. "I hope you've left something for me." Clarice and Lucrezia were having their dessert. Lucrezia laughed at her son. "I thought you were Sandro Botticelli for a minute. Never hungry, always starving. You were so noisy that three stewards went running for the kitchen. Sit down; your meal will be here immediately."

Lorenzo took the chair next to Clarice. She smiled at him, then looked down at the sugared cake in front of her.

"So, Clarice," he said, "have you done something interesting today?"

"We went to mass at the Duomo."

"Good. Did you enjoy it? Is it not beautiful? It will hold almost the entire population of the city."

"Very beautiful," Clarice murmured.

Color flushed her cheeks. She was lying, and she was angry. Clarice had not noticed if the cathedral was beautiful. She was too shocked to see it.

For the Florentines, the eight masses said daily were more than religious services. They were also social and business meetings. Women gossiped with their friends; men made financial deals and then gossiped. People walked around the huge benchless spaces of the churches, moving from group to group, stopping for a minute or five or ten minutes to talk. Only when the priest raised the host, the sacred bread/body of Christ, did they fall silent and face the altar and bow their heads. Clarice considered their behavior an outrage.

For her, for all Romans like her, the mass was a solemn duty to be attended with complete devotion and attention.

In Rome the Church was all-important. Not only for the devout, but for everyone. The Church was the State, the Pope its ruler. All laws, all taxes, all benefits, all power came from the Church. Territories controlled by the Church, the Papal States, covered a fourth of Italy. The taxes and produce and tributes from the subject territories made the Pope the richest ruler in the country. His temporal power was limitless in his territories. His spiritual power stretched across all Europe.

One slighted his priests' sermons at peril to one's safety. The Florentines, thought Clarice, were blasphemous. Their behavior insulted the Church. And it threatened everything she believed in. Her uncle was a cardinal, two cousins were archbishops. Although the Orsini fortune came from the family's tremendous properties from Rome to the outskirts of Naples, its security and power came from family members high in the structures of the Church.

Clarice had been thoroughly drilled in a wife's duty to her husband. Obedience and a meek spirit were requirements. So she lied to Lorenzo. As she had lied to his mother. Clarice's view of religion demanded observance of rites not defense of faith.

She could not know or understand that Lucrezia de' Medici was a profoundly spiritual woman. Lucrezia enjoyed the sociability of mass. She also spent long hours studying the scriptures and the writings of great theologians. As a gift to God, she had been working for years translating the Psalms into Italian poetry, and she followed the biblical injunction by making her charitable contributions in secret.

Lorenzo waited until it was obvious that Clarice had

nothing to add to her two-word remark about the beauty of the Duomo. He was not accustomed to silence at table. Conversation was an art form and a plaything for Florentines. He began to report Verrocchio's news about the della Robbia family's latest project. Clarice listened politely.

A steward brought a bowl of steaming ravioli and placed it in front of Lorenzo.

"The kitchen took you at your word," Lucrezia said. She hid a smile behind her napkin. The bowl was one customarily used for serving, and its contents were heaped high. There was enough food to feed six people.

Lorenzo laughed mightily. He loved practical jokes, even when he was the butt.

"It will take two hours to eat that. Just long enough for Clarice and me to have our rest. We had a busy morning, and your sisters are coming to visit this afternoon." Lucrezia took Lorenzo's bride away and left him in peace.

She came back ten minutes later. "Clarice is terribly shy, Lorenzo. You're a man; you cannot imagine a girl's emotions." She took his hand, a signal since his childhood that she wanted his full attention. "Dear son, you have always been in a hurry about everything. But this time you must rein in your impatience, control your energies. Patience is what is needed. Be a husband to Clarice; she is able to be a wife. But don't expect her to be easy in talking to any of us until she feels at home."

Lorenzo raised his hand, lifting Lucrezia's to his lips. She could feel his smile when he kissed it. "I'll remember, Mamina," he said. "Thank you."

That night Lorenzo visited his wife in her room. Clarice was expecting him. Sweet herbs burned in the pierced brass holder that hung above the silk-sheeted wide bed, and her hair was perfumed. She was wearing an embroidered silk chemise with long lace-trimmed sleeves. Lorenzo was bewildered. All Florentine women and men slept nude except for a night cap.

Clarice turned her head away from the sight of his

body; with her hands she pulled the sides of her chemise to show him the opening in it that would permit intercourse without offending her modesty.

She made no sound when he entered her and the hymen ruptured, but her fingernails cut into her palms. She said nothing when he left her. Then she cried herself to sleep.

It was the only time she cried. She was too proud to allow herself such frailty. The Romans were proud people, the Orsini the proudest of the Romans. Clarice was educated to one aim: she must behave as befitted a member of the Roman nobility, do her duty and show no weakness.

In a matter of weeks, even Lucrezia recognized that Clarice's silences were the product of pride, not timidity. She hoped that Florence's annual Carnival would amuse and please her daughter-in-law. Carnival was famous throughout all Italy. It was the celebration of the feast day of St. John the Baptist, Florence's patron saint, and it offered everything in its four-day festivities. Religious processions moved majestically from all parts of the city to the Duomo. A hundred elaborate gilded towers were presented to the Signoria by the subject-towns of the Republic. A breakneck horse race, the *Palio*, was run from one side of the city to the other. There were parades and trumpeters, competitions between groups of standard-bearers who twirled and tossed their huge, colorful silk banners, and a fierce, day-long calcio contest with teams from the four quarters of the city.

Everywhere shops and houses were decorated with banners, tapestries, lengths of bright silk or cloth of gold, Persian rugs, paintings. Florentines wore their most festive garments, roving through the streets and squares, sharing the holiday spirit and the entertainment everywhere. There were trained animals, jugglers, fire-eaters, acrobats, troubadours, rope walkers, musicians and sword swallowers. Amazement was offered at every corner, and all Florence was in the streets to enjoy it.

Clarice pronounced the spectacle vulgar, and she shrank from contact with the crowds. In Rome, she said, aristocrats were never touched by commoners.

Her disapproval became hysterical condemnation on the final day of Carnival. This was the day of carousel. There was music and dancing in every piazza, merry-making in every street. While unwed women could only look out on the festivities from windows and balconies, married women of all ages and classes could and did mingle with the joyful hordes. Most people were masked, many were outrageously costumed. Youths dressed as women postured suggestively and sang bawdy songs, often to delighted older women they surrounded and held captive. The floats moved ponderously through the streets, stopping frequently to present their poems or plays or narratives. Men exhibited exaggerated padded shoulders and codpieces, inviting observers to marvel and feel. It was a day-and-nightlong celebration of life and sexuality. For those who lost their heads, narrow alleys offered temporary privacy for embraces or hasty couplings.

Clarice endured the noisy jostling crowds for less than ten minutes. Then she turned to Lucrezia. "I wish to be taken back to the house. I am sickened." Her face was masked, but her eyes flashed harshly through the openings in the soft pink satin.

Lucrezia spoke to the stewards who were escorting them, and they began to make way through the crowds for the two women. "Lorenzo hoped that you would be amused by the float he designed," she said in a deceptively mild voice.

"That is not part of my duty!" Clarice's words came out in a piercing shrill scream.

Lucrezia never again spoke to her son about the virtue of patience.

Lorenzo knew immediately when his mother's view of Clarice altered. Lucrezia did not change her behavior; she remained considerate and patient toward Clarice and gave every indication of pleasure in having a new daughter to share her life. But Lorenzo had a gift for feeling the sadness of others, and he knew without words that his mother was disappointed in Clarice and sad-

dened that her choice of a bride for him would bring
him so little happiness.

He had known for some time what Lucrezia learned
at Carnival. Clarice measured her life by her rigid, narrow view of duty. She considered herself superior to
everyone around her because of her birth and, even
more, because she never failed to do her duty. In her
own eyes she was a martyr, like the saints whose allot-
ted days of celebration she faithfully observed with private devotions in addition to daily mass.

The nightly ritual in her bed never varied. Clarice
made Lorenzo's role as her husband as unwelcome a
duty to him as her role as wife was to her.

I expected no more, he told himself, and thought no
more about it. He had his life to live. There was so
much to do, so many things to be enjoyed. The long
days of summer gave precious additional hours, and Lorenzo wasted none of them.

When the city was silent with its traditional two-hour
rest period after the midday meal, he usually rode out
to Careggi, the closest of the family villas, to watch his
horses exercise. His most cherished dream was to win
the famous, dangerous race, the Palio. Three years earlier he had begun a systematic breeding program, buying the fastest horses the Medici bank managers could
find in all the places where the bank had branches:
Rome, Venice, Naples, Milan, Pisa, Antwerp, Bruges,
London, Geneva, Lyons, and Avignon. Agents in Constantinople sent Arabian stallions and mares. The train-
ers mated them, keeping detailed records of every
strength and weakness, looking for the perfect combi-
nation of sire and dam to produce the fearlessness, speed
and stamina necessary for a Palio winner.

He also followed a regular pattern in the evenings.
He visited the beautiful house in the Via de' Pucci and
his beautiful Lucrezia. Then he went home for the leisurely meal that the family ate in the garden as the daylight slowly faded. Piero was often with them, and after
the quiet, simple meal, Lorenzo helped Piero's men
carry him to his room. Before the painful business of
being prepared for bed, Piero talked earnestly to his son

about the workings of the Florentine government, trying to prepare him for the role that would be his. When the effort of speaking was too great for him to continue, Piero sent Lorenzo away. The rasping noise of his agonized breath echoed in Lorenzo's head while he went to Clarice's room and performed his husbandly duty.

Then he found Giuliano and took him along on his revels. With a good sword and a torch and a fat purse for the fines it was possible to overcome the dangers and the laws of the night streets. The taverns were always full and lively. With Gigi Pulci as companion, it was almost possible for the brothers to forget that their father was going to die, and that there was nothing anyone could do to ease his pain.

Shortly after Carnival, Andrea del Verrocchio notified Lorenzo that the della Robbias had completed their work at Antonio de' Pazzi's villa. "We will go tomorrow," Lorenzo told Lucrezia. "I have already sent a messenger to beg permission."

Lucrezia was apprehensive. "Antonio is such a hermit, he may not allow visitors."

"Nonsense, Mamina. He is a strange old man, but he loves art. He'll be overjoyed to show off his prizes. Verrocchio and Botticelli are going with me."

"Oh, well, in that case . . . I hope what you discover there won't be too terrible. I'm worried about those rumors that young Ginevra is so undisciplined. The contracts for the betrothal are almost done, and Pierfrancesco is impatient. If we have to break it off, I don't know what he'll think."

Lorenzo kissed her loudly on both cheeks. "We won't have to. Whatever needs doing I'll see to. Don't worry."

He wished he was as confident as his words. Antonio was a notoriously difficult man, even for a Pazzi.

Chapter Seven

Lorenzo had never been to the Villa La Vacchia. It was not at all what he expected. The huge gates were made of intricately scrolled iron instead of solid wood, and they stood open and welcoming. The gatekeeper and his wife gazed curiously from the window of their small house but said nothing to the visitors.

A road climbed from the gate through an olive orchard to the crest of a hill and the villa. It was small and very plain, nothing like the grandiose palace of Jacopo de' Pazzi in the city. La Vacchia was only two floors high with a small square tower rising from the center of the red tiled roof. There were no crenellations, no decorations except the scrolled ironwork that protected the windows.

And the della Robbia lunette above the simple tall paneled front door.

Lorenzo heard the sharp indrawn breath of Sandro Botticelli at his side, knew that he, too, was gasping. The enameled half circle was breathtaking.

"Welcome, gentlemen."

Lorenzo was so enthralled that he had not seen Antonio in the doorway. The old man was smiling.

Lorenzo dismounted hastily. "I beg your forgiveness, Messer Antonio. I was so . . ."

"No offense taken, Lorenzo. Art should seize the eye . . . You are Lorenzo, are you not? I see so few people that I am never sure if I remember them or not."

"I am Lorenzo. And grateful for your receiving us. May I introduce my friends . . ." Andrea and Sandro had joined him on foot.

"Ha! I already know this brilliant rogue Verrocchio," said Antonio. "He robbed me of a pretty sum for a reading stand. Did good work, so I had to forgive him . . . You must be Botticelli. I bow to your genius, young man." Antonio dipped his head in homage.

Lorenzo was fascinated by the old man. Antonio was tall and thin, like his brother Jacopo, with the long narrow hawklike nose of the Pazzi. But while Jacopo's half-hooded eyes were alert and suspicious, Antonio's were seemingly focused on some internal horizon. They were strangely transparent. It was, Lorenzo recognized, the look of a scholar, out of touch with the world that surrounded him.

His clothing was similarly not-of-the-world. He was formally dressed in a fine silk doublet and tunic over silk hose and shirt. But the tunic hung halfway down his calf, an antique style, and the blue silk was so old that it was mottled green. His sword belt was made of flat gold links, another outmoded fashion, and his sword was in the knightly style, too long and narrow for anything other than display. Lorenzo had to struggle to keep from smiling.

"Come with me," Antonio said. "I insist that you look at the lunette last. Else you will not give just attention to the others. They are on the garden wall. Follow me."

He hurried them through the square entrance hall and an austerely furnished salone to an open door leading to a walled garden.

"Turn and see," said the old man.

Between the tall ground floor windows and the windows of the upper floor seven rectangular plaques glowed in bright enameled colors. They were scenes from Old Testament stories: Daniel in the lion's den, Joseph in his coat of many colors, David and Goliath, Jonah and the whale, the animals entering the ark, the parting of the Red Sea.

"Name of God, they are magnificent!" boomed Verrocchio. "Messer Antonio, do you have a ladder?"

"I'll send for one." Antonio gestured to a steward who was almost as old as he was. The man hobbled away and returned with surprising speed, dragging a ladder. Botticelli ran to him to relieve him of it. Then the three young men moved it from one enamel to another, taking turns to climb up for a close look, shouting at each other.

Antonio listened, smiling, to the agitated appraisals of the plaques. It was agreed at once that these were the best things the della Robbia studio had ever done. But there was heated disagreement about which of the group was superior to the others. And excited demands that everyone look more closely at the modeling on this or that detail or the particular depth of color or the composition of the figures or the extent of foreshortening or the degree of perspective. Some of the comments were so technical that Antonio had to ask for explanations.

Botticelli and Verrocchio then disagreed loudly about the best way to explain.

Lorenzo looked nervously at Antonio. He would have liked to enter the argument himself, but he realized that the noisy, enthusiastic discussion might appear more like a near-brawl than a search for accuracy to an outsider. He was afraid that Antonio might tell them to leave before he learned if the rumors about Ginevra were true. He had to stop Andrea and Sandro.

Before he could get their attention another argument caught his. Two men entered the garden through a small door in the brick wall, both talking, gesturing wildly, almost hissing at each other. They were speaking Latin.

Botticelli and Verrocchio fell silent, staring at the unlikely pair. One was a friar, tiny and fragile-looking in his voluminous shabby brown robe. His tonsure gleamed pink in a circle of wispy white hair. The other was large, but he looked just as breakable as the little friar. His bony wrists showed below the sleeve of his black cotton tunic, and his knees seemed ready to split the black cotton hose on his long skinny legs. He was very blond and very young, his wide mouth as pink as the friar's scalp.

Lorenzo fought the desire to laugh. The entire scene was like a low comedy played on a Carnival float. The antique host, rowdy artists and beggarly Latinists. He wondered which part he was playing.

"Mateo, Marco," called Antonio, "leave off your disputation and come meet our guests." The new arrivals looked away from each other and halted their speech and their movements. Then they smiled and hastened to join the group near the villa.

Antonio made the introductions. Fra Marco was a companion of many years standing. He lived at the villa and said mass for the household in the small chapel on the grounds. "Mateo is my granddaughter's tutor. He has only recently come to join us."

Lorenzo expressed his pleasure at their meeting. Then quickly, before the opportunity escaped him, he asked if he could see Ginevra.

"Of course," Antonio said. "Where is she, Mateo?"

The tutor blinked. "I have no idea, Excellency. Have you, Fra Marco?"

The friar shook his head.

Antonio looked vaguely at a lemon tree near his elbow, as if the child might be there. "She must be with your wife, Mateo."

"No, Excellency. Emilia is visiting her family in Arezzo, don't you remember?"

Lorenzo felt his temper rising. It was true. Antonio let the little girl run wild. And it would do no good to speak to him about it. He was too engrossed in his own internal world of the mind to care. The others were no better. They had the same abstracted scholarly look as Antonio. If Ginevra were eaten by wolves they probably wouldn't notice her absence unless her bare bones were put on top of the text they were studying. His father's reconciliation with his cousin was going to be shattered by these learned fools.

Antonio was presenting the friar and tutor to the artists. Lorenzo ground his teeth.

And Ginevra watched and listened from her perch on a branch high in a tree on one side of the garden.

She would answer if anyone called her, but no one had. Until that happened, she could look at Lorenzo and worship. When he asked for her, she had almost climbed down, but her arms acted independently and held fast to the tree. She could have talked to her friend from the birthday party, but not to the heroic master of the tournament. She was only a child, an ignorant child, too, as her grandfather kept saying. And children do not address heroes.

But they can look at the changing expressions on the hero's face and store them up in memory with the words in the hero's voice and the sound of the hero's laughter . . .

"Ginevra!" Fra Marco's small body made a large sound. "She might be around here someplace," he said in his normal quiet voice. Then he looked toward the shaking leaves of the tree. "She is. Astonishing."

Lorenzo wanted to deny the evidence of his eyes. The little girl came down from the tree like a monkey. She was all brown. Her skin tanned from the sun, her clothing a coarse brown peasant's tunic tied with a frayed piece of rope, her hair half undone from the single braid down her back and dotted with cocklespurs. Her feet were bare and stained with earth.

She stood at the base of the tree and stared at him, brown eyes huge in her brown face.

"Contadina," Lorenzo muttered. Peasant. It was an epithet of despair. It was what Pierfrancesco would think.

Ginevra heard it as the affectionate nickname of the birthday party, and she laughed. Her laughter was fresh and free and happy. "Greetings, Lorenzo," she said. She used the Latin words without self-consciousness.

Lorenzo was intrigued. What was this nest of scholars producing?

He looked at Antonio, ignored his scowl. "May I take your granddaughter for a brief walk, Excellency?"

"If you do not fear contamination. She is disgracefully dirty."

Lorenzo took the child to the end of the garden where they sat on a stone bench and talked. Her Latin was extremely limited, he discovered at once. But her Italian was flawless. And she could still speak the language of the country people fluently.

She answered his questions artlessly, giving him a complete picture of her life with Antonio. Learning was valued above all other things there. She had a breakfast of milk and bread at sunrise, then worked with her tutor until midday. In the afternoons, while Mateo taught Antonio and Fra Marco Greek, Ginevra went to one of the farms on Antonio's property to play with the farmer's children and help with the work in the fields. When the sun was low in the sky, she returned to the villa for a bath and clean clothes. Then she had the evening meal with her elders, listening to their talk and learning from it.

"And do you enjoy your life, Contadina?"

"Oh, yes! I love it." Her eyes were shining, her brown cheeks pink with fervor. "Do you want to know what happens, Lorenzo?"

He hid his amusement. "Very much," he said.

"Then I'll tell you. Mateo shows me something and explains it—grammar or the way a poem is made—and it makes no sense to me. So I turn it around in my thoughts. This way and then that way and then squeeze it some and try it next to what I learned yesterday or the day before or something I heard at table. Then all of a sudden—pop—all by myself, it comes clear. It's very exciting."

Lorenzo looked at the rapturous smudged face of the tiny scholar. It was an odd sensation to feel respect for a mere child; she had described an experience he had had a thousand times. He had felt the excitement, too. He still did.

But scholarship would not reconcile Pierfrancesco to a betrothal. Ginevra had to be trained in life and civilized behavior. "Who is Mateo's wife?" he asked. "Does she give you lessons, too?"

"Emilia? Certainly not. She doesn't know anything. She washes my hair and laces my dress up the back. I wear real clothes in the house. These are my farm things."

"I see. Do you like farming as much as your lessons?"

"More, sometimes. Farming makes so much sense.

If you plant things and take care of them, God will have them reward you. You can see them grow. The plants and the animals. One farm has five chickens. I saw them come out of the eggs. That's where I usually go. There's a girl just my age. Her mother is wonderful. She calls me her orphan child. I usually eat with them because there's never enough to eat at the villa. Grandfather says that a full stomach suffocates the mind.''

Lorenzo was in a dilemma. Ginevra had a life that was totally unsuitable for a girl of good family. Something would have to be done. And yet he wished he could leave her as she was. Her life was a kind of paradise. He had always loved the country and country people. And he never tired of study and learning. He envied this child who had both in full measure.

It would serve no purpose to admonish Antonio. The old man would be offended and would probably forget what was said as soon as he returned to his books. Lorenzo searched his mind for a solution.

Ginevra inadvertently gave him the answer. "Have you seen Bianca? Is the baby growing very fast? I'm glad to be out of that house, but I miss Bernardo. He has our birthday, too, you remember.''

Lorenzo smiled. "I remember. And I'll arrange for you to see him. I'll talk to Bianca tomorrow.''

"You will? Oh, thank you, Lorenzo.''

"I'm happy to do it, Contadina," he said. More than happy, he thought. Bianca will provide the training Ginevra needs. She has daughters, she'll know what to do. He sat very still, relishing the relief of having found a solution. For the moment, he was unaware of the child next to him.

Ginevra was looking up at him, mute, star struck. I should have known Lorenzo would make things perfect, she was thinking. He can do anything. How lucky that I asked about Bernardo. All I had to do was ask . . . What if I asked about the other thing I want . . . ? Would he do that, too . . . ? Would it make him angry . . . ?

Lorenzo's lips curled in a self-congratulatory smile.

I'll ask, Ginevra thought. She shivered, but she

plunged ahead. "Could you talk to Grandfather, too, Lorenzo? Talk to Bianca and to Grandfather?"

Lorenzo was surprised from his reverie. "What? Talk to your grandfather? About what?" Puzzlement made him frown.

Ginevra shivered again. She should not have asked, and now it was too late to stop. Her voice quavered. "About a horse. I do so much want a horse. Grandfather won't let me ride his, and all Fra Marco has is a donkey. Mateo is afraid of horses, so he rides in a cart behind a big fat mule."

Lorenzo was annoyed, but the terror on Ginevra's suddenly colorless face touched his heart. She was, indeed, an orphan child. "It would not be right for me to talk to your grandfather," he said carefully. "He is older than I am, and it would be wrong for me to tell him what his granddaughter should have."

Lorenzo thought of the plans he was making. No consideration of Antonio's rights over his granddaughter is interfering with what I want, he admitted to himself. What hypocrites adults are with children.

"Why are you laughing, Lorenzo?"

"Because I am enjoying myself. I can promise you this, Contadina. The day will come when you will have a horse. Will that satisfy you for now?"

Ginevra's face lit up. "Oh yes," she said.

"Now I must join my friends. Help me find them."

Verrocchio and Botticelli were in front of the house admiring the lunette above the door. "Give me a turn on that ladder, rogues," Lorenzo shouted.

After a close look, he ran his fingers reverently over the intricate modeling of the enameled clay, following the serene curve of the arched top and the forceful curves of the angels' wings. He climbed down, backed away from the wall and gazed up.

Inside the semicircle of blue, two golden-winged angels bracketed the green-robed figure of Christ. He held an open book in one hand, the letters Alpha and Omega on the pages. The other hand was raised, fingers slightly curved. It looked to Lorenzo like a holy blessing for his plans.

"You want me to do what? You must have taken leave of your senses, Lorenzo. The nursery maids would never forgive me if I brought Ginevra back into the house." Bianca lost none of her placidity, but her chin was firmly set under its soft flesh.

Lorenzo was amazed. He had always been closer to Bianca than to his other two sisters, and he thought he knew her well. This adamant resistance was a part of her character that he had never seen before. He wanted to grab her shoulders and shake her. Wisely, he decided to try persuasion instead.

"Sweet sister . . ."

Bianca laughed. "That won't work, dear brother."

Lorenzo threw up his hands. "Bianca, you have to help. The situation is desperate. If you'll just make the child respectable enough for the betrothal ceremony, I won't ask you to do any more."

Bianca's eyes were round and bright. "What betrothal?" she asked, eager for gossip. "Everybody in town is wondering who will get her."

"You don't know? She's to marry Pierfrancesco's son, my godson, Lorenzo."

"Our cousin? That's splendid. Her dowry is immense. And when Antonio dies . . ." Bianca frowned suddenly. "But the girl is an abomination, Lorenzo. We can't have her become a Medici. She'll disgrace the whole family unless she learns how to behave."

Lorenzo waited while his sister convinced herself to do what he wanted her to do.

"That's settled, then. I'll send word to Antonio tomorrow," Bianca said at last.

"You are an angel." Lorenzo kissed her. "I was alarmed there for a minute. I didn't recognize you. Naturally I thought you knew all about it, that Elmo would tell you."

Bianca returned his kiss. "How young you are, Lorenzo. Elmo never tells me anything. You haven't been married long enough to learn it, but men and women live in different worlds. Husbands and wives make babies together and go to parties together and that's the end of it. You'll see.''

Bianca's brisk acceptance of the pattern of married life made Lorenzo feel better. She was obviously content. He need not feel responsible for Clarice's happiness. Wives created their own.

When he left the Pazzi palace Lorenzo looked at sky and shadows to gauge the hour. If he hurried, there was still time to visit his mistress before he went home. He had sent word to Lucrezia Donati that he would be coming, and he didn't want to let her down. He set off along the street at an easy lope.

He still saw Lucrezia almost daily. He had made up his mind to do so, guessing that his marriage would make her feel less important to him and unsure of her safety. As it turned out, he went to Lucrezia less to reassure her than to seek confidence for himself. Until Clarice, Lorenzo had always been welcomed to the arms and the beds of women. The joyless sex act with her made him feel brutal, and it deadened his spirit. The house on the Via de' Pucci had become an oasis of renewal. As he ran, he composed a poem for his beloved.

Chapter Eight

The ceremony of betrothal between Lorenzo de Pier-francesco de' Medici and Ginevra de' Pazzi took place on October tenth. As was the custom, it was held in the home of the bride's family and the groom was not present. Lorenzo acted as proxy for his young cousin. He was also the proxy for his father in signing the contract.

Bianca had done a masterful job on Ginevra. The little girl stood quietly throughout the long process of signing and witnessing the documents. When she was called, she stepped forward and waited, eyes cast downward, to play her role.

She looked demure and charmingly shy. Her face was pale from the quantities of powder Bianca had rubbed into her skin, and her light brown hair gleamed from herb rinses and hour-long brushing. It was wrapped with ropes of pearls. Bianca had made sure that Ginevra would be a credit to the house of Pazzi. Her gamurra was made of yellow silk damask, her cioppa of deep blue wool. The Pazzi colors were blue and gold. Two bellicose dolphins erect on their tails were embroidered in gold on the left sleeve of the cioppa. Each scale was distinct; the eyes were sapphires; the extended tongues were made of minute rubies; the sharp teeth were formed with silver thread. It was the Pazzi coat of arms.

When instructed, Ginevra held out her hand. Lorenzo slid the betrothal ring over her thumb and held it there for a moment. The ring was a round ruby carved with the Medici coat of arms: six balls on a shield. It was a solemn occasion, and Lorenzo did not allow his smile to show. Ginevra's unpowdered hand was as brown as a chestnut.

She looked up at him and smiled. It required all Lorenzo's self-control not to laugh. Her milk teeth were gone but not yet replaced. The center of her smile was composed of bright pink gums.

He removed the ring and handed it to the waiting notary for addition to her dowry. Ginevra curtsied to Lorenzo, then to each of the adults present. Then she walked to Pierfrancesco, sank to her knees and kissed his hand in token of daughterly submission. Bianca held her breath. Pierfrancesco kissed the top of Ginevra's bowed head.

The little girl stood, turned slowly and walked out of the room with her head high and back straight. Bianca expelled her breath in a relieved sigh. Ginevra had performed perfectly.

Stewards came in with trays holding golden goblets of wine and silver plates piled high with little cakes. The formalities were done. Now everyone could enjoy himself with toasts and responses made and mutual congratulations. The entire Pazzi family was in attendance. Jacopo, his smile as fierce as that of the Pazzi dolphins; Antonio, his mind on other things; their younger brother Andrea with his six sons; Elmo and his younger brothers, Giovanni and Francesco. The wives clustered at one end of the room talking about their children. The men talked about hunting.

Lorenzo caught Bianca's eye and winked. She laughed, then whispered to the women, telling them all about the magic she had done to make Ginevra presentable.

When the celebration ended, Lorenzo and Pierfrancesco walked home together, carrying dolphin-crested gold boxes of confetti. Pierfrancesco turned into the Medici palace with Lorenzo.

"I'll just go see your father, Lorenzo," he said. Pierfrancesco was a regular visitor now. There was not much time left to make up for the years of estrangement. Piero was visibly weaker every day.

Lucrezia de' Medici met the men at the top of the stairs. Lorenzo answered her silent question with a smiling nod. All was well.

"Have you confetti . . . ? Good. There's cause for it here, too. Clarice just told me that she is with child. Piero will be so happy. It is what he most wanted. Congratulations, my son."

Lorenzo shouted with joy, capered, lifted his mother and swung her in a circle. Cosimo had said sorrowfully that the Medici palace was too big a house for such a small family. Lorenzo remembered the words when he saw the strong sons of the Pazzi and their cheerful chattering wives. But now there would be new life in the house of the Medici. It was the best cause for celebration that he had ever known.

I knew the little contadina would bring me good fortune, he thought. The following day he rode to his stables and selected the most beautiful yearling. "School him well," he ordered. "Teach him to be gentle. Then send him as a gift to my young friend at the Villa La Vacchia."

"Lorenzo . . ."

He had to put his ear close to his father's lips to hear him. "My son, I love you. I would spare you the burden that will fall on you when I am gone. I would live to carry it longer, but I cannot."

"Father, don't say those things. This is only a bad spell of illness. You've had them before. You will get stronger soon."

"We have no time for lies, Lorenzo. Heed me . . ."

"Yes."

"Take care of your brother. You must be father to him as well as to your son when he is born."

"I will."

Piero struggled for breath. Lorenzo held out his hands to him, helpless, knowing that his touch would cause greater pain. Piero was the color of an eggshell, more fragile than one. He coughed feebly, thin tears welling in his filmy eyes. The rattle in his throat faded.

"Tommaso Soderini," he whispered. "Go to him for

help in governing . . . to your mother for wisdom . . . do you hear me?''

"I hear, Father. I will do all you say." Piero's ravaged face contorted horribly. Then it relaxed. As Lorenzo watched, the lines around the mouth and eyes lost their definition, smoothed into tension-free oblivion. The suffering was erased and Piero slid into a coma.

Three days later he died, on December 3, 1469.

On December 5, he was buried in the sacristry of the church of San Lorenzo, not far from the tomb of Cosimo.

That night, Lorenzo did not sleep at all. He knew what was expected of him, what would happen the next day or the day after. He would be given "the care of the State," become the untitled leader of the Republic. He strode restlessly across his study for hours, his mind and heart in turmoil.

"It's too soon," he said aloud, "I'm not ready."

And, "It's not fair. Piero was forty-seven when it came to him; I'm not yet twenty-one."

The profiles of statesmen on the antique medallions he collected seemed to mock him. You were confident enough when you boasted to Cosimo, he imagined them saying.

He wanted to smash them under his heel.

He paced furiously to the display case and opened its door . . . and began to laugh. Lorenzo, he thought, you won't have to worry about accepting or refusing if the Signoria learn that you hear voices in the middle of the night . . . no, the night's over. Voices at dawn.

He crossed the room again, slowly this time, and stood before the window. His restlessness was done. He watched the sun rise over Florence, and he was motionless. Why was he behaving like a child, what purpose was there in lying to himself?

He smiled at his beloved city and spoke quietly to her. "I want it. The tedium and the demands, the glory and the adventure, the triumphs and the failures. All of it. Yes, and the risks and the dangers, too. I want it all. I will do as I promised Cosimo. I will love you, Florence, and care for you and guide you. I will make you mine."

The delegation came that afternoon. Tommaso Soderini was the spokesman. He extended the condolences of the government and formally requested Lorenzo to assume the care of the State.

Lorenzo replied with a speech as polished as Soderini's, thanking the government for its sympathy and for the honor of the request. He would, he said, ask no greater privilege in life than the opportunity to serve the Republic.

On one condition.

The delegation had expected Lorenzo's speech. They were not prepared for the condition.

Lorenzo insisted that his brother be regarded as equal partner with him. There was a long moment of silence.

Then Soderini accepted on behalf of the citizens of Florence.

Lorenzo had tested his strength, and he had won.

1470–1471

Chapter Nine

His strength was tested again very soon, this time by others. A group of exiled Florentine nobles hired a mercenary army and attacked Prato, a subject-city twenty miles from Florence. They believed that Florence was ripe for the taking with only a youth to rally opposition.

But the citizens of Prato did not join their forces, and their army was easily defeated. Florence did not even know about the danger until after it had ceased to exist.

Lorenzo was exultant. He knew that the displaced nobles were always a threat, always plotting to regain power. Like every powerful family, the Medici had observers and informers everywhere and received regular reports on activities and attitudes over all Europe. Now the dissidents had made their move and been defeated. He could stop worrying about them.

More importantly, the people of Prato had remained loyal, and the people were Lorenzo's main concern. He had been given the "care of the State." In his mind that meant the "care of the people."

He spent more time than ever walking through the streets of Florence, making himself available to the people, demonstrating his preference for their company and their interests above the company and interests of the councillors and legislators and bureaucrats with whom he now had to spend so much time.

He was even patient with the hundreds of petitioners who came to the palace begging his help in securing work or promotion or tax relief. His only concession to the demands of his new position was that he hired a secretary. He could no longer write responses to every letter himself.

"My son, you will kill yourself within a year," Lucrezia fretted.

Lorenzo laughed and embraced her. "Nonsense. I've never felt better. I like being busy."

Giuliano worried about him, too. He knew, even better than Lucrezia, how little rest Lorenzo took, because he was one of his brother's companions for most of his nongovernment activities. They went together to see what their artist friends were working on, and they hunted in the woods around the Medici villas, riding as far as Pisa, two days away, in search of special game. They visited the farms, they planned new floats and spectacles for Carnival, they applauded Luigi Pulci's newest ballads in the taverns, they joined in games of calcio on the Piazza Santa Croce. Lorenzo urged Giuliano to take part in the political process, too, but the younger brother begged off.

"It's more than I can do to keep up with you as it is. Anything more would put me in my grave. Won't you slow down just a little, Lorenzo?"

"But I have," Lorenzo said. His eyes sparked with humor. "Didn't you notice that I passed up the pretty little widow who needed consoling at Pisa? I even spend less time with my Lucrezia. The Signoria should appreciate the sacrifices I make for the State."

Giuliano guffawed. "They're all so old they don't remember what it is you're sacrificing."

Lorenzo smiled. He knew, from the talk at the priors' dinner table, that Giuliano was badly mistaken.

It was no less bawdy than the conversation at his own table. He seldom ate with the women now. In order to see his friends, he held perpetual dinnertime open house when he was at home. Any one of his intimates could come at any time, bringing anyone who had wit and talent. Often the laughter from the lighted room rang in the dark stone street outside until dawn.

Early in June Clarice gave birth to a crimson, squalling, healthy baby girl. Lorenzo was entranced by the tiny creature. He insisted that she be called Lucrezia, the name dearest to him of any that could be given a girl child.

Giuliano teased him gleefully. "You are a clever dog, brother. Now your mistress will have to stop feeling neglected and our mother will have to overlook the way you've turned the house into a tavern."

"Just as she ignores your sins," Lorenzo replied. "Now that I have a child I can understand why. There's some alchemy that makes purple splotched skin beautiful and two ears a rare accomplishment."

"You're besotted."

"I admit it."

In truth, Lorenzo was happier than he had ever been in all his pleasure-filled years. He gloried in his participation in the government, even though it was annoying that the councillors sometimes seemed to regard him as no more than a boy. He enjoyed the pomp and drama of his role as host to ambassadors and visiting dignitaries. He relished the ability to help the deserving with appointments to well-paying government positions. He secretly liked even more to aid a special few undeserving with appointments, because they were talented at music or poetry.

He liked power.

He was careful not to abuse it. At all times his first love was for Florence and her people and her republican form of rule. Cosimo was his ideal. "Father of the State," the title he wanted to earn.

On his twenty-second birthday, he went to Cosimo's tomb again to talk to him. "I believe you must be pleased with me, Grandfather. I am doing all that is asked of me and more for the Republic. I have a child born and another to be born in seven months, so the Palazzo Medici is filled with new life. I am filled with joy that the city welcomes the love I give it and returns love to me."

Lorenzo felt peace in the dim silence of the great church. He knelt for an hour, praying from a heart brimming with gratitude for his blessings.

He saw no omens to warn him of what lay so near in the future.

* * *

Two months later Lorenzo was host to Florence's strongest ally, Galeazzo Sforza, the Duke of Milan. Sforza was fully aware of the importance to Florence of Milan's support, and he was a demanding and extravagant guest. He was accompanied by his duchess, his daughters, their ladies-in-waiting, five hundred foot soldiers, one hundred mounted knights, fifty grooms, dozens of trumpeters, drummers, huntsmen, falconers, falcons and hounds. Lorenzo had to arrange and pay for their food and lodging and entertainment during the eight-day visit. He declared festival in Florence for the entire period and, with his brother's help, put on a series of spectacles that dazzled even the jaded Milanese.

Clarice entered into the festivities with uncharacteristic enthusiasm. To be hostess to a powerful head of state was a triumph, even for a woman from one of the great families of Rome. More and more she was learning to appreciate the pleasures of her position as Lorenzo's wife. Just as petitioners lined the courtyard of the palace waiting to see him, so, too, did Clarice have her share of supplicants. They flattered her, treated her with fulsome deference, begged her to use her influence with her husband on their behalf. Clarice felt that she was respected as she deserved to be, and she liked it. In her way, she became devoted to Lorenzo. She found no pleasure in his visits to her bed, but she received him without revulsion, and her easy pregnancies reinforced her self-esteem. Childbearing was a woman's primary duty.

On the fifth day of the Duke's visit, tragedy interrupted the gala celebrations. The church of Santo Spirito caught fire during the performance of a sacred play, and hundreds of people were killed or injured in the fire and the terrorstruck stampede from the building.

It was God's judgment, the Florentines said fearfully, a sign of divine wrath at the impious Milanese who were eating meat during Lent at the banquets given for them.

Even Clarice was frightened. She spent hours every

day in the small chapel at the palace, praying with the priest who was part of the household.

But Lorenzo continued to devote himself to Galeazzo's amusement. Personal diplomacy was Lorenzo's strongest asset as the Republic's leader. His first diplomatic mission had been a visit to Milan when he was fifteen. There he had made friends with Galeazzo and Galeazzo's sister, Ippolita. Through her, he had become close to the family of the King of Naples, because Ippolita was betrothed to Alfonso, the heir to the throne, and Alfonso's brother was in Milan as proxy for the betrothal ceremony. The friendships strengthened alliances with Milan and Naples that were crucial to Florence's security.

For the three remaining days with the Duke of Milan, Lorenzo was apparently lighthearted and totally absorbed in pleasure.

As soon as the gigantic retinue departed for Milan, his demeanor changed. He initiated a committee for the sober work of locating the victims of the fire at Santo Spirito to provide assistance and support. Santo Spirito was the church of Florence's poorest inhabitants, the laborers in the woolen factories.

Already saddened by the Santo Spirito disaster, he fell into despair when Clarice had a miscarriage ten days after the Sforza party was gone. For the first time in his life, he could not concentrate, could find no joy in his work. Clarice rejected his attempts at condolence. It was God's will, she said, a just retribution for the blasphemy of the Milanese.

Lucrezia de' Medici held her son in her arms while he wept.

Then she sent him out into the city. "Walk," she commanded. "Let the people share your grief, Lorenzo. They will heal your heart's wounds."

Lorenzo did her bidding and discovered that she was right. He was surrounded by love and compassion everywhere he went. In the Mercato, vendors pressed him to accept a wing of fowl or a bit of cheese or a cup of wine or a saffron cake. Their sympathy was mute, expressed only by their offerings and the tears in their eyes. People made way for him on the crowded streets, opening an avenue for his stumbling progress. As he passed among them he could feel their eyes on him and hear stifled sobs. The sharing lessened his anguish; he felt as if every Florentine was taking a fragment of his sorrow and experiencing it for him.

He returned home as dark was falling and sought out his mother. His face was drawn but no longer bitter. He knelt beside Lucrezia's chair, took her hands in his, kissed her palms. "Thank you for your wisdom, Mamina." Lucrezia rested her cheek lightly on his bent head.

"Giuliano, I am going to Verrocchio's studio to start the plans for this year's Carnival float. Move your lazy bones and come with me."

"My bones are promised at a game of calcio. Why don't you come with me instead?"

Lorenzo was tempted, but resisted. He felt a need to create something, not to bruise and be bruised. And he had an idea for a design that should be sketched while it was still fresh in his mind.

Andrea del Verrocchio's workshop was near the river. The breeze across the water carried the scent of freshly tilled fields on the hills beyond the city walls. Lorenzo felt the annual rebirth of the land, remembered that the Feast of the Annunciation and the beginning of the New Year was only a few days away. His step became lighter, and his heart.

He turned a corner into the alley that led to the workshop and collided with a tall, thin young man.

"Forgive me," Lorenzo said. "I hope I didn't hurt you."

His victim shook his head. "No, no, Excellency. I did not look where I was going. Forgive me." He brushed his long fingers across the rumpled folds of his dark scholar's coat.

Lorenzo squinted. He was trying to remember the man's face. Then he saw the cranelike black-stockinged legs and the memory came to him. It was Mateo, the tutor of Antonio de' Pazzi's granddaughter.

"And how is Messer Antonio, Mateo?"

"He is well, Excellency."

"How about Ginevra? Do her lessons go well?"

Mateo grinned. "With me, yes," he said. "But with the music master, listen. She is having her lesson now."

Lorenzo heard a mournful howl from Verrocchio's studio. It was the voice of a man. "Her teacher?" he asked Mateo.

The tutor nodded. "Always the same," he said. "I walk the alley reciting aloud so that I don't have to hear."

Lorenzo laughed. He stepped quietly inside Verrocchio's cavernous workshop and stood in a deep shadow. He looked in the direction of the sound of notes plucked on a lute and held his breath at the beauty that he saw. The young music master had fair hair haloed by the light of a nearby window. The nimbus framed a head and narrow features of classical purity. It hardly seemed possible that this was a human, not an ideal man carved from marble.

Andrea del Verrocchio loomed suddenly from the darkness at Lorenzo's side. "I was amazed, too," he said quietly. "He's a recent apprentice. The injustice of it is that he is as gifted as he is handsome. No discipline, though. He always wants to experiment with something new when I'm trying to teach him the way things are done."

"Is he a good musician?"

"Brilliant. But I think he may have met defeat in the little Pazzi. Watch. It's my weekly amusement."

The apprentice struck a note, then sang it. "Do you hear?" he said to Ginevra. "They're the same, the sound of the instrument in my hands and the instrument in my throat." He repeated the exercise. "A . . . A . . . A . . . Now, you pluck the string, Ginevra . . . Good . . . Now again, while I sing . . . A . . . A . . . A . . . Did you hear? Good. Now pluck it again while you sing."

"A . . . A . . . A . . ."

"STOP!" The word was a shout of pain. The young teacher held his head in his hands. "An abomination," he groaned. He sat up suddenly, grabbed Ginevra's head. "Open your mouth wide." He peered inside at her throat, felt her neck, tried to see inside her ear.

He dropped his hands and shook his head slowly. "I cannot understand it," he sighed. Ginevra's frog voice was a puzzle, and he was fascinated by puzzles. He was sure he could solve this one. Every week he thought of a new approach. And every week he failed.

Ginevra's sigh echoed his. "I can't understand it either. I hear the song in my head. Then I play what I hear on the lute, and you say it's right. But as soon as I sing what I hear, you say it's wrong and start all over with the A's and 'open your mouth.' It's the same tune, on the lute or singing. Are you sure you're not making a mistake?"

"I am very sure. Never in my life have I been so sure. Come, let's try it again."

Verrocchio pulled Lorenzo into the light. "Wait," he said. "I don't want my friend to have to suffer with us."

The musicians stood when Andrea and Lorenzo approached them. "This is Leonardo da Viñci, Lorenzo. You'll be glad to know, Leonardo, that Lorenzo needs no lessons."

Lorenzo laughed. Andrea knew that he could sing no better than Ginevra. He looked down at the little girl. She had grown so much since he had last seen her at the betrothal ceremony that he would not have known who she was. Lorenzo was pleased with what he saw now. She was neatly dressed and silent, as she should be until she was spoken to. Bianca was doing well with her. Pierfrancesco could have no cause for complaint.

"How are you, Ginevra?" Lorenzo asked.

She swallowed and curtseyed. "Well, I thank you." The words were barely a whisper.

Lorenzo was no longer pleased. Ginevra had spoken clearly enough to Leonardo. Why not to him? He did not recognize the adulation that was strangling her. To Ginevra, Lorenzo was a supernatural being, a magician who caused her heart's desire to materialize from thin air. The horse from his stables, a gift he had forgotten long since, was to her a miracle.

"Do you like music?" he asked. Ginevra nodded dumbly. This will not do, Lorenzo thought. She must learn not to be so timid. "Then please play for us," he said. It was an order.

Ginevra did not delay. She would do anything he wanted, grateful for the chance to please him.

Leonardo accompanied her; his subtle counterpoint filled and rounded Ginevra's wavering beginner's plucking and made it sound like music.

Lorenzo nodded to Andrea. Here was a talent indeed. When the little song ended, he asked Leonardo if he would play alone.

"Willingly," he replied. He cradled the lute closer to him, bent his head toward it with the gesture of a lover. His lithe, beautiful fingers caressed and commanded the strings, and sound shimmered in the room. The music he made was strong, yet tender, each note so pure that it pierced the heart. His was not a talent, but a genius.

The other apprentices had come close while Leonardo played. When he finished, his audience paid him the tribute of absolute silence while the memory of his music hovered in the studio.

Then, "Bravissimo," Lorenzo said. "Bravissimo, maestro."

Leonardo smiled. Then his fingers danced on the strings, playing an ancient folk song. The apprentices joined in, singing.

Lorenzo looked at Ginevra and laughed. "Come, Contadina, this is a song we can sing, too." He bawled out the words, using the thick country accent of their origin.

Ginevra stared. Her idol sounded like a donkey braying. The sounds were horrible. She turned to Leonardo. "Is that the kind of noise I make?" she shouted. Leonardo nodded. His forehead was wrinkled from the pain Lorenzo's singing gave to his finely tuned ears.

"I'm sorry, then," she yelled. "I'll never sing for you again . . . after this time."

The rollicking song went on, verse after verse. Ginevra jumped up and ran to Lorenzo's side. His flaw made him approachable. She leaned against his arm and joined her dissonances with his.

When the song was ended, Lorenzo left the studio with Ginevra and delivered her to Mateo. The rowdy interlude had restored his energies, and the sharp spring air promised that anything, everything was possible. He felt a surge of love for life, for all living things.

"Give me your hand, Contadina. I'll walk you home and pay a visit to my other birthday partner. How is Bernardo growing? Does he torment his little brother?" Bianca had given birth to another son, this time without the drama of her hectic departure from Lorenzo's coming-of-age party, and she was hugely pregnant again.

"Bernardo's fat and wonderful, but I'm not going straight home," Ginevra said. "Mateo's taking me by the tailor's shop first. Would you like to walk there with us?"

"Yes. I would. I'd rather be walking than in the house anyhow."

The little girl clapped her hands, then slid one of them into Lorenzo's palm.

"I've grown three inches this year," Ginevra offered. "That's why I'm going to the tailor. He had to let down the hems on my dress-up clothes. I'm to wear them for the procession to the *Scoppio*. I've never walked in a procession. Or anywhere in the dark. It's at midnight, you know."

"Yes, I know."

Ginevra looked thoughtful. Of course he knew. He must know everything. "Lorenzo, what is the Scoppio exactly?" she asked. "All I know really is that I mustn't talk while we're walking there."

"No, you mustn't. It's a very solemn occasion." His smile removed all threat from the words. "You'll love it. There's a beautiful white silk dove above the altar in the Duomo. At midnight mass the Archbishop lights a fireworks rocket that's concealed inside the dove. Bright sparks shoot from its tail, and it flies along a wire the whole length of the cathedral, then out the door onto the piazza. It goes right into the center of a huge pile of fireworks on a cart there, and the whole thing explodes. Rockets go up into the sky, and small crackers swirl around the paving stones until they burn out. The noise is wonderful. The piazza is full of people, and they all cheer. Everyone in the Duomo runs as the dove flies, so they are outside too, cheering.''

''Why are they cheering?''

''Because the Scoppio tells them that the crops will be good and no one will be hungry. The bigger the explosion, the better the harvest.''

''Oh, I'll like that! Grandfather didn't tell me there'd be fireworks and lots of people. I thought it was just a family thing.''

Lorenzo laughed to himself. How like Antonio. For that matter, how like the Pazzi family. The Scoppio ceremony was the most important event of the year to Jacopo de' Pazzi. Probably to Antonio, too. On Easter Eve the entire family formed a procession at the Palazzo Pazzi, all dressed in the blue and gold colors, all wearing the Pazzi coat of arms. Jacopo's surcoat was a blaze of small dolphins repeated a hundred times in gold thread. He led the family to Florence's oldest church, Santi Apostoli, where the Archbishop delivered to him the Pazzi's richest prize: flints from the stones in the Holy Sepulcher, the tomb of Christ. An early Pazzi had brought them back from Jerusalem in 1099 when he returned from the First Crusade. Jacopo carried the flints and led the procession through the torch-lit city streets to the Duomo, the Archbishop and his clergy and his choir following.

Jacopo released the flints to the Archbishop at the altar. They were used to strike the sparks that lit the dove. Many Florentines, including Lorenzo, were sure that when the people along the procession route genuflected as the holy relics passed, old Jacopo thought they were honoring him. And the Pazzi.

Lorenzo wondered for a moment if Ginevra would learn that overbearing family vanity from her grandfather; it might make her a difficult bride for his young cousin. He decided that it was foolish to worry. Bianca's husband Elmo gave no sign of it even though he and his brothers had grown up under Jacopo's direction after their father died.

Besides, the child was being trained by Bianca. And even though Bianca refused to be burdened by Ginevra more than one day a week, Lorenzo trusted his sister to make a stronger impression in one day than the three scholars at the villa could in the other six. Most likely they forgot the girl was there most of the time.

"Do you still visit the farms every afternoon?" he asked.

Ginevra shook her head. "Bianca says working in the fields is forbidden. If I can't help with the work, I'm in the way, so I don't go."

"Then who do you have to play with?"

"I play chess with Fra Marco in the evening sometimes, but I don't need people to play with. I have Caesar."

Lorenzo smiled. The scholars must have named her pet. "Is Caesar your dog?"

"Of course not. Caesar is my horse that you gave me. I love him more than anything in the world. And he loves me, too. He comes when I call, even if I don't have any sugar for him."

Lorenzo thought of his first horse of his own and how special that love was. He was glad that he'd made the child so happy although he couldn't remember giving her the horse.

"He's so handsome," Ginevra boasted, "and so brave. He goes as fast as the wind, and he'll jump anything."

"I'm glad you're pleased," said Lorenzo. They had reached the tailor's shop. "Mateo!" He caught the tutor's arm before he could walk past it. Mateo was deep in his own thoughts. "Goodbye, Contadina. I enjoyed our duet." He bent and kissed Ginevra's hand as if she were an adult.

Ginevra lifted her hand close to her eyes to see if it looked any different. She thought it should, after resting in Lorenzo's hand and being touched by his lips.

Mateo had to tug on her long braid to get her attention. The tailor was waving them into the shop. Ginevra looked critically at her clothing for the first time in her life. She wanted to look her best at the Scoppio. Lorenzo would be there and she might see him.

She caught a glimpse of him when she reached the door as everyone ran after the dove. She shouted his name, but the sound was lost in the screams from the crowds in the piazza.

Tommaso Soderini paced heavily back and forth in Lorenzo's study. As his father had urged, Lorenzo relied on Soderini for guidance in his relations with the government. Usually the older man was calm and decisive. Lorenzo had never seen him so agitated.

"It was the worst Scoppio even the oldest man can remember, Lorenzo. The dove stopped, then its head blew off, then the cart exploded and shot fire into the people. Three of them died and who knows how many were burned."

"I know all that, Tommaso. I was there, too. But it is not up to us to question God's will."

Soderini waved away Lorenzo's words. He continued to pace and to talk. "The people are worried and alarmed by the omens. They need to find a way to return to God's favor. The churches are full from sunup to sundown. There is a shortage of candles because so many have bought them."

Lorenzo nodded, listening attentively, not betraying his impatience at Soderini's recital of things that everyone knew.

"They need to be freed from their despair, Lorenzo. They need to believe that the omens of Santo Spirits and the Scoppio can be overcome, that there is a way to regain the favor of God. They will take heart if we can give them a sign, a sign that God Himself will see. We must complete His cathedral, Lorenzo. We must crown the Duomo."

Lorenzo recognized at once that Soderini had found the perfect answer. The dome that rose above the cathedral was the real symbol of Florence, even more than the lion that was the official symbol. It was the biggest and the most beautiful dome in the world, the most dramatic feature of the city's skyline, the landmark visible from miles away and from almost every spot within the city. Builders from every corner of the world studied it and tried unsuccessfully to copy it. It was uniquely Florentine. And it was incomplete.

Filippo Brunelleschi, the great architect of the dome, had died before he could complete his masterpiece. The Duomo lacked the crowning touch designed by him, a great golden ball to catch and reflect the sun's rays and to serve as a flashing beacon to travelers long before the city was visible.

Andrea del Verrocchio had won the prestigious commission to create the ball. But he had not yet finished it. "Lorenzo, Andrea is your friend," said Soderini. "He will listen to you. Tell him he must hurry."

Lorenzo went to Verrocchio's studio at once. His friend welcomed him with an embrace. "I have just heard a most superb joke; you're in time to hear it before I forget it."

"We can laugh later, Andrea. I have come to talk seriously and urgently."

Verrocchio sobered. He had never seen Lorenzo so worried. "What is it?"

"I need to know about the ball for the Duomo. How is it progressing?"

"Come see. Follow me."

The ball was in the far corner of the floor, screened off by gigantic drapes of muslin. It was huge, seven and a half feet in diameter, and it glowed like a man-made setting sun. It was made of pure copper sheets hammered onto a wooden framework then polished to a satin finish without visible joins or hammer marks. Tension drained from Lorenzo's face and his voice. "Andrea, you are probably the finest craftsman in the history of Florence," he said. "The last time I saw this monster it looked poxed."

Verrocchio basked in the praise.

"So you'll find it easy to have it finished by St. John's Day." Lorenzo grinned at his friend. Andrea sputtered.

"Are you crazy? Have you ever worked with gold? First you have to hammer it into leaves thinner than silk, then each leaf has to be applied with a touch like an angel's kiss, then . . ."

"I know, I know. An insuperable task. But not for you."

"I could drown in the oil you're pouring, Lorenzo. It won't make any difference. There is no way to work that fast."

"How much?"

"Now you offend me. I'm not trying to raise my price. I tell you, it can't be done."

"Andrea, I'm imploring you. Listen. Florence needs you." Lorenzo repeated all the reasons Soderini had given, added his own convictions. "We'll raise it to its glory on the day of the city's patron saint, Andrea. Florence will be speaking to God. You must see how right that is, how much we all need this."

Verrocchio's eyes surveyed the vast expanse of copper. They narrowed while he made mental calculations. "I'd have to take all the apprentices off of whatever they were doing . . . and parcel out jobs to goldsmiths . . . and put up rings to hold torches so we can work at night . . . and pray to all the saints . . . and then perhaps, but only perhaps. One healthy sneeze and we would be ruined."

Lorenzo grabbed his shoulders and kissed him on both cheeks. "You'll begin at once?"

"Almost. After the other work is put away and our bellies are full. Will you stay and eat with us?"

"I can't. I'm promised to the Signoria for a report."

"Then be off and let me get started." Andrea opened an exit in the hangings and pushed Lorenzo through it. "And tell the priors I will need their prayers."

Chapter Ten

Verrocchio did the impossible, and on June 25, the huge golden ball was raised slowly to its place on top of the Duomo. The people of Florence celebrated with a Carnival that surpassed any in memory. As if the great ball were indeed a sun, the grapes grew plumper on the vine than they had for years and the grain was taller than a man.

Then on July 26, Pope Paul II died. The news reached Florence on August 1, and the city went into mourning. In the Medici palace, Lucrezia supervised the servants while they draped the brightly painted walls of the private chapel with black. Then she and Clarice prayed throughout the night while Lorenzo met with the government leaders in the Palazzo della Signoria. The Pope's death was a cause of sorrow for all Christianity. For the Italian states, it was also a source of political anxiety. The Pope was the ruler of the Papal States, commander of the papal armies. The uncertain balance of power, the unsteady alliances between states—all depended on the politics and character of Paul II's successor. Like all other governments in Europe, Florence would send a diplomatic delegation to Rome to meet the next Pope and establish the most favorable relations possible. The most skillful diplomats were finally agreed on. Lorenzo was the youngest and the most experienced.

The delegation left Florence a week later in a downpour that depressed Lorenzo's already apprehensive mood. The election was over and the new Pope named. He was Cardinal Francesco della Rovere, now Pope Sixtus IV. Lorenzo knew his history and his reputation. Born in a poor fishing community not far from Genoa, della Rovere had entered the Franciscan Order very young. He utilized a gift for preaching to advance his ambitions and became General of the Order before he was fifty. Only three years later he succeeded in having himself made cardinal, and now, at fifty-seven, he was Pope. He was known to be shrewdly intelligent, a learned theologian, and rapaciously ambitious for himself and his large family. He was also reputed to revel in battle.

It was necessary that Lorenzo make a friend of this suspicious belligerent man; the peace of Florence required it and the future of his family depended on it. More than half the income of the Medici bank came from its role as collector and administrator of the papal revenues, and the Medici were partners with the Papacy in a business that generated enormous profit and power. The business was a prosaic, uncomplicated enterprise—the mining of alum from the rich deposits at Tolfa, near Rome. Alum, a simple white crystalline powder, was essential to Florence's wool trade. It fixed dyes, making the famous deep colors permanent. Cosimo de' Medici had negotiated the agreements for these valuable links with the Vatican in 1462, when Pius II was Pope. Piero had maintained them when Pius and Cosimo died in the same year and Paul II became Pope. Now it was Lorenzo's turn. He had to succeed. Ten pack mules loaded with gifts were part of his baggage.

He returned to Florence after a month with the same ten mules, also carrying heavy loads. This time they were for him. Sixtus had proved to be extremely amiable. The contracts were renewed; he gave Lorenzo two antique Roman marbles to add to his collection of statuary; and he arranged for Lorenzo to buy, for a very reasonable price, a number of treasures from the collections of the previous Pope. Lorenzo was jubilant but wary. Sixtus had been too easy.

His apprehensions were quieted shortly after he arrived home. Alum had been found in Volterra, one of Florence's subject cities. The Medici bank financed the organization of a mining company. The wool trade would be safe no matter what Sixtus might do.

If only it would stop raining. The Arno was high and so muddy that the wool couldn't be washed. It was piling up in merchants' basements because there was no room left in the warehouses. Special masses were said, but the skies remained heavy and gray, and the rain was incessant. People began to mutter about the Scoppio. Crops were rotting in the fields. The Signoria sent men to reinforce the doors of Or San Michele, the communal granary. They worked in the hours before dawn so that no one would see what they were doing.

But people knew. And they knew what it meant. The government was afraid of a famine. Before the day was over, every neighborhood food shop was empty of flour. Hoarding had begun.

The rain finally stopped, but by then it was too late. When winter came there was not enough food. The city rationed the stocks kept in Or San Michele, gave weekly allotments of bread and flour, barely enough to sustain life. The weak died.

Chapter Eleven

The arrival of spring and the beginning of the New Year were welcomed by the Florentines with reverent gratitude. Already the fields were striped with the fresh green of healthy new growth, the air was sweet, the sun a benison. On Easter Eve the Scoppio sent jubilant color high into the sky. The city resounded for hours with the cheers of its people. They filled the churches the following day to celebrate the Resurrection.

Lorenzo bought forty pounds of candles for the altar of San Lorenzo and pledged the money to rebuild and enlarge the shelter for travelers outside the San Gallo gate. His acts were thanks-offerings. For the survival of his beloved city and for the new child that was growing in his wife's womb.

He was overflowing with energy. "I want to do something grand," he told Lucrezia, "something that will have meaning, will make a difference. I have an idea."

Lucrezia folded her needlework and put it to one side. "I'm listening," she said.

Lorenzo strode back and forth across her room, too excited to stay in one place. "I'll give you the ingredients first, Mamina. Be patient with me . . . Item: the city of Pisa."

Lorenzo held out his left hand. With his right, he turned back the little finger. "A vassal city for the past sixty years or so and angry about being subject to Florence."

He bent another finger. "It used to be a major port, but the harbor silted up and now only small vessels can use it."

With the third finger he said, "When the sea trade left, prosperity left. So did half the population. There are hundreds of empty houses, and they're beginning to decay.

"Marshes covered the silt, and fever came." The index finger joined the others in Lorenzo's palm, leaving his thumb protruding from a fist. He held the thumb up before him like a trophy.

"This is the University of Pisa, the pride of all Tuscany for a hundred years." He turned his wrist and the thumb pointed to the floor. "Dead!" He rounded his shoulders and bowed his head in mourning.

Lucrezia applauded the performance. Lorenzo straightened, grinned and bowed.

"Now!" he said. His open hand went up again. "Item: the city of Florence."

He held the hand to his face and looked between the spread fingers. "Watching Pisa always, worried about insurrection."

Then he lowered the left hand and closed the thumb and forefinger of his right hand around the spread fingers, squeezing. "Walls," he said, "crowding people together, and no room to build more housing."

He writhed the trapped fingers. "University students, more every year, crammed into too few rooms."

The fingers burst free from confinement. "Trouble in the street."

Both hands in front of him, palms outward, sagging from limp wrists, Lorenzo shook his head in dismay. "And not much of a University either," he said. "No good teachers are willing to be burdened with rebellious students and long waits for a lecture hall."

He smiled at Lucrezia. "I suppose you know what my idea is now."

"It's fine, Lorenzo. What will you keep in Florence?"

"Philosophy and philology. Pisa can have medicine, law and theology. Those are the most crowded classes."

Lucrezia laughed. "And the least interesting to you."

"Mamina! A secondary consideration . . . what do you think, really?"

"Really I think it is brilliant."

Lorenzo laughed. "That's what I thought, too. Pisa will have pride again, and Florence's gift will be the source. We'll drain the marshes and plant grass. There will be parks for walking and games, and clean air."

He began to pace again, energized by the future he saw. "Bologna is the seat of learning in Italy, everyone says. What they mean is the great teachers are there. I know that I can woo some of them away. 'You can design your own curriculum, Master,' I'll say, 'and your studio and your lecture hall.'"

Lorenzo's normally sallow skin was flushed; his dark hair clung to his forehead where perspiration had dampened it. "If I can do this, I'll be giving learning to the Republic's people, Mamina. There is no greater gift."

He stopped suddenly. Then he chuckled. "I'll take an oath that I was thinking of the benefits to Florence and Pisa and the Republic as a whole. But it did just occur to me that our estates near Pisa will rise in value when this is done. That will be a good thing, too."

"I agree," said Lucrezia. "Another good thing is that I won't have to worry about you and Giuliano getting the fever when you go hunting there . . . Have you thought about how you're going to get the government's support?"

"Not yet. I've been too busy with the vision of the end to think about the means. Have you time to talk with me about it? Have you any suggestions?"

"I have all the time there is, my dear. And I have two suggestions.

"First, I suggest that you sit down. My neck hurts from looking up at you.

"Second, I suggest that you consider talking to the businessmen in the student quarter. There is a lot of vandalism and pilfering. They'll be interested in reducing the student population. And their influence will offset the howls of the wineshop owners."

They talked for more than three hours. At the end of that time Lorenzo had a clear plan of action. He knew whom to see, in what order, with what arguments to gain support.

"I've never been still for so long in my entire life," he said, standing and stretching. "A walk will feel good. I should be able to see at least five or six men before the end of the day.

"My thanks, councillor." He touched his mother's cheek gently with one finger.

Lucrezia caught his hand in hers. "There's something I want to tell you before you leave." She released his hand, held him with her eyes.

"Your grandfather told me many times that the proudest accomplishment of his life was that he brought Johannis Argyropoulos to Florence. Before, there was no man who knew Greek, who could read the works of Plato as Plato wrote them. Cosimo said, as you have said, that learning is the greatest gift."

Lorenzo was motionless, solemn, silent. After a long minute, he spoke. His voice was hoarse with emotion. "I did not know . . . Thank you for telling me."

"Let's rein in, brother. I love to look from here." Lorenzo halted on the crest of the hill. Giuliano pulled up next to him. Their horses snorted and tossed their heads, throwing off drops of sweat.

The two young men wiped their hands across their faces and snapped the collected sweat off their fingertips. It was August, and they had ridden hard in the heat, covering the hundred miles from Pisa in only two days.

Below them Florence shimmered in a heat haze. The great golden ball on the Duomo flashed brightly in the slanting rays of the late afternoon sun.

Lorenzo breathed deeply. He could feel his heart beating and sensed it there in his chest, strong, surging with life and with love for his beautiful glowing city.

He tasted the salt of his sweat on his tongue, savored it, savored the moment of homecoming, the completion of a successful journey, the elation of success in everything he touched.

His plans for the University were proceeding even more quickly than he had hoped, and they had been received with enthusiasm on all sides. Because of them, his role in the Republic's government had changed. He had become truly a leader, a planner, an initiator, not simply the inheritor of honorary leadership.

Already scholars were writing to ask when the new University would be opened, whether it would have need of them. The Vatican had pledged itself to support the theological college, with funds as well as students and teachers.

It was true that Pope Sixtus had justified Lorenzo's first suspicions of him; he had taken away the Medici share of the alum concession at the same time that he gave his pledge of support to the University. But the loss was much smaller than the gain. After all, there was alum at Volterra.

And the Pope was less important than the scholars. Lorenzo discounted Sixtus as a factor in Florence's future because all reports from Rome said the same thing: the Pope was devoting all his attention to the advancement of his nephews and illegitimate sons. The latest joke along the Tiber asked "Who is the richest man in Rome?" The answer was, "There are two, the vendor of red dye and the hatmaker." Sixtus had already elevated his six cleric nephews to cardinal; he placed the red hat of office on their heads himself.

Lorenzo's horse was restive, sidestepping to avoid the lengthening thin shadow of a cypress tree. "It's getting late," he said, "let's go home."

Giuliano whooped, spurred his horse and galloped recklessly down the steep road. "Try and catch me," he challenged. Lorenzo laughed, plummeted after him.

Florence's wealthy families moved to the cooler air of their villas during the summer months. The Medici women were at the villa in Fiesole, and Giuliano joined them there. Lorenzo rode up daily for lunch but he lived in town at the palace. The trips to Pisa had swallowed almost all his time since spring, and he wanted to get back in touch with the city. He took his evening meal in the open loggia, sharing it with friends, talking with passersby, inviting some of them to stop and take a cup of wine.

Like all the city streets, the Via Larga contained a mixture of buildings. Besides the Medici palace and the big house of Pierfrancesco de' Medici, there were shops, small houses, tenements, workshops. Many of the street's men made a habit of joining the group in the loggia after their meal and talking as the light faded from the day.

They talked about the weather and its effect on business, about the weather and its effect on crops, because all but the poorest Florentines owned a small patch of land in the country to provide them with fresh produce and a little wine. They talked about the winners of the most recent calcio and the last Palio and made bets on the competitions to come. They talked about the garden that Bernardo Rucellai was filling with plants never seen before in Florence and about the Eastern astrologer who had set up a tent in the Mercato. They spoke slowly and sleepily because it was hot and night was falling. And they addressed each other with the familiar "thou" instead of the formal "you" because they were citizens of the Republic of Florence, where every man was the equal of every other, regardless of his occupation or purse.

At the end of August, Clarice gave birth to a son. Lorenzo brought his little daughter down from the villa and rode her on his shoulders through every street in the city, giving confetti to everyone and urging them to share his joy. He named the baby Piero.

To honor his father, he commissioned Verrocchio to design and build a tomb that would be the most beautiful ever created. And he paid for a lavish party at Andrea's workshop to celebrate Leonardo da Vinci's acceptance into the artists' guild of St. Luke.

The young artist fascinated Lorenzo. His skills at music did not stop with the most beautiful playing Lorenzo had ever heard; Leonardo also made his instruments. Several were grotesquely fanciful. A mandolin was the fat belly of a laughing man, a lute was shaped like a horse's head. No matter how bizarre, they all produced an exceptionally pure sound. Especially when Leonardo played them.

Like all educated men, Lorenzo was a musician and a poet. Despite his crowlike voice, his musical ear and skills were as good as any of his peers. As a poet, he was genuinely gifted. Both music and poetry came easily to him and gave him great pleasure; he excelled at both.

But Leonardo's music was of a different order altogether. Lorenzo was tempted to take lessons from the younger man. With most of the government officials away at their villas, he had more free time than usual.

Then he received a scented note tucked in a bouquet of flowers. The sender was the beautiful young wife of a rich wood merchant who had gone on a business trip to Venice. She wrote that she had come to their city house to oversee some changes in the garden. She was bored, and she was lonely.

She was also a skillful, gluttonous lover. Lorenzo decided that the music lessons could wait. The husband would only be away for a few weeks.

The affair lasted only three days. Then a dust-covered courier brought word of an uprising in Volterra. The people there had seized and occupied the alum mine.

"Lorenzo, there is no need for force." Tommaso Soderini was confident that the whole matter could be settled by negotiation and compromise.

Lorenzo was determined to put down the rebellion on his terms. Alum was too important to Florence, and without the Volterran mine, the Pope had a monopoly, could set any price he chose. The Medici no longer had a voice in the operations of the Roman mines.

Also, if Volterra could rebel and not be punished, other subject towns might follow its example.

And there was word that the Florentine exiles were involved, were urging the Volterrans to attack Florence and overthrow the Medici government.

But most important, he was tired of being told what to do by Soderini. Not only must the people of Volterra be forced to recognize Florence as master, so, too, must the old men in the council be forced to recognize that Lorenzo was no longer an inexperienced youth. He had been agreeable, deferential, an apprentice at ruling for almost three years. It was time to assert himself.

He insisted on hiring an army. The best. The most professional. The mercenaries led by the famous *condottiere* Federigo da Montefeltro, Duke of Urbino. The Signoria authorized it.

Volterra surrendered after a month's siege. Lorenzo was triumphant.

Until a second courier rode into Florence, this one with mad, staring eyes and bloodstained clothing. "We surrendered," he cried, "we opened our gates. The army marched in under the flag of truce, and then . . . and then . . . oh God have mercy . . . they destroyed everything . . . Everything. Burning, looting, murdering, raping, even the children."

Lorenzo rode at once to the rebellious town. He could not believe the report. Warfare was conducted by rules, just as tournaments were. Surrender meant safety.

When he neared the hilltop town and saw the open gates, he was sure that everything must be all right. Then he saw the carrion birds on the walls.

The invigorating crisp air of October brought everyone back from their villas to Florence. For days friends greeted each other at mass with the gossip stored up during the summer's separation. Then all the talk was about the change in Lorenzo.

His silks and velvets were gone. He dressed now in the *lucco,* a severe dark colored wool, ankle-length, pleated robe. It was the garment favored by the old men and scholars, and it looked incongruous on his athletic youthful body.

People whispered that he was in mourning for the sack of Volterra. His lucco was usually black.

Lorenzo knew what they were saying, but he gave no explanations. The lucco was not a symbol of mourning for the past; it was a visible pledge to the future. Cosimo had always worn the lucco. Cosimo had never acted impetuously, nor to gratify his own importance. Cosimo had brought peace to the Republic, not pillage. Lorenzo vowed before God's altar that he would preserve that peace. He worked more intensively than ever, slept less. Deep lines etched themselves on his face.

But he continued to make poetry, to make love, to make his companions laugh. And as time passed, people grew accustomed to the lines. And the lucco.

Chapter Twelve

"I wish Lorenzo would wear something other than that dreary lucco!"

Lucrezia de' Medici spoke the words so loudly that she woke herself up. What could I have been dreaming, she wondered, but she could not remember.

She sat up in her bed, then sank back into the pillows. She did not want to get up. "There must be something wrong with me," she said, again speaking aloud. She felt her forehead; it was cool and dry. Then she moved her arms and legs, pressed her throat and her breasts and abdomen. No pain anywhere.

But she did not want to get out of bed. Never in her life had she felt this way. It frightened her. She willed herself to rise and bathe and dress. Then she hurried to Lorenzo's rooms.

"I would see my son," she said.

Lorenzo's secretary spattered ink all over the letter he was writing, jumped to his feet and hastened to report that Madonna Lucrezia was in the antechamber and that she was not like her usual self.

Lorenzo argued with his mother's announced intentions. "Let me get a doctor, two doctors."

"If I wanted a doctor, Lorenzo, I'm perfectly capable of sending for one. I am not ill, only tired and out of sorts. I want to go to the baths at Morba, and I asked you to assign an escort for me. Is that so difficult?"

"No, of course not, but you shouldn't travel if you're not well."

"I am not ill. I told you that I am not ill." Lucrezia felt increasingly irritated.

"Then I'll go with you. I don't want you to be alone."

"You will not go with me. Alone is precisely what I want to be. Are you growing deaf? I told you what I want from you. An escort."

Lorenzo had never seen his mother lose her temper this way. He was alarmed and a little bit frightened. He spoke in the soothing tones he used to gentle a spooked animal.

"Very well, Mamina. You shall go. And alone. But I beg you, not to Morba. There are newer spas, with better facilities. You'll be more comfortable."

Lucrezia ground her teeth. "I like Morba."

Lorenzo capitulated. "Whatever you say, Mama. Anything you want."

Even before she arrived at the baths Lucrezia felt better. She had not made a long trip in years, and she grew stiff and sore in the saddle after the first half day's riding, but the aches and pains were infinitely preferable to the causeless fatigue that had afflicted her. When the captain of the escort asked her if she was ready to halt for the night, Lucrezia ordered him to keep going. It was nearly dark when they turned into the gates of a hilltop monastery for shelter. Lucrezia stayed awake long enough to drink some soup, then she stretched out on a hard pallet as if it were the finest feather mattress, asleep even before she said her evening prayers.

When she woke at dawn, she felt as if every bone in her body was broken. And serves me right, too, she thought. Only a stubborn old fool would have ridden so many hours after she began to stiffen. She laughed at her folly, winced at the sharp pain the laughter caused, was grateful that her sense of humor was coming back.

She needed it when she reached Morba the next day. The bathhouse had lost half its roof and was almost surrounded by a thicket of thorns. The guest quarters were almost as derelict, lacking most of their shutters and doors. She could smell stale cabbage and unwashed linen even before she entered.

Lucrezia remembered the spa as austere but extremely

clean, with beautiful gardens and a large competent staff of attendants. The food had been delicious, too. "I cannot imagine what happened to this place," she said to the hovering captain.

Then she remembered that she had last come to Morba after Giuliano was born. Twenty-two years before.

"There are definite advantages to being a Medici," Lucrezia said. She inhaled the pungent steam from the hot water that covered her up to her chin. "Not the least of them is that people are terrified of me . . . Most people, that is, not you. I don't frighten you, do I?"

There was no answer. The cadaverous old woman she was talking to was completely deaf. And toothless. Lucrezia smiled at the old crone's blissful expression as she sucked on a sugared lemon. Caterina was the woman's name; she was Lucrezia's attendant in the baths. She watched, more or less, to see that Lucrezia did not slide under the water and drown. And she held a towel ready for her when she came out. Occasionally she offered Lucrezia a lemon. When it was refused, she pointed to herself and, at Lucrezia's nod, ate it.

She was useless as a masseuse because her wrinkled old hands were too weak, and she could not obey orders because she couldn't hear them. And yet she represented the greatest luxury to Lucrezia and an inestimably valuable companion. Lucrezia could talk to her.

For more than thirty years, Lucrezia had had no one person in whom she could confide. Piero and the children had needed her strength and serenity. She could never admit to dissatisfaction or fear. And, as a Medici, she had always to guard her words when talking to her friends. Anything that happened in the Medici palace was intriguing gossip for the whole city and potentially valuable information for the dozens of informants to political enemies and commercial rivals.

Now she could talk, talk openly, freely, without having to think before she spoke. Most luxurious of all, she could complain. Caterina didn't know who she was, didn't know that of all the women in the world, Lucrezia de' Medici had least cause for complaint. When the old woman saw Lucrezia's lips moving, she nodded vigorous, ignorant encouragement.

"I am forty-eight years old," Lucrezia told her, "an old woman . . . the problem is, I don't feel old. And I don't like being treated as if I were old . . .

"The effrontery of Lorenzo, trying to call in a doctor! He might as well have pushed me into my grave and been done with it. If you want to die, send for a doctor. He'll find some way to kill you even if you aren't sick . . .

"I had my fill of doctors and then some in all those years my poor Piero was suffering so. They'd come in with their greasy velvet robes and moth-eaten fur trim and gilt spurs and colored glass rings on every dirty finger, and they'd read his stars and tell him lies and feed him some half-poisonous nostrum and by the time they were done, they were wearing the thickest velvet and richest furs and rubies and spurs of solid gold. Thieves, they should call themselves, not doctors. They're nothing more than astrologers with a degree from Salerno that entitles them to dress like a lord and steal from the sick . . . how dare my own son think that I would be such a fool as to listen to a doctor? I'm sure you've never had a doctor in your life, Caterina, and look at you. You must be two hundred years old . . . No, most likely, you're not much older than I am. Your life hasn't been as soft as mine.

"And it isn't soft now. Look at you. You're still working, never mind how little you're really doing. At least you can believe you're useful, that you're good for something.

"I'm no good to anybody." Lucrezia shocked herself; she began to weep. Hot tears rolled down her face into the hot water of the bath. "What's wrong with me?" she sobbed. "I never do this."

The old deaf woman saw Lucrezia's twisted face. She took the lemon from her mouth and smiled. "Good," she said, "good. Clean inside and out." Then she peered closely at her lemon, threw it on the floor and took a fresh one from the bowl at her side.

When Lucrezia had no tears left, she climbed up out

of the bath and accepted the towel from Caterina's gnarled hands. "Thank you," she said.

"Thank you," she said again after she was dressed, "you are a lot wiser than I am, old woman. I do feel cleansed inside." She smiled. "Now I'll go terrify my host some more. That makes me feel better, too."

Lucrezia was overseeing the cleaning and repair of the buildings at the spa. She gave orders, refused to listen to excuses, hinted at terrible consequences if her orders weren't obeyed, demanded ever greater efforts from the slovenly owner and his surly staff.

She was enjoying herself immensely. The place was a challenge; it was her own Augean stable. And she was Hercules.

It had been a very long time since she had met a challenge.

After Lucrezia had been there for three weeks, Morba was almost restored to its former state. The walls were freshly stuccoed and painted, and the roof's new red tiles glowed warmly in the autumn sun. The gardens were almost bare with small mountains of weeds rotting in the corners, and their geometry was visible. Lucrezia pruned the thicket of rose bushes herself. Deep in the heart of it she came upon a tight bud. The pruning allowed air and light to reach it, and it bloomed.

She took it as an omen. Her litanies of complaints to Caterina were a kind of pruning, too. They freed her heart of long-stored grievances. Now that she had voiced them, they seemed smaller, hardly worth caring about.

So what if Clarice was supplanting her in the house and was a disappointment as a daughter? She had given Lorenzo two daughters and a son, all that a wife really had to do. And that made three grandchildren in the house for Lucrezia to enjoy.

And Giuliano's recklessness was not really harmful to anyone, not even himself. He was twenty-two and still more boy than man, even though Lorenzo had staged a coming-of-age tournament for him that was the wonder of the year. But twenty-two was not so very old, not for a second son who needed to assume no responsibility. Giuliano liked being rich and handsome and carefree. Who could blame him? Certainly not the people of Florence. They all adored him, all ages, because of his looks, because he was the best athlete, because he had the unsullied sweetness of a much-loved child for whom all things are easy and all skies unclouded. Lucrezia loved him, too. It was absurd to wish he was different.

Especially when it was exactly that childlike sweetness in her husband that had made her love him so much, that made her long for him still. Piero would want Giuliano to be no different. He had recognized his own nature in the boy, he had understood Giuliano. In truth, Giuliano had always been his favorite of all the five children. He had never been able to love Lorenzo the same way.

Whereas, she . . . Lucrezia thought of what she had accomplished at Morba. She had done very well.

But she was not finished yet. She had avoided it as long as possible, now it had to be faced. All her other troubles were easily evaporated in the hot steam of the baths. Lorenzo was the real canker in her heart.

"Lorenzo, Lorenzo!" Lucrezia cried out, and the walls of the bath answered "Lorenzo."

"Do you know what it is, Caterina, to be betrayed by the one you love most, the one you trust above all others? Do you know the pain of watching him change? Seeing him move away from you?

"Volterra! May a plague take the place. It was Volterra that changed him. Not when the mines proved worthless; it was before that, at the beginning when the army sacked it. What does he think men are like? Men kill, and they plunder, and they rape. Is it his fault that men act like men? He should know. He sits on the council that hears the crimes. He sees the gallows outside the Gate of Justice, the men hung there. He must see the crowds who go to the hangings to laugh and drink and eat while the legs still kick in the air. He must know about the brigands who lay in wait to kill and rob on the roads, else why send such a strong escort with me?

"Why must he be more than a man?

"Cosimo. He wants to be Cosimo. Fool! Cosimo was no saint. I knew him well. Cosimo saw men as they are. He would have forgotten Volterra in a week. No, he would have seen it as a mistake that he should not make again. He made mistakes, the Father of the State, oh yes, and he covered them so no one would know.

"I could have told Lorenzo that, if he had come to me. But he didn't. Volterra was three years ago, and in all that time he has not asked my advice, has not told me his plans. I am nothing to him. I am useless."

Lucrezia tormented herself into a frenzy of weeping. The old woman Caterina watched her and nodded encouragement and sucked a lemon. When Lucrezia was exhausted, Caterina helped her climb out of the bath. She wrapped Lucrezia in a towel, then draped her cloak over her shoulders. "Now you sleep," Caterina said.

Later Lucrezia woke and sat looking out her window at the starry sky until the stars began to fade. The turbulent emotions she had felt faded with them; and she bade farewell to Morba. She was ready to go home.

There was no further need for deaf ears to talk to; her heart was calm, her thoughts ordered. She realized that it was up to her to fill up her life, for herself. And that she could do it. The metamorphosis of the spa was all her doing. She was proud of it.

Almost as much as I was of my children, she thought, a wry smile on her lips. Ah, motherhood, what a deceptive devil you are. Love and vanity all mixed, and impossible to separate.

It was right for Lorenzo to make his own way independent of her. He was twenty-six and had been in charge of the State for almost six years. She would have no respect for a man who ran to his mother before he made up his mind, and neither would anyone else.

She had to let him go. It was long past time for it.

She saw his face in her mind's eye, and her heart contracted with love. My dearest son, she said silently, beauty passed you by. Perhaps that's why you were always my favorite, because other people looked away when they saw that big squashed nose and wide mouth on your infant's face. All the others were such lovely babies.

I embroidered your little shirts myself, to surround you with my love. And I made sure that only the finest wools in the brightest colors went into your clothes when you got older.

She shook her head in rueful amusement. You did yourself no favor, my love, she chided her son, when you decided to wear the lucco. It makes you look even uglier than you are. No wonder it gave me nightmares.

Lorenzo met Lucrezia on the outskirts of Florence.

"How did you know I was coming?" she asked.

"I have my spies. You look wonderfully well, Mamina. Morba was good for you."

"Yes, it was. It's a delightful place. A bit austere, but very fresh and clean. I like it so much that I've arranged to buy it. With a little effort it can be the best in all Tuscany. I'm going to be a businesswoman and make a great deal of money."

Lorenzo tried to smile. "That's good news. For a change. I hope you're not too exhausted, Mama. I have a lot to tell you, and I need your wisdom."

Lucrezia's resolution to let her son run his own life dissolved in a second. "I'm not tired at all," she said.

Chapter Thirteen

"Tell me again, Lorenzo, and don't talk so fast. I can't understand a word you're saying."

Lorenzo crashed his fist down onto his desk. "It's vile treachery to the Republic, that's what I'm saying. To me, too, but they owe me no loyalty. Every Florentine does owe it to the State."

"Start from the beginning . . . You said the Pope applied to the bank for a loan?"

"Yes. Forty thousand florins. A fortune, but of course we would have granted it. We're the Vatican's bankers, and we have no reason to deny loans; we earn ten times more than we ever lend. This was not for Vatican business, though. It was for Sixtus to buy a kingdom for his nephew, or bastard, whichever he is. Now that he's turned all his peasant priest nephews into princes of the Church, he wants to make this Riario a Lord of his own state. And threaten Florence at the same time.

"I didn't believe we had anything to worry about when Imola came up for sale. It's a small city with no importance except that it's on our borders and the route our merchants take to the port at Ravenna. The Republic was going to buy it, but the price was too high; I was negotiating for a better figure. Then Galeazzo entered the picture and bought it for Milan, so we had nothing to worry about. He's a dependable ally because he needs us as much as we need him."

"Then what is the problem? I don't see it."

"Sixtus is the problem. Wily old devil. He offered Galeazzo his bastard son Riario as a husband for Galeazzo's bastard daughter if Galeazzo would sell Imola to be the home of the bride and groom. Galeazzo agreed. The girl has had no takers because she's illegitimate . . . and a shrew, from all accounts.

"Then Sixtus applied for the loan. Smooth as fresh-pressed oil. Prating about the virtues of Riario, whom everyone knows to be a debauched lout. And acting as if the extension of the Papal States to border on the Republic's east was the furthest thing from his mind.

"The Rome branch asked me what to do. I told them to be just as oily when they refused the loan."

Lucrezia's brother was manager of the Rome branch. She knew how courteously and firmly he could say no. "Then Sixtus didn't get the money. Where's the treachery in that?"

"You don't listen, Madonna! The Pazzi are the traitors. There are at least thirty banks in Rome, but the Pazzi have the only one rich enough to make a loan that size. Other than ours, that is. Before I sent word to my uncle, I went to the Pazzi palace. I talked to Jacopo and Elmo and Giovanni. Antonio was in bed with a fever at his villa, and Francesco was in Rome visiting his cousin Renato. I explained the danger of having Sixtus's nephew in Imola and asked for a pledge that their bank would not grant the loan. They all agreed.

"So then I wrote to Renato, told him everything that had happened, and sent the letter to him by the same messenger that took the letter to our branch.

"This morning I received a report that all Rome is whispering that the Pazzi are planning to finance Sixtus. It's only a rumor, but it comes from a reliable man. If it's true, it's the foulest treachery I know."

Lucrezia fully understood the danger to Florence if the Pope controlled Imola. And she agreed that, if the rumor was accurate, Renato and Francesco Pazzi had done serious injury to the Republic. But there was no confirmation of the report, she had seen many rumors prove false, and she had been riding over dusty roads for six hours that day. "Don't waste your energy on anger that may not be deserved, Lorenzo," she said. "Wait until we know something for certain. I'm going to wash, then rest, then visit the nurseries. How are my grandchildren?''

''Well,'' said Lorenzo. He was too angry to think about anything except the Pazzi.

The children were better than well. They were thriving. Lucrezia, five, was big for her age and very noisy. When her grandmother entered the nursery, she was shouting protests against her little brother's systematic destruction of one of her dolls. Piero ignored her; two-year-old Maddalena was sleeping, oblivious of the tempest.

It's wonderful to have the house filling up with young life, Lucrezia thought. It's what houses are built for. ''Good evening, Maria,'' she said to the nursemaid. Piero abandoned the doll and came running to her, his sister close behind.

''Did you bring us anything?''

Less than a month later, on December eleventh, the nursery gained a new center of attraction. Clarice was delivered of a boy, soon named Giovanni.

The baby was several weeks early, but he weighed more than eight pounds and was so strong that his cries were almost as loud as his oldest sister's.

''Like a lion's roar,'' Clarice said, half-frightened. She had already told Lorenzo about her dream the night before Giovanni's birth. It was so vivid that it had to be full of meaning. She was in the Duomo, writhing in agony on the bright mosaic floor, at the very moment of delivery. But when the baby came, it was not a human child. It was a huge lion.

Lorenzo read the meaning at once. Giovanni was destined for the Church. He would be Florence's protector there, her lion, symbol of the city.

The birth of his son, with its portentous dream announcement, broke the uncharacteristic melancholy Lorenzo had been feeling. It had grown darker and darker with each new shock of bad news.

First, the rumor about the Pazzi loan to the Pope had proved true.

Then an official Vatican document had arrived, announcing that the lucrative papal business was being transferred from the Medici to the Pazzi bank. More than half the Medici bank's income was gone.

"I don't know anything about banking," Lorenzo said bitterly. "There was never time to learn. Or interest. And there was always more money than we needed. Now the needs are the same, but there's so much less income. The London branch had to close because the Plantagenet Wars destroyed the country and King Edward could not repay his loans. The same thing is happening in Bruges, with the Duke of Burgundy. What am I supposed to do?"

"You can't do other than what you're doing," Lucrezia replied. "You have to let the branch managers run the branches. It's what your father did and your grandfather. Even if you were the greatest banker in the world, you can't be in ten cities at the same time. Your place is here in Florence, leading the government."

"Yes, yes. And you know what that means: paying for the entertainment of visitors, paying for the fireworks for Carnival, for the floats, for costumes for sacred plays on every feast day, for contributions to this and to that, for gifts to the King of France and the King of Naples and the Dukes of Milan and Urbino and Ferrara and the Doge of Venice and even the old Satan Sixtus, propitiating anyone who might threaten the Republic. How am I going to have the care of the State if I am deep in poverty?"

His mother stroked his dejected shoulders. "Hush, Lorenzo, you exaggerate. Even with half of it gone, three quarters if need be, the Medici fortune is still great enough to do all that you want to do. If the Pazzi are even wealthier now, what difference does it make? They are, after all, tied to us through Bianca's marriage to Elmo and the future marriage of Pierfrancesco's son to Ginevra. It's better to have alliances with the rich; they are not so likely to ask for favors.

"Don't be gloomy, my son. You've been outsmarted in business, that's all. It happens to everyone. As for the Pope's nephew, I've heard you say a dozen times that Riario is a fool. He's no real danger to you or to Florence. You may not be the best banker in Italy, but you are the best statesman. You'll be able to contain his ambitions with no trouble. The Pazzi know that too. Their loan to Sixtus was not really treacherous. Simply sharp business with an edge honed too fine for your liking. Forget your grievance and get on with your life. You have many blessings; think about them, not about your losses.''

Lorenzo kissed his mother's hand. ''You are a comfort, Mamina, even when you voice truths I'd sooner not hear. You're right; I'm acting like a child with a toy taken away. Only a fool wastes time sulking when every hour can be filled with joy. Thank you for reminding me.''

Two days later, Lorenzo rode out to his stables at Careggi; he returned to the city at a gallop, singing raucously and tunelessly. ''At last,'' he told Giuliano, ''there's a horse with the speed of a rocket. I saw him run, so fast my eyes could hardly follow. Next year the Medici will win the Palio.''

Giuliano threw his arms around his brother, turned the embrace deftly into a choke hold. ''And I'll ride him. Say yes, or I'll break your neck.''

Lorenzo broke the hold by stabbing his elbow into Giuliano's stomach. Then, with shouts of laughter, the brothers wrestled fiercely until both were soaked with sweat and lumpy with bruises.

Their mother admired their colorful faces when the bruises flowered blue and purple. ''You are like a pair of majolica decorations,'' she said. ''I like bright color in a room.''

At that, Lorenzo disappeared for a few minutes and returned with the present he had been saving for Epiphany, the celebration of gift-giving. There was no point in waiting; this was the perfect time for this particular gift.

It was a pair of terra-cotta busts. They were life-size and startlingly lifelike. Lorenzo's was wearing the lucco, frowning slightly, impressive. Giuliano's seemed to be about to smile. It was elaborately decorated, wearing a clay replica of the carved silver armor he had worn at his tournament.

Lucrezia cried out when she saw them and held out her hands. "They're so beautiful, I have to touch them." She ran delicate fingertips over the terra-cotta features of her sons, looking at the battered flesh of the living models.

"Of everything I own, nothing has ever pleased me so much," she said. "I thank you with all my heart." Touching, stroking, looking closely from all angles, Lucrezia admired her gift. "Andrea del Verrocchio made these, am I right? He must love you both very much.

"As do I." She left the busts and embraced her sons. Gently, brushing the bruises with her lips to make them heal.

Chapter Fourteen

"This year's Carnival will be the best in all history," Lorenzo announced. He was in high spirits, had been for months. He had kept his vow to turn away from shadows, and life had rewarded him with golden light-filled days of pleasure and peace. He stroked the mane of the racehorse, rested his cheek against his neck and murmured encouraging endearments into its flicking ears. "Morello, my handsome; Morello, my Pegasus; Morello, my beloved; you will leave all the others so far behind that they'll think you were a zephyr of their imagining."

Giuliano grinned nervously and bent from the waist, limbering his tension-knotted muscles. "I wish we'd get started," he said.

All over the city much the same scene was being repeated. The hour before the Palio was a time of rising excitement for all, for the spectators who crowded the route and increased their bets on who would be in the lead at that vantage point, for the judges who traded stories of previous years and concealed their individual partialities, for the owners of the horses whose prestige rode in the coats of arms embroidered on the wool tapestry belted across the horses' backs. Most of all for the riders who knew that they might find glory or disgrace that would haunt them forever. The Palio was in no sense an ordinary race.

The prize was valuable in money, but even more valuable as symbol. The palio was a piece of cloth about a meter long, fringed with gold. Because it was paid for by the subject-cities of the Republic, it represented the power and might of Florence. Because it was a masterpiece of design and weaving, it was a crystallization of Florence's preeminence in the arts and in the manufacture of cloth. It was the most desperately coveted prize in all Italy. The race was the most dangerous.

"Now don't forget about the flowers," Lorenzo said.

"You've told me that a thousand times."

"Morello is a country horse, and young. He won't know what is happening."

"Lorenzo! I am having enough trouble staying inside my skin without your warnings."

"Forgive me. You'll be superb. And so will Morello. Just remember that . . ."

"Silence, for the love of God!"

Jacopo de' Pazzi scowled at the young page who was riding for his house. "Remember, boy, this is no ordinary horse. He's worth more than you and your entire family. If any leg gets broken, it had better be yours and not his."

The boy, whose name was Santino, gulped and swore on his grandfather's grave that he'd remember. But what was first in his mind was the hundred florins the old man had promised him if he brought the strange foreign horse in first. A hundred florins was ten years' wages; the thought made his mouth dry. He swallowed again, trying to make some spit.

The big gray stallion stamped nervously. It was not accustomed to stones underfoot. It had been brought clandestinely to Florence from the soft sands of the Arabian desert.

The great bell in the Palazzo della Signoria sounded. The entire city shivered. It was the first signal, the call for the contestants to move to the starting point of the race.

"Go with God," Lorenzo said. He embraced Giuliano and gave him a leg up. For the Palio, there were neither saddles nor stirrups.

Giuliano laughed. The waiting was almost over. Now he could enjoy the sport.

* * *

The second bell was the signal for the riders to take their places. This year the field was the biggest ever; thirty-six horses and riders formed a long skittish line on the broad meadow just inside the Porta al Prato, almost knee to knee. It was a festive sight. The riders wore the colors of the houses they represented in their parti-colored hose, belted tunics and soft feather-trimmed caps. Giuliano grinned at his friend Matteo de' Tornabuoni. Matteo was wearing green and gold, his face looking green as well. He had taken a dare when he was drunk and wished he were anywhere else. Alberto Palmieri was next to him, wearing blue and black. He was edgy, eager to get started. Alberto was forty, and this was his twenty-fifth Palio. He swore that nothing else in life—not drink, not women, not hunting—gave the same elation as riding in the Palio. He had never come in better than fifth, but he'd keep trying until he died or the race killed him, so help him, God. The Alessandrini twins were both riding, one of them for their mother's house. They were the youngest, only fourteen. Giuliano was between the twins, repeating Lorenzo's warning about the perils of flowers making their horses shy. All along the route expectant spectators leaned from upper windows; often young ladies threw tributes of flowers to their favorites.

The third bell rang and the race began; the crowds around the meadow's edge shouted. "Giuliano" was heard above all other cries.

The meadow stretched for about five hundred yards, and the riders bent low over the necks of their mounts, urging them on with words and spurs, striving to be first at the bottleneck of the street ahead. The Borgo Ognissanti was wide for a Florentine street, wide enough for four horses at a walk, three at a run.

The spectators ran too, adding an additional hazard, eager to see the first winnowing of the field. "Rucellai," they shouted and "Giuliano" for the first to enter. Then the Palio really began. Riders looked for advantage, using elbows and feet to push at the horse and rider alongside. Horses reared and plunged, pressing against one another, scraped and bumped their riders against the stone walls of the houses. It was mayhem. Matteo de' Tornabuoni fell when his horse veered, refusing to enter the fray. He rolled himself into a ball and protected his head with his hands. Four riders jumped their horses over him. One hoof grazed his side, ripping his tunic and breaking three ribs. "Thank God," breathed Matteo. He was safe.

Ahead the race went on. Through the Borgo to the small piazza on the river at the foot of the Ponte alla Carraia with spectators all around and a wider space where speed and daring could move a horse ahead and gain a better position for the plunge into the Via del Parione, narrower than the Borgo. Santino, the Pazzi groom, saw a fortune waiting for him, called on all the saints and let out a fierce yell. It gained him half a length on his nearest competitor. He was ninth entering the narrow street. Giuliano was leading, with Alberto Palmieri scant inches behind. The noise was deafening: hoofs on cobbles, horses snorting, spectators shouting encouragement, riders yelling in pain when legs hit walls at the bend in the street.

The horses surged out into the Piazza Santa Trinita, bigger than the last square but with a dogleg to the left before the next street and the horses wild from the noise and the pelting flowers. One of the Alessandrini twins lost control of his mount and plowed into the crowd. His brother tried to stop. The press behind him piled up sending him and his horse to the ground. He lay still and vulnerable; the spectators surged forward to pull him aside and the next riders swerved desperately to avoid them. Santino made it. Two others were thrown. Their mounts sped on, caught up in the madness around them.

Into the Via Porta Rossa, wider than Parione, with a chance to nudge and force and move ahead. There was a trail of fallen riders behind now and the weaker horses were losing ground. The leaders were blocks ahead, bunched together, evoking wild cheering from windows and the dangerous open doors of ground-level shops. Santino prayed and wept and cursed.

The most perilous part of the course was the right angle turn into the Via dei Calzaiuoli. A wooden barricade protected the crowds behind it. It appeared that the riders were directing their mounts directly into a wall or over it into a wall of people. Morello tried to refuse, and Giuliano skidded forward onto his neck, losing his seat. He kept control, forced Morello to obey, turned the corner. Alberto Palmieri saw victory on his twenty-fifth attempt. He galloped past Giuliano into the broad Piazza della Signoria. It was rimmed with people. The cheering was like a wall of noise. Palmieri snatched off his cap and waved it.

Behind him Giuliano hit the ground. Seeing the open route ahead, Morello had released a burst of speed before Giuliano regained his seat. The young Medici slid ludicrously off the horse's rump, fell on his own rump and rolled backward in a somersault to land on his feet. "Giuliano" shouted the watchers. He smiled, shrugged, laughed, ran out of the way of the oncoming horses and into the center of the square.

The Strozzi horse and rider flew by, then the Soderini, the Rucellai and the Pazzi, with Santino vowing to the Virgin that he would never say another unkind word to his mother if he won. Giuliano began to run. The riderless Alessandrini horse was in the piazza, crazed, eyes surrounded by white, body flecked by white foam. It was confused and its pace was slowing. Giuliano ran parallel to it, closed on it from behind, seized the loose reins and its mane and vaulted on its back. The crowds went wild, but Giuliano was already gone, calming and urging the unfamiliar horse back into the race, followed by eleven riders. Nineteen entrants were gone, lost to accident or injury.

On the Borgo dei Greci, Alberto Palmieri lost the lead to a howling blue and yellow dervish on a gray Arabian. It was Santino, pounding with his heels on the lean flanks of his horse, shouting prayers, flailing his arm at competitors as he caught up to them and passed them. The horse was a marvel, stretched out in a way that could not be matched, wherever there was room to run. It crossed the Via de' Benci into the Piazza Santa Croce as if it had wings. It was the winner. The spectators were thickest here at the finish, the cheering the loudest, the flowers a hail of color. Santino pulled gently on the reins. He was weeping. He leaned forward to kiss the horse's lathered neck. Then he knelt on the animal's back, lifted one foot, steadied it and sprang upright. His hose and sleeves were in bloody shreds, his tunic stained, his entire body trembling. He rode standing to the judges' box, then jumped to the ground. His face was wet with sweat and tears. It shone with triumph.

"Brother, I let you down. I should be hung." Giuliano found Lorenzo in the palace stables dressing a long wound on Morello's flank.

Lorenzo looked up with a smile. "Don't be a fool. It was his first race, and he spooked. Next year, that's different. If you don't win next year, I'll kill you with my bare hands. Now tell me, how was it? How did he go, my treasure Morello?"

The brothers enjoyed Carnival as never before. Their float was acclaimed as incomparably the best. And the song that Lorenzo wrote to accompany it caught the fancy of the revelers. It spread throughout the city and was soon on everyone's lips. Its hedonistic message was the very essence of festival.

> Quant'è bella giovinezza
> che si fugge tuttavia!
> Chi vuol esser lieto, sia;
> di doman non c'è certezza.

> How fair is youth
> and how fleeting!
> Anyone who wants to, let him be merry;
> there is no certainty in tomorrow.

Chapter Fifteen

It was not losing the Palio that bothered Lorenzo, although he hated to lose at anything. It was that the Pazzi had won. It rankled.

He saw them often; Florence's street life made it inevitable. And he wondered always if Jacopo's shark smile was laughing at him or if Francesco was boasting to people about taking the Vatican account away from the Medici bank.

The danger he had feared if the Pope installed his nephew in Imola had not materialized. Riario spent little time in his new domain, and Florence's merchants continued to travel to Ravenna without interference or increased tolls. Sixtus seemed to be concerned solely with the Papal States' southern neighbor. He had made a treaty with Ferrante, the King of Naples, and was reputedly showering his new ally with attention and rich gifts.

It was an uneasy situation for Florence. Shifts in alliances were always cause for concern. As the papal banker, Lorenzo would have been able to consult with Sixtus, perhaps influence him. Now he had no contact with the Vatican. But had the balance of powers in Italy ever been anything other than uncertain and potentially dangerous? Not since the end of the Roman Empire.

Lorenzo told himself to stay watchful but calm. The Pazzi had not really damaged the Republic and he had no right to harbor resentment for a personal business reverse. It was the essence of banking to try and steal accounts from competitors.

Yet still it was hard for him to be friendly with Jacopo. Almost impossible with Francesco. Even with Elmo, he felt false when they were together. And Elmo was a friend of more than ten years standing, as well as his sister's husband.

Why couldn't his horse and his brother have been defeated by anyone other than the Pazzi?

"Lorenzo, you mustn't do this thing!" Elmo de' Pazzi grabbed Lorenzo's arm and pulled him away from the group while they walked around the edge of the church at morning mass.

"What thing? I don't take your meaning, Elmo."

"Don't be disingenuous. Everyone in the city is talking about it. Alessandra was old Borromeo's only living child. When he died, she should have inherited everything he had. And she would have, if she weren't the wife of my brother. You've dug out that old law just to get back at the Pazzi."

Lorenzo resumed his stroll, easing his arm free of Elmo's grip. "I don't make the law, Elmo, you know that. That particular law has been in effect for a hundred years. If a man dies without a written will, his estate goes to his nearest male relations. For the Borromeo, that means the nephews."

Elmo kept pace with him, his voice rising. "Lorenzo, I'm your friend, and your brother by marriage. Don't do this, I beg you. You know that law has been forgotten for decades. Everybody knows it. They know, too, that it's you who persuaded the Signoria to apply it now."

Lorenzo gestured for silence. The bell was ringing to alert the congregation to the climax of the mass. He bowed his head, his lips moving in prayer.

Elmo bowed, too, but he did not pray. He waited until the solemn moment passed and people began moving and talking again. Then he took Lorenzo's arm for the second time.

"I'm telling you for your own good, Lorenzo. You're making enemies this way. Not Giovanni so much, although Alessandra's his wife. It's Francesco. He's so angry he's planning to move to Rome. He says he can't stomach living in the same city with you.''

Lorenzo laughed. ''Is that so? I wish him a good journey, then, and soon is better than later. I have no more love for Francesco than he does for me.'' He answered the hail of a friend, smiled at Elmo. ''I must talk to Luciano. Excuse me, Elmo.''

The ''Borromeo scandal'' people called it, and it kept tongues buzzing for weeks in the early autumn. Almost everyone was delighted by the neatness of Lorenzo's revenge. Jacopo de' Pazzi was notorious as a sour near-miser and it was a great joke to deprive him of the tremendous Borromeo fortune for his nephew.

Lorenzo was too busy to enjoy his success. He was occupied with a different estate. His cousin Pierfrancesco died suddenly, leaving his two sons in Lorenzo's guardianship.

Lorenzo took on his new responsibilities the way he did everything else; he applied his total concentration and energy and made rapid decisions about how best to do the job.

Pierfrancesco's house was poorly furnished and in need of repairs; he did not even own a villa. He had always complained that his poverty prevented him from living comfortably. The two boys would move to the Medici palace and become part of his family, Lorenzo decided.

But Pierfrancesco's will specified that his sons should have their own household, the estate lawyer told him.

In that case, Lorenzo thought, maybe he should accelerate his ward's marriage. Young Lorenzo was betrothed to Ginevra de' Pazzi, and her dowry was immense. It could easily support the kind of life he thought the boys should have.

True, Lorenzo was young, only thirteen. But his betrothed was thirteen, too, and many girls married at that age. It was old enough to have a baby, and Lorenzo couldn't imagine that his ward wouldn't be glad to carry out his duties as a husband in that respect. As he re-

membered himself at thirteen, he would have been happy
to have had ten wives.

Lorenzo laughed. It was a neat solution, with a delightful dividend. It would make Francesco de' Pazzi
furious to know that the little heiress was repairing Medici property and adding to it. The boys should have a
villa. For that matter, it might not even be necessary to
buy one. Old Antonio de' Pazzi would probably be very
happy to have the young people use La Vacchia as their
summer home.

The more Lorenzo thought about the marriage, the
better he liked the idea.

Provided that Ginevra had not become too much a
Pazzi. His young cousin was his responsibility; he
couldn't rush him into an early marriage with a female
version of Francesco.

Lorenzo tried to remember how many years had gone
by since he last saw Ginevra . . . It must be at least
five. Was she still the engaging little contadina or had
she learned Pazzi haughtiness from her family?

He decided to ride out to Antonio's villa and see for
himself. It was a beautiful day, after almost a week of
rain.

The gates to the villa were open and untended. So
was the door to the house. Lorenzo wrapped his horse's
reins around the iron ring beside the door and stepped
back a few paces to look at the della Robbia lunette. He
had forgotten how perfect it was.

Everything was very still. There was no wind, and
the leaves of the olive trees were silent. He would have
thought the place deserted if he had not heard the low
mumble of voices from someplace inside the house. He
drew breath to shout a greeting, then slowly exhaled. It
seemed wrong to intrude a loud noise into the peaceful-
ness all around him. He walked quietly in the direction
of the voices.

They grew louder as he approached, and clearer. Lorenzo recognized the words. A man was reciting in
Latin, a passage from Cicero's *On the Nature of the*

Gods. Lorenzo paused in the doorway that led to the dining room until the speaker had finished.

The scene before him was curiously appropriate for the words of the great Roman stoic. It was scholarly and austere. The long, polished oak table in the center of the room was covered with stacks of paper and neatly arranged pens, ink and a penknife. The four people having their midday meal were seated at a smaller table in front of the windows on the left wall. They were eating soup and bread, the soup in wooden bowls.

Mateo, Ginevra's tutor, was the orator. He and the old friar were seated on a bench directly beneath the window. They were as shabby as Lorenzo remembered them.

Antonio de' Pazzi sat facing Lorenzo. The light from the window gleamed in his white hair and made deep shadows in the folds of his antique-styled velvet doublet. It illuminated his thin, hawklike, patrician face. Lorenzo smiled at Antonio's rapt concentration. His smile faded when he saw the old man's pale blue eyes. They were milky and unfocused. Antonio was blind.

Mateo finished, and the others drummed on the table with their fingertips in muted applause. Fra Marco suggested that the Roman gods were less godlike than the Greek gods. He spoke in Latin. Antonio and Mateo began to argue immediately, one speaking Latin, the other speaking Greek. Ginevra laughed at their sputtering outrage. Fra Marco grinned with pleasure at his successful teasing of his two friends.

Ginevra was seated with her back to Lorenzo, opposite the friar and the tutor. Lorenzo could see that her back was slender and straight, her hair neatly arranged in a single thick braid that fell to her waist. It was obvious that she understood and enjoyed the men's talk. He was impressed. Education for a woman was considered a good thing in Florence, but few were taught to discuss Cicero at meals. And hardly anyone, man or woman, knew Greek. Even he had studied only Latin translations of the Greek writers. My young cousin, he thought, will be getting a remarkable wife, if her disposition is as fine as her education.

"Forgive my interruption," he said, "may I join your discussion?" His spoken Latin sounded like music.

"Who is that?" said Antonio.

Ginevra had spun to face the door. "It's Lorenzo de' Medici," she said.

Lorenzo saw that she had changed very little. She had the same long nose and pointed chin in a face that would have been hopelessly plain were it not for her deepset large brown eyes and nicely shaped full mouth. She was, he thought, unhealthily pallid.

He couldn't know that the color had drained from her cheeks when she heard his voice. In the years since she last saw him, Ginevra's childhood hero worship of Lorenzo had grown, magnified, become confused with the stories she was learning about Jason and Ulysses, Achilles and Hercules, Perseus and Bellerophon. For him to appear on the threshold was a legend come to life. She had almost fainted.

"Welcome, Lorenzo," said Antonio. "Please come in."

Lorenzo thanked him, greeted the others, walked across the room and sat on the bench next to Ginevra. To the girl, it was as if the sun had left the sky and come down to rest beside her. She could not believe it had happened. It was almost impossible to pay attention to the debate about the gods; she heard only Lorenzo's voice.

Stop mooncalfing, she told herself, gathering all her powers of self-discipline. She made a small gesture, and the old steward brought a steaming bowl of soup to set in front of Lorenzo. And she watched Antonio carefully, as she always did, placing a cup of mineral water in his hand when his voice grew hoarse, replying to his questions in a firm, clear voice with well-reasoned answers, signaling an end to the conversation when his energy ran out.

"It's time for your rest, Grandfather."

Antonio sighed. "You're a tyrant, Ginevra." But his words were heavy with love.

There have been many changes here, Lorenzo thought. From Antonio's irritable acceptance of responsibility to a closeness and affection greater than any I've ever seen, other than the love between my mother and father. What an extraordinary nest of scholars this is.

Ginevra pulled her grandfather's chair back from the table then turned so that his extended right hand fell on her shoulder.

"I have enjoyed your company, Lorenzo," Antonio said. "I hope you will be here when my rest is done. I'd like to talk some more."

"Thank you, Messer Antonio. I would like that, too." It was true. Lorenzo had liked the spirited discussion very much.

Antonio smiled and bowed. Then he walked slowly and confidently from the room with Ginevra's support and guidance. It was obviously a long-practiced routine.

"A delightful young woman," Lorenzo remarked. Fra Marco and Mateo competed loudly in singing Ginevra's praises. They loved her as much as Antonio did.

When she returned, Lorenzo asked her to show him the della Robbias in the garden again. "It's been a long time since I've seen them."

He was in a mild dilemma. Ginevra's quiet composure and advanced education made her seem much older than her years. Perhaps she would intimidate his young cousin. Lorenzo had seen marriages where the wife ruled; it was abominable.

On the other hand, she was obedient and deferential. Would she be that way with young Lorenzo, too?

He needed to know the girl better.

Her body was like a boy's, not a good sign for childbearing. But she looked strong, and she was not as pale as he had thought. Lorenzo realized that the girl was blushing. His scrutiny embarrassed her.

"Forgive me, Contadina. I was just looking at how grown up you are. I suppose I shouldn't call an educated young woman by childhood nicknames."

"Oh, but I like for you to call me that!" Ginevra's cheeks grew even redder, and she looked at her feet.

Without Antonio to think about, she was fast losing her disciplined calm. She felt clumsy and gauche. A

furtive glance at Lorenzo made everything all right. He
was smiling, and it was a smile of pleasure at her response; he wasn't laughing at her. His eyes were warmly
friendly, interested, encouraging. She had a sudden conviction that she could tell him anything and he would
not disapprove. He was her friend.

"No one else has ever called me a nickname," she
confided. "It makes me feel as if we're special friends,
like having the same birthday . . . I always love the
confetti you send me. Do you get the letters I write to
thank you?"

"Of course." Lorenzo remembered now that he did
receive a careful, formal little letter every year in response to the small remembrances his secretary sent.
That was more than Bernardo did, his nephew who also
shared his birthday. He'd have to speak to the boy. He'd
be eight soon, plenty old enough to write. "I enjoy
them. Most of the letters I get give me work, not pleasure."

Ginevra smiled. She looked very young and eager to
please. She'd make a good wife for Pierfrancesco's boy.

"You do know, don't you Ginevra, that you're going
to marry my cousin one day?"

"Yes." She blushed again. She was completely spell-
bound by Lorenzo, but there were some secrets she
couldn't share. Until very recently, she had believed
that he was the Lorenzo she was to marry. She remembered that he had put the ring on her finger at the betrothal ceremony, and she could not imagine that the
world held more than one Lorenzo. Too ignorant to
wonder what "wife" meant or how a man could have
two wives, she had invented a future where she lived at
the Medici palace, part of his family, every day a mag-
ical blend of birthday parties, songs with Verrocchio's
apprentices and exhilarating rides together on horses that
never grew tired.

"Caesar is well," she blurted. "Would you like to
see him? My horse, that you gave me."

"Very much. Do you still ride?"

"Every day, while Grandfather rests."

"Then you're missing your ride today."

"I don't mind. Really, honestly. I'd rather be walking with you."

"Why not ride? My horse has had a long rest."

Ginevra drew in her breath sharply. "Really? Together?" She seized Lorenzo's hand and ran pell-mell toward the stables, pulling him with her.

She rode bareback, explaining that she and Caesar were closer that way and could understand each other's wishes without using the reins.

And she rode like no one Lorenzo had ever seen. With her skirt tucked up over a strip of leather tied around her waist, her bare knees and legs molded to Caesar's sides, Ginevra and her horse became a near-centaur, a single being. Her face was illuminated by a total abandon to happiness. She galloped alongside Lorenzo, sometimes moving ahead of him, calling to him to catch up, and she was like a mystical spirit-creature, part of nature's world, not man's. When the road grew steeper and wider, she challenged him to race. He agreed and dug his spurs into his horse's flank, feeling a gypsylike wild gaiety, caught from Ginevra. He raced full-out, but she reached the top of the mountain first. She threw her arms high, spread wide, in a gesture of triumph and joy that Lorenzo recognized in his soul as the very meaning of freedom.

He rode slowly back to the city when he left the villa. He wanted time to think before reentering his busy, complicated world.

How did she do it, that child? She lived a life of seclusion, long hours of study, ceaseless devotion to the needs and comforts of others, and it made her happy. She said as much when Lorenzo asked her, astonished that he could question her satisfaction with her lot.

And yet, at the same time, her restricted life did not constrain her emotions. Ginevra had passions instead of feelings. When she told Lorenzo that she loved the three men she lived with, he heard in her simple statement a fierce protectiveness that was frightening in one so young.

Mateo's wife had left him, Ginevra explained, because she hated the quiet of the villa. She returned to her family in Arezzo and, according to the cook, lived in a form of marriage with another man. She had come to La Vacchia twice, to demand money from Mateo. Each time, he gave her all he had and experienced again the weeks of despair that her departure had caused.

"I told her that if she ever came back, I'd kill her," Ginevra said, her voice flat, and Lorenzo believed that she could do it.

How, then, did she reconcile the conflicting aspects of her nature? How did that wild heart exist in that quiet domestic life of premature old age? And find content?

Lorenzo felt a coldness run up the nape of his neck. He was certain that the answer to his questions was a mystery. Not a puzzle to be solved, but a mystery like the mysteries of ancient times that men found in hidden springs and caves and made propitiating sacrifices to.

He felt an eerie bond to this child-woman-spirit, as if she were finding for him the ultimates that he could never attain. She knew the tranquillity that he often longed for, and the uncontrolled emotion that he never dared release, and the absolute freedom of nature that he had thought was only a poet's imagery.

She shared his stars. Then perhaps she shared his soul, was an extension of himself, the part that was missing in him.

He didn't know what to do about the marriage. An unpleasant image of a bird with broken wings came into his mind, but he forced it away.

Pierfrancesco's lawyer called on him later that day and solved his problem for him. The boys' inheritance was a stupendous fortune. Pierfrancesco's miserly close-fistedness had retained and invested virtually every florin he ever touched.

The wedding could be delayed indefinitely.

"And a good thing, too," said Lorenzo. "Agnolo, you've got to help me. My young cousins are the most ill-educated boys in all Florence. Their father economized on their training the same way he economized on everything else. To think of Lorenzo marrying a wife like Ginevra when he can barely manage to read the Gallic Wars and doesn't even know a good horse from a bad one. It's abominable. Will you help me find a tutor?''

Agnolo Poliziano looked solemn. "I'll try, Lorenzo, but I can't say I feel hopeful. If there's no desire to learn, it's impossible to teach a boy that age. And if the desire is there, he would have learned no matter how poor his tutor might be.''

"I don't suppose you would . . .''

"No! Your sons are one thing. For love of you, I'll love them and tutor them. Not your young cousins. Particularly after your description of them.''

Lorenzo grinned. "You're right, of course. I shouldn't have told you about them. It would have been a great joke to see you break your head on the rocks of their ignorance.''

Poliziano hesitated, then laughed. He did not always know when Lorenzo was joking. As a result, Lorenzo took great delight in teasing him. He only did it when they were alone together; Agnolo was touchy, and Lorenzo was careful not to make him feel ridiculous in front of his other friends. He had infinite respect for Agnolo's mind; he could be tender with his sensitive feelings.

They had met eighteen months earlier, when Poliziano sent Lorenzo an epic poem he wrote about the tournament Giuliano held, repeating and surpassing the spectacle of Lorenzo's tournament. Poliziano was seeking patronage.

Several dozen poets had the same idea. But Poliziano's talent separated his offering from all the others. The poetry was sublime, with graceful metaphors, startling images, learned and witty allusions to the classic mythology that was an integral component of the Neo platonic philosophy that Lorenzo loved so well.

He sent for Agnolo at once. The young poet was twenty, six years younger than Lorenzo. He looked more like a soldier than a scholar, with a strong, muscular body and a craggy face, dominated by a large beak of a nose. He was not humble, like so many of Lorenzo's supplicants, and Lorenzo admired him for his self-confidence.

He had been studying for years with the scholars Lorenzo respected most, the men who made up the "Platonic Academy." When Lorenzo asked Poliziano why he had not persuaded them to recommend him, Agnolo replied that he wanted no advancement unless his own abilities earned it.

Lorenzo invited him to live at the Medici palace and granted him a yearly income. In the months that followed, Agnolo became Lorenzo's closest friend after Giuliano. He was also a favorite of Lucrezia's, and of the four children.

Lorenzo had little difficulty persuading Agnolo to take on the delicate job of finding a tutor for Pierfrancesco's sons. Agnolo was devoted to Lorenzo and dedicated to his service. He admired Lorenzo's energy and wide range of activities, respected his political and diplomatic skills, appreciated his wit and imagination. Most of all, he recognized, better than anyone else, Lorenzo's astonishing gift of poetry. He thought it a near-tragedy that Lorenzo could not give all of his time to serious work as a poet.

"So you'll solve my biggest problem, Agnolo. I'm deeply grateful. When you've winnowed the field, I'll join you in making the final choice. In the meantime, I'll manage the lesser matters."

Lorenzo hired workmen to repair and improve his cousins' house. He spent as many hours as he could with the boys, getting to know them and introducing them to the pleasures of being a Medici in Florence.

By the end of the year, he was more than ever eager to turn them over to a tutor. In spite of all his efforts, the boys were still hostile to his plans for them and resistant to his attempts to impart a desire for education.

"Anyone at all will do," he groaned to Poliziano. "Surely you have some suitable candidates by now."

"I'll bring you at least three next week. Then you can choose."

But by then, Lorenzo had more vital demands on his attention.

1477

Chapter Sixteen

On his birthday, Lorenzo received the news that his strongest ally, Galeazzo Sforza, Duke of Milan, was dead.

He had been assassinated in the doorway of the church he was entering for mass on the day after Christmas.

Lorenzo sat as if frozen. Bruno, his secretary, took the courier away and rewarded him for the perilous speed with which he had traveled on the frozen mountain roads from Milan.

In his office Lorenzo stared numbly at horrible visions of the future. "The Republic is in mortal danger," he whispered into the empty room. "Only a few more steps would have saved him. If only he had entered the sanctuary of the church. A few steps . . ."

The news reached Rome three days after it arrived in Florence. Pope Sixtus moaned and sank to his knees. "The peace of Italy is dead."

That evening in a palace on the Palatine Hill, Sixtus's nephew Girolamo Riario entertained his friend Francesco de' Pazzi with dinner and music. Like everyone in Rome, in Florence, Venice, Perugia, Assisi, in cities great and small, they talked about the murder of Milan's duke.

"I can hardly believe it," Francesco said. "Sforza was always surrounded by armed guards. If it had been Florence, it would be different. Lorenzo de' Medici goes everywhere with no protection at all . . ." His voice trailed off into resonant silence, and he looked at Riario.

The absentee Lord of Imola looked back at him.

In that exchange, spawned by an idle comment, the plot to assassinate Lorenzo had its beginning.

After the initial minutes of shock at the news from Milan, Lorenzo acted. He was a whirlwind of decisions made, orders given, letters written, conferences held, meetings called.

Galeazzo's heir, the new Duke of Milan, was an infant, the government in the untrained, weak hands of his mother, the Duchess Bona. And Galeazzo had three younger brothers, each of whom would try to seize control, none of whom had any record of loyalty to the Milan-Florence alliance.

Lorenzo sent his old advisor Tommaso Soderini and Luigi Guicciardini, a practiced diplomat, to Milan at once. They carried with them authorizations to draw on the Medici bank's Milan branch for any amount and letters to Bona that pledged Florence's support and expressed Lorenzo's grief and sympathy. "I have sent," he also wrote, "two wise heads and noble hearts to counsel you. You can trust them absolutely to guide you on the best path for the safety and future of your State and your orphaned son."

At the same time that he wrote to Bona in his own hand, Bruno was transcribing dictated letters from Lorenzo to the heads of state in all Italian and European principalities. They expressed Florence's determination to stand behind the widowed regent.

After that Lorenzo could only wait. For reports from Milan and from the informers he had everywhere. For action by others to which he would have to respond. For indications of shifts in the shattered balance of power in Italy and threats to the suddenly vulnerable Republic. Now, as never before, information was essential to him. He reserved the hours of the night for work at his desk, sorting through the floods of dispatches that arrived every day. He studied them, compared them, analyzed patterns, drafted urgent demands for details and sources of whatever seemed important.

He did not concern himself with the report of an unsubstantiated rumor in Rome that there was a plot to murder him. There were always such rumors, and he was sure that he had nothing to fear. The Republic was not a despotism, and he had no need for caution, nor for guards to protect him. The citizens of Florence were his guards.

In the meantime, until events called for government action, there were other things that needed his attention.

At the end of January, a new daughter was born, with all the celebrations that such a happy occasion demanded. Luisa slept peacefully through them all.

And there were all the traditional celebrations of saints' days, with the processions and sacred plays that had added significance because they offered prayers to the saints to aid in the protection of Florence.

And it was necessary to pay added attention to his mistress, even though the necessity grew ever more onerous. Lucrezia Donati was distraught because she was going to die. She was twenty-one and very beautiful, but she had noticed tiny lines at the corners of her eyes and swore that she could detect a roughness in the texture of her silklike skin. She was growing older, she cried to Lorenzo, and wept in his arms.

Two years before, her reign as Florence's greatest beauty had ended abruptly when Marco Vespucci returned from Genoa with his bride. Simonetta Vespucci became, overnight, the unattainable beloved of all the men who had courted Lucrezia. The poems, songs, flowers, candies, trinkets all went now to the Palazzo Vespucci.

Lucrezia bore the defection with outward calm. Lorenzo was assiduous in his gifts and visits, and Lucrezia said gaily that her forced abdication was a blessing because it gave her more time for him and some long-desired privacy.

She smiled radiantly from the throne of Queen of the Tournament at Giuliano's joust, even though Simonetta was enthroned next to her as Queen of Love and Beauty.

But then, after only a year and a half of triumph, Simonetta died. No one had known that she was consumptive, not even she. The end followed the onset of symptoms by only a few weeks.

Lucrezia was terrified. It was the first time in her life that she was forced to recognize that death comes to all, even the beautiful and young. If not suddenly, as with Simonetta, then slowly by the accumulation of years. It would come, one day, to her.

Lucrezia was not the only person deeply affected by Simonetta's death. Giuliano had been in love with her, and his grief was desperate. It was also short-lived, burnt out by its intensity.

But Sandro Botticelli was still mourning, a year after Simonetta's burial.

At first, Lorenzo mourned what he regarded as a facsimile of death in his old friend. Sandro had not worked at anything during that year. Then Lorenzo raged.

"You were at the top of your profession, Sandro, the height of your powers. I still love you, but my respect is dead, because you are dead. What is a painter who does not paint?"

Botticelli turned his head away. Weak tears fell onto his hollowed cheeks. "Don't torment me, Lorenzo, I beg you. I'm tormented past endurance already."

Lorenzo stalked across the darkened studio and threw open the shutters. "Let some light and air into this grave you've made for yourself." The sunlight struck the bright colors of dried-out paints on the worktable beneath the windows. Sandro covered his eyes.

Lorenzo pulled the artist's hands away from his face. His grasp was tight, painful on Sandro's wrists. "Listen to me," he shouted, "you cannot do this thing. You were touched by God, given a gift that you have no right to leave unused. It is a blasphemy to hide from your art. Look at your paints. Dry, useless now. Just like you. You are an abomination in the sight of the saints."

Sandro tore away with a madman's strength. "Then let heaven strike me dead," he cried. "It is all I long for. I could see her again, among the angels."

Lorenzo backed away. His hot anger was gone, and he felt the chill of fear for his friend's sanity.

"Leave me," Botticelli said. "If you love me, I beg of you, Lorenzo, leave me."

The sound of the shutters closing followed Lorenzo along the street as he hurried back to his house.

"I cannot understand madness," Lorenzo told his mother. "Sandro was never sane after Simonetta came to Florence. He saw her in the Mercato, riding in a litter, and he fell in love with her perfection of beauty. Very well. So did every lover of beauty in the whole city.

"But . . . do you remember, Mamina, he refused to meet her? Even to be in the same room with her? We made such jokes about his timidity.

"If he had been her lover in fact. If he had possessed her body. If she had returned his love. Then, perhaps, this exaggeration of grief would make sense. But this . . . It is lunacy."

Lucrezia began to pull on the shoes she used outdoors. "I had no idea things were so bad," she said. "I'm going to go bring him home. And you will be patient with Sandro. This is partly your fault, you know, Lorenzo."

"My fault? You're as mad as he is. Did I kill Simonetta?"

"You introduced Sandro to your Platonic Academy. You excited his imagination with the concept of the ideal. He's not a philosopher, he's an artist. When he saw a woman who was to him the very ideal of beauty, he didn't sit around a table and discuss the works of Plato on the subject. He surrendered his heart and his soul.

"I intend to rescue them both."

Lucrezia surrounded Sandro with the healing care and acceptance of a mother's love, and his body grew stronger.

But it was Lorenzo who rescued him.

Several times each week Lorenzo and Giuliano rode out into the countryside, searching for a villa that could be bought for Pierfrancesco's sons. Lorenzo was determined that the boys get out of the city in the summer and that they experience the pleasures and challenges of the outdoors. Agnolo Poliziano had found a young tutor who was far from brilliant as a scholar but who made up for his classroom deficiencies by his willingness to teach his pupils to ride and hunt and take the risks expected of men.

In early May Lorenzo bought Villa Castello with money from Pierfrancesco's estate. It was a small elegant castle, three miles toward Prato at the foot of a gentle meadowed mountain. He persuaded Botticelli to go there with him one afternoon. The mountain was carpeted with color, delicate wildflowers rippled by soft breezes.

"It is very near perfection, isn't it, Sandro?"

The artist's bemused eyes were an affirmation.

"Will you paint the perfection for me, my friend? For this place, to hang between the windows that overlook the mountain? Will you, can you, put your heart into line and color and story?"

"I want to try," said Botticelli. "I want to see the windows, the space between them. Is it big enough? The painting must be big."

Lorenzo controlled his impulse to embrace his friend. He must not pressure him now, when he was beginning to return to life. "Let's go inside," he said. "If the space is too small, I'll have the windows moved."

"Our Sandro is cured," Lucrezia said. "I thank God."

Botticelli had rushed into the palace after the visit to the villa, shouting for Agnolo Poliziano. For two weeks he worked in a frenzy, Agnolo at his side, making sketch after sketch for the painting he saw in his mind. Agnolo was honored by Sandro's need for him. The artist wanted to use many of the allegorical images that Agnolo had fashioned in his poem on Giuliano's joust.

"I can't tell you what he's doing," Poliziano said to the family. "He made me give my word."

Lorenzo was consumed with curiosity, but he wasn't offended by his exclusion. He was too happy that Sandro was working.

Lucrezia was gratified by the artist's complaints that

he was always hungry. It was like the old days when Sandro was a boy growing up in the household.

When the heat of summer clamped down on the city Lucrezia and Clarice and the children moved up to the villa at Fiesole. Giuliano stayed at Careggi; the stables were there, and the Palio was only weeks away. "I'm going to coax Morello into loving me as much as he does you, Lorenzo," he said. "This year the Medici will win."

Lorenzo would have liked to help with the training, but he had to be in the city, weighing the daily reports from Milan. With Florence backing her, the Duchess was maintaining control in spite of a bloody uprising in Genoa and the agitation of the three Sforza brothers.

Lorenzo followed his usual summertime routine of long sociable twilights in the loggia. They were a respite from the daytime demands on his powers of dissimulation. At mass, in the streets, in the government meetings, everyone wanted reassurance that Florence was safe, even though Milan was in turmoil.

He made time for happier activities. The Villa Castello needed designs for furnishings, orders for renovation, plans for gardens, and he did them all. By far the best, he had to decide on the paintings. Ever since the loss of the papal account to the Pazzi, he had had no money to commission any art.

He spent freely from Pierfrancesco's estate, buying for Pierfrancesco's children, reviving the Medici patronage that was so necessary to Florence's artists. At Antonio Pollaiuolo's studio, he listened respectfully to the suggestions of the painter. Piero, Lorenzo's father, had considered him the greatest of the age. Lorenzo thought him the greatest storyteller in any form and commissioned a rendering of the battle between Hercules and Antaeus as a painting and as a bronze statue.

He was less formal when he went to see Luca Signorelli. Luca was Lorenzo's age and not yet considered a master by anybody, but Lorenzo believed in his talent.

Luca wanted to do a huge madonna and child. Lorenzo wanted classic heroism. They wrangled noisily, ate some bread and cheese and radishes and reached a compromise that made them both happy. The Villa Castello would have a *guardaroba,* a room lined with wardrobes, in which the siege of Troy decorated the doors. And a small madonna and child to hang above the altar in the chapel.

Lorenzo lingered in Verrocchio's huge studio, selecting lamps, knives and forks, goblets, reading stands, tapestry designs, garden benches and fountains and all sizes of storage chests, *cassone.* "How I love your company!" Andrea shouted. "Ho! My little chickens, we are all going to be rich." The apprentices cheered.

"Don't celebrate yet," Lorenzo laughed. "I'm not going to pay until the work is done. I want decorations in tempera not in wine."

But he had no objections when they were all drinking together and one of the apprentices sketched on the scrubbed wood table with a finger dipped in the Chianti. Piero Perugino immediately won the monopoly on all the cassone paintings. The chests would show scenes of Florence's festivals.

Lorenzo also commissioned frescoes for the walls of the chapel at the villa from Filippino Lippi. The young man's father was the notorious profligate monk Fra Filippo Lippi who had been a close friend of Cosimo's. Filippino was only twelve when his father died. For the eight years since then, he had been studying with Sandro Botticelli and, during the year of Sandro's withdrawal, the youth had done his best to hold the workshop together.

Botticelli himself, Lorenzo left alone. He had moved back to his studio and was working at fever pitch. The shutters were wide open.

The expenditures Lorenzo made were huge, on a Medici scale, but they made barely a dent in the income from Pierfrancesco's estate. Lorenzo drew up papers for a loan to himself of sixty thousand florins. Keeping peace in Milan was costly. And in Burgundy, Charles the Bold had died, owing the Bruges branch of the bank ninety-five thousand.

* * *

Lorenzo's wards were thrilled with the villa and the bright new furnishings that were arriving. They decided that their cousin was a wonderful guardian, and Lorenzo's visits to them were actually pleasant for him.

They learned to ride sufficiently well to go with him once to Careggi to watch Giuliano training for the Palio. And they were even more disappointed than Lorenzo was when Giuliano fell ill and could not enter the race. A Medici horse ran, ridden by a groom, but it finished far back. Lorenzo wouldn't allow anyone other than Giuliano to ride his prized Morello.

Alberto Palmieri won, after twenty-six years of trying. He filled the fountains in four piazzas with wine, and Carnival was more flamboyant than ever before. Day and night the streets rang with Lorenzo's song of the year before. It had become the accepted theme of all revelers . . . "How fair is youth and how fleeting . . ."

Lorenzo smiled when he heard it. "I see that you enjoy immortality," his friend Luigi Pulci grumbled. "I'm sick with envy. Injustice bothers me. After all, I'm a much better poet than you."

Lorenzo pushed him into a wine-flowing fountain. Pulci said he'd found his home at last.

"I thought I smelled something good." Sandro Botticelli walked through the door with his nose pointed upward and sniffing.

Lorenzo leapt up from his chair and ran to his friend. After they embraced, he looked Botticelli up and down. Sandro was well groomed, well fed and smiling; his old self.

"Come eat," said Lorenzo. He brushed the snow from Sandro's shoulders. The December day was bitter. Agnolo Poliziano moved to one side, making room beside him on the bench. Botticelli seated himself and calmly began to eat Agnolo's dinner.

A young envoy from Milan was a guest in the Medici palace. He gaped at the artist's boldness. But he was not surprised. Nothing could surprise him anymore in the house of this unconventional head of the Florentine Republic. At the castle of the Duchess of Milan there was a strict courtly formality and protocol. Here there was anarchy. Everyone addressed Lorenzo by his given name, called him "thou," spoke so freely that they would have been sent to the dungeon in Milan.

"Ambassador," Lorenzo said, "this lout is the great painter Sandro Botticelli . . . Our visitor is the Marchese Stefano Vallambroso, Sandro. He brought us the good tidings that all is quiet in Milan. I hope you have some good news, too."

Botticelli nodded to the Milanese, declared himself delighted to meet him, then started mopping up the gravy on the plate in front of him. He used elaborate care to break the bread, to apply it precisely to the center of the plate, to move it in even circles.

"I feel the dagger twitching in its sheath at my side," Luigi Pulci observed. "It wants to kill Sandro. Shall I allow it?"

"Help it," growled Andrea del Verrocchio. "I have never liked competition."

Agnolo made a great show of edging away from Sandro. "No splashing on my clothes, please. Blood leaves stains."

"I'm trembling with fear," Sandro mumbled from a full, chewing mouth.

Lorenzo rapped on the table with the back of a spoon. "Attention," he said. "Watch this." He lifted the lid of the tureen and waved the steam that rose from its interior toward Botticelli. Then he replaced the lid with a crash. "Plenty more for anyone who's hungry, if that anyone will quit driving me crazy."

Sandro smiled. "It's finished," he said. "I invite you all to the studio tomorrow to see it." He held out Agnolo's empty plate.

Lorenzo pushed the tureen to him. "Bravo!" he cried. "Bravissimo." He gestured to the steward in the doorway. "Bring more bread for the hungry painter."

"And a plate for the hungry philosopher," added Poliziano.

Chapter Seventeen

Botticelli's studio was not very big, not even a quarter the size of Verrocchio's tremendous converted warehouse. It was also his home, with his bed and cooking facilities in one corner; his apprentice Filippino lived in a small shed attached to the building. To make room for the friends Sandro had invited, the bed and stove and cassone were stacked one on top another against the wall.

Even so, there was not nearly space enough. Verrocchio had told everyone he knew, and they had told others, and the news had spread throughout the art-loving city. The street outside the studio was packed with people, eager and patient at the same time, waiting for their turn to see what Sandro had done.

They made way for Lorenzo to pass through, and he accepted the favor because he had the Milanese ambassador with him. Also because he was avid to view the painting.

It was breathtaking. Unlike anything Sandro had ever done, unlike anything being done by Florence's other artists. Huge, almost eight feet high and over ten feet wide. To see it, it was necessary to move to the very back of the studio where the unsteady tower of furniture threatened to fall at any minute.

The envoy from Milan was normally a timid man, but he forgot the danger the instant he saw the painting; he even understood how a head of state could allow such familiarity at his table. The man who could create a work of art like this need be subservient to no one.

Beside the ambassador Lorenzo stood with his arm

across Botticelli's shoulders. He didn't say anything; there was no need.

The painting was an allegory of Spring. Venus stood in a bower of fantastic trees that bore golden globes of oranges and bright sprays of blossoms. Underfoot the ground was carpeted with the wildflowers of the meadow near Castello.

The symbolic figures from Poliziano's poem were superbly rendered. Eros, Mercury, the goddess Flora, Zephyr. And three graces. Solemn. Transported by their dance. Separate from the other figures and linked with each other by intertwined fingers. They were the embodiment of beauty and youth and eternal celebration of life. With differing stances, differing ethereal robes, differing coils and billows of exquisite pale hair, the three graces were three portraits of Simonetta.

Sandro had expressed and possessed his love for all time.

"Did you see Sandro's painting, Lorenzo? It's great. And he's in fine form." Giuliano was pink-cheeked from the cold and from excitement when he charged into Lorenzo's office.

"I saw. It is. And I know. He came to eat with us last night. I wish you had been there. Pulci made up a ballad about artists and models and things to do with paintbrushes that gave the Milanese a fit."

"I'm sorry I missed it. I was with my mistress." Giuliano's chin stuck out defiantly.

Lorenzo frowned. "Are you joking? You must be."

"No, brother, I'm not. I know what you told me, that mistresses are more demanding than wives, that I shouldn't obligate myself. But Fioretta isn't anything like Lucrezia Donati. She doesn't expect attentions, she doesn't make demands at all." Giuliano spoke rapidly.

Lorenzo held up his hand. "Wait a minute. Slow down. I can hardly understand a word you say. 'Fioretta'? Who is Fioretta? Fioretta who?"

"Fioretta Gorini. Her brother is Gorini the tailor, the calcio player."

Lorenzo laughed. "Thanks to God, now I know

you're joking. I remember Gorini's sister who watched all the games. She's as plain as mud. You shouldn't scare me like that. I thought you were serious."

"And you shouldn't laugh at me. I am serious. I've made Fioretta my mistress. I talked to her brother about the arrangements because her father's dead. She's living at home, no little palace of her own like Lucrezia; Fioretta doesn't want to take advantage of me." Giuliano's hands were balled into fists.

"All right, all right." Lorenzo felt as if he were having a preview of future conversations with his sons. "You don't have to tell me your business. You're a grown man . . . I do want to ask you one thing, but you don't have to answer. I'm just curious . . . Why this girl? Florence is full of beautiful, amusing, educated girls, and most of them are half in love with you. Why pick one who is . . ." He stopped, afraid of offending his brother.

Giuliano smiled. "That's just why, because she's not beautiful or educated or witty. All she has to offer is a heart full of love, and no one puts much value on that . . . Don't you see, Lorenzo, if I don't love her, she'll never have anybody who cares about her. Those beautiful girls will."

Lorenzo said, "Yes. I see." No wonder I love him so much, he thought. No wonder everybody does. "Come on," he laughed, "let's go see if the way is clear to Sandro's studio. I'll get him to do a portrait of your Fioretta. Sandro will make her look beautiful. I promise you, she'll like that. Especially as she grows older."

"Thank you, brother, I wouldn't have thought of it. Better get your cloak and boots. Look out the window. It's snowing."

The snow was falling steadily, small flakes that turned as if dancing as they floated down through the dim gray light.

It piled into crowns on the stone dolphins that were mounted on the corner of the Pazzi palace. A window next to them was lighted, although it was only two o'clock in the afternoon. The light made the snow glitter when it fell past it, cast a golden glow onto the crowns.

Inside the lighted room three men were huddled around a table in front of a bed of embers in the fireplace. Servants could not replenish the fire because the door to the room was locked.

"I don't like this," Jacopo de' Pazzi was saying. "The whole family should decide."

Francesco managed to hold his temper. He spoke in a voice of cool reason. "It doesn't concern the whole family, Uncle. Not until it's done, and then they'll be grateful. The Pazzi will be what they have a right to be . . . We three are the only ones who count now. And we can keep our counsel. If too many know, there will be no chance of secrecy, and surprise is essential."

Jacopo nodded, granting the point. "How do I know that you're telling the truth, that the Pope is behind us?"

Francesco's face reddened, but his voice remained calm. "I'll send confirmation to you. A soldier, a captain of the papal army. He is the one who will use the sword. He's experienced in killing. And he went with Riario and me to Sixtus. He knows Sixtus is supporting us. With arms and with money if necessary."

Francesco turned to his brother. "Elmo? You're the only one left. Our uncle has agreed, am I right, Jacopo?"

Jacopo nodded again.

Elmo pushed away from the table, shaking his head. "I can't agree. I can't."

Francesco put a hand on his brother's chair to hold him still. "You must. Think what it will mean to your family, to your children. Our uncle will be your councillor, but you will rule. You're the eldest. Florence will be a kingdom again, as it should be, with the lower classes below us, where they belong. And you'll be ruler, Elmo. And your son a prince."

"But Bianca is their sister!"

"Yes. And the children are her children. Where is a woman's loyalty greater, as a sister or as a mother? Don't you see the beauty of it? If there are any Medici supporters who are wavering, it will be easy for them to give you their allegiance because the heirs to the kingdom will be half Medici.

"You won't have to strike a blow, Elmo. You won't even have to see it happen. All you have to do is gather support from the people after it's done."

Elmo's face was shiny with cold sweat. "Then I vote yes."

"That's it, then," said Jacopo. "Go back to Rome and send this captain to me. What is his name?"

"Montesecco."

"All right. If he confirms your claim about Sixtus, we will proceed. Have you made a plan? Chosen a time?"

"Not yet. We'll find a way that will be above suspicion. I'll send word."

Elmo wet his lips. "Is it really necessary . . . Giuliano, too? He has nothing to do with the government."

Jacopo exchanged looks with Francesco. Without a word they agreed that Elmo's role would be no more than decorative when the power was theirs.

"It is necessary," the old man said. "There must be no one for the people to look to when Lorenzo is gone. No one but you."

1478

Chapter Eighteen

"Which one is she, Lorenzo? You promised you'd show me."

Lorenzo responded to the tug on his sleeve. "Oh yes. Let me find her." He was standing just inside the door of the Duomo with his wards Lorenzo and Giovanni on Easter Eve. He had mentioned to young Lorenzo that his future wife would be in the procession of the Pazzi carrying the flints for the Scoppio, and the boy had insisted that Lorenzo take him to the ceremony and point Ginevra out to him.

Lorenzo could understand his young cousin's curiosity, but he wished he could have come without the boy. He wanted to watch every moment of the Scoppio to see what the omens were. They were supposedly a foretelling of the year's harvest, but why not use them for the health of the State as well as the health of the vines and fields? The news from Milan was disturbing.

"Lorenzo! Which one is she?"

"Not yet. Wait . . . there. There she comes. See the old man in gold velvet with his hand on the girl's shoulder? The girl is Ginevra."

She did not notice Lorenzo in the crowd. Her eyes were directed straight ahead, her expression reverent, her back straight and strong as support for her grandfather's weak arm. The jeweled golden dolphins on her sleeve glimmered in the light of the thousand candles in the cathedral.

"She looks mean," Giovanni said.

"Quiet," ordered his guardian. "This is a very important mass."

Giovanni hopped from foot to foot, giggling. "She

looks mean . . . Lorenzo's bride looks like she'll bite his head off.''

Before Lorenzo could silence him, young Lorenzo grabbed his brother's arm and twisted it. ''Be quiet or I'll hurt you,'' he said. ''And she doesn't look mean, you stupid, she looks important. All of them with their gold insignia, they all look important. The Pazzi are very important, aren't they, Lorenzo?''

''They think so,'' Lorenzo said under his breath. More loudly he said, ''Look there, Lorenzo. There's your cousin Bianca, my sister. You know her.'' He smiled. Bianca could always make him smile, usually without knowing why. The stately pace of the procession suited her, because she was monumentally pregnant. Her Pazzi regalia was designed with the dolphins embroidered from breast to knee on a blue-brocaded silk cioppa, one on each side of the open front. It looked as if they were supporting her yellow-silk-covered, protruding belly on their backs. She was holding Bernardo, Lorenzo's godson, by the hand, ignoring his attempts to pull free with the majestic obliviousness of the experienced mother. Bernardo will be ten on our next birthday, Lorenzo thought. I'll take him out to Careggi to choose a young horse. It's ridiculous that I let my irritation with Francesco keep me from seeing my sister and my godson. And my friend Elmo. He avoids me these days.

Tomorrow, he decided. I'll go see them tomorrow. It will be Easter, a day for rebirth and reconciliation.

During mass he pondered the eternal mystery of the Resurrection and the lesser but somehow equal mystery of birth. Bianca's proud motherhood, his own growing family, the infant daughter, Contessina, only three weeks old and already an individual, distinct and different from her two brothers and three sisters. My children are my fortune, he thought, and he offered up humble prayers of thanks.

As if in benediction, the dove flew true into the fireworks and they exploded in glorious bursts of color. A weight of worry lifted from Lorenzo's heart. The Republic would be protected, he was confident now. The troubles in Milan would be resolved.

He stood on the steps of the cathedral and cheered, joining his shouts to the pandemonium of joy in the thronged piazza. Rockets climbed and exploded, and the lights—white, red, green, blue—showed him to the crowds. "Lorenzo! Lorenzo!" they cried. He opened his arms to his people, laughing, cheering, celebrating with them, a Florentine among Florentines, a Tuscan among Tuscans, a Republican among Republicans.

A hundred yards away, a tall man with a strong, weathered face craned to see above the heads of the people crowded close around him. He was a Roman, a captain of the papal army. Montesecco. He had entered Florence in the midst of a group of pilgrims come to celebrate Holy Week in the capital of the Republic. The city gates were open wide, and the guards did not ask what business brought visitors as they usually did.

Twenty Perugian soldiers entered the same way.

Once inside the walls, they had only to wait until it was time for them to act.

Chapter Nineteen

"I tell you, Francesco, we've got to call it off," Elmo whined. He grabbed his brother's shoulder. "Pay attention. Listen to me!"

Francesco slowly reached up and lifted Elmo's clutching hand by the wrist. He turned his body away, dropped the hand as if it were a dirty object. "I have listened," he said, "and I've heard nothing but a coward's imaginings."

"I'm not imagining anything. Lorenzo is suspicious. He's been too agreeable, too friendly. For two weeks, ever since Easter, he's been seeking me out, inviting me to eat with him, coming by the palace to see Bianca, visiting my children. He must know something. He must be laying a trap." Elmo held out his hands, beseeching the other men in the room.

"Don't you see?" he cried. "We've got to stop before it's too late." His hands were trembling.

The men all looked at Francesco.

"It's already too late, Elmo," he said, biting the words. "Our armies are only a day's march from Florence. Everything is ready, and nothing will go wrong if you will only control yourself." He waved a sheet of paper at his frightened brother.

"You've seen this. It's an invitation from Lorenzo for dinner at his villa in Fiesole. It's precisely what we planned. Jacopo wrote and told him that the Cardinal and Archbishop had arrived here at our villa, and Lorenzo wrote to them immediately, inviting them to come to dinner, with any companions they cared to bring. It will be done today. Go to your rooms and wait. We'll

147

tell you when it's over." Francesco sneered, gave Elmo a push.

Elmo stumbled, but did not move. "It's a trap. He'll have guards, soldiers."

"Fool. The Archbishop has ten 'servants,' all of them professional men-at-arms. Montesecco's Perugians will be just behind us. The Cardinal's priests are armed. And Lorenzo suspects nothing."

Elmo began to argue. A man near the window began to laugh. "Look here, my worried friend." He pointed. The rich purple silk of his sleeve gleamed sumptuously when his arm rose. He was the Archbishop of Pisa, Francesco Salviati, a lean man with a vulpine face that proclaimed his avarice and his vicious nature. "Here comes your suspicious brother-in-law now. He's not setting any traps; he's such a good host that he's saving us the trouble of riding out to kill him. He's coming to us. With only two companions, one a boy."

Francesco and Elmo rushed to the window. "Giuliano," Francesco said, "is Giuliano with him? Where is Montesecco? What a stroke of luck."

The other two men in the room were priests in simple black cassocks. One of them ran toward the door. "I'll find Montesecco," he said.

The second slid one hand into his sleeve. "If you don't find him, it doesn't matter," he said. His eyes were glittering, his lips stretched in an evil grin. He pulled out a thin, shining dagger.

Francesco grunted and turned from the window. "Put it back, Stefano. I don't recognize the other man, but it's not Giuliano. Go get the Cardinal."

Elmo scurried across the room. "I'm not here. You haven't seen me." He was babbling. "I'll hide in my bedroom."

Francesco cocked his arm at his brother's retreating back. "Disgusting," he said. "I'd drown him if we didn't need him. He's popular with the rabble and he has the Medici wife. I'm ashamed."

Salviati shrugged. "No need for apologies, my friend. We don't choose our brothers any more than we choose our fathers. He's useful, that's all that matters." He smoothed his rich robes into even folds and adjusted his hat on his head so that his face was in shadow.

"How I look forward to this evening," he said. There was voluptuous pleasure in his deep voice. "I hope Lorenzo is slow in dying. I have hated him for a long time."

Rafaello Riario was the Cardinal's name. He was only seventeen years old, and his life had been so full of changes that he was in a state of perpetual confusion and amazement. First his simple farming family had become the most prosperous in their village; then he had been made a priest, although he could barely read and write; then, when he was fifteen, he had suddenly been sent to the University of Pisa, where the instructors were astonishingly patient with him; and two months ago, he had been named a Cardinal, with the enormous incomes of the region around Perugia.

Rafaello's great-uncle was Pope Sixtus IV.

The boy Cardinal looked down at Lorenzo de' Medici's bared head when the older man bent on one knee to kiss his ring, and he felt like a child dressed up in adult clothes that did not fit.

Lorenzo made him feel much better when, the obligatory homage done, he stood, smiled and asked him how he liked the University. "I only hear what the teachers think," Lorenzo said, "and I'd be grateful if you'd tell me what things are really like for the students."

Rafaello was happy to oblige. He had a lot of complaints, and no one else had ever wanted to hear them. Lorenzo was genuinely interested. He could tell. So was the man with him; Lorenzo introduced him as his son's tutor, Agnolo Poliziano.

"And this is my son, Eminence. His name is Piero, and he is almost six years old. He'll be a student at the University himself when he gets older."

Piero was small, dazzled by Rafaello's new crimson robes and huge sapphire ring. He made the young Cardinal feel extremely grown up. For the first time, he began to enjoy being an Eminence and to have a good time on this trip that the Archbishop had planned for him.

He knew nothing about the conspiracy, the real purpose of his elevation in rank or the journey, by way of Florence, to his ecclesiastical territories in Perugia: as head of the Republic, it was axiomatic that Lorenzo would entertain any visitor of Rafaello's distinction.

"We are looking forward to having you as our guest at Fiesole, Eminence," Lorenzo said. "We rode over to escort you and your friends there ourselves. There are some interesting sights along the route."

"The Cardinal is looking forward to the visit," the Archbishop said to Lorenzo. Rafaello bit his lip. He could have said that himself. Salviati continued, "He's particularly looking forward to meeting your brother. He'll be there, of course."

Lorenzo spoke to Rafaello. "I'm afraid my brother is not going to be with us today, Eminence. He's not feeling well and he's staying in the city."

Salviati spoke again. His voice was warm, smooth, with no hint of the frustration he was feeling or the urgency to have both Medici brothers together and vulnerable. "His Eminence has heard such marvelous reports of your collection of antiquities, I know he's been hoping to see them, but he's too unassuming to press his hopes on you."

Rafaello couldn't remember ever hearing anything about Lorenzo's collection, and he did not particularly want to see it. But he did want to be with Lorenzo, to tell him about the many ways the University could be made a happier place. When Lorenzo responded to the Archbishop's blatant hint by inviting Rafaello to the Medici palace on the following day, the young Cardinal accepted with unfeigned gratitude.

"I'll be in the city," he added, attempting nonchalance. "It has been arranged for me to assist at high mass in the cathedral. I'll be wearing my full vestments. Will you come?"

"Of course I will," said Lorenzo, "and then we'll go back to my house for the midday meal. You can see my collections then. And meet the rest of my family."

Salviati glanced casually in Francesco's direction. Well done, said Francesco's eyes.

Sunday morning the awakening birds roused the young Cardinal before the sun was more than a promise in the chill gray light. He woke in a fine humor, wondered why, then remembered the pleasure of the evening before. There had been a very funny minstrel at the Medici villa, singing songs full of wickedly sexual puns. Rafaello had gotten very excited, felt very sophisticated. His new friend Lorenzo had promised to write the words and tune on paper for him. He'd be able to learn them and play them for the other students when he returned to the University. "My friend Lorenzo de' Medici taught this to me when I was his guest in Florence," he'd say. "He wrote this song."

Rafaello left the warm bed without his usual reluctance. He was eager for the day to start.

The sky was streaked with rose and gold when Ginevra de' Pazzi woke. She held the warm feather cover close to her for a moment, then bolted from bed. The tiled floor was cold, and she skipped from foot to foot, shivering, while she washed and dressed. Then she pushed her windows wide and breathed in the intoxicating fresh scent of dew-dampened flowers. It was going to be a glorious day.

I'll arrange for breakfast in the garden, she decided.

After early mass, she led her grandfather from the chapel to his chair at the garden table, then took her place at his side. She felt the sun's warmth on her back, and she closed her eyes to enjoy it even more, free of the fascinating distractions all around her in the garden.

Antonio and Mateo and Fra Marco talked about the portrayal of death and the underworld in the legend of Persephone.

Ginevra half-dozed in a happy semistupor of warmth and fragrance. She became suddenly alert when she heard Fra Marco say, ". . . Lorenzo de' Medici."

"What about Lorenzo? I was half-asleep."

"I went to the city yesterday, and I heard that Lorenzo was entertaining a Cardinal. I wondered if perhaps he would bring him to see our della Robbias . . . I've never met a Cardinal, you see."

"I doubt that he will, Fra Marco. There's so much art to see in the city." Ginevra's tone was gentle. If she'd known that it meant so much to the old friar to meet a Cardinal, she would have written to Lorenzo and begged him to come, or to invite Fra Marco to the city.

"I suppose it was terribly bold," said the friar, "but I left a small note at the Medici palace. I said we'd be happy to show them if the Cardinal wanted to come."

Ginevra laughed. "You are wonderful," she said. "It wasn't bold at all, just generous."

Fra Marco shook his head. "I'm afraid not. I'll have to go tomorrow to my confessor. Now, I will polish the altar candlesticks." He stifled a sigh and stood. The heavy silver candlesticks were so intricately carved that polishing them thoroughly was a long, exhausting task. Fra Marco often imposed it on himself as a penance for worldliness.

Mateo stood also and put his arm around the elderly friar's thin shoulders. "As you know, Father, I have more sins than I can remember. I'll polish with you."

"Good men and good friends," Antonio said after they left.

"Yes, indeed," said Ginevra. "As are you, Grandfather."

Antonio extended his hand toward her. "Bless you, child. Hold my hand and share the day with me. Tell me what I see."

Ginevra held Antonio's knotted fingers between her two smooth palms. "It's a wonderful day," she began, "and you see the world full of new life. The olive trees have turned up the silver sides of their new leaves to feel the breeze, and the vines have fresh little fingers of growth curling around the trellis. There are baby birds in the nest in the fig tree. Their mother is feeling proud and nervous all in one. Listen to her . . .

"And did you hear that? One of the goldfish in the fountain basin just jumped. He must be celebrating spring.

"There's a bee at the lemon pots on the terrace. The lemon trees have fruit and flowers both. The bee looks dizzy from the scent, or maybe just from the sweet air." She rested her head against Antonio's arm and inhaled deeply. "Try it, Grandfather. The air has bubbles in it."

Antonio smiled and breathed, seeing through Ginevra's eyes. In a curious way, his life had become fuller since his blindness. He "saw" things that he had never noticed when he had eyesight, and he appreciated things that he had taken for granted. The world came to him through the perspective of youth, and he was rejuvenated.

"Thank you, my dear child; I'm ready to go in now." Antonio rose. Ginevra led him into the house. She smiled when her keen young ears heard the sound of Mateo and Fra Marco singing as they worked in the chapel.

In the city Bianca de' Pazzi heard singing, too, when she entered her house, but she did not smile. "Be grateful that I'm the one who caught you making that racket and not the master," she said to the kitchen maid who was pulling up a bucket of water from the well. "Now put that down and help me up the stairs. Silently." Bianca was thirty-four and near the end of her twelfth pregnancy. She felt very old, heavy, and out-of-sorts.

Halfway up the long stone staircase she was nearly knocked flat by Francesco, who was running down. "For the love of God, Bianca, can't you keep your belly out of people's way?" he shouted.

"Can't you watch where you're going? Are you trying to kill me?" Bianca's shouts were even louder.

Francesco felt as if a fist had struck him. Did she know something? Had Elmo told her? He pushed the maid away and took Bianca's arm, apologizing, insisting that she allow him to help her.

Bianca regretted her outburst. It wasn't like her to raise her voice or to lose her temper. She thanked Francesco and made a great effort not to lean too heavily on him. "I apologize," she said, "I shouldn't have screamed at you like that."

"No, no, it's all my fault." Francesco breathed more easily in spite of the weight on his arm. Clearly his alarm had been unnecessary.

Bianca was chattering sociably, trying to smooth over the ugliness of her outburst. When Francesco realized what she was saying, he felt another blow. This fright was not imaginary.

"May God send Giuliano de' Medici to eternal perdition!" he swore when he entered his uncle's study a few minutes later.

There were seven men in the room. They all gasped at Francesco's words and crossed themselves hurriedly. Death, even murder, was a commonplace event, but damnation was too terrible to think about.

Francesco stalked across the floor, waving his arms and cursing. Giuliano, he told them, was still feeling ill. Bianca had seen her mother at early mass and learned that the younger Medici brother was not going to attend the dinner Lorenzo was hosting for the young Cardinal. "There are too many servants and men-at-arms in the palazzo for us to go looking for his room without causing suspicion," Francesco sputtered. "We have to have the two brothers together and off guard."

The conspirators looked anxiously at each other. Francesco had been, until now, the leader, the confident one. His anger and uncertainty were demoralizing.

Archbishop Salviati stepped forward into the center of the room. "Calm yourself, Francesco," he said. His low voice was soothing. He looked from face to face, a small, self-assured smile on his lips. "There is a simple solution, a better plan than the one we were following." He walked slowly to Francesco's side and stopped. Taller, older, more in control of himself, he eclipsed Francesco and took away his dominant role. Salviati was suddenly in command. "This is what we will do," he said.

Francesco's sputtering subsided into a sulky pout. The other men ignored him.

They were a strange group, with motives that ranged from a fervent revengeful patriotism on the part of Antonio Maffei; a priest from Volterra, to a hope to share in the plunder of the Medici estates.

The plunderers were two fashionable wastrels named Baroncelli and Bracciolini.

Jacopo de' Pazzi wanted power; the second priest in the room, Stefano da Bagnone, was his private secretary and his creature. He would do anything his master wanted, including murder.

Salviati had no difficulty in gaining the agreement of them all to his plan. The only dissenter was Montesecco, the professional soldier.

"Killing," he said, "is my work. But I will not take a man's life before God's altar. It is a blasphemy."

Salviati's proposal was that the two Medici be murdered during mass. Giuliano might easily refuse to attend a dinner, but he could not omit attendance at mass on a Sunday unless he was far more ill than Bianca reported.

The Archbishop roared at Montesecco. Who was he, a layman, a common soldier, to set himself above an Archbishop and two priests and the wishes of the Pope himself in his interpretation of what was acceptable to God?

But Montesecco was adamant, and time was passing. Finally Salviati had to capitulate.

"Then this is it," he said. "Francesco, you and Baroncelli will dispatch Giuliano. The two priests will take care of Lorenzo. The signal will be the bell when the priest elevates the Host and all heads are bowed. I will leave just before then and lead the Perugians to the Palazzo della Signoria where we will kill the priors and seize the stronghold. I'll ring the great bell in the tower when I have taken it; the Florentines will rush to the piazza in response, and I will tell them that the tyranny of the Medici is over, that the Pazzi have taken control. The bell will also be your signal, Jacopo, to lead your men-at-arms through the streets arousing the populace to our support. It will all be over before the noon hour, and the armies will be at the walls before day is done to occupy the city and control any rebellion . . .

"Now, the sun is high. The little Cardinal must be on his way to the city to prepare for mass. Let's be about our business. Francesco, bring your craven brother here to me. I will say a prayer to bless our enterprise and ensure our success."

Chapter Twenty

"Do I look all right, Lorenzo?" The boy Cardinal's hands fluttered in front of him. He was afraid to touch his ceremonial robes. The rich gold brocade cape was embroidered with wide borders of red and green scrolls surrounding Maltese crosses made of pearls.

"You are splendid, Eminence," Lorenzo said. He settled the robe more comfortably on the boy's thin shoulders. "Perhaps the biretta is not quite straight. I'll adjust it for you." He pulled the square red silk hat down on the Cardinal's head.

"You're very kind," said the boy. "I couldn't do this by myself. And I'd hate to have to ride into town all dressed up in a litter. Thank you for letting me change my clothes at your house."

"You do my house honor, Your Eminence."

The boy blushed. "Couldn't you please call me 'Rafaello'?" he begged.

Lorenzo smiled and shook his head. "I'm sorry," he said gently, "but it would be wrong. The Pope can call you by your given name, perhaps other cardinals, but not a priest of lower rank and certainly not a layman. High office has its rewards, but it has its price, too. There are things a man has to give up when he becomes a prince of the Church, Your Eminence. Intimacy is one of them."

"Did you give up a great deal when you became prince of Florence?"

Lorenzo laughed, saw that his laughter was wounding, stopped. "Forgive me," he said quickly. "I wasn't laughing at you, only at the idea of anyone being called

157

a prince of Florence. We are a Republic, Eminence, and proud of it. We have no princes. Except today, when a prince of the Church visits us. Come along. The Duomo will be filling up with Florentines eager to see you.''

Rafaello followed Lorenzo obediently. On the short walk from the Medici palace to the Duomo, he made the sign of the cross in the direction of the people in the street who bowed low at the sight of him. Lorenzo had showed him how to do it while he was dressing. The young Cardinal discovered quickly that it was extremely pleasant to have everyone bowing to him. By the time he entered the cathedral he was walking with his shoulders held back and his red-stockinged step was firmly assured.

Lorenzo led him through the long nave to the octagonal raised platform in the center of the transept that held the altar. The officiating priest hurried to open the gate in the low balustraded marble rail that surrounded the altar's platform. He knelt quickly and kissed Rafaello's ring. ''An honor, Your Eminence,'' he murmured. The boy Cardinal bent his head in gracious acknowledgment.

Lorenzo hid his smile and edged away. As he had predicted, the Duomo was rapidly filling with people who wanted to see the Cardinal. Lorenzo moved through the crowds, greeting, responding to greetings, stopping from time to time to talk for a minute. All three of his sisters were there, all of them pregnant. Bianca was the most advanced. Her brow was glazed with perspiration, and she was leaning heavily on Elmo's arm. He does not look at all well, Lorenzo thought, even worse than the other times I've seen him lately. He tried to make his way to Elmo, planning to take his place as Bianca's support, but Sandro Botticelli waylaid him.

''Your young guest makes a pretty picture, Lorenzo,'' Sandro commented, ''and so, may I add, do you.'' The artist tilted his head to one side while he admired Lorenzo's sumptuous clothing. In honor of the Cardinal's visit Lorenzo had put aside his usual lucco and was wearing a deep green, watered silk doublet with sleeves slashed to show their crimson lining. His hose were parti-colored green and yellow, his surcoat crimson with gold-embroidered suns centered with sewn-on clusters of emeralds. Larger emeralds and rubies glowed on the gold hilt and scabbard of his sword.

Botticelli nodded his approval. "I enjoy color. You should wear it more often. But I didn't stop you to deliver compliments. I wanted to complain. Giuliano hasn't shown up for sittings, and I can't finish his portrait until he does. Where are you hiding him?"

Lorenzo pretended to be hurt. "Why do you accuse me? I don't control Giuliano's comings and goings."

"You do when you dangle pleasure in front of him. He abandoned me last week to go hunting with you."

Lorenzo chuckled. He moved closer to Sandro and spoke into his ear. "And was punished for it. His horse scraped him against a tree, and he has hardly been able to walk. He's giving out a story that he has a sore throat so that no one will know what a fool he was. Imagine Giuliano unable to master a horse."

Sandro laughed with delight. Everyone knew Giuliano's reputation as the finest horseman in Tuscany.

"What's so amusing?" Agnolo Poliziano pushed through the crowd to join them.

"I was just telling Sandro about Giuliano's sore throat," said Lorenzo. Poliziano laughed with them. He had been one of the group hunting.

"The mass has started," Agnolo said. "You'd better get closer to the ceremony, Lorenzo, or the little Cardinal will be offended . . . Will you come with us, Sandro?"

"No, I want to find Giuliano so I can ask him how his throat feels."

"You're a wicked creature, Sandro," Lorenzo said. "Luckless, too. Giuliano's not coming."

Botticelli shrugged. "I'll see him tomorrow then. In the meantime I can tell thirty or forty people the story. I don't have to waste my time on princes of the church."

Lorenzo and Agnolo left him. Within seconds Sandro was leaning close to a friend, whispering.

The people in the transept were moving in a more orderly way than the milling crowds in the body of the cathedral. It was customary to walk slowly and speak quietly near the altar and the choir, progressing always in a clockwise direction around the great octagon. Lorenzo and Poliziano joined a group of five young men whom Lorenzo was grooming for political office. Antonio Ridolfi was the eldest of them. He was twenty-nine, the same age as Lorenzo, and he took his place by Lorenzo's side as if he had rights of seniority. The others walked slightly in front, Agnolo among them.

Lorenzo caught the young Cardinal's eye and smiled. Rafaello started to smile in return, then remembered where he was and assumed a solemn air of attentiveness to the words and music of the mass. Lorenzo moved on, with a brief nod of approval. "Tell me, Antonio," he said to Ridolfi, "do you think you have trustworthy friends in Venice? There has been no reliable news from there in weeks, and I'm planning to invent a diplomatic mission and send someone to find out what the Doges are planning."

"I don't know Venice that well," Antonio said ruefully. "Nori has relatives there; he'd be a better emissary."

"I'll talk to him, then. Don't worry. There'll be a mission for you, too. Think about where you'd be most effective and let me know. All Italy is unsettled these days." Lorenzo turned to look again at the Cardinal before he stepped ahead to talk to Francesco Nori. For an instant he thought he saw Giuliano on the opposite side of the choir, but he decided he must be mistaken.

He wasn't. Francesco de' Pazzi and Bernardo Baroncelli had gone to the Medici palace and persuaded Giuliano to come to the Duomo with them. They were walking on each side of him, very close. At the rear of the cathedral a tall figure in purple-trimmed white silk slipped quickly through the door and ran down the steps. It was Archbishop Salviati.

Lorenzo noticed that the mass was nearing its climax. People slowed their steps, prepared to stop. I'll wait, he thought, and talk to Nori afterward. He looked to see if the young Cardinal was managing all right; the boy was a touching figure, so young and uncertain and lost in his voluminous rich vestments. The priest, Lorenzo saw, was holding the bread, the Host, ready to elevate it for worship as the body of Christ. Lorenzo bowed his head.

As he did, he glanced from the corner of his eye to see who was standing so uncomfortably close behind him. He saw a black garment, black sleeve. A priest, he thought, pushing near to get a better look at the Cardinal. From the altar he heard a thin tinkling sound, the bell rung when the Host was raised. He lifted his fingers to cross himself, felt a hand grasp his shoulder, opened his eyes, halted his prayer, saw a flashing glint.

His reflexes acted faster than his mind, jerking his body away from the stranger's grip, the flash of metal. Something cold, then hot, touched his neck, and his left hand ripped his cloak from his shoulders and whirled it around his arm while his right hand, the sign of the cross half made, reached for his sword. His body turned, and he was facing his attacker, his sword almost drawn, his cloak-padded arm raised in defense. Two priests, not one. Two daggers jabbing at him, one of them stained with blood.

How many more? Where? Lorenzo could not afford to look away from the nearest enemies. He slashed his sword at them, felt swirls of air at his sides, behind him, heard screams, felt a jolt and a push, saw Agnolo Poliziano spread his arms and leap in front of him, a human shield between him and the priests. "Run, Lorenzo," Agnolo panted.

"Quickly," cried Antonio Ridolfi, "to the Sacristy. There must be more of them."

Lorenzo grabbed Poliziano's arm. "With me, Agnolo," he cried, "not in my place. Come." He vaulted the choir rail and ran across the altar platform, Poliziano at his side, pushing the Cardinal out of his way—across the rail on the other side and toward the door to the Sacristy. The murdering priests followed, their pace hampered by their skirted cassocks, their faces pale, eyes burning. In front of the Sacristy door Francesco Nori was fighting with someone, sword blades clanging. Lorenzo had barely time to recognize Francesco de' Pazzi as Nori's adversary. Then he was inside the Sacristy, shoved by Poliziano, with Ridolfi shouting, "You're wounded," and three more of his protégés struggling to close the massive bronze doors against the onrushing priests and a group of hulking men-at-arms wearing the Pazzi colors and brandishing daggers and swords.

"Nori!" Lorenzo shouted. "Come inside." But as the doors swung slowly, so slowly, together, he saw the sword penetrate Nori's chest, heard his terrible, gurgling scream, then the clashing metal sound of the doors slamming shut.

The thick bronze panels muffled the noises in the cathedral but did not close them out. There were screams, pounding on the doors, running footsteps. Antonio Ridolfi grabbed Lorenzo's shoulders, shook him. "You've been cut," he cried, "the blade may have been poisoned. Don't move, Lorenzo." He fastened his mouth to Lorenzo's neck and sucked blood from the wound.

Lorenzo was barely aware of Ridolfi. He could think of only one thing. Had he seen Giuliano? Or had he imagined it? Was his brother there? Wounded?

"Giuliano," he said, "did anyone see Giuliano? Is he safe? Let me out. I must go find him." His cries were lost in the sound of the great bell in the tower of the Palazzo della Signoria. Its tolling vibrated and filled the air around them all.

When it stopped there was a ghostly stillness.

Then the doors rang from fists pounding on the other side. "Friends," Lorenzo heard dimly. "We're friends." But the voices were distorted by the barrier of the doors, unrecognizable.

The tiny group of six inside the Sacristy could not know if they were rescued or being drawn into a murderous trap.

"The organ loft," said Poliziano. "Where's the ladder?"

Antonio Ridolfi and a youth named Cavalcanti dragged a ladder from the rear of the Sacristy and leaned it against the doors. Lorenzo's gorge rose at the sight of them. Cavalcanti's doublet was stained with blood from a wound in his side; Ridolfi's lips were pale beneath the streaks of blood that might have poisoned him when he drew it from Lorenzo's wound into his mouth. The Pazzi must pay.

The youngest of the group, Sigismundo della Stufa, climbed the ladder into the organ loft. From there he could look down into the cathedral. He crept on hands and knees toward the carved marble balcony. The floor vibrated beneath him; the great bell was sounding again.

A mile to the south the only sound to be heard was an angry fretful twittering of birds disturbed by the proximity of a cat to their nest. Ginevra de' Pazzi shooed the cat away when she entered the garden. "There," she said, "you can stop your hysterics. You're very silly birds, you know. That's the kitchen cat. He's much too lazy and well-fed to bother you." She tied an apron around her waist and pulled on a pair of gloves before she went into the cutting garden where flowers for the villa's vases were grown.

She sang off-key while she cut tulips and laid them in a basket, began to fill a second with daisies and iris. The crunch of footsteps on gravel caused her to stop. She never inflicted her singing on the others.

Fra Marco was in the archway that led to the garden. Ginevra smiled at him. Then she turned her head quickly to the side and listened.

"What is it, Ginevra?"

"I thought I heard a bell. It was very faint; I must have been mistaken." She clipped some stalks of larkspur and added them to the brimming basket.

"The flowers are earlier than usual this year," said the old friar. "We'll have summer before we know it."

"It looks that way." Ginevra smiled again. Fra Marco said the same thing every year. "There'll be beautiful bouquets for May Day," she said, then she remembered that she said that, too, every year, and she laughed.

Fra Marco laughed with her, remembering as well. He took one of the baskets, Ginevra another, and they went to a table on the terrace where vases waited to be filled. They talked idly while Ginevra did the flowers for the house and Fra Marco created arrangements for the chapel. There was a restful, musical hum of small bees hovering above the completed vases and an occasional small splashing sound of fish in the pool around the trickling fountain.

A single gust of wind set the leaves of the trees to rustling, then it vanished. "There," said Ginevra, "did you hear that? I'm almost sure there was a bell in the breeze . . . No matter . . ."

Sigismundo reached the edge of the balcony and slowly raised his head. Below him the great spaces of the cathedral were almost deserted. Opposite he could see a priest leading the young Cardinal away; the boy's hands clutched the priest's stole, and his stiff robes glittered, stirred by the trembling body beneath them.

Immediately under the balcony was a group of a dozen young men. Sigismundo heard them clearly now, recognized the voices of friends. But he could not look at them or call to them. He was paralyzed by horror. The light-hearted green and pink and white mosaic floor of the cathedral was horribly marred. A pool of darkening blood marked the place where Francesco Nori had fallen.

And, in front of the altar, a body was sprawled in the grotesque awkwardness of brutal death. Stained, silks torn, once-shining hair matted to broken skull, hands empty and beseeching, Giuliano de' Medici savagely murdered.

Lorenzo must not see this, Sigismundo screamed soundlessly. Desperation gave him the strength to look away, to call down to the men below, to control his voice so that he could not be heard in the Sacristy. He told the others what to do, learned that Nori's body had been taken away by his father. Then he turned and shouted down into the Sacristy. "Open the doors to our friends. The Duomo is deserted."

Surrounded, rushed, tormented by worry and ignorance, Lorenzo ran through the ominously empty cathedral without seeing his brother's mutilated body. There was no one in the piazza, no one on the streets around it. The shutters and doors of all the houses were closed, barricades against the danger let loose in the city.

Four guards stood outside the Medici palace. They ran toward Lorenzo's group, swords drawn, then saw Lorenzo and ran faster, to protect him until he reached the house and the small door beside the barricaded great wooden entrance.

Once inside, Lorenzo continued to run. "I am not hurt," he called over his shoulder to the armed men gathered in the courtyard. "I will be back shortly with orders for you."

He found his mother waiting at the top of the stairs.

"Lorenzo! Your throat."

"A scratch, Mamina. Thank God you are safe. Clarice? The children?"

"All well. Let me dress your wound."

"No time for that. I must find out what is happening in the city." His bright green doublet was stained with rust blotches of dried blood; his neck was wrapped with the white silk sleeve torn from Poliziano's shirt, the white streaked with brown and with red from the still-flowing cut. "Mamina, where is Giuliano?"

Lucrezia could only stare at him.

"Mamina?"

Her lips trembled, and she held out her arms to him. "My poor darling. I thought you knew."

Lorenzo backed away from her comfort.

"No!" he roared. "No! It cannot be."

"Bianca saw him, Lorenzo. There's no mistake."

"Bianca? She is here? Wed to a Pazzi and here? She lies. A Pazzi lie. I'll shake the truth out of her."

"Lorenzo." Lucrezia's voice was the sound of authority and of reason, a mother speaking to her son. Lorenzo looked dumbly at her, momentarily a child again, overwhelmed by grief and confusion and rage. "Lorenzo," she said again, her heart in the soft syllables. "My son, you are alive. I thank God for that. We will grieve for my other son tomorrow. Now there is no time for sorrow. Florence needs you. This is what I have learned . . ."

Bianca had brought Elmo to her mother for protection. He sobbed and babbled and confessed every detail of the plot.

Lorenzo listened carefully to Lucrezia's report. His face was pale and hard as granite. "Keep him out of my sight or I will kill him," he said when Lucrezia finished. "I spare his miserable life only because you ask it; the other Pazzi will not be so fortunate."

He rushed back down to the courtyard then and issued orders without emotion. Within minutes men were on their way to every corner of the city to learn what was happening. A strong guard accompanied the priest who lived in the palace on his mission to administer the last rites to Giuliano and bring his body back to his home.

Lorenzo did not trust himself to see his brother. Not yet. He returned to the floor above, used the grand salone for headquarters, saw to the dressing of Cavalcanti's wound, wrote messages for delivery to Pierfrancesco's boys, to Lucrezia Donati, to the managers at the nearby Medici villas, to the Signoria. If it still existed.

He was still writing when the men began to return with their reports. He finished a sentence with extraordinary care, delaying the moment when he would learn if the Pazzi were in control of the city, if he was a prisoner in his own house. Then he looked up, and the expressions on the faces before him told him that the Pazzi had failed.

Salviati and his followers had been captured by the priors. The ringing bell had been an alarm to the city, a warning of the rebellion.

Jacopo, believing it was a signal of success, had ridden through the city with a hundred followers, shouting for people to follow him. They had responded with the cry, *"Palle! Palle!,"* the rallying cry of the Medici. When he reached the Palazzo della Signoria he was greeted with a fusillade of stones thrown down from the tower, and he had fled the city accompanied by Montesecco. Guards at the gate had seen them racing away.

Francesco and the other assassins had fled the Duomo after Lorenzo's escape, but there was no news of their whereabouts.

The city was boiling with news of Giuliano's murder, rumors of Lorenzo's death, rage and lust for revenge against the Pazzi.

Lorenzo went to each of his men, shaking his hand, thanking him for a job well done. "Deliver these messages," he said. "And find the Pazzi and their men. Bring them to the Signoria. I will go there after I talk to the city militia. There are armies marching against us, and there is much to be done." He tilted his head toward the sounds that were rising from the street outside.

"Many people followed us here," said a guardsman. "They refuse to believe that you weren't killed."

Lorenzo walked toward the window.

"You look so battered and bloody. Shouldn't you change your clothes before you show yourself? The mob might slaughter everyone who has ever been friendly with a Pazzi."

Lorenzo touched the bloodstained silk around his neck. "Let them see," he said. His eyes were red and terrifying. "This is nothing. My brother . . ." He threw open the window and stood exposed, his face awful with anger.

Agnolo Poliziano carried Lorenzo's message to the Signoria. He had to force his way through the mass of people in the streets leading to the piazza. When he got to the piazza itself, it was solidly packed with Florentines all shouting demands for justice.

They did not have long to wait. Agnolo, pushing, elbowing, begging to be allowed to pass, stopped all effort, fascinated against his will by the drama being played out before him. He knew by the cries of the crowd when Francesco de' Pazzi was dragged into the palazzo. He had been discovered in Jacopo's palace, hiding under a bed.

He heard himself shouting in primitive triumph when the Signoria guards marched out onto the raised platform in front of the doors. They bore the dripping severed heads of the Perugian soldiers on their lances.

Then his eyes followed the pointing hands of the mob

to the tower windows and he saw the Gonfaloniere and
the priors standing there. He cheered with the people
around him and, like them, he thundered out the chant
"Justice! Justice! Justice!"

With joy in his heart he watched the priors tie a rope
to the window's stone mullion, wrestle with Salviati's
accomplice Bracciolini, tie the other end of the rope
around his neck and throw him from the window. His
cries as he fell filled Agnolo with satisfaction; his jerking body as he strangled made Agnolo bare his teeth in
a snarl of triumphant revenge.

Archbishop Salviati was next. He was still wearing
his rich ecclesiastical robes, and the shining silk fluttered like a banner of celebration in the wind when he
struggled against the rope.

Francesco de' Pazzi followed immediately. He had
been stripped naked before he was hung. The crowd
exulted in his humiliation, shouted insults about his sagging belly and death-throes erection. They gasped with
joy at the grisly spectacle above them: Salviati, in a final
dying spasm, collided with Francesco and fixed his teeth
in his naked body. The two conspirators left life joined
together.

Salviati's servants did not hang. They were thrown
from the windows. Their screams seemed to hang suspended in air, higher than their plummeting bodies. They
struck the stone platform with a sickening sound, part
liquid, part solid, and the crowds were silent; then the
cheering rose again, with a deeper, frenetic roar. Men
and women ran to the broken bodies and stripped them
of their clothes. Fighting broke out over possession of
the booty, a strangely friendly kind of fighting. The
Florentines were united against a common enemy. They
had no anger for each other. In the end, hundreds of
people left the piazza with scraps of cloth or handfuls
of hair or broken teeth, ghastly souvenirs of the defeat
of their enemies.

They ignored the bent figure of Agnolo Poliziano. He
was on his knees, vomiting, ridding himself of the sickness that had made him exult in the hangings. He could
not disgorge the horror of the realization that there were

such hidden depths in the soul of every man, even a philosopher.

When he had nothing left in him except shame, he staggered to his feet and stumbled to the fountain near the palazzo where he plunged his head into the water again and again. Then, at last, he felt cleansed enough to deliver Lorenzo's message.

Chapter Twenty-one

The sound of hooves on gravel brought Fra Marco to the small porch in front of the chapel.

Ginevra heard them, too. She was in her grandfather's room, putting a vase of flowers on the table between the windows. She looked down at the handsome red and white uniforms, the tall riders on their fine horses. "We have visitors, Grandfather. There are three Medici men, outriders I guess. Lorenzo must be bringing the Cardinal to see the della Robbias." She wished she was dressed in something better than the old clothes she wore for gardening. She wiped her hands on her apron and reached behind her back to untie the strings.

Fra Marco smiled at the visitors. He looked back over his shoulder at the tiny chapel. Yes, it was fit for a Cardinal. The flowers were God's own gift to His children, and their scent was as rich as incense.

The riders dismounted and approached the tall door to the villa. They formed a tight group, ready to defend themselves against attack if the door concealed armed, desperate men. The first of them knocked with his sword hilt. "Open," he shouted.

In the window above, Ginevra frowned. What ill-mannered men, she thought. She'd tell Lorenzo. She looked toward the road, watching for him.

Fra Marco stepped out of the shadows under the chapel's porch, his hand raised in greeting. The three men turned quickly, startled by the sound of his steps behind them. His raised arm cast a long, menacing shadow on the pale gravel.

Ginevra saw the men rush at Marco and knock him

to the ground. She could not believe her own eyes. Her hands left the apron strings, found the windowsill and held on to it for support.

The front door opened; the old steward ran out, shouting. The men turned. Ginevra gasped at their bright unsheathed swords. "No," she whispered. A uniformed arm moved, the servant staggered, his arms thrown up, his mouth a soundless black hole, a gleaming silver blade through his chest.

"What are you doing, Ginevra?" Antonio's voice was querulous. "I must go down and greet our guests. Come, take me down."

"Yes, Grandfather, yes. We must go." We must go, she repeated to herself. There is no sense in it, no time to try to understand . . . danger, danger . . . run . . . oh God, what is happening?

She heard a scream.

The tower. I can lead Grandfather to the tower. I can bar the door, pile all the barrels of grain against it.

"Grandfather, listen to me. We must go very quickly and with no noise. Come, put your hand here, on my shoulder. Now, we'll walk as fast as we can. And quiet, quiet, we must be very quiet."

"What are you talking about, Ginevra? Who is that making that awful noise?"

"Shhh. Come on, come on. There are men . . . thieves . . . they've broken in. We're going to the tower. But we must hurry, and be quiet."

"Thieves? What do you mean?"

"Hush! Please, Grandfather, we must be silent."

She led him through the hall, onto the stairs. The door to the tower was on the landing, halfway down to the grand salone and the sounds of chaos below.

Ginevra put her hand over Antonio's and tapped gently, the signal for the old man to step down, one step at a time.

Slow, his steps were so slow, careful on the stone stairs. She had always begged him to be careful.

They reached the landing. Ginevra heard Mateo's voice, shouting, cursing.

I must move, I must. The door is just there. She turned

and led her grandfather into the exposed half of the landing above the stairs into the salone. Her shoulders hunched, braced against shouts of discovery from below. There were none.

Her hand touched the handle of the door. Thank you, Heavenly Father, she prayed.

Don't look, she told herself. But she could not obey. While her fingers turned the handle, her eyes turned leftward and down.

Oh, dear Mother of God! The cook was sprawled on the floor at the door to the dining room. But it wasn't the cook, it was a horrible mass of blood and hacked flesh with her head and staring eyes. At the foot of the stairs, Mateo was falling, slowly, slowly, crumpling, folding, his hands held out, sliced by the sword they had tried to stop, the sword that went up through his neck and made his falling so slow, held as it was by the strong arm in red and white, the white spattered redder than the red.

Ginevra wrenched her gaze away, fixed her eyes on the handle. The door would not open. It was locked.

Don't, she told herself, don't rattle it. It won't help. She saw the key clearly in her mind, lying carelessly on Antonio's desk . . . in his study, beyond the salone.

It couldn't be locked. It was never locked. She pulled, pulled, refusing to accept the truth. But she had to. She had to think of something else.

There was a small roof garden on top of the kitchen. A door from Fra Marco's room led to it. If she took her grandfather there, if they were very quiet, if they lay on the tiles, lower than the parapet, invisible from below . . . It was the only chance. She touched Antonio's hand, signaling for his attention, and moved quietly, slowly, slowly, turning back toward the stairs they had just descended.

"There he is!" A shout from the salone. Ginevra looked down, began to run at the sight of the man pointing at them.

Antonio's hand fell from her shoulder when she fled. Ginevra sobbed, turned back, caught his arm. "Run, Grandfather, run with me." She put her arm around his waist, half-pulled, half-pushed him up the stairs, supporting his weight when he stumbled.

Behind them boots pounded up the lower flight.

Ginevra stopped inside the hall, slammed the door, turned the tasseled key in the lock. "Ginevra," said Antonio, "I need to know."

She put his hand on her shoulder. "Hurry," she whispered. She could hear their pursuers beyond the door, pounding on it, shouting. She walked quickly, Antonio at her heels.

"I need to know, Ginevra."

"They want to kill us, Grandfather. I don't know why. They're killing everybody—Mateo and the servants." She could not tell him about Fra Marco. "I'm taking you to the roof. Maybe they won't look there."

Antonio stopped her. Ginevra grabbed his wrist and pulled. "No," he said. "You go. I'll stay here and stop them while you hide." He put his hand on the hilt of his decorative sword.

"No." Ginevra held her grandfather's hand firmly and led him along the hall. Antonio's resistance was futile against her determination.

The barrier behind them splintered as they entered Fra Marco's room. "We are lost, Grandfather," Ginevra said, "but we must try." She hurried him across the corner of the room, onto the roof terrace, into the shadows behind the open shutters and doors.

The three men raced onto the terrace only seconds later.

"Hold her," one said. He seized Ginevra by the upper arm and flung her toward the others. One of them caught her to him, her arms imprisoned by his arm across her.

"Let me go," she cried.

"Release her," ordered Antonio. He drew his sword. One man's sword licked out and touched Antonio's.

"Don't!" Ginevra cried. "Look at his eyes. Can't you see he's blind and old? He can't hurt you." She struggled against the iron-hard grip that held her.

"Blind? A fine fighting cock and cannot see?" The two men near Antonio laughed. "A Pazzi to play with, then." Taunting and mocking, they pranced in front of the old man, parrying the thrusts he aimed at their voices, flicking their sword tips across his chin and cheeks, leaving dotted red lines of blood that mingled with and colored the tears rolling from his milky eyes.

Ginevra saw his torture in fragmented moments while she fought her captor. She twisted, trying to free her arms, and she kicked savagely, but her soft slippers made no impact on his legs. She succeeded at last in sinking her teeth into the shoulder behind her head, and he threw her from him against the rasping stucco wall of the villa. Ginevra raced toward Antonio's tormentors.

The men near him looked around, careless of the blind man's seeking sword. It struck one man's chest and glanced off his chain mail. He spun and cursed and drove his blade into Antonio's heart at the moment that his companion took the full weight of Ginevra's attack, staggered and fell against the low parapet.

Before she could fling herself on him, Antonio's killer struck her on the side of the head with his fist. The other two clubbed her to her knees.

Pain and dizziness and blurred views of the red squares of the tiled floor and her grandfather's hand, open and reaching and strangely limp. Rough hands and harsh voices and her arms pulled, wrenched, tearing at their sockets. Ginevra tried to shake her head, to clear away the blackness that streaked across her vision. But when she moved it, nausea gripped her throat, and the blackness grew worse.

Her hair was twisted and her head pulled back. "Look at your master now, wench," she heard. She saw her grandfather, then, his arms and legs splayed, knees bent, without life, without dignity. She felt pain greater than the pain in her head or her arms, an agony of pain for his degraded death and for her failure to prevent it.

"A gift from Lorenzo, old man," she heard, and saw the boot hit Antonio's face. Rage washed pain from her. She lunged for the booted leg, her hands curled into talons, and tore free.

Before she could grasp the leg, she felt a crushing

weight on her shoulders and back, and her chin hit the hard floor.

Laughter roared in her ears and words. "The old man gave us a game, how about this doxy? She has spirit and needs taming."

". . . should welcome a man's cock after that ancient withered stem."

"You took the bite, Guido, you get the first blow."

"The bitch might bite me again. I'll hold her for you."

"Both of you hold her for me. My sword needs sheathing."

Ginevra breathed gratefully when the weight lifted. Then her arms were wrenched again, and the back of her head struck the tiles, and she felt nails scratch her throat, heard a tearing sound, felt sudden warmth and chill at once as her bare breasts met the sun-filled air.

Sharp teeth closed on the tender exposed flesh. Ginevra heard a scream, felt rawness in her throat. I must have made that sound, she thought; she swore silently that she would scream no more, nor cry. She saw a face approach hers and found moisture in her dry mouth to spit. A hand hit her mouth, then her jaw. More hands, striking, slapping, grasping, holding, pulling arms and legs apart. Faces, voices, the gleam of metallic links, the red and white squares of silk.

"From the Medici," she heard, and a new pain pierced her body, arched her back. "Medici, Medici, Medici, Medici." The name with each new ripping pain, and foul breath expelled on her face.

Forgive me, Grandfather, she cried inwardly, I cannot keep my oath, and she screamed. She kept screaming until she was unconscious.

The three men at the villa were half of a band of six commanded by a lieutenant. He had led the other three on a search of the farmhouses, looking for Jacopo de' Pazzi's hiding place. They found nothing, and the lieutenant was in a bad temper when he rode up to the villa to claim his prisoner and collect his men. The carnage that he saw made him furious. He stormed through the house and finally arrived at the roof garden.

"You fools," he growled, "I told you to arrest him, not kill him."

"He drew his sword. What could we do?"

The officer shrugged. He was outraged by the flouted order, not by Antonio's death. The Pazzi had killed; they deserved killing.

He walked over to Ginevra's battered, inert body. Her bare spread legs were stained with blood. "Couldn't you find more than one woman? You made a mess of this one." He nudged her head with the toe of his boot, and the bruised face rolled up into view.

His jaw dropped. "Mother of God, do you fools know what you've done? This is no serving girl. I know her. I brought her a horse as a gift from Lorenzo. She is betrothed to his nephew. You'll be hung for raping her."

"But she's Pazzi."

"Betrothed, I tell you. Property of the Medici. Jesus help you."

The oldest of the rapists knelt by Ginevra and gathered her into his arms. "She can't tell anyone if she's dead." He carried her to the edge of the terrace. "She could have been running away. She could have fallen. They should have built this parapet higher." He threw her over the low wall. She looked like a bundle of rags falling through the air.

The lieutenant grimaced. "I'll report the accident," he said. "They probably would have broken the betrothal anyhow."

Chapter Twenty-two

It was late afternoon when Lorenzo returned from his meetings with the militia and the Signoria. He was exhausted, as he had never been before. The turmoil of the day, the pain and loss of blood from his wound, the demands for decisions about the city's defense, the uncertainties and fears—all had taken their toll. But primarily he was drained by the effort of will required to keep all thoughts of his brother from his mind until his work was done.

The table in the grand salone was covered with stacks of paper. Reports from hundreds of sources about happenings in the city. Lorenzo looked at them, and he swayed on his feet, collapsed into a chair. "Lorenzo, you must rest," said his secretary. He was shocked by Lorenzo's haggard face and slumped shoulders.

"When I finish," Lorenzo replied. He lifted the first report off the pile nearest him.

A half hour later he came to the lieutenant's account of the "accident" at the Villa La Vacchia. The bottled-up grief in his heart erupted. He could not afford to think about Giuliano; there were too many memories; there was too much love. But he could feel the lesser pain of Ginevra de' Pazzi's death. He saw in his mind a kaleidoscope of memory, rapidly shifting scenes of the comic waif in her steeple hat, the giggling, happy child at her music lesson, the wild, free spirit clinging bareback to her horse and raising her arms to embrace the world and the future that now she would never know. He felt, as he had before, that Ginevra, born under the same stars as he, was a part of him, that she shared a

177

corner of his soul. And she was dead; her innocence and joy in life were gone, destroyed in an instant. So, too, were his. He felt that all happiness, all trust, all gentleness was gone from his heart forever. His soul was dead. His hands were fists, the report crumpled in one.

He threw his head back and shouted, an incomprehensible animal cry of loss and agony and despair. It was a protest and a prayer.

There was no answer.

Finally he looked at his frightened secretary. Lorenzo's eyes were red-rimmed, ringed by the shadows of suffering. But they were dry. The release of tears was not granted him. When he spoke, his voice was calm. Lifeless.

"Give this paper to Agnolo Poliziano," he said. "Tell him I asked that he take a priest and some women to prepare the bodies for burial."

Chapter Twenty-three

Lucrezia de' Medici interrupted Lorenzo's work, something that she had never done before.

But, then, this endless day was unlike any day that had ever been.

"Lorenzo," she said breathlessly, "Agnolo has just come in. He has brought Ginevra. Lorenzo, she lives! She is terribly hurt, but she is breathing. She isn't dead."

Lorenzo stood, knocking over his chair, all fatigue forgotten. His contadina was alive. His star-sharer, the shadow image of himself. More than ever she seemed to him an omen embodied, her life entwined mysteriously with his. She had been wounded on the same day he was wounded. When he believed her dead, he feared the omen of his own death. But she was not dead. Hope and energy raced through him. God had not let Ginevra die. He had not turned His face from Florence, from the Medici, from Lorenzo.

"Send for doctors," he commanded his secretary.

"No!" Lucrezia cried. "I won't allow any doctors to torture her further. Send for nursing sisters from the Hospital of the Innocents. I will cure Ginevra with their help."

Lorenzo struck the table with his fist. "You will look to your own health, madam, not to this girl's. We may be attacked any day, any minute. There will be war, and I want my family out of it. Clarice and the children will go to a safe place, and you will go with them."

"I will not."

Mother and son faced each other across the wide room. Lorenzo's secretary held his breath.

Then Lucrezia walked slowly across the space that separated them. She laid her hand gently on Lorenzo's rigid arm. "My son," she whispered, "my only son. Don't send me away. My heart would break to lose both sons in one day."

Lorenzo cried out. His mother's words pierced the wall he had built to protect himself from thoughts of Giuliano.

He caught his mother to him; Lucrezia held him close; they wept together, sharing loss and grief.

Lorenzo's secretary left silently; he went himself to escort the nursing sisters to the palace.

Ginevra was broken. A priest administered the last rites because it seemed impossible for her to live. The sisters whispered together while they bathed her, praying and exclaiming in horror at the extent of her injuries. Both arms were broken and one leg fractured in three places. Collarbones, ribs, pelvis and jaw. They set the bones and bound them, grateful for the deep coma that kept Ginevra from stirring even while it held her on the brink of death.

Lucrezia helped the nurses apply salve to Ginevra's lacerated skin, and it was she who packed the girl's torn and bleeding vagina, weeping at the damage and the certain cause of it. She would not tell Lorenzo that Ginevra had been raped. It would not make the bleeding stop if he punished the men who had done it. She joined the nuns in their prayers and mixed a potion of herbs and bathed the wounds exposed when Ginevra's hair was clipped close to her scalp.

Then she helped the sisters wrap a turban of bandages and lay an eiderdown over the girl's pitiful mummylike body.

"Take these and burn them," she told a servant, pushing the bloodstained remains of Ginevra's clothing with her foot. "Then tell my son that he can come in if he still wishes."

Lorenzo gasped when he saw the swollen bruised face that was the only visible part of Ginevra. "I would not have known her," he said. Then he put his hand over his mouth. He leaned close to Lucrezia and murmured into her ear. "Will she live?"

"With God's mercy," said Lucrezia, speaking aloud. "You need not lower your voice; she can hear nothing. And feel no pain. The coma may save her."

Lorenzo knelt by the bed. "Contadina," he said. Despite Lucrezia's words, he whispered. What he had to say was for Ginevra only. "Contadina, be brave. You must live. You have been my good omen many times. Do not give up when I need all my strength." He peered at the inert form on the bed, searching for some response, a movement, a flicker of an eyelid. Ginevra lay as if dead. Even her slow, shallow breathing made no sound, did not disturb the quilt that covered her. She was profoundly sunk in darkness.

In the weeks that followed she floated in unconsciousness as if it were a warm, comforting sea. From time to time she neared the surface, heard sounds, felt the silver tube the nurses put between her cut lips to feed her. Always she slipped away from the pain that accompanied consciousness, grateful for the oblivion of the deep blackness that erased the pain in her body and in her mind.

Against her will the periods of awareness grew longer and more frequent. Her bound legs and arms did not move, her bruised eyes were too swollen to open, but her mind registered the throbbing, tearing agony that racked her body, remembered the nightmare of the attack on her, relived the powerless desperation, saw the vicious assaults on the people she loved most, witnessed her grandfather's degraded death.

She heard the nurses talking, and their words added new horrors. Jacopo de' Pazzi, they said with relish, had been found near the border of Tuscany. Brought to Florence in chains, tortured, hung from a window in the Palazzo della Signoria. "With his last breath," said Sister Serafina, "he consigned his soul to the devil."

"A fit companion for all the Pazzi," her companion said emphatically.

"Renato de' Pazzi made a proper end," Sister Serafina offered. "He confessed his sins and kissed the cross
before he was hung."

"They should all be hung. Sending all the men to the
dungeons at Volterra is too easy a punishment."

"Sister Constantia! That's not Christian."

"The Pazzi are the devil's spawn. Bad blood, all of
them."

Ginevra swam into darkness, but it was no longer the
nothingness of peace. Everywhere, agonized pendulous
figures jerked in death throes.

There were other nurses sometimes, less damning than
Sister Constantia. But the voices of them all conveyed
the same satisfaction at the destruction of the Pazzi.
More than two hundred servants and supporters were
dead, their heads carried through the streets on pike-
staffs . . . the name Pazzi was declared a badge of shame
. . . the Signoria decreed that any Florentine who married a woman of the family would lose his rights as a
citizen . . . the Scoppio was abolished . . . the proud
dolphins were destroyed wherever they appeared, and
all Pazzi properties were confiscated, becoming the
property of Lorenzo de' Medici.

Ginevra abandoned her attempts to lose herself in unconsciousness. She was, she was sure, in too much danger to allow herself the luxury. Lorenzo had killed all
her family so that he could seize their wealth, she believed. But she had no riches.

Why had he kept her alive, a prisoner in his palace?
Did he enjoy the knowledge of her suffering? She forced
herself to stay conscious for longer periods. She accepted the pain of awareness because it was the price
for the ability to listen and to think. And she devised a
way to survive. She feigned coma as protection against
Medici justice, submitting to the ministrations of the
nurses without crying out at the agony they caused,
keeping her eyes closed even when the swelling subsided. She willed her body to remain limp and heavy
even when her knitting bones sent firelike itching
through all her nerves.

Her senses grew more and more acute, her mind more

clear. In time she learned that she was in the Medici palace, but not, as she first thought, a prisoner. Lucrezia de' Medici wanted her to recover. She visited the sickroom a dozen times a day, and there was real concern in her voice, real comfort in her gentle cool hands. Ginevra longed to respond, to give herself over to Lucrezia's healing touch and spirit.

But she could not. Her memories were stronger than her need for comfort; she visualized the boot kicking her grandfather's face, a "gift from Lorenzo"; felt again the rough hands on her flesh and the stabbing tearing between her legs, heard the chant "Medici, Medici, Medici" while the soldiers used her; and her heart hardened.

Hour after hour, while she lay as if lifeless, her mind worked, progressing from fear to frenzy to cold determination. She felt her body's fevers abate, the end of hemorrhaging, the diminution of pain. And she knew that she had been healed by hatred, not by kindness. The hate was hers, a searing curettage that gave strength to her will to live.

There is nothing left for me, she thought. I lost everything and everyone, including Ginevra, on the day the Medici men rode up through the olive grove to La Vacchia. But I cannot die yet, I cannot die until I have avenged us all—grandfather, Fra Marco, Mateo, the servants at La Vacchia, the honor of my family, my own injuries and shame.

Ginevra moved her fingers, curved them, cursed their weakness. I will make you strong again, she vowed silently, as strong as my hate, and I will kill him. I have nothing to live for save that. When it is done, I can die and be free of remembering.

I will make him pay.

I will kill Lorenzo.

BOOK TWO

Ginevra
1478–1483

Chapter Twenty-four

Ginevra had become an adept at deception. After the superhuman efforts necessary to pretend unconsciousness for weeks, the new role she had to play was laughably easy. In fact she did, sometimes, laugh quietly to herself. When her nurses asked why, she always replied, ''I'm just happy that I'm getting well.'' Her role was prolonged recuperation.

Her real activity was secret regaining of strength. Even before she opened her eyes and croaked a request for water she was stretching and flexing her wasted muscles in the night hours when her nurses dozed off. After the wrappings and splints were removed she concentrated on one area at a time, hiding the movement of knee or ankle or abdomen under the mound of lightweight bedcovers. Her efforts were constant and so fierce that they produced another period of high fever. It weakened her even more.

But she was never so weak that she forgot or gave up her goal. And the purpose gave her the ability to conquer each of the many setbacks in her recovery. While always pretending to be feeble and pathetic and grateful even when her heart burned with rage for revenge and her emaciated body grew wiry and precisely controlled.

So controlled that she was able to make it limp and lifeless when Lorenzo lifted her in his arms and carried her down to the ground floor bedroom that had been his when he was young.

''I think you'll be happier here, Contadina. You can look at the big painting of horses that faces the bed and think about getting well enough to ride again very soon.''

Ginevra produced a few weak tears and a faint "thank you." Then she closed her eyes in a mock faint while Lorenzo put her gently on his old bed.

Behind the lowered lids she was seeing his chest, vulnerable next to her cheek when he carried her, and his arms, burdened by her body and unable to defend himself. If only she had had a dagger. And the strength to drive it home.

She doubled her surreptitious exercises.

She soon discovered that the new room had many advantages. It was late summer, and the door that was left open for ventilation allowed her to hear the conversations of the men-at-arms in the courtyard and the comings and goings through the entrance to the palace.

She learned that Lorenzo was always surrounded by guards when he went out into the city, and she laughed because she was inside his house where he was vulnerable.

She heard about the war that was raging, with the armies of Rome and Naples capturing one and then another of Florence's subject-cities. The guards were worried. Florence had only a ragtag army made up of small contingents sent by Milan, Bologna and Clarice de' Medici's relatives, the Orsini. The King of France, a longtime Medici ally, had sent an envoy with a letter of support and a pledge of five hundred lances, but the soldiers had not materialized, while the envoy, Philippe de Commines and his retinue, stayed on as Lorenzo's guests in the palace, creating extra escort duty for the guards and constant grumbling.

Ginevra, knowing nothing about war, was delighted by the guards' anxious chatter. She'd be happy to see Florence taken by the enemy if it meant the destruction of the Medici.

Provided that her hand and hers alone delivered the death blow to Lorenzo.

Although she was educated in the writings of the Greek philosophers and the Roman poets and statesmen, Ginevra knew nothing about the ways of the heart. If anyone had told her that her consuming hatred for Lorenzo was intensified because she had held him as hero since childhood, she would have dismissed the speaker as a madman. She wanted revenge for mortal injuries to her and those she loved. She never suspected that she also thirsted to avenge a dream betrayed.

The nurses were not needed so much now that Ginevra was visibly out of danger. Only one stayed by her side, and at night she slept in the room adjoining the sickroom. Ginevra was able to increase her activity, exercise more vigorously, even take her first tottering steps around the bed, leaning on the high mattress for support.

The night-hours' efforts exhausted her, and she slept during most of the day. The sleep replenished her energies and maintained the fiction of her invalid condition.

Lucrezia was alarmed. "I hoped she would have a rapid recovery once the crisis was past," she told the nursing sister. "It has been almost six months since she was hurt, and she's still so weak. Too weak to resist disease and yet too fragile to be moved to safety."

The plague had broken out in Florence. Everyone who could leave was fleeing the city in panic. The first victim had been found on the steps of the church of Santa Croce on the first day of October. Now, a week later, the death toll was up to nine a day.

Lucrezia had every floor and every wall in the palace scrubbed with lye and vinegar, all windows were sealed with wax, and pierced metal balls filled with herbs burned day and night in every one of the seventy-six rooms, whether occupied or not.

There were three censers in Ginevra's room. Lucrezia also made thick soups of minced cabbage and scraped beef and shook the girl awake every two hours of the day to feed her.

"You must force yourself to eat," Lucrezia begged. "It's the only way to build up your strength."

Ginevra cooperated eagerly. She had been desperately hungry for weeks, her hard-worked body demanding more sustenance than the thin broth and warm milk that was an invalid's diet.

Lucrezia watched Ginevra eat, and tears filled her

eyes. "My poor child," she said, "that must be what you've needed all along, and I didn't know. I beg your forgiveness."

Ginevra said nothing. She was too occupied with feeding herself to speak. And she would not say "I forgive you" to a Medici, not even this woman who was so much like the mother the orphaned Ginevra had invented for herself when she was a child.

The nourishing soup satisfied her for only a short while. It made it possible for her to exercise with less fatigue, and her limbs strengthened so that she could walk, then bend, then jump from the floor to the high bed. She could almost lift the wooden steps at the side of the bed; she knew that soon she would be able to raise them an inch, then two inches, three and eventually as high as her head if she wished.

But she needed more food, something substantial. She longed for a hard crust of bread or a thick spiced sausage, something to chew, something that would not slide down her throat before she could relish the taste. She couldn't tell Lucrezia what she wanted because she did not dare reveal how far her recovery had actually gone. If anyone knew that she was almost well, she would be sent away from the city and the plague.

And it was vital that she stay in the Medici palace because only here could she catch Lorenzo off guard and unguarded.

I must be dreaming, Ginevra thought. She pinched her arm, winced, sniffed. The smell of cheese was richly sharp. Her mouth watered.

She walked softly and surely in the near-darkness of her room. Her eyes had long ago become accustomed to the faint illumination from the smouldering herbs overhead. She turned the handle of the door slowly, ready to run to her bed if it made a noise, wondering if the nurse had locked it when she closed it at night. She felt the latch open, pulled cautiously.

Light poured through the narrow crack; Ginevra drew back, sure she'd been discovered. Then she recognized the sounds beyond the door. Someone was snoring, just as Fra Marco used to do when he nodded off in his chair after the evening meal.

The vivid memory caught her unawares, and her throat filled with stinging tears. She swallowed, regained control and concentration, opened the door wider.

Five men in Medici uniform were sleeping in the courtyard, their bodies stretched across the floor in front of the doors to the street, the garden, the loggia, and the arched entrances to the staircases that led to the floors above and below. They slept with their hands holding a sword and a spear.

Ginevra grabbed the door for support, her strong legs suddenly weak. She had eavesdropped on the guards for weeks without thinking of them as anything other than disembodied voices. But the sight of these men made her tremble with fear. The torches that lit the courtyard made the red and white silk tunics glow brightly; chain mail on their arms glittered; their weapons seemed to move in the flickering light.

It all came back to her in a horrifying rush. That white silk spattered red with blood, the metal links of the armor pressing into her naked skin, the swords clashing and cutting and killing. Fra Marco clubbed, Mateo's life bubbling out of the hole in his chest, her grandfather . . .

She sank into a crouch, covered her head with her arms, bit her own shoulder to stop the noise of her chattering teeth and whimpering cries.

It seemed to her that she stayed there for an eternity, reliving her horror, expecting it to begin again, paralyzed and helpless with fear.

The snoring stopped; fear became terror, and Ginevra scrabbled deeper into her room on her belly.

At dawn the nurse found her under the bed, writhing in convulsions, her eyes rolled back in her head, her lips bitten and raw. The nun screamed for help. A guard answered, looked, ran for Lucrezia. "We must get her into bed and warm," Lucrezia said. "Then we must pray."

She sent word to the rest of the household, asking for their prayers as well.

Lorenzo hurried to Ginevra's room when he got his mother's message. He knelt with her for a minute by Ginevra's bed, then he went upstairs and paced the long hallway that led to his study, unable to rest. He had received a message only the day before, telling him that his godson Bernardo was dead of the plague. The boy should have been safe, isolated as he was in the country at the villa to which Elmo and Bianca had been exiled. But he was dead, the child born on Lorenzo's birthday, Ginevra's birthday, the day she had arrived in Florence, the day Lorenzo came of age.

And now Ginevra was afflicted with an illness equally as mysterious and capricious as the Black Death. Just when she was improving so markedly.

Lorenzo felt crushed by his powerlessness before fate, by his inability to understand the meaning of these portents. If there was any meaning. If the collapse of Ginevra and the death of Bernardo were portents.

He didn't know. He felt that there was nothing that he could be certain of.

Uncertainty and helplessness were strangers to him; they were not part of his nature, nor of his past life. They were intolerable to him and so he walked back and forth along the hall for hours, trying to shake them off, crush them under his heels, regain the decisiveness that was expected of him. By the Signoria. By the people of Florence. By himself.

Couriers found him, messengers, representatives of the Council of War. They all had questions, and he answered them. They all needed orders, and he gave them. They all looked to him for leadership and drew on him for confidence, and he satisfied them.

Then he strode into his study and sat at his desk, ready to attack the mass of correspondence that required his attention. There were so many things, so many people that depended on him, and he could not waste precious time worrying about unanswerable questions.

The contadina would be all right. He knew it. She was a part of him in a way that Bernardo had never been, and she would no more give up the struggle to win than he would. He spread out a map of Tuscany and marked the latest reported positions of the armies of his enemies.

Three hours later Ginevra sighed. Her shuddering ceased and she relaxed totally. Lucrezia kissed her closed eyelids. "She sleeps. Thank God."

When Ginevra woke she was rested and calm. Her sleep had been undisturbed by nightmares for the first time, and she knew that she had undergone a major change in her life. She lay quietly, musing, until she reached understanding.

The thing that terrified me beyond reason, she thought, was the past, what has already happened. It is over. Done. So it need not be feared. And there is nothing that anyone can do to me in the future that will hurt as much. I've already known Hell; what have I to fear now? Nothing. I am afraid of nothing, not even death. Death is only a deeper unconsciousness, and I know that it is restful. There is pain only when it is necessary to come back to life.

She stretched slowly, appreciating the smooth obedient response of the muscles that she had worked to build, luxuriating in her newborn feeling of invincibility.

That night she prowled the silent courtyard, found the small room where food and drink were set out for the guards, ate her fill of cheese and olives and bread.

Three nights later she discovered the armaments room. She selected a small-hilted, perfectly balanced dagger and a sharpening stone and took them to her room. She hid them on top of the deep baldachin above the bed that held the heavily brocaded silk draperies designed to keep out drafts. It was easy to climb the carved bedposts; they were as thick as a tree. She could sharpen the knife every night while she waited for the opportunity to use it.

"I'm ready," she whispered aloud to the fantasy pastel horses that decorated the walls. And she laughed.

Chapter Twenty-five

Lucrezia noticed the change in Ginevra immediately. "Our patient is happy, Sister. See, there's a smile on her face as she sleeps."

When she woke Ginevra to give her the soup, she suggested that Ginevra might enjoy getting out of bed, out of her room. "I've had a chair brought down for you. It was my husband's. He couldn't walk, you see, so it's made to be carried. If you like, I'll assign two stewards to you, and you'll be able to get around the house, even go into the garden on nice days."

"Oh, thank you, Madonna Lucrezia. I'd love that." Ginevra was genuinely grateful. She needed to learn the house, know where to find Lorenzo alone and unsuspecting. This way no one would know that she was able to walk. It would give her an advantage.

To her dismay she had barely begun to see the upper floor when Lorenzo went away.

"He misses his children terribly," Lucrezia explained, "and he's going to our villa at Cafaggiolo to spend some time with them. Clarice took them there for safety from the war when it began last June. It's a remote spot, and the villa has good thick walls and a moat with a drawbridge."

"Is the war over?"

"No." Lucrezia's face was suddenly shadowed and gray. Then she smiled. "But it's stopped for several months. Armies have very definite rules about what they will and won't do. In the winter they retire to a city where men and horses can be sheltered and comfortable. They'll start to fight again next spring.

"In the meantime we'll have the house practically to ourselves. When Lorenzo is away, there are few visitors. I intend to enjoy the peace and quiet, especially with such good company. Lorenzo told me that you are quite a scholar, Ginevra; perhaps we could do some reading and discussion. Our library is rather fine. And there are many things I'd like to learn, if you'll help me."

Ginevra was astonished. She had never thought that an older person would look to her for education. She looked at Lucrezia with suspicion, but she could find no trace of condescension or trickery in Lucrezia's still-beautiful face.

"I'll be happy to do anything I can," she said.

And the winter was happy. It was a gift of time, free from hate, from plotting, from the pursuit of death. First Lorenzo's. Then, inevitably, her own. Ginevra accepted the gift without anger. She could wait for her revenge. It would not lose its sweetness. She put all thoughts of Lorenzo out of her mind and gave herself over to Lucrezia's guidance. "We'll go first to the library," Lucrezia said. Ginevra hadn't realized how much she missed the tranquil hours of reading until she entered the room and felt her heart pounding with excitement. She had never seen so many books at one time. A household was considered rich if it contained five books. There were at least five hundred in the Medici palace.

The riches did not stop there. The palace was a treasure-house of art. Lucrezia introduced her to the paintings and sculpture and tapestries and Oriental rugs one at a time so that she had time to study and savor each one. Lucrezia also told her wonderful stories about the artists who had made many of the beautiful things.

"Donatello was perhaps the closest friend of my husband's father. He was a sweet, loving man as well as a great sculptor. The fountain in the garden—Judith triumphant over Holofernes—he made that. My father-in-law commissioned it at a very high figure because he worried about Donatello's way of life. He never seemed to have a warm cloak or a decent meal. Cosimo paid him in advance in gold, and he gave Donato the name of a manager at the bank. 'Go see this man, give him your money and tell him to invest it for you,' he said. 'Then you'll have enough income to be comfortable.' ''

Ginevra's mouth twisted. "No wonder he was such a close friend after such generosity," she said.

Lucrezia laughed. "Money meant nothing to Donatello. He took Cosimo's gold and did with it what he always did with anything he earned. He put it in a basket that hung from the ceiling of his workshop. His cook, his apprentices, his friends all helped themselves from it when they needed anything. They could hardly believe it when they took out a coin and found that it was a florin instead of a scudo."

Ginevra joined in Lucrezia's laughter. "What did Cosimo do then?"

"He commissioned the statue of David that you like so much, the one near the door to your room."

"With payment in advance?"

"Of course. He never quit trying."

"And did it go into the basket?"

"Of course."

Ginevra loved the stories, and the art. She substituted a hesitant gait for the pretense of immobility, so that she could move around on her own and look at her particular favorites whenever she liked.

One of them was the brightly colored Procession of the Magi that covered three walls of the small family chapel. It was full of surprises, and every time Ginevra looked at it she saw something that she had not noticed before, an exotic flower or animal or a detail of the kings' elaborate costumes or a tiny insect perched on a feather of an angel's wing.

Lucrezia was told that Ginevra often sat alone in the chapel for as much as an hour. The news relieved her, because she was concerned about the girl's spiritual health. Often Ginevra did not come to the daily mass celebrated in the chapel, and when she did come, her face often wore a harsh expression.

But if she went to the chapel when no one else was there, she must be making her devotions in some private fashion, Lucrezia thought. She could understand that.

Father Paolo was a fussy, nervous man and he made everyone around him nervous as well. When he said mass, he raced through it, garbling the sacred words, clattering the vessels of the sacrament.

Lucrezia wished that she could invite another priest to serve as the house cleric, but it was impossible. It would be too cruel a blow for Father Paolo. He had lived in the palace for almost twenty years. And, to be fair, it must be admitted that his nervousness came from a sincere spiritual dilemma. It had begun immediately after the Pazzi rebellion when the Pope excommunicated Lorenzo and demanded that the city give him up to Rome's jurisdiction or suffer interdiction.

The Signoria refused to deliver Lorenzo to certain death, and the interdiction, an excommunication to the entire Republic, was pronounced. Churches were to be closed, no sacraments given, no Christian marriages or burials performed. The bishops of Tuscany refused to recognize it. Instead they wrote a condemnation of the Pope and circulated it throughout all Europe.

Father Paolo, dutiful son of the Church, feared that he was risking his soul every time he performed mass. He was trained to follow the laws of the Pope, not the schismatic defiance of the bishops. But he was not able to regard a man like Sixtus who conspired to murder in God's cathedral as a legitimate Pope. His conflicting emotions were the source of his nervousness.

Lucrezia understood and was patient with him. She was also patient with Ginevra and did not expect her to understand. How much the girl knew about the Pazzi conspiracy was a question Lucrezia did not dare to ask. She chose to believe that Ginevra was innocent of any complicity because she was very fond of her, and growing fonder every day.

Her affection was obvious when she took Ginevra's hands in hers on the day after Christmas and led her to a low bench near the warm fire in the grand salone. "Please sit with me, my dear, and help me with a difficult task."

Ginevra agreed without hesitation. "Just tell me what you would have me do."

"What you must do, my child, is listen carefully to what I am going to tell you. I'm afraid the listening will be even more painful than the telling. I'll make it as quick as I can . . .

"Ginevra, your betrothal to my young cousin has been broken. You will not be married to him."

Ginevra smiled. "Is that all? Madonna Lucrezia, you shouldn't frighten me so. I was afraid that you had some really bad news. It doesn't matter to me that I won't be marrying someone that I've never even met."

Lucrezia's clasp grew tighter. "That's not all, Ginevra. It will be difficult to find you any husband worthy of you."

Ginevra pulled her hands away and turned her head so that Lucrezia couldn't see her face. "I know about that," she said. Her voice was harsh. "I heard the nurses gossiping. No man can marry a Pazzi. It's a law."

Lucrezia held back her tears. "Laws can be circumvented. It's easy to change a name, and not unusual. A dowry can be arranged. But there is nothing that can be done to cure the damage done to you. My poor darling Ginevra, you will never be able to bear a child. I tried to stop the bleeding. I used every medicine, every art I knew . . ." The tears flowed freely over Lucrezia's cheeks.

"Ginevra, you no longer have a womb. You are forever barren. A man takes a wife so that she can give him children. The most we can hope is that the father of children whose mother has died will consent . . ."

Ginevra turned to face her. "Please," she said, "please, Madonna, don't cry. Your sorrow breaks my heart." She put her arms around the older woman in a clumsy embrace. "It doesn't matter. Truly it doesn't. I don't care about a husband or children. I'm alive, thanks to you, and happy, thanks to you. There's no reason for you to weep."

She placed her cheek alongside Lucrezia's and felt tears, hers mingling with Lucrezia's. I should never have let her love me, Ginevra thought, or let myself love her. It will be so much harder now to kill her son.

Chapter Twenty-six

Lucrezia couldn't believe that Ginevra was not desolate because she was barren. Children were a woman's joy as well as her duty. She didn't stop to think about Ginevra's history. Isolated in the country with only old men and elderly servants for companions, the girl had no experience of children, no idea of what it meant to be a mother, no desire for something that she could not imagine.

On a warm, springlike day in February Ginevra learned.

She felt the sun's strength through the thin panes of the library window and was seized with a wrenching longing for the garden at La Vacchia. She needed the smell of earth, the sight of growing things, the sound of birds and splashing water. She had thought the garden behind the palace a sorry thing except for Donatello's statue. It had been bleak and colorless and cold.

But on a day like this, it would surely be different. At the very least there would be birds drinking from the fountain and sunlight on her shoulders. In her haste, she forgot to return her book to its case. She didn't want to miss even a minute of sunlight.

She thought she heard the call of a bird unknown to her when she approached the garden, and she ran for the final few steps. Then she stopped abruptly in the doorway. Directly ahead of her a bright green woolen blanket was spread out on the still-brown winter grass. A baby lay on it, gurgling with delight and playing a game of capturing its own toes. It was almost naked, its swaddling undone and bunched around its rosy satin skin.

Ginevra looked from right to left. There was no one else in the garden. She dropped to her knees beside the child and cautiously put out a hand to touch its fat bare foot.

"You're so soft," she exclaimed.

The baby chortled.

Lucrezia found Ginevra a half hour later. She was nuzzling the baby's stomach, laughing at its shrieks of joy, pretending to resist the tugs of the chubby little fists that were clutching at her kerchief and the short curly hair beneath it.

"So you've met Giulio," Lucrezia said. "Isn't he delicious?"

Ginevra's smile was radiant. "I think he likes me."

"I'm sure he does. I could hear him laughing when I got to the courtyard . . . What a little devil. He always manages to get out of his bindings. Heaven help us all when he learns to walk." Lucrezia seated herself on the grass by Ginevra, extricated the baby's hands from her hair and kissed the dimpled fingers. "I thought he'd be howling by now. It's past the hour for his feeding."

As if he had been reminded, the baby puckered his face and looked woeful. Ginevra tried to tickle him into laughter, but he began to cry.

"Oh, no!" she wailed. "What did I do wrong? Did I hurt him? I didn't mean to."

Lucrezia laughed. "He's just noticed that he's hungry, that's all . . . Maria!"

A young woman ran into the garden, her fingers untying the laces at the neck of her gown. "I'm sorry, Madonna," she said. "I didn't notice the time." She bent and scooped up the baby and his wrappings; his loud screams seemed to disturb her not at all.

Ginevra watched with fascination while Maria sat on a garden bench and lifted out a full, globelike breast. Giulio's crying changed to loud sucking noises.

"Greedy little monster," Lucrezia said fondly. "What do you think of him, Ginevra?"

"I think he's wonderful. I didn't know there were babies here. Are there many others?"

Lucrezia was confused by the question. "Lorenzo and Clarice have six children, but they're all at Cafaggiolo."

"I didn't mean that. I meant the servants. Maria is a servant, isn't she?"

"Oh. Now I understand. No, the servants' children don't live in the palace. When a girl has a baby we move her, and her husband if she has one, to one of the villas. There's no place for a child to run here in the city. Lorenzo's own children spend most of the year at the Fiesole villa."

"But . . ." Ginevra looked at Maria.

"She's Giulio's wet nurse. He is my grandson, the son of my younger son Giuliano. His mother was Giuliano's mistress. Lorenzo persuaded her to let him have the baby after he was born. Giulio will be raised with Lorenzo's boys, just as if he were Lorenzo's own son."

"Why doesn't Giuliano take him? How can he bear to let his brother raise his child?"

Lucrezia's breath was uneven, her face very pale. "Giuliano is dead," she said.

"I'm so sorry. I didn't know. I hope I didn't make you feel sad."

Lucrezia stroked Ginevra's hair. "That's all right. I'm sure you didn't mean to." She could feel the jagged scars on the scalp. Giuliano wasn't the only casualty.

She returned to a happier subject. "Giulio came to us in August. He's six months old now. I find that an excellent age for babies. Younger ones sleep all the time; older ones are always on the move. When his stomach is full he'll nap for an hour or so, then be ready to play all afternoon. We'll have Maria bring him to us in my sitting room. Would you like that?"

"Oh yes. Very much."

Ginevra became the baby's adoring slave. She gave up her pretense of illness and openly enjoyed life. For more than a month she was in a demiparadise, sharing the approach of spring with Giulio, naming birds and flowers for him, patiently removing bits of grass and twigs and leaves from his mouth, playing games of peekaboo, teaching him to clap, wave goodbye, make a sound that she was sure was her name. Lucrezia often joined them in the garden. She made tiny stitches on a tapestry while she shared the laughter and happiness.

The idyll was shattered in early April. Lorenzo came home.

Suddenly the palace was a beehive of activity. People came and went at all hours; the courtyard was crowded with men-at-arms standing guard over men waiting to see Lorenzo; the garden held the overflow; the passage-ways and stairs were busy with messengers and pages, secretaries and councillors. Even the library was occupied by scholars from the University of Pisa whom Lorenzo had met on a visit and invited to come stay and study at the palace.

Less than twenty-four hours after Lorenzo arrived, Maria brought Giulio to Ginevra's room to say goodbye. Lorenzo was sending them to Cafaggiolo. The baby waved as Ginevra had taught him, then burst into a startled wail when she hugged him too tightly. Ginevra's last sight of him was a red face above Maria's shoulder, the round dark eyes brimming with tears.

Lucrezia offered no sympathy. "But it's always been intended to have Giulio join the other children. The roads were full of soldiers when he was born, and the winter was too cold for a baby to be carried that distance." She hurried away to the kitchens. A houseful of people demanded careful management.

Later, when she had a few minutes to think, she regretted her abruptness with Ginevra. The girl was terribly attached to the baby. Possibly too attached. It was probably just as well to break the attachment before it became too strong.

In any case, she had no time to worry about it. Lorenzo needed her. The cost of the war meant higher taxes, and the Florentines were beginning to wonder if supporting Lorenzo in his battle with Pope Sixtus was worth the price. Especially when it was obvious that Florence was losing the war. Lorenzo had to plan his moves carefully if he was going to remain the leader of the government. He and Lucrezia talked throughout the night, assessing possibilities and making plans.

* * *

Ginevra, too, passed a sleepless night. Alone. Lucrezia's brusque dismissal of her had left a bitter taste of disappointment. But she knew that Lucrezia's presence, even her affection, could have been of no help.

Because the loss of Giulio made her realize the meaning of all that Lucrezia had told her. She was barren. She would never bear a child. She knew now what it was to hold a baby, to feel his small arms around her neck, to experience the melting rush of love for him when she saw him asleep or when he pressed a kiss on her throat. If a stranger's baby could be all that to her, how much greater must a mother's love be? Ginevra held her hands against her small breasts until they ached, as her heart ached at their emptiness. They would never fill with milk, never know the eager sucking, never give nourishment and contented sleep.

She was sixteen years old. A woman, and yet not a woman and never to be one.

There would never be life growing in her womb; even though she walked and breathed and spoke, she was lifeless.

She laughed aloud, a ragged counterfeit of humor. I was so certain that I did not fear death, she thought. Why should I? I am already dead.

She felt the stored-up cold of winter seep into the room from its thick stone walls, and she shivered, wrapped a quilt around her hunched shoulders.

A hot thrill of hate raced throughout her body; it warmed her and dispersed the chill of her surrender to despair. Lorenzo. His victims cried for vengeance. Everyone she had ever loved and all those she would never have to love, the babies who would never be born, the children forever denied her.

She climbed quickly up the bedpost and reclaimed her knife. It had rusted and dulled during the months it had lain hidden. Ginevra spit on the blade and began to hone it.

It was not as easy as Ginevra had thought it would be to kill Lorenzo. He was out of the house the better part of the day, sometimes for days at a time. When he was at home there were always people with him and people waiting to see him. She had learned the palace well, knew where to find him, but there was no way to find him alone. That was vital. She had to strike unawares, when his back was turned; she'd never win a contest of strength with him. And she couldn't risk a shout of warning from a third person; Lorenzo's reflexes were too quick. There'd be no second chance. Everything had to be perfect.

He was most vulnerable on the evenings when he and Lucrezia conferred privately in his study. Ginevra was sure that Lucrezia would be so unsuspecting that it would all be over before she knew what was happening. But Ginevra could not bring herself to betray the affection and trust of her only friend.

At first the challenge of finding the opportunity was exciting, almost like a game. But as the weeks raced by, she grew increasingly frustrated. She could not bear to fail.

The days grew longer and warmer. Lucrezia told Ginevra that she had given instructions for alterations in the usual routine of the season's changes. The lemon trees in their great terra-cotta pots would be brought out from their glass-enclosed winter house as usual. But they would not be put in the garden. They were to be taken upstairs and placed on the flat roof of the glass house to make a hedge for the terrace there. "The garden is always full of people now, but we should not have to give up our sun and open air. The terrace will be our private place."

The windows of Lorenzo's study were only a few feet above the terrace. At last, Ginevra thought. At last. All I have to do now is wait there and listen for my opportunity.

The very first day, the moment arrived.

Chapter Twenty-seven

". . . thank you for coming to see me, Luca. You were right, as always. The codex is beautiful, and I'm grateful you let me have first refusal. It will be one of the treasures of my library . . . Bruno, please escort my friend down to the street. Protect him from the horde in the courtyard. A bookseller is too valuable to be jostled by a politician."

Ginevra heard the shuffling gait of the old man and the firm step of Lorenzo's secretary.

"And keep everybody out for as long as you can, Bruno. I'd like a little time with Saint Augustine."

The door closed. There was the sound of turning pages. Ginevra touched her sleeve. The stiletto was safely concealed. Her blood raced, and she felt lightheaded with excitement. It seemed to her that her entire body was buoyed up, that it almost floated when she pulled herself up onto the deep windowsill.

She heard Lorenzo shout, saw him leap from his chair, turn, reach for the dagger strapped onto his calf. She would have sworn that she had made no sound.

"Contadina! Wounds of the Savior, but you frightened me." The knife slid back into its sheath. Lorenzo shook his head. "You should never surprise a man from behind like that, Ginevra. I might have killed you before I knew it was you."

He walked across to the window just as two guards burst into the room, their swords gleaming. "It's all right," he told them. "Go back to your posts . . . Come in, Contadina. I'm happy to see you." He smiled and held out his hand to help her down.

Ginevra hadn't seen Lorenzo for months. He looked tired, she noticed, and there were deep lines on either side of his mouth. She jumped down easily, ignoring his hand.

How could you, she wanted to shout, how could you dare to pretend to be my friend, to be so glad to see me? What degree of fool do you take me for?

She was barely able to listen to Lorenzo's pleased account of the bookseller's discovery of the forgotten pages in an abandoned monastery, to make the appropriate sounds of interest, to smile when he led her to the door and opened it. "This is the way to enter the room," he said with a laugh.

Lucrezia saw nothing amusing about the incident. She berated Ginevra for an hour, calling her foolish, reckless, ungrateful, spoiled, thoughtless, wild.

"Lorenzo is busy with matters of the gravest importance," she said. "He doesn't have time to play games with you. He's not unconcerned, Ginevra. He keeps up with your progress through me. And despite the weight of serious concerns on his shoulders he's even made the first moves to find you a home and a husband. Without success as yet, it's true, but you've not been forgotten. Your behavior was childish and shameful. I'm bitterly disappointed in you . . ."

Ginevra stood quietly through the tirade, her eyes meekly lowered. At the end, she said, "I'm deeply sorry, Madonna Lucrezia. I'll never do anything like that again."

And it was true; she never would. Because it would clearly be unsuccessful. She had to find another way . . . In mid-November she did.

She eavesdropped under Lorenzo's windows every night. Darkness saved her from detection, and she was able to learn the confidential plans and information that he shared only with Lucrezia in urgent, secret strategy-drafting conversations after the palace was supposedly asleep.

No one in Florence was allowed to know how badly the war was going, not even the priors and the Council of War. Nor were they aware of the full extent of the dangerous situation that had developed in Milan. The Milanese had been weak allies under the shaky rule of the Duchess-Regent, but in September there was a real possibility that the neighboring state might become an active enemy. The Duchess was under attack from all three of her brothers-in-law; Florence was unable to divert men or money from its own defense to help her. She accepted the offer of the strongest of the three brothers to join forces with him and destroy the other two. Ludorico Sforza became co-regent for the young Duke. He immediately began to send hints to King Ferrante of Naples that Milan might be willing to consider changing sides. Ferrante responded immediately.

Lorenzo's spies were able to intercept many of the letters and copy them for him. The correspondence suggested a daring possibility.

"Mamina, I am sure that it is worth the gamble."

"I wish I could see it, Lorenzo, but I don't. I think you're reading your own desires into those letters."

"And what if I am? The situation is desperate. The armies of Rome and Naples are less than thirty miles to the south; Sixtus's accursed nephew has an army inside the borders of Tuscany to our north; our royal ally, the King of France, sends couriers with requests for gifts and favors, but the five hundred lances he promised are all at work for him in his battles with the Hapsburg Emperor; Venice is so weakened by war with the Turks that no help can be hoped for there.

"The only thing that saved us from annihilation was the calendar. The winter truce has begun. If I am to do anything, it must be done in these four months.

"Now I say that Ferrante shows a lack of enthusiasm about Sforza's overtures, and he does not praise his ally the Pope with convincing fervor. I believe I could persuade him to abandon Sixtus and renew his old treaties with Florence. Sforza would have to stay our ally then. I want to go to Naples. I'll go in disguise, leave Florence unobserved, take only a handful of companions. The audacity will appeal to Ferrante. He's always had a taste for drama."

"And for treachery. I fear for you, my son."

"As I fear for our State, Mamina. Sixtus wants to destroy me, and he's going to succeed, ruining the Republic to get at me. Naples is my only chance. I must take it."

Ginevra nodded silent unseen encouragement. He'd be in disguise, thinly protected, away from Florence. She'd see to it that Lorenzo never reached Naples.

The plan was for Lorenzo's small band to leave Florence one by one, wearing monks' robes that would cover their armor and weapons and hide their faces inside the deep hoods. The gate that led to the road to Pisa was the Porta San Frediano. A monastery lay in the fields just beyond it. No guard would question a monk passing through, particularly near sundown when the traffic was heavy. They'd meet just beyond the monastery where horses would be waiting.

Ginevra stole one of Father Paolo's monk's robes. She put it on inside the empty lemon house, eased her way into the garden, through the groups of men walking its paths and out the small gate that led to the street. The guard at the gate crossed himself when she passed. She controlled her urge to laugh until she was several paces down the street. Her spirits were so elated that it was hard for her to keep her pace slow and her gaze lowered. She wanted to run, to dance, to sing, to laugh loudly and shout her joy.

It was not only because she was at long last within sight of accomplishing her goal. It was also because she was free of walls, of confinement. No matter how luxurious, the Medici palace had been her prison for more than a year. Unmarried young women did not go out on the streets of Florence except to go to mass, and Lucrezia had not permitted even that. She had thought it dangerous for a Pazzi to appear in public.

Ginevra longed to look around her, to investigate the sounds and smells that came from all sides. But she restrained her curiosity. First she had to get into Lorenzo's small group. Then kill him. Then she would be really free.

She arrived at the rendezvous well in advance, so that she'd have daylight to see by. Unlike the men Lorenzo was expecting, Ginevra had never seen the monastery or the road they would be traveling. She also had to locate the best place for an ambush. Five men were expected. A sixth monk would be noticed at once.

It was December sixth. The dusk brought a chill wind, but Ginevra sweated in her shadowed hiding place. Her hands were slippery on the thick piece of wood she held at her side. Now that she was acting instead of imagining, she realized for the first time what she was about to do. Murder. Maybe more than one. Lorenzo has earned it, she told herself, and his guards, too. Any one of them may be the one who killed Fra Marco, the most innocent creature that ever lived. Or Mateo. Or my grandfather.

But would she be able to do it? Lift her hand. Strike. She was shaking. Her arm felt weak.

You must. You have the strength. You can. She drew on all her fierce willpower, the determination and discipline that had overcome pain and the sweet luring call of restful death. She had made her body obey, she could control her fearful mind's imaginings.

She rubbed her sweaty palms against the rough-textured robe. The roughness felt good against her skin, brought her back to the present, to reality, away from the squeamish visions in her head. She arranged her hands in a firm grip.

One monk figure walked past her to the stableyard, a few moments later a second. The wind rattled the leaves of the bushes that screened her, and it was difficult to hear the lowered voices of the two men. One of them, she thought, was Lorenzo.

Then the third hooded shape passed, and she knew she had been wrong. The quick step and proud bearing could only belong to one man. So, too, the quiet voice of command. "Untether the horses. We must be ready to ride as soon as Sebastiano and Guido arrive."

Which will I be, wondered Ginevra. She felt a giddy desire to ask, to speak aloud.

Then her breath caught in her throat. Approaching

steps told her it was time to act. I hope he's not tall,
she thought. I hope I can do it. She raised her club.

Luck was with her. The man outlined against the
crimson-streaked sky was little taller than she. Intent on
his goal, he didn't hear her behind him. When she hit
him on the side of the head, he made only a soft grunt-
ing sound. He fell into a pool of shadow in the inclined
turf and rolled down away from the path. Ginevra
ducked back into her hiding place.

"What was that?" she heard. She put a hand over
her mouth to muffle her rapid panting breath.

The last of Lorenzo's attendants arrived only a moment later. He was almost running.

"Quiet, Guido," someone hissed. "Your feet are like
drums."

"There's no time for quiet," Guido said, "I think I
was recognized. Let's go."

"We can't. Sebastiano isn't here yet."

"We go." It was Lorenzo speaking. Ginevra heard
the noises of harnesses squeaking and hooves moving
nervously sideways as the men mounted. She pulled the
hood low over her face and ran to the yard.

"Here, Sebastiano." Someone threw her the reins of
two horses. She saw that each man was riding one mount
and leading a replacement. The first rider was Lorenzo.
He was already out of the gate and galloping along the
road. The others followed, Ginevra in the rear position.

Her hands and body adjusted to the horse's gait and
nervous temperament as if she had been riding him all
her life. Under the deep hood her face was wet with
rapturous tears. How I've missed this, she thought. If
they catch me and kill me in the next five minutes, it
will be worth it just to have been able to ride again.

They rode hard, too hard for conversation. The road
paralleled the course of the Arno, often ran along its
banks. It was flat, and there was light from a full moon.
We look like ghosts, Ginevra thought with a thrill. The
dusty road muffled the sound of the hooves, the wind
billowed the dark robes into cloudlike shapes behind the
riders, the cold air made silvered plumes of their breath.
From time to time the man ahead of Ginevra turned his

head to make sure she was keeping up with them. There seemed to be no face in the deep shadow under his hood, only darkness.

She saw that each man switched to his fresh mount on his own initiative, and she waited to be the last to change so that she would automatically remain in last position.

On and on they rode until the moon grew pale in the river, the water a cold steely rose color. Lorenzo called out. "We stop at the farm just ahead."

Chapter Twenty-eight

The door of the house opened just as Lorenzo dismounted. He embraced the man who ran out. "Well, I thank you, Mario," he answered the farmer's question. "There was no trouble. We are all well but fatigued, especially these brave horses. Have your sons rub them down with the care they'd give a beautiful woman. And then feed them as lavishly as you're going to feed us . . . where is Claudia, the beloved of my heart? Ah, there you are." He kissed the farmer's wife on both cheeks. "This time you will leave your brute of a husband and come with me for a gypsy life in the open air, will you not?"

Claudia was an elderly, thin, stern-looking woman, but Lorenzo made her blush like a girl. She covered her smile with her hand to hide the near-toothless gums, but her dark eyes were laughing in their nests of wrinkled skin.

"You ask me that every time you come here," she said, "and one day I'll say yes, and then where will you be, you rascal?"

Ginevra heard the words through a mist of exhaustion. Her physical strength and her nerves were stretched to their limits; her perceptions swung dizzyingly from extra-acute to dull and back again. The language Lorenzo and the farmers spoke was the accent and vocabulary of the contado, the peasant dialect that was the first Italian she had learned. It was confusing, then suddenly clear and right to her ear. A befuddled sense of well-being warmed her stiff, half-frozen body, an amalgam of love for her earliest nurse and this kindly couple, of relief that the punishing all-night journey was over, of eager response to the smell of hot food and the dancing firelight that came from the open door of the small house. I'm happy, she thought, bewildered by the ill-timed emotion.

She dismounted and stumbled toward the warmth.

". . . and this is Sebastiano, the last of my companions and the least in size, but not in courage." Lorenzo's voice was very loud. Ginevra shrunk inside the protection of the hooded robe. "Are you still so cold, then Sebasto?" Lorenzo said. "Come over by the fire and warm yourself." He tweaked the pointed end of the hood, and it slid backward onto Ginevra's shoulders.

When the light reached her face she felt a manic surge of strength and energy. She straightened her spine, lifted her chin, laughed with wild bravado.

Lorenzo's jaw dropped; his stare was unbelieving. Then he shouted with laughter. The others in the room looked puzzled and alarmed. He turned to face them, and he looked ten years younger. "I have good news," he said, laughter bubbling through his words. "Our mission is certain to succeed; we have been sent a sign. This person who is not Sebastiano is my star-sister. Always she has meant luck to me. Now she will bring good fortune to all of us."

Below the exclamations of his companions, Lorenzo spoke quietly to Ginevra. "How did you come to be here, Contadina? And why? Did the angels send you? Where is Sebastiano?"

Ginevra grinned wickedly and told him about her eavesdropping and what she had done to Sebastiano. She was half-drunk from fatigue, from the shock of Lorenzo's reaction, from her confused realization that she was, in some incomprehensible way, a heroine.

"But why?" Lorenzo insisted. "We're going into great danger."

"I wanted to ride. Pictures of pretend horses aren't enough. And I wanted to escape. I cannot bear being closed up indoors. And I don't care about danger. I want the adventure." She heard her own words, in the dialect of the contado, and she recognized them as true. Before she could blurt out the deeper truth, the compelling reason that drove her, she found the guile she needed to survive. She yawned and sighed. "I'm hungry, Lorenzo. And very, very tired."

The travelers all ate voraciously, then fell onto the straw-filled mattresses on the floor and slept. Lorenzo woke after only an hour. He was refreshed, ready to push on, but he knew that the others needed rest. He wrote a letter to his mother, telling her that Ginevra was with him and safe. He wrote a letter to the Signoria, telling them—and through them, the city—that he was leaving Tommaso Soderini as his deputy, was going to Naples. He promised to secure peace. Through diplomacy if possible. If not, by sacrificing his life and thus satisfying Florence's enemies. Two of the farmer's sons left at once for Florence to deliver the letters.

"I'll take your boys' places, Mario," he said. "Let me help you in your vineyard."

While he cut new supports for the grapevines and tied up the sagging, dry gray vines, Lorenzo enjoyed the touch of the sun on his shoulders and the crisp frosty air in his nostrils. This is what I have needed, he thought. Honest labor and its sweat. Not the world of spies and politics, arguments, bribery, intimidation and compromises. And not the endless meetings and committees, with the evil sweat of fear at every turn because I can no longer trust any man.

Ferrante is my avowed enemy, and I know what I face with him. I will win or I will lose. It will be my doing. Not a majority vote bought with money and scheming. Not a battle fought by men purchased from another province.

He stood tall, stretched the knots out of his muscles, shivered from the cold on his sweat-soaked shirt. He felt free. The risk of death was a cheap price to pay for the feeling.

Adventure, the contadina called it, he remembered. How can I blame her for seeking it?

But how can I allow it? She's only a woman. She'll

have to stay here. I'll leave money with Mario. He can
buy her an escort back to Florence.

"You said she was our luck, Lorenzo. You can't leave
our luck behind."

"Guido's right. I told you I'd follow you anywhere.
But this changes everything."

"I'm not a superstitious fool like these two. I say
we're better off without her."

Ginevra listened while Lorenzo's guards argued. Her
expression was bland, but her heart was celebrating. The
opinion was two to one in her favor. Three to one if she
counted Lorenzo, and she was certain that she could.
He had been glad to see her, she knew it. And no one
in his right mind would turn his back on luck. For the
first time she felt powerful, certain of success. Lorenzo was no awesome figure to fear. He had to be a
fool if he mistook the hand of vengeance for the embodiment of good fortune.

Before he would change his mind Lorenzo took Ginevra outside for a private talk. "Contadina, you must
think seriously about this now. No more games. You
wanted an adventure. You've had one. The disguise, the
ride through the darkness, all that is very exciting. But
there was no real danger. Soon the adventure will be a
gamble for life. You cannot know what that means."

Ginevra looked him in the eye. She worked her
mouth, then spat on the ground between them. "Don't
tell me what I can and cannot know, Lorenzo. I have
been closer to death than I am to you. Can you say the
same? No, you cannot. I tell you I am not afraid of
dying."

He looked away from her intense stare. "There are
other things . . . dangers that do not exist for a man
. . . things that are worse than a quick death . . ." He
was uneasy, embarrassed, unable to find the words to
say what he meant to a young woman he believed to be
still a virgin.

Ginevra did not help him. She could not have spoken
if she wanted to. She was paralyzed by rage. He had,
she thought, forgotten what his men had done. He had

ordered the destruction of so many lives that hers was undifferentiated from all the others, so unimportant that he did not even remember it.

". . . cannot guarantee even the conduct of my own men," Lorenzo was saying, "and there will be dozens of seamen. If you come with us, you must stay close by my side at all times, day and night."

Ginevra's heart jumped. She could have asked for nothing better. She found her voice. It throbbed with sincerity. "I give you my word, Lorenzo."

Ginevra kept her monk's robe. Lorenzo gave her a history to go with it. "We cannot take the chance that someone might ask the friar to say mass or give a blessing," he explained to them all, "so we are traveling with my personal charity, one of God's fools named . . . Tino, a shortening of *cretino*, idiot." He laughed, pleased with the simple joke, pleased that it felt so natural to laugh. He had not known easy laughter for months.

"Tino is a fool, so any peculiarities in his behavior will be attributed to that. Also the pitch of his voice. Remember at all times that Tino is a man. If you forget, our lives may be forfeit once we are at sea. Sailors believe women are a jinx on a ship.

"People will wonder why Lorenzo carries a holy fool with him. Tell them he believes that Tino brings him good fortune. That part, at least, is true."

"If I'm going to be a fool, I'm going to enjoy it," Ginevra told Lorenzo. She rode at his side, leading the group, enjoying everything about the journey. A few hours after they left the farmhouse they turned off the main road onto a narrow track that led through the mountains. When it began to snow the men behind them cursed. Lorenzo reminded them that evidence of their passage would be covered, which would aid the secrecy of their mission, and that the brigands who preyed on travelers were not likely to leave their fires in such weather. Ginevra had never, in her memory, seen so much snow. She caught it on her tongue, marveled at the beauty of the white-clad trees, begged until Lorenzo agreed to stop and let her slide down a gentle slope.

The path took them above the storm into blinding sunlight on a glittering white landscape. "Oh! So beautiful. This must be what the angels see when they look around them." Ginevra threw her hood back, her arms wide, greeting the brilliant world.

Lorenzo had seen the gesture before, when she rode to the top of the hill at La Vacchia. He recognized again the free spirit that was Ginevra. It was right for her to come, he thought. His worry evaporated, and his old envy of her freedom. He was free, too. He began to sing.

Ginevra laughed, joined her tuneless voice to his, gave her heart over to joy.

Three days later they reached the coast.

"I thought I'd never see anything as beautiful as the snowfields," Ginevra said. "I was wrong."

They were on the crest of a hill above the narrow strip of flat land that bordered the sea. The Mediterranean filled their view, stretching forever to a horizon that merged with the sky. Blue turned to blue to blue in an infinity of shifting color so rich that it paupered every jewel ever taken from the earth.

"I want to touch it," Ginevra said.

"So you shall." Lorenzo spurred his horse.

Ginevra was in an ecstasy of discovery. While the others ate the last of the bread and cheese in the saddlebags, she waded in the warm shallows, felt the sharp sand between her toes and sliding through her fingers, ran from side to side on the beach exclaiming at the wonderful delicacy of each shell she found.

"I hate to leave," she cried when Lorenzo called to her.

"It's time," he said.

They rode for miles on the beach. Lorenzo had planned their route well. The sands were narrow, with no inlets or coves, therefore no fishing villages. They saw no other living creature, except the great white birds that rode the air currents above the waters. The solitude and warm air and salt tang were intoxicating. They were all infected by a kind of childish glee, and even Maurizio, the glummest of the guards, was soon racing in and out of the water's edge, playing a game of his own devising with the uneven advance and ebb of the low surf.

The sun moved down toward the horizon, growing larger, staining the blue sea with violet. Without a word they all slowed their pace until the horses were walking soundlessly in the soft sand, and they were surrounded by the expectant hush of the end of the day. The bottom of the crimson sun touched the purple sea and they drew in their breath in a collective whisper of awe.

A wind came across the water in reply, pushing the pink-rimmed surf before it. The sun widened, flattened, shimmered, bobbed upward for an instant and was swallowed by the suddenly dark sea. Ginevra shivered.

The pale sand stretched ahead, like a perilously narrow bridge. The horses stopped.

Lorenzo's quiet laughter made her jump. "Now we make our own light," he said. "Follow me." He spurred his horse into a run, guided him into the water's edge, and the splashing sounds were lit by unworldly green sparks.

"Magic!" cried Ginevra, racing in pursuit. The others came soon after. Their laughter pushed away the fearful dark presence of the sea while they played with the phosphorus-laden gentle surf.

Lorenzo silenced them when they approached a seeming wall of rock. "We're almost there," he said. "You'll see a fire ahead when we get past that headland. Some fishermen are meeting us, with our evening meal. Tino, remember who you are. Everyone, listen more than you speak. Sound travels over water, and Ferrante's men are not far away."

The fire was a welcome beacon in the darkness, the aroma from the cauldron suspended over it a reminder that salt air sharpens the appetite. Ginevra had never tasted anything as delicious as the spicy stew and the chunks of seafood in it. She felt no desire to speak, only a gratified tiredness at the close of a perfect day. She wrapped the folds of her robe around her and curled her body against a still-warm hillock of sand. The rhythmic whispering of the surf carried her into sleep with a smile on her lips.

She awoke at dawn, heard the lullaby sound, remembered where she was, and her smile widened. She turned her head slowly to look at the sea.

A ship was riding at anchor on the slow swells. It was only an outline in the gray half-light, a low dark shape with tall bare masts veiled by mist, floating on tendrils of fog that moved eerily across the surface of the sea. It had a row of black slits along its side, like watching eyes.

The game is over, she told herself. This is the adventure. Watch your step, Tino.

Chapter Twenty-nine

Ginevra's eavesdropping had given her a full picture of
the riskiness of what Lorenzo was doing. Ferrante, the
King of Naples, was a tyrant with a monumental capri-
ciousness and a taste for the macabre that surpassed even
the fabled cruelty of the former Duke of Milan. He was
totally untrustworthy; the year before he had violated
one of the unbreakable rules of war by inviting an op-
posing general to parley, sending him a written safe
conduct, then executing him when he arrived in Naples.

She wondered if Ferrante's generous gesture of sending a ship for Lorenzo's voyage was the equivalent of a
safe conduct. Or better. Or worse.

She looked for Lorenzo. Maybe his face would hold
the answer.

He was sitting with the fishermen near the low-burn-
ing fire, eating, talking quietly, laughing.

Ginevra scrambled to her feet and ran to join them.
Her own mission could wait a bit longer. She could
hardly wait for the adventure to begin.

Lorenzo had sent baggage ahead, and the fishing boats
pulled up on the sands were stacked high with chests,
leather pouches, oiled-silk-wrapped bales. Lorenzo
climbed up to a bright red cassone and lifted its lid. He
threw down even brighter colors, reds, blues, yellows,
greens, elegant livery for his men, a sumptuous fur-
lined blue velvet lucco for himself.

One of the pouches gave up gold coins for the fishermen and a massive gold link chain studded with sapphires.
Ginevra saw that the links were fashioned in the shape of

the fleur-de-lis, the symbol of the French king. A reminder to Ferrante that Louis XI was Lorenzo's ally, a
self-appointed kinsman who had granted the Medici the
privilege of displaying the emblem of France on their coat
of arms.

Bravo, Lorenzo, she thought. No supplications for
peace, but threats of a greater power. She had learned,
under the windows above the terrace, that France had a
claim to the kingdom of Naples that it could use as a
pretext for conquest at any time. Ferrante's throne sat
on shaky legs. His father had been the first king of his
line, capturing Naples from its French rulers. Ferrante
was only the second; and he was an illegitimate son. He
was always worried about the intentions of France.

Ginevra smiled and ate her breakfast with a hearty
appetite. She had never felt so hungry in her life or so
alive, as she did in the brisk salt-spiced air of the sea
that was dancing now under the new-risen sun. She was
sorry only that her role required that she wear the dull,
dusty monk's robe. She would have liked to be in colors
as bright as her spirits.

The ship was commanded by a "gentleman-captain,"
the Count of Ardenza, Filippo Gambassi. He was the
very picture of opulence in furs, brocades and jewels.
He even had a large pear-shaped pearl hanging from one
earlobe. His face was lean and darkly sardonic. He
looked as if his boots might hide cloven hooves. It was
not hard for Ginevra to gibber like an idiot when Tino
was presented to him.

"This holy fool is my mascot, Count, my good luck
charm. He thinks he is a priest, as you see. His name is
Tino."

Gambassi bowed his head. He was amused and impressed. All rulers had fools, but they were usually men
of wit and courtly accomplishment. He thought Lorenzo
very original to have a fool who was a fool.

His amusement grew when Lorenzo told him that the
fool would share his guest quarters. Gambassi was a sophisticated man from a libertine city. A wealthy man's
protégé was nothing out of the ordinary to him, but he had

never heard of a simpleton would-be priest for a plaything. He thought that Lorenzo was very original indeed.

Ginevra felt his interested eyes staring at her, and she was grateful for the concealing deep hood. She was sure that her face would give her away. It must be glowing with excitement. Everything was falling into place. The adventure had become hers alone, now that she knew she was sharing Lorenzo's quarters. Alone with him. All she had to do was wait for him to go to sleep, and then . . . He had even given her a knife to carry hidden in her robes, never suspecting that she already had one.

But first she had the entire day to enjoy the beauty of the sea and the novelty of being aboard a ship for the first time. As if he were reading her thoughts, Lorenzo told Gambassi that he would like to see all around the craft.

It was a galley, luxuriously appointed with an upper deck built over the area where the rowers were. The sails were striped blue and red, and the same colors decorated the cushioned benches in the saloon and the beds in the big cabins. Blue and white squares of silk were sewn together to make an awning over a table and chairs on deck. Ginevra sat silently while Lorenzo drank wine and gambled with Gambassi. She was glad to have a quiet moment after the stimulating morning. There were so many impressions and experiences to assimilate: the crack when the sail was raised and caught the wind, the breathtaking sight of it, billowing blue and red against the blue of the sky and sea, the motion of the deck and the triumph of balancing on it, the sound of the water rushing past the hull, the sting of salt in the drops that splashed onto her face, the wonder of the speed at which they were moving, faster than anything she had ever known.

She wanted it to go on forever.

"How long will it take us to get to Naples?" she asked Lorenzo when they retired to the suite of cabins assigned to him.

"It depends. We had good winds today. Tomorrow there might be none, and the oars are not as fast. Or a gale, and we'd have to put in to shore. A perfect passage is about six or seven days.''

So short, Ginevra thought. One day is gone already. She started to speak, then saw that Lorenzo was asleep, his head against the tall back of a thronelike chair under the swaying oil lamp. The clasp of his lucco was unfastened at the neck, exposing his throat.

I can do it now, Ginevra thought. Her right hand moved slowly toward her left sleeve and the dagger strapped to her arm inside it. Her breathing sounded very loud to her.

Her fingers closed around the hilt.

Then released it and withdrew. There are days and days to go, she said to herself. Let me have a little more time on the sea. I'll have many chances like this, and only one ship voyage.

The next night the same thing happened, and the next, and the next, and each time Ginevra let the chance slip by. She was too greedy for the hours on board the ship. She had known pleasure, contentment, but never before in her life had she known what it was to have fun. Every minute of every day on the galley was crammed with light-hearted pleasure.

Lorenzo wanted to see everything, learn everything, try everything. Ginevra felt the same. And, she discovered, everything was possible for her. Everyone believed she was a man. Lorenzo talked to the seamen, asked them questions about the sails, the rigging, the way to read the wind. Ginevra, at his side, learned with him. And when he joined the deckhands in hauling on a line, she grabbed hold behind him.

They learned knots at the same time, and how to make the flat coiled circles of rope, and they climbed to the lookout on top of the mast, one on each side. The arc of sway at the top was terrifying and exhilarating. Their eyes met and they laughed, each glad to see the tear on the other's face.

They saw a pair of porpoises and watched them silently for timeless minutes, sharing the wonder of the animals' grace and beauty, remembering the rich mythology attached to them.

In the evening, in the suite, they talked about the mystery of the sea, of the magic of the wind, of Odysseus and Jason, the Hesperides and Zephyr, their favorite books and poetry. Ginevra recited passages of Homer. Lorenzo said one day he intended to learn Greek.

"I'd like to learn to swim," Ginevra said. "It looks like such fun. The porpoises."

"It is fun. And simple. I'll teach you when we get home to Florence."

Neither of them acknowledged that they might never see Florence again.

Ginevra was very conscious of the change in Lorenzo when he was with the Count. She thought of him then as the Naples Lorenzo. At meals or when the two men walked the deck talking, she remained silent and let her mouth hang slack, made her eyes vacant. But she watched the contest between them, Gambassi sleek and subtly threatening, Lorenzo seemingly unaware of any undercurrent, confident of his position and power. It seemed to her that Gambassi was shrinking a little every day, diminished by Lorenzo's presence. He stayed in his cabin for longer and longer periods, as if Lorenzo were taking command of the ship. Ginevra was glad. She never tired of discovering some new corner of it.

Lorenzo, she believed, was glad, too. He could be more human when the captain wasn't around. On the morning of the fourth day, Gambassi did not appear for breakfast. Lorenzo winked at Ginevra. "Come on," he said. They went below where Gambassi had forbidden them to look and saw the ranks of oarsmen, slaves chained by the ankles. Lorenzo talked to several of them, called Ginevra to translate the words of a Greek for him, put his hand over hers when he saw pity twist her mouth. Then he asked the men to teach him songs they sang when they rowed, and when he sang with them Ginevra led the laughter at the hideous sounds he made.

Later the wind died, and Lorenzo took the Greek's place. He rowed for an hour. Ginevra stood by the drummer who set the pace, angry that her hands were too soft to take a turn.

"You were smart," Lorenzo said afterward. "I was

ready to stop five minutes after I began, but I didn't dare
admit it." He showed her the broken blisters in his palms.

"Tino will have to roll for me," he told Gambassi
when they began the dice game that they played each
day before dinner. "My hands are a mess."

Gambassi chuckled. "I had heard about your Republic and its theories, Lorenzo. When you told me you
wanted to take an oar, I was afraid you were going to
incite republicanism on my ship."

"I had no politics in mind, Filippo, only excessive
curiosity and masculine bravura. I've been punished to
excess, too. I hope the dice won't add to my pain. Roll,
Tino. Bring me luck."

Ginevra did. She also caught the feverish thrill of the
game, of watching the dice turn and willing the number
she wanted to come up.

Lorenzo gave her the coins they won and a pouch to
keep them in. He made her swear an oath that she would
not gamble with the seamen.

But she did while he was napping. And she lost all
her money. She didn't care. She was playing with three
deckhands, all of them her age or younger. It was the
first time she had companions of her own age.

Lorenzo gave her a stern lecture, but Ginevra was not
upset by it. She saw the quivering at the corners of his
mouth and knew he was barely controlling his laughter.

"Now promise me you won't do it again," he concluded. "And this time mean it."

"Of course I won't do it again. I don't have any more
money."

Lorenzo could hold the laughter in no longer.

Ginevra looked at him, at his wind burned face and
battered hands and the tiny white lines at the corners of
his eyes when he squinted in the light and where the
sun could not brown his skin. She wondered if the pale
skin was soft, his ruddy cheek rough. The sound of his
laughter seemed to recede and she heard her own voice
hollow and echoing inside her mind. I've been lying to
myself. I cannot kill this man. I love him. No matter
what he has done or what he may ever do. I've always
loved him, and I always will.

Chapter Thirty

"Ginevra. Contadina." Lorenzo nearly shouted.

"What? I'm sorry. I didn't hear you, I was thinking of something else. What did you say?"

"I asked you if you'd like to go on deck for a walk before bedtime. The night is warm now that we're so far south."

"Yes, I'd like that." Ginevra felt the need for space. She was cramped, held in a vise of emotion, confused by the discovery of feelings too strong, too new. She wanted so desperately to touch Lorenzo that she was afraid to be in the cabin with him, afraid that she'd lose control of herself. She needed to get away from him and from her strange self.

"Come along, then." He held out his blistered hand, offering to pull her up from her crouched position on the bench. Ginevra leapt to her feet and scurried to the door. If he touches me, I don't know what I'll do. Cry. Tell him. Run away.

She walked along the decks, her steps urgently fast, hounded by her turbulent heart, blind to the sights and deaf to the sounds around her. Lorenzo caught up with her and stopped her by holding the folds of her robe in the back. "I suggested a walk, not a run," he said. His voice was warm, indulgent, amused. "Look, Contadina, look at the heavens."

The southern sky was different, Ginevra thought, the stars closer and warmer, soft radiances rather than distant sharp brilliances. Or is it that I am different? I don't know this person inside me; I don't understand her passions that make the me I knew so weak.

226

Lorenzo put his arm carelessly around her shoulder, still looking upward. Ginevra steadied herself against an awning support. You must not lean against him, she told herself, or you are lost. She didn't know how she could be so sure, but she had an absolute certainty that she must not tell Lorenzo about her love.

"Those are our stars," he said, "moving to their own purpose into the conjunctions that make our sign and govern our lives. I believe that it was meant for me to meet Ferrante on the cusp, when Capricorn is entering. It means that my strength will be on the rise. Yours, too, Ginevra, and you are with me. It means my strength is doubled. I'm grateful to have you here." His arm tightened in a brief hug, and he looked down into her face with a smile.

"Have you enjoyed yourself, Contadina?"

"Oh yes."

"I have, too. It was a good thing to have these days at sea, away from the world, with no responsibilities, and all cares postponed. I felt almost like a child again. It's odd, but sometimes I almost called you Giuliano. He and I did so many things together, had so many good times, laughed so much . . ." Lorenzo's voice blurred.

Ginevra clasped her hands tightly together to keep her arms from holding him while he wept.

After a minute Lorenzo cleared his throat. "Now we must make our plans for Naples," he said. "We will arrive tomorrow."

"So soon?" Her cry was full of pain.

"We've had a perfect voyage. Very fast. Tomorrow we'll probably make less speed. Gambassi landed men tonight to ride ahead to warn of our arrival; he'll give them time to deliver their message, probably weigh anchor after breakfast and use the smaller sail. In all likelihood he'll be watching closely, looking for signs of fear that he can report to Ferrante. There'll be little time to talk.

"I am going to appoint Guido your guardian. He'll be at your side to protect you. I imagine I will be taken to Ferrante at once. He's too crafty to begin the game of nerves by making me wait for an audience."

"When will I see you?"

"I don't know, Contadina. I don't know what to expect."

"Are you afraid?"

Lorenzo laughed. "No," he said, "not yet. There'll be plenty of time for that later if I've bet wrong . . . Are you frightened, little sister?"

Ginevra's laugh sounded real. "Why should I be? Who would hurt one of God's fools? Particularly one as dirty as Tino. I have to get some new robes. I smell like a goat."

"Do you? That's excellent. No wonder the good captain stayed in his cabin so much. This nose of mine, you know, has blessings other than its beauty. I have no sense of smell at all. It makes Rome and Naples tolerable to me. You'll see what I mean tomorrow. It's nothing like Florence."

The galley dropped sail and entered the Bay of Naples with its banks of oars pulling in perfect unison. A flotilla of flag-fluttering smaller ships was waiting to escort it to its landing. On the bow of each of them trumpeters blew salutes and pages waved banners with the coats of arms of Ferrante and Lorenzo. It was a royal welcome.

Lorenzo raised his arm in reply to the salutes. He was wearing full court dress, the lucco set aside, the fleur-de-lis chain in prominent display. He looked calm, but his eyes were searching the ships' decks for familiar faces. He had friends in Naples, and he knew he would need them.

Ginevra was some distance away, standing with the three liveried guards. She barely noticed the welcome; she was thunderstruck by the panorama of the deeply curving bay. Its waters were the blue she had seen all week, but they were streaked and patched with other blues, turquoises, greens. The galley moved majestically over a field of jewels. Her eyes followed the waters to the shore where other colors clamored for attention: houses like slices of the rainbow, flowers, the costumes of the people crowded on the long broad quay. The sweeping curve of the shoreline led her gaze hypnotically to its farthest point and, beyond it, the mysterious smoking mountain of Vesuvius. She stared at the pale plume in wonder and fear, half-believing that Vulcan was at work in the earth beneath it.

The galley neared the land, and Ginevra inhaled ecstatically. Lorenzo must be mad, she thought. The odor of Naples is the perfume of its flowers. On December seventeenth it is Spring. How sad not to be able to smell it. Lorenzo. She held the word in her mouth, the taste as sweet as the perfume in her nostrils. With her face hidden by her hood, she feasted on the sight of him. How straight his back was, and how broad his shoulders. His hair gleamed as richly as his jeweled silk cap, and his legs in white silk hose were as strong as columns of Carrara marble.

He said he was glad to have me with him, she thought, and he put his arm tight around me.

Her heart was filled with a Spring even sweeter than the one before her eyes. All the poetry she had read without understanding flooded her soul, and it was rich with meaning, and its music sang in her heart.

The perfect happiness lasted until the galley stopped at the broad stone steps of the quay and Lorenzo leapt easily over them onto the dressed stone platform. He was immediately lost in a circle of smiling, talking, gesticulating people, and he embraced one after another, women as well as men, then walked away from the ship, never looking back.

Ginevra felt as if the sun had gone behind a cloud.

King Ferrante and his court lived in a bulbous brick castle overlooking the bay. He assigned a small palace opposite the castle to Lorenzo. A pompous chamberlain from the Neapolitan court led Lorenzo's small group of attendants there from the ship with an expression of disdain on his face. Only four, and one of them a rank, stumbling idiot. He assigned quarters; Ginevra was given a room near the chapel. The chamberlain sniffed ostentatiously at a clove-studded orange pomander whenever he came within five feet of her.

Ginevra suppressed the urge to giggle at the man's

dandified gestures; she also bit back the sharp words that came to her tongue. On the walk from the quay to the palace she had discovered what Lorenzo meant when he warned her about Naples. A wide paved avenue led to Ferrante's castle, but the streets on each side of it were morasses of mud that reeked of the garbage and slops thrown out of house windows. In comparison, she wanted to say, her unwashed monk's robe was positively fragrant.

She explored her room and then the palace. It was light and airy, with balconied windows on the seaside, and polychromed or gilded decorations of seashells, nymphs, porpoises, fish and fantastic vegetation in every room. The colorful frivolity of it made her spirits soar; it was impossible to believe in danger here. Behind the closed doors of her room, she whirled in a spontaneous merry dance. Even though her room was far away from Lorenzo's. Even though he had forgotten her as soon as he saw his friends. It was springtime and she was in love.

The following day Ginevra did not want to move from her bed. She had slept hardly at all. Too excited to rest at first, then kept awake by the turmoil in her heart and mind.

I have to make some sense of what has happened, she told herself. What does it mean to be in love? What should I do? What can I do? What does Lorenzo think of me, feel for me?

I know he cares for me . . . or does he? He brought me with him, said I was his luck . . . left me without even saying goodbye the minute we arrived.

As lovers have done throughout time, she examined every memory of every word, every look, every action of Lorenzo's, turning the incident in her mind to see every facet, trying to read significance into each gesture or intonation, searching for the meaning and message she longed to find.

Her emotions soared, then plunged, then rose again. I'm torturing myself, she thought, and I've got to stop. I'm just getting more and more confused.

But the torture was sweet, and she could not stop. She invented conversations between them, little dramas where she confessed her love to him and he was surprised, then overcome by the joyful realization that he loved her, too. Or where he admitted at once that he had always loved her but never hoped that she would return his feelings. Or where he said nothing, only swept her into his arms and . . . she could not complete the scene. Her shining dreamworld did not allow any memory of the touch of hands on her skin or the ugly, brutal lust of the men who had raped her.

She knelt by her window and looked at the stars that Lorenzo said they shared, and she prayed incoherently to them, to God, to all the saints, the Virgin and the Blessed Jesus, to the moon and the sea. Make him love me . . . not the way I love him, that's asking too much. Make him love me just a little . . . or if that's too much, make him let me love him.

She was still kneeling there when she finally fell asleep. The cries of hungry gulls woke her at sunrise. She moaned at the stiffness of her back and legs and twisted neck, staggered to her bed, fell across it, and dropped into a deep sleep.

It seemed to her that it was only seconds later that she heard the pounding on her door. But when she opened her eyes, glaring sunlight assaulted them, and she understood that it must be late.

"I'm coming," she called. "Just a minute." She pushed the hair back from her face and put on her redolent monk's robe.

She unbolted the door and jerked it open. "What do you want?"

The maidservant outside looked terrified and backed away, jabbering in an accent that Ginevra's tired mind could scarcely make sense of. She had to ask the woman to repeat herself three times before she understood. Then her fatigue and ill temper vanished. Hot water and a tub and fresh garments were waiting for her in the room the maid would lead her to. The Excellency, honored guest from Florence, had commanded them for his priest.

Lorenzo had not forgotten her.

* * *

An officer of Ferrante's guard escorted the three servants and holy fool from Florence on a tour of the castle before the midday meal. It turned Ginevra's world upside down.

The throne room, reception halls, banquet hall, ballrooms were immense, lavishly decorated and furnished. Exactly what a Neapolitan king should have, said Maurizio, one of Lorenzo's men. The other two laughed. Florentines, proud of the austere stone beauty of their city, considered the abundance of gilded cherubs comical.

The officer's face darkened. He decided to expand the tour.

"This is our King's favorite area of his castle," he said. He opened a thick wooden door and ushered the Florentines into the rooms beyond it.

Then began an hour of horror. The officer showed them the devices used for torture, many of them ingenious devices that the seasoned Medici guards had never heard of. Then he led them into a tremendous walled garden. Ginevra thought that the tour was over and congratulated herself on having maintained her composure.

Until she saw the first cage. It held a man, naked, gaunt, with filthy matted hair and beard. His eyes were crazed, and he made pitiable animallike cries, stretching his hands through the bars toward her.

"He thinks it's time to eat," the officer said with a laugh. "Usually people come to see the captives at feeding time. It's very amusing. Sometimes we throw them pieces of wood painted to look like meat or bread. This one will bite so hard that splinters fly."

"How many . . . ?" Maurizio pretended to be unaffected and mildly interested.

"It varies. Right now there are only four or five. We'll see them all. Follow me."

Ginevra thought that these must be Naples' insane. She was uneasy about her masquerade as an idiot. Guido, the guard who was entrusted with her care, worried about the same thing. After the third caged man was proudly exhibited by the officer, Guido asked if all of Naples' crazy men were kept in cages.

"Crazy?" the officer echoed. "They're not crazy when they get here. These are enemies of the King. They were all nobles once. He likes to see them beg to be released, then beg to be killed, then beg for food to stay alive. He wagers with his friends about how long it will take to break each one down."

The officer smiled at the visitors from Florence. He knew they were all imagining Lorenzo de' Medici in a cage. "Enough of the captive garden," he said. "It becomes boring."

They were glad to follow him along the ribbonlike clipped grass path, away from the cages.

He had accomplished his purpose, but he was enjoying himself too much to omit the climax of the tour.

Ginevra thought at first that the officer had made a mistake, that he had blundered into a reception. The elegant long room they entered was hung with rich tapestries; enormous vases of flowers sat on the deep window ledges; elaborately dressed men sat in gilded armchairs or stood all around the edges of the room.

Then she smelled the odor that the flowers failed to mask, and she gagged. "These are the King's most valued enemies," their guide said. "All men he admired, regarded as friends. When their friendship proved false, he had to execute them, naturally. But he didn't want to lose the pleasure of their company. By embalming them, he was able to keep them available any time he wants to talk to them . . . An excellent piece of work, don't you agree? You'd swear any one of them might move or speak any moment . . . Would you like to be introduced? We have three generals, two dukes, a number of counts . . ."

And this is the king that Lorenzo intends to reason with, to persuade to stop his war against Florence, Ginevra thought. At this very moment Lorenzo is probably with him, the mouse to Ferrante's cat.

She despised herself for worrying about anything so inconsequential as her own lovesick yearnings when Lorenzo was at the mercy of Ferrante, with nothing but his own wits for protection. In an instant she made the leap from self-centered romantic daydreams to a true recognition of Lorenzo as a man. Here was courage. And boldness. And statesmanship. Care of the State.

And I share his stars, she said proudly to herself. I must find some way to help. Surely the heavens will show me how.

Chapter Thirty-one

There was a sizable population of Tuscans in Naples.
The Medici bank had a branch there; so did several
smaller banks, wool traders, shipping firms, traders in
jewels and spices and wine. In addition, there were
wealthy Tuscans who preferred the more relaxed style
of living in the south and some who were addicted to
the sophisticated vices that flourished there.

Lorenzo was eagerly welcomed by them all. Invita-
tions flooded into the palace even before he arrived.

His closest friends, however, were not among his
countrymen. They were members of Ferrante's family.
Almost fifteen years earlier, when he was fifteen, he had
represented Florence on a diplomatic mission. He met
Ferrante's younger son Federigo when he landed at
Genoa and went with him to Milan to meet Ippolita, the
daughter of the Duke who was ruler at that time. Federigo then escorted Ippolita to Naples to marry his older
brother Alfonso, heir to the throne and Duke of Calabria. On the way to Naples the entire wedding party
were Lorenzo's guests in Florence for over a week.

The three young people were all about the same age;
they shared the enthusiasm and energy of youth. Also
more enduring traits. Federigo was a poet, as all educated young men were expected to be, and he was pas-
sionately interested in Lorenzo's fierce advocacy of
vernacular Italian as the best language for poetry. Ippolita was a brilliant young woman, fascinated by the ideas
of the Platonic Academy that Cosimo de' Medici had
started.

Strong friendships were born, and they grew stronger

over the years. Letters and manuscripts went back and forth between Florence and Naples with regularity.

Lorenzo had wondered how Ferrante's war might have affected his friends. The general of the army that threatened Florence was Alfonso, Federigo's brother and Ippolita's husband.

"Treaties and wars come and go, but poetry endures forever," Federigo said. "It is wonderful to repay your hospitality at last. I only hope we will enjoy ourselves as much in Naples as we did in Florence."

Ippolita said that she was determined that they would. Her smile suggested that she might offer Lorenzo hospitality of a kind that Federigo could not match.

Lorenzo had won his first gamble.

He found Ginevra in the chapel, praying fervently. "Come with me, Contadina. I want to show you a specialty of Naples." He had just left his friends, and he was in high spirits.

Ginevra had just returned from the ghoulish tour. She wanted to cry out a warning, beg him to flee from Ferrante. But she smiled and went with him. It would do no good to tell him what he already knew, and it was certain that he would never run away.

They went together to the cathedral to see the astonishing moving mechanical Christmas pageant. Life-size, lifelike figures of the Holy Family were grouped in the stable, with beautiful angels suspended above them and worshipful animals looking on. A slowly rotating track carried the shepherds and their sheep from behind a hill to the creche, then past it and into a grove of trees. As the shepherds vanished, the procession of the Three Kings appeared from behind the hill. Each king was accompanied by pages, knights, slaves. There were camels and elephants, zebras, horses of every color. Ginevra had never seen anything like it. She gaped at the beautifully crafted figures, at the clothing they wore, at the real hair on their heads, at their jewels and saddles and the gifts for the Christ Child.

When the last page glided into the wood, she looked at Lorenzo. He was as dazzled as she was. "I'd heard about these creches, but I didn't believe it. I have to get one for Florence."

"Oh, look, Lorenzo, it isn't over. There's a bagpiper."

"Yes. And a farmer with a scythe. His wife, too, leading a goat."

"That old woman behind her. She looks like Claudia at the farmhouse we stayed at when we rode out from Florence."

Dozens of men, women, children moved before them. They represented all classes, all occupations, all varieties of the people who lived in the region of Naples.

Lorenzo and Ginevra exclaimed at the naturalness of each one. It was art, a homely art, perhaps the only art not practiced in Florence. Lorenzo wished that his artist friends could see it, and his determination to have one increased.

The first shepherd appeared again. Ginevra sighed. "I could see it a hundred times."

"I wish we could, but I have so little time. I wanted to tell you that the stars are working for us, and you must not worry. Are you comfortable? Did they give you a pleasant room?"

"Yes. It's very nice. And I feel much better in my clean clothes. Thank you, it was very thoughtful of you to order them."

Lorenzo grinned. "Self-defense," he said. "I didn't want to be thrown out in the street." He became serious. "Listen closely, Ginevra. Everything we do or say is observed. Don't talk to the servants any more than you have to, and keep your door locked at night. You are a religious, remember, so it is important that you attend mass at least twice daily. You can come here with Guido as your guard as often as you like to look at the creche.

"I'll be busy, but I'll try to stop in the chapel at about sundown whenever I can. If you need to ask me for anything, look for me there.

"I hope my mission here will be completed in a week or two. Can you occupy yourself?"

Ginevra nodded. "I'll be fine. I can always find something to do."

"Good girl. Now we must hurry back." He kissed her quickly on both cheeks.

I won't think about that now, Ginevra vowed. I'll save it for tonight when I'm alone and frightened. But her cheeks were burning. She touched them with her fingers, marking the spot for later remembering.

Lorenzo was in a rage. "He wants peace, the bastard, and he knows full well that his throne is safer with Florence for an ally than with the Pope on his borders and ravenous for expansion. But he likes pulling the strings with his monstrous sausage fingers, seeing me dance like a marionette. Damn Ferrante."

Ginevra cautioned him to lower his voice. "There are bound to be spies listening outside the door, Lorenzo. You're supposed to be in the chapel for devotions, and I'm supposed to be an imbecile, not anybody who could understand the problems of diplomacy."

Two weeks had gone by, and Lorenzo was no nearer the end of his mission. The forced idleness was galling to him. He had filled his hours. He gave banquets for Naples' Tuscans, attended banquets given for him. He bought the freedom of the galley slaves who had transported him to Naples and contributed money for dowries to a dozen maidens selected by the Archbishop. He wrote letters to his family, his friends, the Signoria, the managers of his stables and villas, the professors at the University of Pisa. He read, wrote poetry, went hawking with Federigo, began a polished dalliance with Ippolita. But he was not accomplishing anything.

Ginevra's warning forced Lorenzo to concentrate on her instead of his anger. "Forgive me," he said quietly. "You're right. If I lose my temper I'm playing into Ferrante's hands. I'll think about more cheerful things. Tomorrow is our birthday, did you remember? What would you like for a gift?"

"Money." Her answer was immediate.

It offended Lorenzo. "Why not?" he said in a bitter, sharp voice. "That's what everyone else wants." He untied a heavy pouch from his belt and dropped it on the floor in front of Ginevra. The gold coins in it made a dull clanking sound.

She felt like Judas, as he intended, but she picked up the pouch with a simple, murmured "Thank you." She had a plan, and it required money. It was more important to her even than Lorenzo's disgust.

Chapter Thirty-two

She put her plan into action the next day. For more than a week she had been wandering around the castle, her gaze vacant, steps aimless, talk disjointed and punctuated with meaningless laughter and abrupt ravings about religion. Her masquerade invited suspicion at first, but it was so convincing that soon the castle servants and soldiers accepted it and began to enjoy the sport of mocking "Tino" with cruel jibes and insults. Tino did not understand, only smiled idiotically and clapped with pleasure at the attention. The game had grown boring, Tino an unimportant, unnoticed presence. Now Ginevra could begin.

She had identified Ferrante's valet Carlo, learned his habits, knew where he was likely to be found when he was at liberty. She was sure that it was fate; the valet was an inveterate and unlucky gambler. Ginevra put one of the gold coins in her mouth and walked near the corner of the stableyard where Carlo played dice with the Master of Horse and his head groom.

It was not difficult to allow them to discover her treasure and persuade her to play. The cheating was blatant, but Tino was too stupid to see it. Tino was also too dumb to be a cause for discretion. The three men talked freely, Carlo lording it over the others by his special knowledge of the king and his moods. Ferrante boasted to his valet, even confided in him.

Ginevra lost a florin almost every day. She told Lorenzo what she had learned every evening when they met in the chapel.

He was delighted and impressed by her audacity. "By all the saints, you are a marvel, Contadina! I'm glad you're on my side." The information she gleaned was often nerve-wracking. Ferrante was under constant pressure from his son to increase the army's strength and conquer Florence when the war resumed. The king was also a monster of vanity, and he was tempted by the vision of being the conqueror of Lorenzo de' Medici, of adding Lorenzo to his ghastly museum of embalmed figures.

But Federigo's pressure was also constant. Also Ippolita's. And Ferrante was shrewd, knew that Naples would be more secure if the Pope's ambitions were constrained, if Florence to the north and Naples to the south held Sixtus in check. The barrage of letters from Sixtus had an irascible, commanding tone that offended Ferrante's self-importance.

And so the king seesawed, temporized, toyed with Lorenzo, tested his patience. Weeks passed, became months.

While Ginevra served as Lorenzo's anchor and conspirator. She learned his complex, contradictory nature, his despondencies and elations, his impetuousness and iron control, his playfulness and sober sense of duty. Her respect and admiration for him grew, enriched the consuming love she felt. She was nourished by the intimacy of the shared danger, relived the whispered meetings in the chapel a hundred times in her memory. And she wept when she was alone in her room because she saw clearly that Lorenzo did not return her love, did not think of her as a woman at all. She was his partner in the dangerous enterprise, a companion, almost an equal.

We are friends, she told herself, and that's a lot. He trusts me, admires me, loves me with the love of a friend. I am lucky to have that. It is enough. It will have to be enough.

If only I weren't so tired. These masquerades are draining all the life out of me. I hate pretending all the time, watching every word I say, every blink of my eyes, eternally listening and trying to read what is behind what I hear. I hate playing the fool with the despicable Carlo and acting like a younger brother to Lorenzo.

I don't know if I can last it out until Ferrante lets us go. But I must.

At the end of February, after ten interminable weeks, Ferrante signed a treaty of peace and alliance with Florence.

"We did this, Contadina, you and I together. Now we can go home."

The ship for the return voyage was a trading vessel owned by a Florentine businessman in Naples. It was not luxurious, like Ferrante's galley, but the captain and crew were not in the pay of an enemy. Lorenzo could relax; so could Ginevra. Tino was left behind, forever. Except for the monk's robe disguise that Ginevra continued to wear.

There was no tension, no febrile gaiety. Both of them were exhausted and made lazy by the sense of a task completed, rest well earned. They walked the deck or sat comfortably on the stacked bales and barrels of the cargo, looking at the sea, breathing the sharp air, reveling in the limitless space around them after the caged atmosphere of Naples.

They talked sometimes, were more often silent, making no demands on themselves or each other. Lorenzo said idly that he wished Giuliano could have been with them. He would have loved the intrigue and the adventure.

"I don't think I ever met your brother," said Ginevra. "I know you miss him. How did he die? Was it the plague?"

Lorenzo told her about Giuliano's murder, her family's attempt to seize the State.

Ginevra was too shocked to say a word.

Hours later she was able to tell him how deeply sorry she was. "And despite what the Pazzi did to you, you and your mother took me in and cared for me. Why didn't you just let me die?"

"You were innocent. I never wanted the innocent to

be hurt. Hundreds were, but you were the only one who was brought to us. Besides, how could I celebrate my birthday without my contadina?''

The hours slipped away like sand through her fingers. Ginevra tried to hold on to them, to stay awake late into the night the way Lorenzo did, to keep the sun from setting and rising by sheer force of will. When they arrived in Livorno, she knew her time with Lorenzo would be over. She stared at him when he was writing or reading or sleeping, trying to memorize everything about his face, his body, his hands and feet, the way his hair swirled at the crown, the thin scar on his neck, the square shape of his nails.

''No!'' she cried when he told her they would dock the next morning. ''I love the sea so much,'' she added quickly.

''You'll have other sea journeys, I'll make sure of it. What else would you like, Ginevra? I owe you a great debt for your help in Naples.''

I want to stay with you, her heart said. But Ginevra remained silent, her eyes lowered to hide the tears.

Lorenzo forced her chin up. ''No shyness permitted,'' he laughed. ''It doesn't suit you. Now speak up. There must be something you want . . . What is it, Contadina? Are you crying? What's wrong?''

Ginevra tried to turn her head away, but his fingers were firm on her chin. His face was very near hers. ''Tell me,'' he said.

''I want to stay with you,'' she whispered.

Lorenzo released her and drew back as if he had been scalded. Ginevra knew somehow that other women, perhaps many women, had said those words to him before, had tried to hold him, tie him to them. She had ruined everything, even the way he would remember her.

''It's been such fun,'' she said, ''so exciting and so strange. Playing the holy fool, gambling with the dice, being a spy. I wish it would never end. Life will be so dull for me, while you'll be having more adventures all the time.''

Lorenzo believed her. It was evident in his face, in

the relaxation of his body. "I certainly hope you're wrong," he said, smiling. "I can do very well without another adventure like that one.

"Wipe your face, Ginevra, and stop sniffing. Let's see what we can think of to keep your life from being dull . . . My wise and wonderful mother wants me to find a husband for you. I'll have to look for a man who's slightly mad, I suppose. One who likes a steady diet of adventure. How about a sea captain? You could travel with him, virtually live on his ship."

"I don't intend to marry." She was angry now. He was going to dispose of the rest of her life as if she were one of the poor girls in Naples for whom he had given dowries; he'd buy her a husband as a reward, as a good-bye gift, as a souvenir of Naples.

"But of course you'll marry. That's what women do."

"I'm not a woman. What women do is have babies, and I'm barren."

Lorenzo tried to take her hand. "I know, Mamina told me, the fall you took . . ."

Ginevra pulled away from him, furious. "The fall I took be damned! I'm barren because of the way your soldiers raped me. I'll never let any man touch me because I'll never be able to forget. Look, Lorenzo." She pulled her robe open to bare her breasts. "See those marks? They're scars from the bites. And those others, here, the places where the links of their armor tore off the skin. You're a man. Would you like to have a wife who carried the marks of other men? Who had been used worse than any whore and then thrown away like refuse? What kind of degraded nothing of a man could you buy to be my husband?"

The swaying lantern above their heads was like a spotlight on Ginevra's horribly marked white skin. Lorenzo tried to look away from the scars, to deny the tragedy they evidenced. He dropped to his knees in front of her bench. "Let me cover you," he said. "My poor little contadina. I didn't know, I didn't know." His fingers lifted the folds of her robe and pulled them together without touching her.

Then his hands dropped, helpless, and he looked up to meet her dry, raging eyes. "I can't ask for forgiveness. Some things cannot be forgiven. I'll find out who they were, and I'll kill them."

Ginevra shook her head. "I don't want that. I only want to put it behind me." Her eyes were dull, rage spent. She put her hand on Lorenzo's head, a featherlight brushing. "I forgave you long ago. But I'll never be able to forgive you if you force me to marry."

"You have my word."

Ginevra closed her eyes and sighed. "Thank you," she said.

There were flags and music and cheering crowds to greet them in Livorno. News of the treaty had preceded them. The city councillors were waiting nervously, in full ceremonial dress. They bowed, bowed again, looked at Lorenzo as if he were a deity. "Magnificent," said their leader, "the city of Livorno welcomes her savior and pays humble homage and grateful tribute to the Republic." A group of white-clad boys presented a gold-fringed banner embroidered with the symbols of Livorno, Florence and the Medici.

Lorenzo delivered an eloquent extemporaneous speech of thanks for Livorno's welcome and for the mercy of God, who would not suffer the righteous to be defeated by the ungodly.

Ginevra covered her grin with her hand. Lorenzo had written the speech three days before and rehearsed it, using her as audience, to perfect the pauses and half-sentences that would make it seem impromptu.

Standing on deck, she could see over the crowd to the men in Medici livery behind the mob. They were holding lead ropes of three strings of horses, some saddled, others with heavy packs. The return to Florence would be more leisurely than the departure from it.

Lorenzo was making another speech, a flowery, flattering rejection of the invitation to a banquet of celebration. Ginevra ran down the gangplank. She wanted to be on horseback again, to ride like the wind, to express her elation in speed and wordless shouts. "You'll share all my adventures,'' Lorenzo had promised. ''You'll be as my brother, free from the restrictions of a woman's life, my companion and my friend. It will be a law if necessary.''

And he knew a river only a few hours away where he would teach her to swim.

Chapter Thirty-three

"Magnificent." "Magnificent." "Magnificent." Every town and village along the road was decorated with bright streamers and banners. Their squares were crowded with people waiting to see Lorenzo, present him with flowers and wine and cakes. Everywhere he was addressed with the title "Magnificent."

It was not an honor created for him. Throughout Italy grandiloquence was the normal mode of expression. In the Republic there were no titles of nobility and no official master or *signore*, so a man of wealth or power was called "Excellency," "Patron," "Highest," "Honored," "Illustrious." And "Magnificent." Lorenzo had been called by all of those honorifics before. But now, in some mysterious unplanned unanimity, he was "the Magnificent" throughout all Tuscany.

Ginevra teased him about it. She gathered some new-growth pliant branches from a laurel shrub and plaited a wreath. "Here," she said, setting it on his head. "A crown for your magnificent self; in future, I shall call you 'Lauro.' "

It was the Italian word for laurel; it was also an acceptable nickname for Lorenzo. Ginevra couldn't imagine why Lorenzo reacted so strangely. He turned pale, then his face flushed. He lifted the wreath off his head and held it in his hands for a long time. "I hope I have truly earned this," he said. He was looking at the symbol of victory.

Then he looked at her, smiling. "Thank you," he said, "for more than you know. I haven't heard that

247

name in years. It's what my grandfather used to call me when he was pleased with me.''

"Why are we turning off, Lorenzo? We're almost there. I can see the golden ball on the Duomo.''

"We'll stay the night here and enter tomorrow. I sent word to make it a holiday. It'll be a busy day, and I want to be rested . . . Also, Careggi is my heart's home, more than any other place. I want to see how my vines are.''

Ginevra understood at once why the villa named Careggi had such importance for Lorenzo. It was a small house, nestled in a grove of olive trees and surrounded by the homely buildings and fields of a working farm. It reminded her so strongly of La Vacchia that she felt weak. Careggi was a home in a way that the great city palace could never be.

After Lorenzo greeted each of the servants and listened attentively to their reports of conditions while he was away, he took Ginevra with him to the stables. When they neared the low building, he whistled. He was answered by a loud, prolonged neighing. His wide smile illuminated his face.

"Morello hasn't forgotten me,'' he said. "Come meet him.''

He caressed the big stallion and led him into the fenced stableyard. "No, you great brute, I don't have any sugar. You'll have to be happy to see me for my sweet self alone. Now pay attention to what I tell you. This is Ginevra. She can ride anything that runs, including you and all your nasty little tricks. I expect you to be friends.''

Ginevra held her palm under Morello's nose while he sniffed warily. Then, before he knew what was happening, she caught a handful of his mane and scrambled up onto his back.

Lorenzo stepped away and watched while horse and rider battled for control. Morello trembled all over, prepared to bolt; Ginevra spoke urgently to him with low-pitched sounds and tightened legs. In less than a minute, she had won.

"Brava, Contadina. I expected just that. He'll know you now . . . Morello, you've earned some sugar. Show Ginevra where we keep it."

She slid off the horse's back and, her hand on his neck, walked beside him to the latched cupboard. "He's a beauty," she said while she fed him. "I can hardly wait to ride him; I could feel the power in him."

Lorenzo nodded proudly. "He's the prize of my stable. No one rides him except me. And now you. And, before he died, Giuliano."

Ginevra stood very still, ignoring Morello's insistent nudges. "I'm honored," she said. The words were barely audible.

I don't want to fill a dead man's boots, she screamed internally. I want you to love me, as I am, not as a ghost come back. She looked at Lorenzo, bit her lip. If she could be with him, she wouldn't care about the reason for it. He'll forget Giuliano in time, she told herself. Then I'll be the one he wants. I mustn't destroy my happiness by making conditions for it.

"You must dress properly, Ginevra. The time of the monk's robe is over."

"But it was so comfortable. And easy."

"You don't need a disguise anymore. We're home now."

"Well I won't ride sidesaddle, and that's final."

"You will. We're making a ceremonial entry, and I won't have you shocking the city . . . What are you laughing about?"

"Don't you believe that everyone in Florence already knows all about me? Maurizio and Guido went on to the city yesterday. By now they've told all kinds of wild stories about their heroism, their exploits in Naples and the Magnificent's peculiar woman."

Lorenzo struck his forehead with the heel of his hand. "You're right of course." He began to laugh. "I suppose you're my mistress, a witch and a simpleton all in one. There are probably a hundred poets with epics to give to you and a half-dozen marble cutters frantically carving statues of you as Pallas Athena."

"Or a crowd waiting to stone me. I think I'll stay here until it's over and then go in quietly by myself."

In the end she persuaded Lorenzo that her idea was best. She entered Florence the same way she had left it, passing through the gate on foot, the hood of her robe pulled forward to hide her face. But this time she was not afraid. Or intent on revenge. All around, she heard the excited voices of Florence's people vying with each other to praise Lorenzo in the most elaborate superlatives. She drank in the words like strong wine, agreeing with every one of them.

It's very different from what Tino overheard in Naples, she thought happily. She could hardly wait to tell Lorenzo.

The gate to the garden was guarded but ajar. For me, thought Ginevra. She smiled at the sentinel, not caring that he could not see it.

One of the maids was waiting inside the gate. "Madonna Lucrezia asks if you will join her," she said. She was trying not to stare. "Oh yes," she added, "she is in your bedroom."

The courtyard was crowded with well-wishers who wanted to see Lorenzo. Ginevra edged along the outer walls in the shadows, feeling more like a spy than she ever had felt in Naples. She was giggling when she darted through the door to her room.

Lucrezia walked across the floor, her arms extended. "Welcome home, my child."

Ginevra inhaled the gentle fragrance of Lucrezia's hair and skin, felt her warm hug. "I'm so happy to be back," she said. "I'm sorry I left without telling you."

"Hush," said Lucrezia. She held Ginevra away from her, her smooth hands pale against the brown robe, and kissed both cheeks. "Lorenzo sent word, so I had only one day to wonder. Now let me look at you. Brown and healthy with good color and bright eyes. The sea was a tonic for you."

"Oh, yes. I loved it. Everything was a tonic, Madonna Lucrezia. I have so much to tell you."

Lucrezia nodded. "I know. Lorenzo was all but incoherent with all the stories of your adventures. He was loud in your praises, Ginevra. You were a godsend to him.

"I have a tray with cakes and wine. We can celebrate your safe return . . . Will you do me a favor first?"

"Anything."

"Thank you, my dear. I'd be more comfortable if you discarded your costume. Your things are laid out on the bed. I'll look at the paintings while you change. I'm very fond of them and see them too seldom. Let me know when you're ready for me to tie your back laces."

The clothes were all new, a chemise of satiny white silk, pink silk gamurra, and cioppa of heavy white watered silk embroidered in full-blown pink roses and lined with velvet in the tender green of the flowers' leaves. There were hose, too, of white silk, and green velvet slippers.

Ginevra was enchanted by the delicate beauty of Lucrezia's gift. But the clothes seemed to be more a disguise than Tino's robes had been. Her skin was browned by the sun and wind, her body hard and muscular. Her picture of herself was as an adventurer, not a pink and white maiden.

Still, she could not offend Lucrezia. She pulled off her boots, discarded her other garments on top of them on the floor, and put on the chemise and gamurra. They felt strange, chilly against her skin, awkwardly close-fitting when she turned toward Lucrezia.

"I'm ready now."

Lucrezia adjusted the laces with nimble fingers. "Some cut lemons will whiten your skin," she said. "I'll tell the kitchen to prepare some."

Ginevra stiffened. "Madonna Lucrezia, I've talked to Lorenzo. It's all agreed, all planned. I'm not going to live the way a woman does, indoors and in silk . . ."

Lucrezia interrupted, "I know all about that. Lorenzo told me . . . There. The lacing's done . . . Come sit with me, Ginevra, and let me talk to you."

Ginevra wanted to run, to find Lorenzo, to laugh with him about the foolishness of Tino in pink silk. She was afraid to hear what Lucrezia was about to say, that Lorenzo had regretted his promise to her, had gone back on it, abandoned her to a life of domestic imprisonment in a convenient marriage.

But Lucrezia was holding her hand, leading her to a table with her favorite almond cakes on it and a cushioned bench beside it.

"Dearest child," Lucrezia began. "I think of you as a daughter of mine, and I love you, Ginevra. I beg you to believe that. The first time I saw you, you were a tiny, frightened little creature, and I wanted to take you in my arms and comfort you. I feel the same way now.

"I can imagine many of your emotions . . . anger, confusion, fear. Even the thrill of what you accomplished in Naples and how you did it.

"But my dear, you cannot live the rest of your life as a masquerade. You are a woman, with a woman's heart and a woman's needs. You should have a home and a husband to take care of you."

Ginevra jerked her hand from Lucrezia's soft clasp. "I won't marry. I won't. I want to be free."

"None of us is free, Ginevra, not women and not men either, no matter how it may appear to you. There is the world around us, and its rules confine us all. What you want is to act like a man. No, not a man, a carefree boy. That's impossible, unnatural. You are not a boy; you'll never be one; God made you a woman. If you tried to live a boy's life, you'd be like one of those mythical combined creatures, with the head of one animal on the body of another. A monstrous thing. It cannot be."

Ginevra looked away from Lucrezia's caring expression, desperate to escape the trap of her wisdom and love. The walls of the room seemed to be closing in on her, the air stifling. She wanted to put her hands over her ears or across Lucrezia's mouth so that she wouldn't have to hear any more.

". . . more sensible," Lucrezia was saying. "He's always been impetuous. And imperious too, sometimes. But you can see reason, your mind is more disciplined, less carried away by enthusiasms."

Ginevra clutched Lucrezia's arm. "Are you saying that Lorenzo doesn't agree with you?"

"No. He doesn't. He simply set that granite jaw of his and said something about a promise."

Ginevra threw her arms around Lucrezia's neck and kissed her cheek again and again, laughing, crying, gasping. "He's not going to leave me."

Lucrezia held her, stroking her back and her hair.

When Ginevra's uncontrolled outburst was over, Lucrezia brushed away her tears with gentle fingers. "Dearest daughter, do you love him so much?"

Ginevra tried frantically to recover, to deny anything other than a longing for freedom and adventure.

But she could not lie to Lucrezia.

"You won't tell him?" she said at last. "Please, Madonna, I beg you. Promise you won't tell him."

Lucrezia's eyes glistened with tears. "Oh no, my child, I won't betray you. Not that way. But if I encourage this insane wish of yours to live a man's life, it will be another kind of betrayal. I cannot believe you'll find happiness, Ginevra. And if you begin, there'll be no going back. You'll be outcast from the normal world."

"I don't care. I don't want to go back. I only want what I've had these past months. I was so alive, so happy. Beyond any happiness I ever knew or ever dreamed of."

"Because of Lorenzo?"

"Yes, but not only that. I felt the life in me even before I loved him."

Lucrezia bowed her head. "I have nothing to say, then. You see, Ginevra, I'm torn. I'm afraid for you. But I fear for my son, too. He has lost his faith in people; he trusts no one because he once trusted too much and Giuliano paid with his life for it."

"He trusts you."

"Yes, of course. The family is different. But he has abandoned his friends, he has become distant. Careful. You've earned his confidence; he's not afraid to be relaxed with you. I hope he'll regain his old ways with his friends through his easiness with you.

"And I want so much for him to have that. He needs it . . . Using you as a bridge to his friends, it's a poor bargain for you, Ginevra. You know he doesn't see you as a woman."

"I know. I don't care. That's not what I want."

Lucrezia shook her head slowly. "I don't understand." She looked at Ginevra and smiled, her eyes overflowing. "But you have my blessing, my child, and my gratitude. I believe you'll bring happiness to Lorenzo. I pray you don't break your heart doing so."

Ginevra kissed Lucrezia's hands. Her sunbrowned face glowed. "Thank you, Madonna. I promise you, everything will be wonderful. I want to tell Lorenzo about my walk through the city. Where is he?"

"He's in the grand salone with the children and Clarice unpacking the presents he brought from Naples. Come. We'll go up together."

Ginevra sat as still as stone. Of course, he'd want to see his wife and children, she told herself. Until that moment, they had not been real to her. She forced herself to move, to speak. "I must finish dressing. I'll be up soon." She ran to the bed and picked up the thin silk hose. When Lucrezia was gone, she held them against her breast as if to hide the hurt in her heart.

Chapter Thirty-four

Ginevra hated Clarice on sight. She hated the older woman's arrogant sneer when Lucrezia introduced Ginevra to her; she hated the irritated complaints from Clarice that Lorenzo was encouraging the children to misbehave; she hated the way Clarice drew the folds of her cioppa away from her children.

The children were overwhelming. So many of them—eight—and so boisterous. All of them were shouting; even the baby Giuliano, only six months old, howled in his cradle. They climbed all over Lorenzo, pulled at his clothes and his hair, demanded rides on his shoulders or his back, yelled for his attention, "Look at me. Look at me."

Ginevra thought she'd have to ask Lucrezia to identify them for her. Except Giulio. Her first love, even though the time with him had been so short. She recognized him immediately. He was more than a year older, as noisy as the others and as active, but the sturdy little legs that he walked on were still as fat and dimpled as they had been, and his nose was the same button in his pink round face.

Lorenzo saw Ginevra standing near Lucrezia's chair and shouted louder than the children, demanding silence. Except for uncontrollable giggles, they obeyed. He presented them, one by one, with solemn-toned introductions that made the children giggle even more.

"My elderly daughter Lucrezia, who is ten years old and who thinks we're very silly . . . Piero, almost eight and thinks he's twenty . . . Maddalena, seven very soon if she doesn't burst from eating too much candy . . .

Giovanni, five, and the despair of his tutor . . . Luisa, already the most beautiful woman in Florence at the age of three . . . Contessina, almost two and a superlative dancer . . . Giulio, the best singer of the lot . . . and Giuliano, who has the good sense to be fast asleep on his pillow.

"Behave yourselves this once in your wicked lives and say hello to Ginevra. I told you all about her. She helped me row the ship all the way to Naples."

The children crowded around Ginevra, the older ones asking to see her monk's robe . . . please, would she show how she made faces like an idiot . . . was it true that she climbed to the top of the mast on the ship . . . could she really ride Morello without being thrown . . . The younger children simply stared, Giulio with his thumb in his mouth.

"They'll pester the life out of you if you let them," Clarice said after the children were herded away by the nursemaids, under protest. "Lorenzo indulges them outrageously."

"I spoil everyone outrageously," Lorenzo said. "Now that the army's gone, it's safe to bring out the rest of the gifts." He opened a cassone and took out a velvet-covered, flat square box. "To celebrate peace," he said. With a kiss on her cheek, he placed the box in Clarice's lap.

"And for Mamina," he said, lifting an armful of lace.

"Lorenzo! How beautiful." Lucrezia held up her face for her son's kiss.

"Thank you, Lorenzo," said Clarice. She held the necklace of huge pearls up against the light to gauge their luster.

Lorenzo was reaching into the chest again. He looked up and smiled at his wife. "I watched the boys diving for pearls. They must have even bigger lungs than our children." He pulled out a large wad of quilted silk. "And this is a souvenir for Lorenzo." He carefully unwound the wrappings to reveal a vase carved from rose-colored jasper.

He caressed the smooth stone with loving fingers. "It was worth making the voyage just to find this," he said.

"I'll have it mounted on silver, with designs of shells and porpoises to remind me of Naples."

He gestured to Ginevra. "The rest is for you, Contadina. I'm too tired from wrestling with the young to unpack it for you."

She ran to him. The cassone contained many more objects wrapped in padding. Ginevra was almost afraid to touch them. Her hands were trembling so much that she was sure she'd drop the first one she picked up. She knelt, holding on to the open chest.

Lucrezia came and knelt beside her. "I adore presents," she said. "Let me help you."

Ginevra's souvenir was a collection of figures to make a manger scene. They were about one fifth the size of the moving figures in the Naples cathedral, the shepherds being a foot tall. But the detail of the carving was as fine, and the costumes. Lucrezia and Ginevra exclaimed over each sleeve, each pair of boots, each lace collar or tiny sewn-on jewel. Clarice joined them, as fascinated as they were.

Lorenzo left. "At the pace you're going, you'll unwrap the last piece just in time for Christmas," he said. "I have people to see."

"I forgot to thank him," Ginevra said later. "How awful. I was so engrossed . . ."

Lucrezia laughed. "There's no higher tribute to a gift. Lorenzo was suitably thanked by our absorption. I'm quite sure he spent just as long choosing them, or he wouldn't have been able to leave."

He admitted as much when Ginevra thanked him later that day. "I'll tell you all about the figures another time," he added. "I have special plans for them." There was no opportunity to ask what the plans were. Lucrezia took Ginevra away.

"I want you at my side when the family arrives. That way I can be sure you meet everyone." Lorenzo was attending a banquet in his honor with the Signoria that evening, but the family came first.

And they all seemed to come at the same moment. Ginevra lost all hope of remembering names and faces within three minutes. Lorenzo's sisters, their husbands and older children, an uncle she didn't know existed, his young cousins, the extended family who lived at the palace or had ever lived there, the new priest for the palace chapel and the Medici's astrologer, Lorenzo's former tutors and the managers of the family bank, wool business, shipping firm . . .

She did not realize until she was in bed that night that the stout woman who had hugged and kissed her was Lorenzo's sister Bianca de' Pazzi. The last time she had seen Bianca was at the Pazzi family gathering before the procession and Scoppio. Gone, Ginevra thought, all gone . . . She fell asleep at last, exhausted from weeping.

In the weeks that followed Ginevra became part of the family at the palace. Lucrezia was the mother she had always longed for. Clarice was like a distant, uninterested older sister. Most important, Lorenzo lived up to the promise he had given her with such energy and effectiveness that she felt as if she were caught up in a whirlwind.

He took her along on his tour of the Medici farms and villas, and she relived the thrill of riding through unknown country, free to test the power of her horse in exhilarating gallops on unfamiliar roads.

At the country houses she regained fluency in the dialect of the contado and learned the folk songs that Lorenzo maintained were the genuine poetry of the Tuscan people. She shocked the farmers and amused Lorenzo by trying to learn to play the bagpipes that were traditionally reserved for shepherds. "You could sing and make exactly the same horrible squeal," he said.

"You could sing and have all the donkeys follow you home," she riposted.

They had a mirthful, carefree time together.

Back in the city, Lorenzo took Ginevra to the Medici bank and gave instructions that her signature was sufficient authorization for the delivery of any money she requested. Then he led her into the nearby house of a notary.

"What are we doing here?" Ginevra asked.

"Signing some papers. I'm transferring La Vacchia to you. It's a place you know, and with good management it will deliver a good income. If you want freedom, Contadina, you must have your own money. Take what you want from the bank as long as you need it, but build your estate, too."

There was no need for him to say more. She did not have the supportive web of family ties to fall back on. Her family was dead. And the Medici were not really her family, no matter how much she felt that the palace was home. If anything happened to Lorenzo . . . She refused to think about it, pretended there was nothing unusual about the armed guards that accompanied them on the city streets.

She signed the documents with a flourish. "There. That's my new name." The notary's eyes gleamed.

"That will require additional documents, Magnificent," he said to Lorenzo. "And, of course, the customary fee for executing a change of name."

Lorenzo smiled and shrugged. "Talk to the lady. She conducts her own business; she'll give you a draft on her bank."

When they left the notary's house, Lorenzo bowed to Ginevra. "So Ginevra di Antonio della Vacchia, would you like to use your new title at the workshop of an old friend? I'm going to see Andrea del Verrocchio."

"I'd like that very much, Lorenzo di Piero de' Medici. I really would. I was sorry when my music lessons ended and I stopped going there."

Verrocchio's studio was in a pandemonium. "Hello!" Lorenzo shouted. "Andrea, what's going on?"

Andrea's face lit up when he saw his visitor. He threw down his armload of long paper rolls and rushed toward the arrivals. His steps slowed when he was halfway there. "I'm glad to see you and congratulate you on your success, Excellency."

Lorenzo struck Verrocchio in the chest with his fist. Not an angry blow, but strong enough to make the artist totter. He then caught his unsteady friend in his arms and embraced him. "That's what you deserve for your chilly welcome," Lorenzo said. "Is our friendship dead, you buffoon?"

Verrocchio's laughter was joyful. "I would flatten your nose as proof of my affection, but the good Lord was there before me. How are you, Lorenzo? I've missed your beauty all these months. I had no model for the goblins in my paintings."

He put his arm around Lorenzo's shoulders and pushed him toward the door. "Come. Let's go outside away from the noise so we can talk. I'll have one of the apprentices bring us a bottle of wine . . . What? Who is this?" He stopped in front of Ginevra. "All Florence is talking about Tino. Is this he? She? Is it really the same Ginevra who used to grind colors for me when she had finished tormenting da Vinci? Do you drink, little hero? I want to hear all about your superb hoax on Ferrante."

Lorenzo edged Andrea and Ginevra through the wide doors. "You can hear nothing," he shouted, "even if she tells you. First because of the racket inside and second because you never stop talking. Use your voice to order the wine and then give us a minute's peace." His eyes were dancing. He had missed exchanging insults with Andrea.

They sat on the stone steps that led from the end of the street down to the Arno, dipping up water to mix with the wine and talking. Lorenzo's guards made a human wall at the top of the stairs.

Ginevra spoke seldom. She was content to listen to the men, hear the happiness in Lorenzo's voice. She watched the current, full and rushing with spring's flood.

At other sets of steps, and on the stone jetties that ran out into the river, men were washing wool. Lengths of it stretched from their hands into the water, pulled and scoured by the river. The pieces that had already been dyed released their excess color in streaks of red, green, brown, blue, yellow. They were like ribbons, fading as they moved, making new colors where they merged, becoming tinted bubbles when the currents swirled and foamed.

Ginevra was entranced, hypnotized. She barely heard Verrocchio's goodbye. Lorenzo nudged her to attention. "Goodbye, Maestro," she said. "Tell Leonardo I send my greetings."

"I'll tell him. You must come again and make some music for us. We haven't forgotten you."

"Thank you. I'd like to." She waved until Andrea disappeared around the corner.

"I like him," she said to Lorenzo. "I'd like to come again."

Lorenzo agreed. "He is a good man. If I lost his friendship, I'd be impoverished. This war with Naples and Rome cost me dearer than I knew. I have lost touch with so many of the people who mean most to me. Did you see Andrea? He was formal, distant. I didn't realize how much time went by when I saw no one but generals and politicians. Andrea reminded me. I've been missing the best part of my life, my friendships.

"There's still time to go see Botticelli before my next conference. He hardly stayed five minutes at the family party. Come on, Contadina."

Lorenzo stood, then staggered.

Above him, the guards stepped forward, but he waved them back. He put his hand on Ginevra's shoulder for support.

"What is it? Are you hurt?" She was terrified.

"Don't be a Tino. It's nothing. The dampness by the river made my legs a little stiff, that's all. Help me up the steps; then I'll be myself."

Lorenzo talked quietly and without effort as they walked. "Did you hear what Andrea said? The hubbub at the studio is because he's moving. His guild has granted him the lease on the workshop behind the Duomo that once was Donatello's. He's in a fever of excitement and pride. I'm sure he thinks that the dust in the walls will make his work as great as the Master's. He apprenticed with Donato.

"I've made him swear to let me have the first sculpture he does there. Maybe a fountain for Careggi. What do you think? The garden in front of the villa is looking overgrown and shabby. I might get Andrea to make a new plan, with his fountain as the center.''

Ginevra suggested a Saint Francis. "Then when the birds come to drink, they would be like part of the sculpture.''

But Lorenzo didn't seem to hear her. He was still talking, almost to himself. "It's not only my friends . . . I've lost touch with the city. Everyone must know that Andrea is moving, but I didn't. I used to know everything that was happening. Before . . . this.'' His eyes flickered from side to side, glancing at the guards.

"I'll have to let them go. I can't be cut off from Florence.''

He concentrated on Ginevra again. "So, Contadina, what do you think about Andrea's fountain?''

He listened attentively, talked with enthusiasm about the varieties of birds he had seen in the garden and the others that might be attracted if he planted more shrubs with berries. He was, as he had said he would be, himself.

But Ginevra's perceptions were sharpened by love. She saw that there was the slightest limp in his left leg.

And no more was said about going to see Sandro Botticelli before returning to the palace.

Ginevra told Lucrezia about the incident on the steps. "I was afraid he was going to fall. And then he was almost limping. Do you think he should see a doctor? I'm worried.''

Lucrezia's gentle face looked grim. And old. "There'll be no doctors if I can help it,'' she said. "I've been waiting for this and praying it would not come. It's the gout, Ginevra, the Medici curse.''

She looked at her hands, discovered that they were twisting together, made them relax. "Don't say anything to Lorenzo or to anyone else. I'm going to make him take the baths. That will help. I'll tell him that I need to see my investment at Morba; that has the advantage of truth. Who knows what may have happened

during this absurd war, when I couldn't get there myself? I'll ask for his advice. Men always like that.

"Thank you, my dear, for telling me . . . But, of
course, you didn't. Do you know what I mean?"

"Yes. Of course, Madonna. Remember, I'm an old
hand at conspiracy and playing dumb."

Chapter Thirty-five

Lucrezia and Lorenzo were away for two weeks. It seemed much longer to Ginevra.

At first, the minutes dragged because she was shut up in her room, wallowing in self-pity. Why wasn't I asked to go? she moaned to herself. Madonna Lucrezia knows how much it would mean to me, even if Lorenzo doesn't. I had a right to go. I was the one who saw that he was in pain. He leaned on me when he was hurt. I should be with him.

The thought of Lorenzo suffering made her suffer. She even felt her leg becoming stiff as if she could take away his affliction and bear it for him. She yearned after him, imagining him riding, hunting, jolting his leg on the rough road, and she was anguished by her inability to help, by the idea of his pain.

Gradually her image of Lorenzo on horseback slid from imagination to memory, and she saw his broad back ahead of her, as she had seen it so many times. She watched the supple shifting of his shoulders as he adjusted to the motion of the horse, the sudden crouch when he urged it from a walk to a gallop, the light, then shadow, then light, shadow, light as he rode beneath the trees in the olive groves at the farms they had visited . . .

Then the meals around the tables in the farm kitchens, and the songs, and Lorenzo's face warmed by firelight and contentment.

Ginevra turned over her memories one by one, counting her wealth. And her heart raced along the road to Morba crying don't leave me, I need to be with you.

She heard the cry in her mind, and it was like cold water thrown on her face.

You must not say that, she told herself; you mustn't even think it, or you will lose him. You saw it on the ship, when he asked what you wanted and you said you wanted to stay with him. He was repulsed.

And why shouldn't he be? It's parasitic, that kind of demand. Draining. Sucking the life from him to sustain your own.

She looked around the room, remembering, and she told herself that she had conquered the weakness of her injured body by discipline and determination. She would conquer her emotions the same way.

After that, time did not drag. She was so busy that there were not enough hours in the day.

She asked one of the stewards to escort her while she did some shopping. Women did not go into the streets unescorted. Not women of her class. She went to the bank, then the Mercato, joined the crowds of bargainers around the booths selling used clothing, was escorted back to the palace with a mound of lumpy parcels that the steward was obviously embarrassed to carry. And after that, she no longer had to have an escort.

She had bought a patched and mended thin wool gamurra and unornamented cioppa, the kind of clothes worn by working-class women, who were not expected to obey the rules of palace-bred ladies.

She had also bought a secondhand lucco, the ankle-length men's garment that Lorenzo preferred. It was customary for students to wear them, too, although theirs were never made of fine materials like Lorenzo's. Ginevra put on the one she had bought. It was more like fifthhand than secondhand, she decided, laughing. She could go wherever she liked now. She had two disguises, not one, as in Naples. She was making progress.

She opened the other parcels, put away the apron and darned hose, put on the *cappuccio,* the student's hat, and the worn boots. Her hair was still short, no longer than most men's. Ginevra clapped her hands, applauding her own cleverness.

She could make the city her own, learn its streets and

neighborhoods, listen to its people, be Lorenzo's eyes and ears, make him a gift of what he had lost when the guards surrounded him.

Florence fascinated her. She had seen so very little of it when she was growing up; she was astonished by the size and diversity, excited by the life in the streets, amused and infuriated by the gossip she heard on all sides.

She was scandalous, people said. And courageous . . . idiotic . . . pathetic . . . ridiculous . . . brilliant . . . simple . . . romantic . . . brazen . . . tragic . . . outrageous. To her surprise, everyone knew that she had been near death from her injuries and that the official version of her accident was a lie. The speculation about what had really happened often came very near the truth. The consensus was that she had suffered so much that she had become slightly mad. That accounted for her reckless bolt to Naples and her success in posing as a fool. It also allowed almost any aberration of behavior now.

Ginevra was delighted to learn that.

What she heard about Lorenzo made her want to mount a platform and lecture the Florentines about their ingratitude. They were all complaining that he had not pressed King Ferrante hard enough, that the peace treaty was too hard on Florence. Naples should have paid for peace, they said. Instead, taxes were higher, because the armies had to be paid and there was an annual indemnity to pay Ferrante's son, Alfonso, who still held Siena, only forty miles to the south. Lorenzo should have made the Pope bend his knee, too. It was not enough that Sixtus recognized the peace and had withdrawn his army. The captured towns had not been returned to the Republic. And Sixtus had not withdrawn the excommunication he had proclaimed. All in all, Lorenzo had not done as well as he should have.

At the same time, people said, he had done better than any other leader could have done. He was the bravest man in all Italy. And he had brought peace back to the Republic, with reopened trade routes, the crops and farmhouses safe from war's destruction, renewed prosperity for all. He was the Magnificent, and he was theirs. Only Florence was great enough to deserve him.

Ginevra spent most of her days learning Florence, but not all. She went several times to La Vacchia.

The first time it took all the self-discipline she could summon to enter the villa's grounds, and she almost turned back three times on the road up from the gates to the top of the hill where the house sat. She forced her mind to concentrate on the condition of the olive trees that bordered the road. They needed pruning; she'd have harsh words with the manager Lorenzo had hired.

He came out of the house when he heard her knock. Ginevra turned her eyes away from the shadows in the entrance hall beyond the open door and attacked the manager's inadequacies with such heat that he rushed off to begin immediately to improve his care of the property.

Then she went inside to confront her memories and exorcise her ghosts.

After that, it became easier each time she went to the villa. She could recall the good times, recapture her pleasure in the garden and the enchanting story plaques that della Robbia had made, shut out the bloodstained conclusion of her life at La Vacchia. Her life was no longer here; it was with Lorenzo. La Vacchia would be beautiful and productive again, she'd see to that, but it would never be her real home.

Her home and her family were at the Medici palace.

In the evenings, Ginevra got to know the children. Lorenzo had made her a heroine in their eyes, and they shouted their pleasure every time she appeared.

Agnolo Poliziano scowled. "I'm tutor to Piero and Giovanni," he said through thin, disapproving lips. "I cannot allow their study hours to be disrupted."

Ginevra was crushed. Agnolo, she knew, was Lorenzo's closest friend. On the trip to Naples Lorenzo had spoken so often and so fondly about Poliziano that she liked him long before she met him. She had read his poetry, too, in the library at the palace, and she wanted to tell him how much she admired it. She expected that they would be friends.

Agnolo was cold and rude.

Ginevra found the explanation. He's jealous, she thought, because Lorenzo is closer to me than to him. How childish of him and how silly. If you truly care about someone, you want him to be happy. And you love the people who make him happy; you don't hate them for doing it.

I'm certainly glad that I'm not as small and selfish and petty as Agnolo is, she thought smugly.

Her self-righteous, swollen vanity was ripe for puncturing. The deflation came only a few days after Lorenzo's return.

"How well you look! Welcome home."

"Thank you, Contadina. I feel rejuvenated. Mamina's baths are everything she promised. Including the exorbitant fees. She's the best businessman in the family . . . Now, my dear Ginevra, talking of how people look, what is that disgusting rag that you're wearing?"

Ginevra doffed her hat and swept it in an arc before her as she bowed. "A lowly student at your service, Magnificent. Oh, Lorenzo, I have been having such a wonderful time. I feel like a real Florentine at last. Let me tell you what I've heard . . ."

He was amused, then pleased and finally interested. "Wait, Ginevra. I want Mamina to hear all this. Information is what we've been lacking before she could help me with my plans."

Thus Ginevra became the third member of the Medici inner circle.

Lucrezia had to hold back her disapproval of Ginevra's wanderings; the information was too valuable and the girl's pleasure too important. Ginevra needed to build a life apart from Lorenzo, Lucrezia believed. She did not, however, have to dress like a tramp to do it. "Wear the lucco if you must, but have a decent one made."

Chapter Thirty-six

"This is my student friend Tino," Lorenzo said when he took Ginevra to Sandro Botticelli's studio. Sandro and his apprentice Filippino were loud in their praise when Lorenzo explained Ginevra's costume. "Think of it. She can go anywhere in Florence, something no woman has ever done. I half expect her to be elected a prior one of these days."

Sandro's compliments made Ginevra flush with pleasure. So did the more restrained approval of the younger painter Ghirlandaio, whom Lorenzo visited next.

Best of all was when Lorenzo playfully suggested they test her disguise by stopping in a tavern. She took him up on it, wheedled him into actually doing it.

Later she said that the *Sandracca* was so dark that she could have walked in naked and no one would have known she was a woman.

"I should never have agreed to go in," Lorenzo said. "Your mind has been thoroughly tainted by Gigi."

Luigi Pulci had been in *Sandracca* and spent the hour with them. As usual, he was superbly witty. Also as usual, his humor was ribald. Lorenzo could do nothing to protect Ginevra's feminine sensibilities without giving the masquerade away. She found his discomfort even funnier than Gigi's poems.

"Don't be so squeamish," she told Lorenzo. "I hear much saltier stories in the streets. They're just not as amusing." In fact, at first the boasts men made about their conquests and virility had horrified her, made her remember the soldiers at La Vacchia. But then she overheard women talking, too. With equal lustiness. And she had come to the conclusion that her own revulsion had best be kept private; other people were different.

"Ginevra," Lorenzo said, "you are a perpetual surprise and treasure." She held the words in her mind like a gift of pearls. "But no jokes now," he added. "We're going to see an elderly sculptor who would be insulted to be fooled. You'll be Ginevra the eccentric, not Tino the masquerader."

"I'll behave. Who is he?"

"His name is Bertoldo. He worked with Donatello and never left him. He's a humble man; he said that he'd give more to art by polishing Donatello's bronzes than by anything he could make himself. I inherited him from my grandfather. Cosimo was Donato's patron; I take care of Donato's assistant. Old Bertoldo learned contempt for money from his master, so he doesn't make it easy for me. I can't just give him what he needs; I have to find work for him to do. I'm hoping that the manger we saw in Naples will be the answer. If he will copy your little figures in life size, it will occupy him for years."

But Bertoldo said no. He was insulted. "Copy some Neapolitan confection? I, who worked with the great Donatello? Go away, boy, and commission a toy-maker. I don't want your money. I do very well with my students. There are still some in this world with a respect for the standards of real art. They come to me to learn."

Lorenzo made the best exit he could. When the old man's pitiful lodgings were behind them, he stopped and laughed. "Did you hear him call me 'boy'? I feel lucky he didn't cane me. He must terrify those students, if they exist."

"What will you do . . . boy?"

"I'll stick your head in that fountain, hat and all, if you don't show me proper respect. And I'll come up with something for Bertoldo.

"Maybe Andrea will have an idea. Let's go visit the new studio."

Verrocchio's noisy joviality was the perfect antidote to the old sculptor's sourness. "Come in, man," he bellowed. "I've just been thinking about Carnival. We haven't much time to find a theme. What about Pallas and the Centaur for the float? We can make the beast with Ferrante's bloated face.''

''And let my friend here be Pallas, if she ever wears a dress again.'' Lorenzo put his arm around Ginevra's waist.

''What is this?'' Andrea leaned close to peer under her hat. ''Not a student. She looks too intelligent. I wouldn't be fooled for a minute.''

''Gigi was.''

''Surely you lie. Not Gigi. Tell me all. When? Where? What did he say?'' Verrocchio stamped his feet with glee.

Ginevra was certain that she had never been so happy. She was accepted, liked, one of Lorenzo's group, the closest to him of any of them.

That evening she joined the men at Lorenzo's table instead of eating with Lucrezia and Clarice. Lorenzo seated her at his right hand.

Agnolo Poliziano said hardly a word. Ginevra paid no attention.

The following morning she had to pay attention. ''You will meet the most important people in my life,'' Lorenzo said when he invited her to accompany him to Fiesole.

They went to a small house, no bigger than the smallest farmer's house at La Vacchia. Ginevra wondered if Lorenzo was joking. But his face was eager with anticipation.

Three men came out of the door at the sound of the horses. One was wearing the robes of a bishop. Lorenzo jumped down and ran to kneel on the ground in front of him.

The bishop made the sign of the cross on his forehead. ''Blessings, Lorenzo,'' he said. ''And welcome.'' His smile was radiant.

How handsome he is, Ginevra thought, and how young his face is beneath his white hair. Yet, there's something not young at all about it. His eyes look so wise. He could be a hundred years old. Who is he?

He was Gentile de' Becchi, Ginevra learned. Lorenzo's tutor when he was a boy, now bishop of Arezzo. The other men were Cristoforo Landino, a later tutor, and Marsilio Ficino, owner of the house.

All of them embraced Lorenzo and welcomed Ginevra with warm greetings. "There is wine," Ficino said, ushering everyone through the house and onto a terrace that overlooked the Arno, a silver ribbon, and Florence.

Agnolo Poliziano was waiting there. "Ave," he said. These men made up the Platonic Academy, and Latin was their customary tongue.

"It would be Greek," Lorenzo explained, "except that I do not know it. Out of generosity to me, everyone pretends to prefer Latin. You'll have to be as kind as they are, Ginevra, although I'm sure you'd rather use Greek, as they probably do when I'm not around."

Ginevra was out of her depth, and she knew it. She swallowed, searched in her mind for a graceful Latin phrase in response to Lorenzo's Latin words. She found only confused fragments of poetry, conjugations, irregular verb forms, declensions. Panic had erased almost everything she knew.

As time passed, her vocabulary returned, and the lessons she had learned. She was able to understand practically every word the philosophers said. But the meaning of their words was tantalizingly elusive.

They did not discuss Plato and Aristotle the way her grandfather and tutor used to do. Antonio and Mateo had talked about the works as academic subjects; these men talked about them as components of their daily lives. Plato's ideal beauty and ideal good were applied to art and to government, to nature and to man.

They argued, laughed, encouraged and criticized. All of them were eloquent and learned and creative. But Poliziano was the most brilliant of them all. He spoke Latin with greater ease than he spoke Italian, and he was at home in the world of the intellect the way he was in no other setting. The older men listened to him with full attention and admiration. Ginevra listened with attention; and shame that she had ever considered herself superior to him in any way.

* * *

"Did you enjoy yourself?" Lorenzo asked her when they were riding back to the city. "You were very quiet."

"I am very ignorant," she replied. "But I enjoyed myself very much. I had forgotten how exciting it is to study and learn. I'm going to make a corner for myself in the library as soon as we reach the palace." She settled her hat lower on her head.

"How sensible I was to buy student's clothes. Now I'll have even more reason to wear them."

Chapter Thirty-seven

Gigi Pulci laughed uproariously when he heard about the hoax Ginevra and Lorenzo had pulled off. He announced to everyone in earshot that "by the wounds of Christ, a man has to fall in love with a woman like that!" and he marched off to the Medici palace with an armload of spring flowers to woo Ginevra.

To the surprise of everyone, especially Gigi, he did fall in love with her.

Characteristically, he made a joke out of his emotions, swearing that he had succumbed to perversity. "It's the idea of a woman wearing man's clothes," he declaimed. "Everyone knows you can tup a student and find a shining pink bottom, but the thought of breasts and the soft round belly of a woman . . . It makes me break out in a fevered sweat."

He wrote a poem for her. Not a sonnet or love lyric. Being Pulci, he wrote an epic, a brilliant, witty parody of an epic, crammed with spoofs of chivalric romance, outrageous puns and jokes and lyric passages of heart-stopping beauty.

"The title is *Morgante*," he said when he presented Ginevra with the thick sheaf of manuscript. "I want you to make no mistake about who the hero really is. The story is, of course, autobiographical."

Morgante was a giant, so immense that he tore fir trees from their roots to use as toothpicks. He was the very incarnation of mischief, constantly interfering with the struggles of the heroic sons of the Chiaramonte family, Orlando and Rinaldo, to conquer evil in the world.

Ginevra tried to read it aloud to the group around the

dinner table, but she was soon laughing so hard that she had to pass it back to Gigi for him to read.

Morgante became the favorite entertainment of the dinners. Every evening someone would offer a new incident in the epic or demand that Gigi add one.

Pulci never failed them. And he always prefaced the latest installment with an outlandishly flowery dedication to "Tino, my muse and my maddening desire."

He had, he declared mournfully, only one ambition. He longed to be permitted to be Ginevra's lapdog. "Kick me, my unattainable beloved," he would cry, "so that I may lick the adored foot that cracks my ribs." He wore a ribbon around his neck and often followed her across a room on his hands and knees.

Lorenzo and his friends applauded Gigi's antics and his poetry. Only one person knew how much real passion was disguised by them. Gigi's unlikely confidante was Lucrezia de' Medici.

"For many years you urged me to give up my foolish wastrel life, Madonna Lucrezia. You used to warn me that the day would come when I would regret the squandered years and yearn for respectability. Now it has arrived.

"I love Ginevra's bravery and bright spirit. If I were a suitable suitor, I'd woo her with all the poetry I could command. I'd wash away all she has suffered with tidal waves of devotion, and I'd spend my life making her happy.

"But I have nothing to offer her save laughter. I'm only Luigi Pulci, buffoon, tavern poet, court jester at the Medici palace."

Lucrezia smiled and shook her head. "More hyperbole, Gigi. You've made more than one successful diplomatic journey for Lorenzo. And negotiated skillfully, too. There are many who respect and love you, including myself."

Pulci kissed her hand. "You do me honor, Madonna. But you know that what I say is true. I'm no knight to joust for Ginevra's favors. I have no fortune, no profession, nothing to offer her.

"And, besides, she loves Lorenzo. I am not magnificent."

"Who told you that?" Lucrezia asked, too quickly.

Gigi laughed at her. "You gave yourself away, Madonna. But no matter, I knew. Love sharpens a man's sight. When she thinks no one can see, she looks at him in such a way . . . The way, I suppose, that I look at her when I am unobserved. A situation as old as time, the stuff of farce. Why, then, does the humorist Pulci weep when he should be laughing?"

He sat at Lucrezia's feet and put his head against her knee. She stroked his tousled hair. "I weep with you, poet," she said softly. "With you and for you. And for Ginevra."

Ginevra would have found Lucrezia's sorrow incomprehensible. She was sorry only that she had to lose any hours in sleep. Life was too wonderful to waste a minute of it.

Gigi's attentions were only a joke, she was sure, but it was thrilling to be admired. It made her feel different about herself, more womanly even though she usually dressed like a man.

She believed it made Lorenzo admire her, too, because his friend did. Or professed to. Or whatever. It made no difference. All that mattered was that every day was filled with exciting things to do and see. And every evening she was one of the group at Lorenzo's table.

He was busy most days. There was no war, but the threat was always there. Ferrante's son was still in Siena, his army with him. And Girolamo Riario, the Pope's nephew, was adding to his troops in the north, preparing, people said, to attack Ferrara.

Riario also backed another assassination plot against Lorenzo. The conspirators were careless, and their plans became known. They were captured and executed, but Lorenzo had to give up all his plans to dismiss his guards.

Ginevra's reports on what she heard in the streets became more valuable than ever. The talk was mostly about Sixtus. What were his intentions? Why had he refused to lift the interdict? Was it true that the King of Naples was going to renew his alliance with Rome?

The people of Florence were anxious. There were rumors of calves being born with two heads, and for two consecutive nights there were showers of falling stars. A sorceress was seen on the streets near Santa Croce, removing her eye from its socket and holding it in her hand while she wailed predictions of doom. Eleven new astrologers set up booths in the Mercato, and people crowded noisily around them, shoving and pushing to get inside and learn their future.

"Carnival must be better than ever this year," Lucrezia said. "It will renew their faith in the Republic."

"It will be the best ever for me," said Ginevra. "It will be my first." She was like a child, her excitement at fever pitch. She haunted the secret workshop where Lorenzo's float was being built, working at any menial task that Verrocchio assigned her.

She was also taking music lessons again from his apprentice Leonardo, practicing the traditional carnival songs and trying to compose one of her own.

There were visits to La Vacchia, too, to watch the progress of the crops and remind the manager of his duties.

And when she had a free moment, she studied Plato or the commentaries on his works. Unless she was playing with Giulio and the other younger Medici. She kept out of Poliziano's way.

Carnival surpassed Ginevra's wildest heights of anticipation. She saw everything, cheered every spectacle, ate everything offered by the street vendors, sang, danced, slept not at all.

The best, she told Lorenzo, was when she went out with Gigi and a group of his friends to parade behind the float. All of them were in traditional carnival garb, masks and women's clothes. It was a double disguise for her, a woman pretending to be a man pretending to be a woman. That made it doubly exciting.

She did not tell Lorenzo about Gigi's arm around her

waist to keep her from being swept away by the crowd. Or about the things he whispered into her ear.

"The only thing I didn't like," she said, "was that the Strozzi won the Palio. I wish I could ride for you. Then we'd win."

After Carnival, Florence slowed to a summer pace. Clarice and the children moved to the villa on the hill in Fiesole. Lucrezia went to Careggi. "I want some quiet time to myself," she said. Ginevra chose to remain in the city with Lorenzo. She would miss the dinners and the continuing adventures of *Morgante* if she went away, she explained.

Lorenzo chuckled when she told him. "Gigi would manage to get to wherever you might be," he said.

But you wouldn't, Ginevra thought.

She had invented daydreams about the summer months, idyllic scenes of the two of them together, alone, the way they had been on the ship to Naples.

The reality came close.

She helped Lorenzo with his newest scheme to find work for the old sculptor Bertoldo. They scanned maps and records of odd pieces of property owned by the Medici, visited any that seemed likely, chose a disused garden area near the monastery of San Marco. "My grandfather rebuilt San Marco," Lorenzo told her. "It was his favorite of all the things he did for the city, even more than enlarging our family church, San Lorenzo.

"He built a library in the center of the monks' cells; I still add to the collection of religious works he gave to it. He had a cell reserved for his use, too. He used to go there to study and meditate, to get away from the world. His cell is kept ready for me, but I've never been able to retreat into stillness. I have to be active. Maybe I'll learn when I'm older.

"This garden will be Lorenzo's addition to Cosimo's contribution. The monks no longer grow vegetables there. I'll use it to grow artists. I'll see to it that Bertoldo will have all the students he wants. If he doesn't send me packing when I suggest it.''

The old sculptor accepted with grudging pleasure, allowing Lorenzo to understand that it was a great favor when the keeper of Donatello's tradition condescended to teach at the Medici garden.

Lorenzo was eloquently appreciative; then he set men to work clearing the debris from the garden, building a shelter for the old man, moving some of the antique Roman and Greek statues from the palace to the freshly landscaped grounds. ''Donatello himself studied them for inspiration. I suppose Bertoldo will allow them room.''

At the same time that he was coaxing the sculptor to accept his support, Lorenzo decided to tackle an even more irascible artist.

He was Antonio Squarcialupi, the organist for the Duomo. Antonio was famous throughout Europe as a musician and composer. He was also legendary for his foul temper and slashing invective.

''They call me a diplomat,'' Lorenzo said, mocking himself. ''This will be a much greater test than the episode in Naples. I want to persuade Squarcialupi to become a teacher.''

Ginevra felt a lump in her throat. When Lorenzo was enthusiastic about a new idea, he seemed to have a light inside him. His eyes were brighter, his smile more frequent, his skin glowing with color. He paced as he talked, the words tumbling from his mouth faster and faster, his long graceful fingers sketching on the air what he saw in his mind.

''Music is art, perhaps the most perfect art,'' he said, ''because it alone can capture true harmony, perfect balance . . .'' His hands shaped equipoise. ''Why not make music another tool of the artist who expresses life with his brush or his chisel? Doesn't it follow that the man who can create beauty in paint or bronze or marble must have a greater gift than ordinary men for the art that is music?

''Take your da Vinci. He paints trays in Verrocchio's workshop. And cassone. Pictures, too, I suppose. Perhaps those talents are the reason his gift for music is so nearly genius.

"I want Squarcialupi to direct a school for me, a school of harmony. The students will be painters and sculptors. We can have recitals here in the garden, where the walls will give resonance. Or in the city's piazzas, where all the people can hear and have the gift of harmony in their lives . . .

"What do you think, Contadina? Won't it be splendid?"

"Splendid," Ginevra agreed. What I think, she said to herself, is that I love you so much I can hardly breathe.

Squarcialupi was composing, said a nervous assistant. He couldn't be disturbed, not even for the Magnificent.

"My reputation as a diplomat is safe for a while," Lorenzo said. "Let's go talk to the lion-keeper. I have a store of respectful phrases in my head for Squarcialupi. I hate to waste them."

The lion was the symbol of courage and power, hence the symbol of Florence. The city maintained a complex menagerie behind the Palazzo della Signoria where a dozen lions lived in beautifully crafted cages surrounding a large deep pit where they could exercise. There were other animals in the menagerie, three bears and an elephant, but they were mere curiosities. The lions were regarded with awe.

It was a crime to touch one. The penalty was the loss of the hand that had touched. If a man injured a lion, the penalty was death.

Everyone watched them for omens. Sickness or death foretold catastrophe; birth, particularly a big litter, was a guarantee of prosperity to the city.

The man who fed and tended the lions was venerated, approached with the awe once awarded high priests of ancient, pagan religions. He was an enormous, muscular man with thick hairy arms and hands, and a luxuriant tawny-colored beard, the only beard in the Republic. He was not known to have a name; he was called "the lion-keeper."

Lorenzo and Ginevra leaned on the iron fence around the pit and watched the lions sleep in the shade of the awnings that were stretched over the corners of the pit in the summer months. Ginevra was privately much more interested by the elephant, but she knew that such sentiments were best not spoken aloud.

The lion-keeper left the shadows of his house and approached them.

"Greetings, lion-keeper," said Lorenzo. "Your charges look exceptionally fine today."

The lion-keeper granted him a nod.

"How is the young male's paw doing?" Ginevra asked.

The lion-keeper leaned on the fence next to her and described in detail the new poultice he was using: which herbs, how finely certain ones were chopped, how long others were boiled, what proportion of each went into the mixture, how often it was applied, how long left on how large an area. "It is definitely drawing the poison," he concluded happily. "He used the paw to tear his meat this morning."

Lorenzo added his congratulations to Ginevra's.

"And they call me a diplomat," he said to her when they walked away. "How did you become so friendly with the lion-keeper?"

"I don't really know. I often stop and talk to the elephant. One day the lion-keeper started talking to me."

Lorenzo's diplomacy was tested to its limits when Squarcialupi finally finished his composition. The outcome was successful; the school of harmony was initiated in September.

But before that, Lorenzo's reputation as a master of diplomacy soared to a level that carried his title of Magnificent throughout all Europe.

The first news that reached Florence was ominous: Alfonso, Duke of Calabria, was mobilizing the army he had camped around Siena. Soldiers were readying for a march, cannon being outfitted for hauling.

Lorenzo's spies kept watch on the columns day and night; couriers rode on relays of horses to report the advance.

Then it became unmistakable that Alfonso was not going to attack the Republic. He was returning to Naples.

On the same day, a messenger arrived at the Medici palace with a dispatch from Pisa. There had been a disaster that affected all Italy. The Turks had sent their navy, had captured Otranto, a city southeast of Naples, had slaughtered more than two thirds of its population. A Turkish army of seven thousand men was firmly positioned on the heel of the Italian boot.

Alfonso's army was needed to protect Naples. All Italy was threatened if the Turks were opening hostilities.

The Pope sent messages to every State, urging that all quarrels be forgotten and all forces organized for defense against the infidels. He indicated to the Florentines that any kind of apology would gain the Pope's forgiveness and release from the interdict.

"Lorenzo the Magnificent arranged the Turkish attack," ran the rumor. "It is well-known that he has friends at court in Constantinople. His reach extends past that of any monarch, his influence has no limit."

"Lorenzo, is it true what they're saying in the streets? Did you call in the Turks to save Florence?"

"I did not, and couldn't have even if I wanted to. But that's our secret, Contadina. It does no harm to have people believe it."

Chapter Thirty-eight

With the safety of Florence secured and his reputation at such an elevation, Lorenzo decided that it was a propitious moment to look to the future of his children. He rode out to Fiesole or Careggi daily to consult with Clarice and Lucrezia.

The oldest child, Lucrezia's namesake, had been considered a valuable bride by all the fathers of sons in Florence ever since her birth. Lorenzo had stalled off all suitors, uncertain as to the best alliance. But Lucrezia would soon be eleven, only three or four years away from marriage, and a decision had to be made. He agreed to begin negotiations with the Salviati. They were one of Tuscany's wealthiest families, and their expectations about dowry were modest. They were anxious to prove that they were Medici supporters, that they had nothing to do with the actions of their relation, Archbishop Salviati, the conspirator in Giuliano's assassination.

Lorenzo wanted to heal all the ruptures the conspiracy had made in Florence's society, too. But he had no intention of smoothing the breach with the Salviati without impressing them with the magnitude of the crime he was ostensibly ignoring. Before the first meeting to discuss Lucrezia's marriage to Jacopo Salviati, Lorenzo let it be known that he had agreed to a union between his two-year-old daughter Contessina and the son of Antonio Ridolfi, the friend who had risked his life by sucking the blood from Lorenzo's wounded neck.

Luisa, a year older than Contessina, was betrothed to Giovanni, the second son of Pierfrancesco de' Medici.

Clarice insisted that only a bride from the Roman nobility was good enough for her son, and Lorenzo agreed. He had learned, at terrible cost, what it could mean to have the papacy for an enemy, and he had not forgotten the army sent by Clarice's family when Florence needed help. The Medici had to develop more influence in Rome.

He wrote to Clarice's uncle, the head of the Orsini family. In the letter he was frank about his desires, a bride from among the Orsini for Piero and all possible assistance at the Vatican for advancement in the Church for his second son, Giovanni. He intended to educate the boy to the service of God, Lorenzo said. He wanted his son to become a Cardinal.

Lorenzo's preoccupation with family affairs was understandable and natural, Ginevra told herself. It was childish of her to feel sad and abandoned. Especially when she had Gigi Pulci's company whenever she wanted, and Lorenzo always returned to the city for dinner with the group of artists.

Then one night Lorenzo did not return.

But the dinner was served and attended anyhow. "Tino" was elected host.

Ginevra looked around the table, her eyes misty. She had been accepted, she realized. She was one of them, by herself, not only as Lorenzo's shadow. This assembly of genius and wit, these poets and painters and sculptors, they were her friends. She was the luckiest, the richest woman in the world.

Chapter Thirty-nine

"I'm the luckiest woman in the world," Ginevra boasted to Lucrezia when the summer ended and everyone moved back to the city. "I have my freedom, wonderful friends, everything I wanted. You see, Madonna, I was right. I am happy with my life."

"Then I am happy for you, dear child."

"Lorenzo is my friend, too," Ginevra said, answering Lucrezia's unspoken question. "He includes me in practically everything he does, except the government." She took Lucrezia's hand in hers. "It's what I wanted, and it's enough. Really."

A week later, Ginevra put her head in Lucrezia's lap and sobbed.

"He should have told me to stay home, to do something by myself. It was cruel to make me go there."

Lorenzo had taken Ginevra to a party given by Lucrezia Donati, his mistress.

Lucrezia de' Medici tried to reason with Ginevra. There were other guests at the party, many of them the friends she was so proud of. Sandro Botticelli was there, and Andrea del Verrocchio. Agnolo Poliziano accompanied her and Lorenzo. Every one of the guests was a poet or an artist, the very people she enjoyed so much at Lorenzo's dinners.

"Besides," Lucrezia said, going to the core of Ginevra's misery, "the love affair is a thing of the past. Lucrezia Donati became Lorenzo's mistress a dozen years ago. She still holds that position, but there has

285

been no passion between them for a long time. Lorenzo continues the fiction because he feels responsible for her.''

"But she's so beautiful. And I'm so ugly."

Lucrezia shook Ginevra's shoulder. "Stop that," she commanded. "You can't have it both ways, Ginevra. You chose to be a companion, a pretense boy. You cannot measure your worth by feminine standards." She tilted Ginevra's tear-streaked face upward, took pity on the misery she saw there.

"Beauty is the least durable of all human attributes, Ginevra. Just think. Would you trade places with Lucrezia Donati? Would you like to know that the man who once loved you now visits you only when duty prompts him? A mirror is not very good company."

Ginevra dried her eyes on her sleeve. "You're right. And I'm sorry. I won't be silly anymore."

It was a vow she couldn't keep. She returned to Lucrezia's rooms again and again, seeking solace and Lucrezia's stern, compassionate wisdom.

The acceptance that she prized so highly brought her penalties, too. Lorenzo's friends, and Lorenzo as well, treated her as one of themselves. She learned things from their bawdy raillery that were like knives in her heart. About the complicated ruses Lorenzo had devised to facilitate his affair with Ippolita in Naples. About the amazing skills of the Egyptian prostitute who had recently arrived in Florence. About the love sonnets that Lorenzo was writing to several women who were neglected by their husbands. About the short journeys he made with Gigi Pulci to nearby villages in search of eager, fresh young country girls.

It was no comfort to Ginevra that all the other men behaved the same way, that the rules of society gave them wide latitude for carefree sexuality. Least of all did it help when Lucrezia explained that probably Gigi had deliberately drawn out Lorenzo's laughing account of their exploits. "Gigi wanted you to know that Lorenzo is no saint, Ginevra. He hoped you would appreciate him more if you valued Lorenzo less. Gigi is jealous. He's human."

"He's a devil, tempting Lorenzo to be as wicked as he is."

Lucrezia decided that Ginevra needed to get away. "I would like for you to come with me to Morba," she said, the request really an order. "I'm going to take the baths for a week before winter makes it too difficult to travel."

With distance, Ginevra gained the perspective Lucrezia hoped for. She was able to reexamine the choice she had made, incorporate her new understanding of the price she had to pay, and still find it the best way for her to live. The freedom she had talked about with such glibness was real and precious. And to be Lorenzo's friend was to be constantly entertained, stimulated, educated, stretched to the full extent of her intelligence and imagination. Because of him, she was in the very center of everything that was exciting in Florence, in Italy, in all Europe.

On the evening before their return to Florence, Ginevra went to Lucrezia's room to thank her for her wisdom, for the chance to think clearly.

She tapped on Lucrezia's door and opened it, the words on her lips.

An attendant was inside. The woman rushed to the door and pushed against it. "Go away," she said urgently. "Go away."

Ginevra retreated, propelled by the weight of the closing door. But before it shut, she heard the deep, tearing coughs. And over the woman's shoulder, she saw Lucrezia's bent form and the bloodstained cloth at her mouth.

"It's true," Lucrezia told her later. "I have consumption. It's been going on for a long time, but it has only become serious this past year. That's why I wanted the summer alone at Careggi. Hiding it is so tiring.

"Ginevra, you asked me once to keep your love a secret from Lorenzo, and I have. Now I ask you to keep my illness from him as long as possible."

"I'll do anything you ask, Madonna. Anything at all."

"Then do this. Promise me there'll be no doctors. And try not to grieve, my daughter. I have time, perhaps a lot of time, before the end."

Everyone in Florence was laughing when they got home. Lucrezia laughed, too, when she heard the reason for the hilarity. Ginevra followed her lead.

The story on everyone's lips was the report of the final reconciliation between Pope Sixtus and the Republic. He had insisted on a public demonstration of Florence's contrition. The delegation had to kneel on the steps of Saint Peter's and receive a symbolic blow from the rod he carried while they apologized aloud for the sins that had brought about the excommunication.

"We knelt, as ordered," the delegates told everyone. "And he touched our shoulders. But what we mumbled was not an apology, no matter what he may have thought he was hearing."

The churches had never closed, despite the Pope's orders, but the official welcome back into the Church was a relief to everyone, even the people who had been most loudly defiant. Many of the baptisms and marriages and funerals of the years under the interdict were quietly held for a second time.

And then it was nearly Christmas. Lucrezia and Ginevra arranged the Neapolitan manger scene on a platform in the loggia so that all the people of Florence could see it as often as they wished. There was a constant, slowly moving line in front of it all day every day.

1481

Chapter Forty

"I hate to admit it," Lorenzo said, "but I admire the old pirate's gall." He shook his head and gave a grudging laugh. The Pope had written asking him to send Florence's best painters to Rome to decorate a chapel he had built.

"He did his best to destroy us, his nephew is to our north, trying to make an alliance with Venice so that he can take our border territories, and Sixtus wants me to turn over Florence's glory to him."

"What will you do?" said Ginevra.

"I'll ask the artists. It's no small thing to be a painter for the Vatican. A man can become famous. Every church in Italy that needs decoration will want to hire a man who has painted for the Pope."

"And he will be making a gift to God of his talent," Lucrezia interjected. Lorenzo's increasing worldliness distressed her. He thought too much about money, too little about spiritual matters.

He had never said anything to her or anyone else about the desperate state of the Medici banks. The Bruges branch, once one of the strongest, was about to close.

But finances were never part of the policy discussions he had with his mother. Diplomacy and politics were the subjects. Ginevra was frequently included in the meetings. At first because of her role as information gatherer. Later, because it had become a habit. She never offered an opinion unless asked. Lorenzo was surprised when she spoke up.

"The Pope will owe you if you help him. He must care a great deal about his chapel if he's willing to be under obligation to you."

"Astute contadina. I'll make it easy for him. What I really want is for him to muzzle his nephew. An impossibility. So what I'll do is simply call Giovanni to his attention. I want no obstacles to his advancement in the Church when he's older."

Lucrezia nodded her approval.

"Which artists will you send?" Ginevra asked. "I mean, which will you talk to?" She had private reasons for hoping he was not thinking of Sandro Botticelli.

Lorenzo answered immediately. "Ghirlandaio, of course. Sixtus wants frescoes of stories from the Testaments, and Domenico is the finest narrative painter we have . . . Verrocchio, no. Fresco is not one of his strengths. He leaves most of the painting to Perugino, so he'll be one. And that recent apprentice, Bernardino Pinturicchio. Andrea thinks highly of him."

Ginevra suggested Leonardo da Vinci.

"Absolutely not," Lorenzo said. "He's a fair painter, but too undisciplined. Since he left Andrea, he's spent more time experimenting than he has working."

Ginevra bit her lip. She couldn't deny what Lorenzo said, but she wished he would help Leonardo. She still went to him for music lessons, and she knew that her payments were virtually his only source of income, small as they were.

"And of course," Lorenzo continued, "Sandro. He can be the director of the project."

Ginevra suppressed her protest.

The next day she ran to Botticelli's studio as soon as the sun was up. It was cold in the shadowy stone streets, not a great deal warmer in the studio.

"Brr," she said through chattering teeth, "I feel sorry for your barely clad goddess, Sandro."

Botticelli laughed, thinned the gauzelike silk draperies he was painting with a sure stroke of the brush. "Goddesses have ichor in their veins, not mere blood like you mortal creatures. They never feel cold."

Ginevra made a grotesque face at him and went to the corner where the tiled stove was. It was hardly warm. She raked a few coals into a brazier and added wood to the stove. Then she arranged herself on a stool between the two sources of heat and waited quietly. She came often to watch Sandro work. Alone of all the artists, he didn't mind an audience. Ginevra was fascinated by the moment-to-moment development of the painting.

She had also discovered that sometimes Botticelli liked to talk while he worked. With very little prompting, he would reminisce about the years that he lived in the Medici family, about Lorenzo when he was young.

This did not seem to be one of his conversational days. He was concentrating on a detail of the goddess's gown. Ginevra kept herself still with great effort. She felt like squirming with urgency.

Filippino, Sandro's apprentice, came in with fresh bread from the Mercato stuffed inside his doublet to keep the bread warm and to warm himself. Sandro put his brush down at once.

"I'm ravenous," he cried. "Let's eat."

Filippino warmed some sausage and brought out a cheese from his room. "A feast," Ginevra said. "Thank you, Filippino." She liked the young painter; he was an earnest, dedicated worker, and he was, at twenty-three, the closest of them all to her own age.

While they ate, Ginevra swore them to secrecy, then told Sandro that Lorenzo would be coming to talk to him soon and for what purpose. "So you see, everything has to be completed much earlier than we thought. You might be in Rome for years."

The painting on the easel was a gift for Lorenzo from the Signoria. It was Sandro's version of the theme that Lorenzo had used for carnival, Pallas and the Centaur. The centaur did not, this time, have a caricature of King Ferrante's face, but the meaning of the allegory was unmistakable. The goddess wore a circlet of laurel on her head, and the background was the Bay of Naples. Lorenzo had tamed the beast of Naples, it said.

"I don't have many days' work left on this, Ginevra. Don't worry so. No one can travel anywhere until it gets warmer."

"But the other painting, Sandro. You haven't begun."

"Maybe it's better to wait on that one. More time will soften the shock."

Botticelli had promised to complete the portrait of Giuliano that he was working on at the time of the younger Medici's murder. Ginevra wanted to give it to Lucrezia for her birthday in June.

"No," Ginevra said, "it can't wait. I have my heart set on it."

She had revealed Lorenzo's plans without a second thought. But nothing would make her betray Lucrezia's confidence. She couldn't tell Sandro that she was afraid Lucrezia might die before he returned from Rome.

Four days later, she left the house again at dawn, this time to go to the Mercato and listen to what people were saying about the artists' going to Rome. Lorenzo had talked to the men he had chosen, and they had all agreed. The criers would be announcing the news to-day, beginning in the Mercato. There was no predicting how the Florentines would react. Would they be proud that the Pontiff recognized that the artists of Florence were the greatest in the world? Or angry that their artists were being sent away from them, sent to the ruler with whom Florence had so recently been at war? Whatever the reaction, the praise or blame would be laid at Lorenzo's door.

She had covered half the distance, could hear the market noises ahead, when she stopped, tilted back her head and sniffed the air.

There was spring in it.

It was still bitterly cold; January was not yet done. But in the air there was an elusive hint of softness, a change from the day before, a promise of birth and growth and tender green.

Ginevra jumped as high as she could and laughed aloud. Her step was light and swift when she hurried the rest of the way.

Florence responded positively to the criers' announcement. Ginevra was not surprised. Nothing but good could happen on a day so full of promise.

She listened with practiced skill until she was confident that she need listen no more. Then she ran back to the palace.

"I need a horse," she told the guard at the door. "Order one for me, please, while I get ready. If anyone asks for me today, I've gone to La Vacchia."

It was time to plan, to apportion crops, to order seed and stock. This year, for the first time, she would be deciding what was to be done on the land. Her land. Her chance to make La Vacchia better than it had ever been before.

"Our Ginevra is obsessed," complained Gigi loudly.

Lorenzo smiled. "It's a good obsession. She's happy."

"But so abstracted. I don't think she heard a single stanza of tonight's *Morgante*. And look at her. Her fingernails are rimmed black. She's getting worse every day."

"Your poet's pride is wounded, Gigi. Let the contadina be. She's in her element, hounding the manager, talking to every farmer in the region, learning about the land. When the fields have been planted and the vines pruned, then she'll scrub her nails and applaud your wit. For now, it doesn't matter to her, and it shouldn't matter to anyone else."

On March 25, the official beginning of the New Year, Florence said goodbye to the four artists. Their train of horses, packhorses, outrider guards for the dangerous roads left the city in a rain of flowers and a bedlam of cheers.

There had been a banquet the night before at the Medici palace, complete with musicians, clowns and a play written by Agnolo Poliziano for the occasion.

Botticelli presented Lorenzo with the painting that commemorated his triumph in Naples, and the celebrations began all over again.

"They won't ride far today," Lorenzo remarked when the last horse rounded the bend in the road. "They all had too much wine and too little sleep . . . For that matter, I could do with a nap right now. Shall we go home until it's time for the procession to the Duomo, Contadina?''

"You go on. I'll meet you at the house. I have something to do first.''

She had to go to Sandro's studio and talk to Filippino. The portrait of Giuliano was finished, the final strokes of the brush applied only minutes before the banquet began. Now it had to cure. Ginevra needed to remind Filippino to keep it out of sight and to let her know as soon as she could come get it.

I hope he's here, she thought, when she pushed on the door. "Filippino," she called as the door swung open. "It's Ginevra.''

She walked inside and stopped abruptly. "Forgive me," she said. Filippino was working.

He did not even look up. His hand was moving rapidly across a sheet of paper, sketching with a piece of charcoal, making preliminary drawings for a portrait.

The subject was a young man. He turned and looked at Ginevra.

There was something about his lazy stare that made her wish desperately that the day might reverse itself and begin again so that she could scrub her nails and wear a dress instead of a lucco.

Chapter Forty-one

His name was Franco Soranzo, and he was from Milan, he told Ginevra. "I have been in your beautiful Florence for only a few weeks, and I feel very much a stranger."

Ginevra stammered with a clumsy, incoherent welcome on behalf of the city.

What is wrong with me? she said to herself. I can hear my voice; I sound like a fool. And I'm gaping like an idiot, staring. She turned her head and looked toward Filippino. But she saw only the sketches he had made, the face of the Milanese. The chin was rounded, with a curious padding of flesh that curved to a shadowed hollow beneath his lower lip. His face had molded hollows, too, under prominent slanting cheekbones. His mouth seemed to be made of the hollows, as if a sculptor's fingers had pressed into clay and moved it forward. His lips were full, sharply outlined, almost pouting. The bottom lip was indented, a line rising across the center to the pointed bow of the upper lip. It was an exaggerated mouth, too curving, too full, too sensual.

A mouth that matched his eyes. They were set unusually far apart under high, arched, cleanly marked brows. The irises were light brown in color, like topaz, with a strange transparency that made them seem bottomless, mysterious, secretive, challenging. Knowing.

"Perhaps you'll have the kindness to show me today's celebrations, Madonna Ginevra," Soranzo said. His voice was thick and heavy, like honey. "We have a different New Year in Milan; yours interests me very much."

Ginevra's gaze was drawn magnetically back to meet his eyes. Her breathing was shallow, unsatisfying.

The Milanese rose from his bench with a powerful fluid motion. His thick leg muscles worked visibly under his tight-fitting red silk hose. He turned and bent to lift a fur-lined cloak from the bench.

He wore the short doublet fashionable in Milan. It reached only a handspan of inches below the belted waist then ended in an embroidered border that framed his tight muscular buttocks.

Swinging the cloak around his shoulders, Soranzo turned to face Ginevra. "Shall we go?" he said. His strong fingers fastened the clasp of his cloak, then smoothed the pleats of his doublet over his flat stomach. The doublet's bright blue border was repeated in the ribbons that tied his thickly padded yellow silk codpiece to his red silk hose.

He looked briefly toward Filippino. "I'll be back in the morning, painter." Then his lips curved in a slow smile for Ginevra, and he held out his hand to her.

She stepped backward. "I cannot," she said. "I . . . I'm meeting . . . a friend."

Soranzo frowned his disappointment. "Another time, then," he said.

His shoulder brushed Ginevra's when he went through the door. It started the turning movement that she was incapable of halting until she was facing the street, watching him walk away.

He moves like a lion, she thought.

"Milan," Lorenzo groaned. "Nothing but trouble ever comes out of Milan."

Ginevra's arm jerked, and her wine spilled. "Why do you say that?"

Lorenzo folded the message that had just been brought to him. "The Duchess and her son are out," he said. His voice sounded weary. "Lodovico Sforza has grown tired of being joint regent. He's taken over the State and exiled the boy and his mother. It was bound to happen, but I hoped it wouldn't be now. It means a new alliance to make, and a new Duke to woo. I wonder what his price is.'' Lorenzo pushed his plate away and put his arms on the table, his forehead resting on his hands.

"I'm tired, Contadina."

Ginevra shook her head in protest. Never had she seen Lorenzo tired like other men, never, never dreamed that he would admit to fatigue. She held out her hand, drew it back, afraid to touch his bent shoulders, afraid of everything in this suddenly unstable world.

He raised his head and smiled, and Ginevra's frightened heartbeat slowed to normal. "Finish your meal," Lorenzo said. "We don't want to be late for the procession." He touched her nose with his finger. "Such a pale little rabbit. Don't be alarmed. I have a touch of gout, and it makes me gloomy."

"You shouldn't go out if you're in pain. You should rest your leg."

"Eat, and stop being foolish. I'm not in pain. And the people expect me to be at the celebration."

Ginevra stayed close to him, watching his every step and gesture, ready to offer her arm and shoulder for support. Lorenzo showed no pain, and his dark mood was gone. He left his guards behind and pushed through the crowds, talking and laughing, drawing strength from his contact with his people.

But that evening when Ginevra and Lucrezia met with him to talk about the meaning of the events in Milan, Lorenzo's leg was outstretched on a bench, supported and cushioned by pillows. The knee was swollen and pulpy.

"You must go to Morba," Lucrezia said, "at once."

"I cannot do that, Mamina. I have to be here for messages from Milan."

"Then go to Bagno a Ripoli. It's not far. The couriers can take your letters to you there. Your secretary can go with you to answer them. You must have the sulfur baths, Lorenzo. You must. I know these things better than you do."

Lorenzo agreed. "I'll leave at first light. Now we have to consider Lodovico Sforza. What do we know about him, other than his dark complexion? 'Lodovico

Il Moro.' It sounds more like a clown than a ruler.''
Lorenzo's eyes were bright from pain, but his voice was
even and his expression amused.

Ginevra waited until Lucrezia went to her rooms.
Then she asked Lorenzo if she could go with him to the
baths.

"No," he said.

"Please, Lorenzo. It's important.''

He rubbed the bridge of his nose, smoothing out the
lines of his frown. "No, Ginevra. I may take the older
boys and Agnolo, but that's all. Why do you want to
go? Are you ill?''

"No, I'm fine. I just feel like getting away from the
city.''

"Then go to one of the villas. Or La Vacchia. See
how your vines are growing. Do whatever you like. Now
be a good contadina and let me be. I want to go to bed.''

"Let me help you.''

"I can manage.'' His irritation was growing. Ginevra
said goodnight.

She had trouble falling asleep, a rare experience for
her. The bed felt lumpy, she could find no comfortable
position to lie in; her body was strange, the skin tender
to the touch of the covers, the muscles unable to relax.

Maybe I am sick, she thought. Maybe that's what is
wrong. But she knew that wasn't so.

The tavern near the University had locked its doors
long since, when sundown brought curfew. The three
men inside would have to stay all night or risk arrest
when they went out onto the streets. The proprietor was
sleepy, but he didn't mind. This group looked as if they
would drink until dawn, and they were paying for the
best wine.

"I met the Magnificent's crazy mistress today,'' said
Franco Soranzo. He was sprawled across a bench, his
head propped against the wall, his feet up on the table.
"A funny-looking, scrawny thing she is, too. Either this
Lorenzo is strangely perverted or she has some very
well-hidden talents. I think I'll find out what they are.''

"You're the crazy one, Franco," said one of the men. He had difficulty pronouncing his words. "Lorenzo de' Medici owns this city. He'd cut off your balls."

"That makes it more exciting, doesn't it? It always adds spice if there's danger in discovery."

The third man laughed raucously. "Listen to the world-weary voice of Milan. What makes you think that a woman would look at you, Franco, when she has Lorenzo the Magnificent? You're nothing but a pretty pup. He's a man above all other men."

Franco raised his eyebrows. "So you Florentines say. This Milanese says that she can be had. I'll wager anything you like."

"A thousand florins."

"And another thousand from me."

Franco smiled. "Two thousand it is, then."

"Bring another flagon, tavern keeper! I want to celebrate the fortune I'll have soon."

"I won't go there!" Ginevra cried the words aloud, and the sound woke her. She sat up in her bed, tried to straighten the tangle of bedclothes that her restless sleep had made. Her efforts only made it worse.

You're behaving like an imbecile, she told herself. Tino, she thought, you're being Tino again. The idea made her smile. She was proud of what she'd done in Naples.

She lit a candle, scrambled down from the bed, pulled all the covers off onto the floor, replaced them one by one, pulling them smooth. Then she puffed up the pillows and arranged them in a neat pyramid. She stepped back to inspect her efforts. The soft mounded quilt and pillows looked warm and inviting.

She climbed quickly into the nest that she had made. She had barely time to blow out the candle before she was asleep.

Sunlight slanted through the high windows onto her eyelids and wakened her.

Ginevra blinked and turned her head away from it. She never slept so late.

But she had slept well; I'll walk to La Vacchia, she

thought, or maybe run. She stretched, pointing her toes, feeling the pull in her legs, anticipating the pleasure of the steep path up the hills, the sweet air of springtime.

She left the palace an hour later after breakfast and a reassuring talk with Lucrezia: Lorenzo had been much better that morning; he and Agnolo and the boys had set out for Bagno a Ripoli in a holiday mood.

I'll cut flowers and bring them down for Lucrezia, Ginevra thought. The iris should be ready, and the tulips. She was arranging colors in her mind, choosing from Lucrezia's collection of vases, when she realized what she was doing. She was walking in the wrong direction. No, she told herself, but it did no good. Her steps slowed, but she did not turn back. She walked, as if mesmerized, to Botticelli's studio.

Chapter Forty-two

It was always the same. Ginevra struggled against herself, and she lost. Her mind had no power over her actions, her willpower deserted her. She could not keep away from Franco Soranzo.

She despised herself for her weakness, and she told herself again and again that she should despise him. He was everything she hated: he was a student at the university, but he had no interest in learning; he drank too much; he was lazy and self-indulgent; he had no wit, no humor; he treated ordinary people like servants, servants like animals.

But he treated her like a woman, a woman he desired.

He never told her so. He had no conversation, no poetry. Only his pale eyes that watched her lips when she talked with false, nervous gaiety to fill the silence and maintain the distance between them. And his mouth that seemed always about to smile at her transparent excuses for appearing at the studio during his sittings. And his compact, muscular body that daily came closer to hers when he walked to the table to refill his cup or stood near her to drink the wine.

"This portrait will be finished soon," he said one day, "and then you will come to my rooms . . . to choose the best place to hang it."

And Ginevra knew that she would.

Ginevra wanted to talk to Lucrezia, to confide in her, ask her help. She was confused and frightened by her inability to control her behavior, afraid that she would lose her mind the same way that she had lost her will, terrified by the insistent new sensations of her body, by the dreams that disturbed her sleep and could not be remembered when she woke.

But Lucrezia was ill. She looked well; her eyes were bright, and color bloomed on her cheeks. Yet, her skin was hot and dry when Ginevra took her hand, and she spent many hours alone in her rooms. Ginevra knew that Lucrezia must be in there, bent and racked and coughing, just as she had been at Morba. She could not add her problems to Lucrezia's burden of sickness.

She spent most of the day at La Vacchia, trying to blot out the turmoil she felt by concentrating on the work that was closest to her heart and by laboring in the vineyard and stables until her body throbbed with fatigue instead of incomprehensible, unwanted demands.

Often she stayed the night at the villa. The dinners at the Medici palace were different, now that Sandro had gone to Rome and Lorenzo was not there. Andrea del Verrocchio complained that he could not get all his work done without his two best apprentices. Other artists, who had been content to be included in the group, now asserted themselves with loud arguments about technical points and caustic commentaries on one another's projects.

Gigi tried to sustain the comedic tone. His humor lacerated Ginevra's nerves. She couldn't bear the underlying sensuality, the pointed sexuality.

She wouldn't allow herself to admit that there was a connection between Gigi's stories and what was happening to her.

I'll be all right again when Lorenzo gets home, Ginevra told herself. We'll go hunting and tour the farms like last spring, and I'll show him what I'm doing at La Vacchia, and the dinners will be fun again, and every day I'll know that he's here and I'm going to see him and I won't think about anything or anyone else. When Lorenzo comes home.

But he stayed at the baths for more than three weeks. When he did return, he was preoccupied with the threats from the north, with the erratic progress of the diplomatic mission he had sent to Lodovico Sforza. At the meeting with Lucrezia and Ginevra on the evening he arrived, he talked constantly about Milan.

Every time he said the word, Ginevra's heart stopped beating for a long, sickening moment. Milan meant Franco to her. His coarse reddish-brown hair that changed texture and became silk in the narrow line of it that began between his shoulder blades and disappeared into the cleft between his buttocks.

Lorenzo had stayed away too long. Franco Soranzo's shuttered rooms had become the center of Ginevra's life.

She did not pretend to herself or to Franco that she went there for an acceptable visit to a new acquaintance. Not even the first time. Franco said he wanted her to approve the light on his portrait, but Ginevra did not even look at it. She stood in the center of the room and waited for him to stop talking. She was there because, against her will, she had to be. To be touched by his wide hands, to feel his skin under her palms, to taste his full lips and smell the arrogant masculinity of him.

He grasped her arms above the elbows and looked into her eyes and the surrender they spoke. "So," he said. His tongue lazily traced the outline of her mouth. Ginevra shivered and opened her lips to his probing kiss.

When Ginevra told herself that Franco moved like a lion, her perception was more accurate than she knew. Franco was a predator, and his prey was women. He lived lavishly in Florence at the expense of a Milanese nobleman who was willing to pay well to keep him away from his wife.

Franco's mother died when he was twelve. His father's second wife had not waited for many months before she began her stepson's education in the art of pleasing a woman. He was then fourteen. When he was sixteen, he delivered a cloak that his father, a tailor, had made for the widow of a merchant. He never went home again.

His accent improved, and his manners. His victims were like a ladder of increasing wealth and power. When he was twenty-two, the Countess Alessandra hired him as her personal bodyguard and bought him so many clothes and jewels that her husband had to bid very high to convince Franco to leave Milan for Florence.

The women in Franco's life were usually older than he, although he amused himself sometimes with young serving girls in the houses where he lived. They were all hungry for sex and responsive to Franco's repertoire of pleasures. He had become a virtuoso at lovemaking.

But nothing in his wide experience had prepared him for Ginevra.

His first kiss unlocked a passionate flame of woman, a voluptuary who set him on fire by the intensity of her quivering response to his touch on her body. Her breasts rose to meet his hands when he opened her clothes, nipples tall and hot, half-moon scars red and burning. Her warm skin flushed, became so feverish that his palms felt scalded. The invisible downy hairs on her body stood upright, stiff, like minute nails that scraped and inflamed his fingers, his lips, his chest when he ripped his shirt away to hold his bare skin against her. Her abdomen leapt under his hands in waves of muscle contractions that vibrated, called forth vibrations in his entire body, propelled his hands downward through the raking triangle of erect hair. Between her open legs there was a thick, hot dampness and his fingers penetrated swollen fevered flesh to trigger a convulsion of shudders and spurting liquid fire. She screamed, and he heard his scream meet hers, felt his own tearing climax erupt like molten fire from deep within his shaking body.

The cry of release was the only sound Ginevra made, and she covered his mouth with her fingers when he tried to say the practiced phrases of love that he knew so well. She permitted no invented romance, no dissembling, no denial that the force that crackled in the air around them was the white-heat-lightning of carnality.

Carnality unresolved. She would not allow him to enter her. She pushed him away with such strength that he believed the legend that she was a madwoman, and he was chilled with fear.

Then she silently touched and tasted his body with her burning hands and arms and legs and lips until he was as fevered as she and willing to meet her mute urgent demands with the heat of his caresses.

Over the weeks of daily assignations, he became her servitor, captive to her passions, ensnared by his own failure to dominate. The predator became prey to an elemental force he could not comprehend.

And then she told him it was over. "I have used you, Franco," Ginevra said, "and I am ashamed. You let me learn what it is to be a woman, and I'm grateful, but now I'm finished."

"It's worth the money to be rid of her," Franco said with a laugh when he settled his debt to his drinking companions. "I was afraid she'd be hard to cut off." He acted the way he always had, except that his walk had become a swagger. But his friends agreed that he was somehow different.

There was a difference in Ginevra, too, but it was so subtle that only Lucrezia noticed it, and even she could not define it.

Ginevra believed that she could. I'm burnt out, she said to herself, and I thank God. Now I feel at peace. I don't even feel disgusted by my weakness and my furtive, sordid desires. There is a beast inside all of us, as the mythmakers understood so well. If it gets free, its power is too great to control. My beast has had its day and is dead; I don't have to fear it anymore.

When Carnival came, with its insistent display of sexuality, she took part in the celebrations with enthusiasm. Aware of meanings, no longer confused by excitement she could not understand, but removed from true involvement by passions spent, she felt immeasurably older and wiser.

"How fair is youth and how fleeting . . ." she sang with the rollicking crowds in the streets, and she was glad that her youth was past.

She even found it possible to understand why Lorenzo fell in love with a masked woman he met in the Piazza Ognissanti.

Despite the leaden jealousy in her heart.

Chapter Forty-three

"Lorenzo, who is this woman, Luisa Felceroccia?" Lucrezia demanded. "Clarice's message to me was hysterical. Someone told her that you have been making a spectacle of yourself."

"Mamina, I won't tolerate being questioned by you or criticized by Clarice. She has no right to interfere with my private life, nor do you." Lorenzo's voice was shrill, with a tremolo of suppressed fury. He was angry at his mother's inquisition, angrier because he knew that there was justice in her accusation. His affair with Luisa Felccroccia was not the conventional discreet alliance that his other adventures had been. His infatuation was like a disease; it dizzied him and destroyed his judgment.

Ginevra rescued him from Lucrezia's wrath. She stuck her head around the door to his study and asked if she might interrupt. Lucrezia glared at her son and said she had to leave.

"What is it, Ginevra?" Lorenzo aimed his anger at her when Lucrezia was gone.

Ginevra ignored it. "I want you to come to my room and look at something," she said. "It's the gift I'm giving your mother for her birthday tomorrow, and I don't want you to be unprepared . . . It's Sandro's portrait of Giuliano, Lorenzo."

Lorenzo forgot everything else. "You got him to finish it? Contadina, you are a wonder! How happy she'll be. I, too. Come, show it to me." He sprang up from his chair, then grabbed the desk for support.

Ginevra started toward him, but he waved her away.

"It's not bad. I forget that I can't do what I used to do, and then I aggravate it."

The most recent attack of gout affected both knees.

"Lend me your strong arm, and hand me that cane. Then I'll manage."

Ginevra put her arm around his back, her shoulder under his arm. "I can bring it up to you."

"No, this is better. I have to get used to moving. I'm afraid that if I don't, the joints will stiffen until they lock and become useless."

"Ah yes," Lorenzo said under his breath. His hold on Ginevra tightened. "Giuliano, my brother."

They looked at the portrait together.

"I wish I had known him," said Ginevra. "I can see why everyone loved him."

The painting showed a young man in three-quarter profile. He was about to smile, perhaps laugh, and the good humor would be contagious.

His skin was golden, flushed with youth and health, but his gaze was downward, eyelids almost closed. It was the symbol of his true state; it was a portrait of a man who was dead.

He was placed in front of a window with interior shutters, one shutter closed, another representation of death. The second shutter opened outward into space and a luminous distant blue Tuscan sky. Eternity, the destination of his departed soul.

The painting permitted no grief.

"I loved him so," Lorenzo said. Ginevra settled her shoulder closer to him and silently gave him her strength.

"You have made me very happy, Ginevra," Lucrezia said. "I shall treasure this gift above all that I own."

She kissed Ginevra and Lorenzo, then sat facing her younger son's likeness. "I'd like to talk to Giuliano now," she said, and they left her alone.

"What do we know about death?" said Lorenzo. He held a short branch he had broken from an olive tree in the garden outside Marsilio Ficino's small house. There were five olives among the leaves, and his long fingers plucked them one by one while he spoke.

It was early December, the time of the olive harvest and the time when all other growth in the garden was brown and lifeless.

Agnolo Poliziano was the first to reply. While his poet's voice quoted Plato's teachings, Ginevra looked at the absorbed faces of the men seated around the table. She was comfortable now with these philosophers, this Academy. I'm very lucky to be part of this, she thought, to be able to leave daily concerns behind and spend some hours sharing their search for larger meanings and eternal truth.

Her mind followed Agnolo's words, then Ficino's commentary on them. At the same time it pursued a parallel sequence of speculation. Why did Lorenzo raise the question of death? Had he noticed Lucrezia's increasing weakness? He didn't seem to. Was he pretending to be unaware of it because he guessed that she wanted to hide it from him? Or was it his own illness that made him think about mortality? The bony knobs on his wrists were concealed by a lace ruffle on his shirt, but Ginevra knew that they were inflamed by the gout. It no longer attacked only his knees.

She concentrated on the discussion, contributed a passage from Aristotle, laughed with the others at Lorenzo's mock-sobbing rendition of a funeral oration he had heard a peasant deliver for a sow who died farrowing.

He is wonderful, Lorenzo, she thought. Landino and the others deserve all the respect in the world for their brilliance, but they are narrow next to him. His mind matches theirs and encompasses a thousand things besides. He is the warmth in this room.

Last time the Academy met, he was the heat, she thought. "What is love?" he asked then and spoke too long about his opinions. That was the summer romance with the Felceroccia woman. The talk in the streets is that it's over.

Ginevra's satisfied smile went unnoticed in the general merriment.

1482

Chapter Forty-four

"Happy birthday, Lorenzo."

"Happy birthday, Contadina. Do you see the gift the heavens have sent us?"

It had begun snowing during the night, a rare occurrence for Florence.

After breakfast they all went to walk in the falling snow: Ginevra and Lorenzo, Lorenzo's guards, Agnolo, the nursemaids and the children. The streets were crowded, everyone slipping, laughing, catching the snow in their hands, on their tongues. The snowfall was gentle, with no wind, but the fat wet flakes were already piled nearly a foot deep.

"We can build a statue," Lorenzo said. "Who will help me?"

The children crowded around him, shouting, "I will, I will."

"I will," Ginevra shouted with them.

They built three in the garden behind the house. Lorenzo sent the three oldest children inside to get hats for the statues when they were finished; he lifted the three youngest children in turn to put them on the lumpy figures.

The two middle children, Luisa and Giovanni, watched sadly. Ginevra knelt quickly beside them. "Luisa," she said, "the Judith fountain looks cold. If you'll brush the snow off her head, then Giovanni can put my hat on her." She picked the little girl up in her arms.

Giovanni, soon to be seven, scorned any help. He climbed the snow-covered bronze statue by himself, Ginevra's hat clamped between his teeth. Everyone clapped when he crowned Donatello's masterpiece with Ginevra's red cappuccio.

"Giovanni will have the red hat himself one day," Lorenzo said that afternoon. The snow had stopped falling; the sky was a clear blue, with a bright sun that made the snow glitter and flash.

Ginevra was surprised by the certainty in his tone. "Have you heard from the Pope?"

"I've received word that he is very pleased with the decoration of his chapel . . . and that he is favoring a new nephew now. Giuliano della Rovere has his ear, and Giuliano hates the old favorite Girolamo. Since Girolamo is my enemy, Giuliano is my friend. It looks favorable for my son. Giovanni will almost certainly be made a cardinal when the time comes." Lorenzo grinned and stretched out his arms.

"Enough of politics and ambition. I'm going to glide. Do you want to race me?"

Ginevra didn't pause to answer. She stretched her arms and pushed away from the wall in an unbalanced, windmilling slide along the ruts that a cart had made in the street.

"Unfair!" Lorenzo shouted, skidding after her.

They ended up sprawled in the same drift of snow, laughing, spitting out the snow that fell in their open mouths, then laughing at their own sputtering. Ginevra pointed at Lorenzo's guards, who were slipping and falling as they tried to run to him, and they laughed harder than ever.

How happy I am, Ginevra's heart sang. It's our birthday. I'm nineteen years old, Lorenzo thirty-three, and we're having as much fun as children. More, because we know how seldom these moments come . . . and how few days are free of gout for him.

Lorenzo helped her up, and they brushed each other off. Then they proceeded to their goal, Bertoldo's sculpture garden and school. As they had hoped, the old man was using the snow as a medium for instruction in modeling figures. The nine students were making copies of the antique marbles that Lorenzo had placed in the garden.

"For the love of God, don't tell Bertoldo that you put your hat on Donatello's Judith," Lorenzo whispered when they neared the elderly sculptor.

They watched the rapid creation of ephemeral beauty until the lengthening shadows made the snow look blue. Then they went home.

As if winter had spent itself in the snowstorm, the weather became springlike. Day after day, people said, "It can't last, we'd better enjoy this while we can." But it did last. By the beginning of February, the hills around Florence had a tender haze of fresh green.

The artists returned from Rome, blessing the warmth that made travel possible.

"You can't imagine how happy I am to be home," Sandro Botticelli told Ginevra. "Tell me all the gossip. Lorenzo's letters were woefully inadequate, all about politics and Plato . . . Where is he? I want to tease him about his great romance. Luckily, I have other friends who wrote news more to my taste than his. I'm going to recommend spectacles. My friend said the famous Luisa was as plain as a wall."

"He's at the Signoria," Ginevra said. "He'll probably be back any minute. He knows you were expected to arrive today and told me to arrange a special dinner tonight. Gigi has written a song of welcome, and I'm playing the accompaniment. It has more than thirty verses, so don't plan to be early to bed.

"And, Sandro, don't be too rough with Lorenzo. He's suffering. Madonna Lucrezia is terribly sick."

"What is it? Can I see her?"

"Yes. She wants to see you. But you must prepare yourself. She's dying, Sandro . . . Forgive me, I'm crying again, and I promised her I wouldn't. The only thing that worries her is that we are all so unhappy." Ginevra put her hand to her lips, unable to speak anymore.

"How like her," said Botticelli. "Mamina. I'll go to her and tell her shocking stories about Rome. I'll laugh at them myself." He wiped tears from his eyes, smiled broadly. "I can do anything I must, if it will make her happy . . . I know what to do. I'll beg her for something to eat . . . I'll even eat it."

Lucrezia de' Medici died peacefully in her sleep just as the sun was rising on the first day of the New Year, March 25. The church of San Lorenzo could not hold all the people who had loved her and came to mourn her.

Lorenzo was so controlled that Ginevra was alarmed. He accepted the condolences of all the mourners personally, wrote responses to every letter of sympathy in his own hand, comforted the children, composed an elegy and designed the memorial on which it was to be carved, chose the location for it in the hospice that was Lucrezia's preferred charity, selected the architect to rebuild and enlarge the hospice in her name. All this in addition to his regular work on behalf of the Republic. He was like a stranger to Ginevra.

Until the day that she received a summons to his study. He was at his desk, a mass of papers in front of him. When he looked up at her, his eyes were full of the pain he had been hiding. "This is Mamina's estate," he said. He held out a folded, ribbon-tied sheet of vellum. "She has willed Morba to you. Here is the transfer." His hand was shaking.

"No," Ginevra said, believing that he was hurt because Lucrezia had trusted her with the spa instead of him. His next words proved her wrong.

"You must take it, Contadina. This is what she said." He read from the document on the desk; his voice trembled, like his hand. "I leave the sulfur baths at Morba to Ginevra della Vacchia with the hope and trust that she will persuade my son to go there for treatment of his infirmities . . ."

Lorenzo tried to smile. "I can see her now. She hated doctors so much. Remember how she'd make her hands into little fists and wave them about when she talked about them? This makes her so real . . . Ah, Ginevra, I have such an emptiness in my life without her."

He looked to her for help; his face was desolate.

"I know," she said. "I know." She went to him and took him in her arms, cradling his head against her breast.

Lorenzo's arms circled her waist; he held her tightly, his head heavy against her. And then he wept.

Ginevra rocked him gently. Her fingers stroked his hair, pulled tendrils away from his mouth and eyes. His tears dampened her dress, soaked it, were warm upon her heart, and a piercing joy mingled with the grief she shared with him. This is all I ever wanted or needed, she thought. To love him and to have him want my love.

When Lorenzo's shuddering breaths became exhausted sighs, Ginevra moved her hands to hold his face and turn it upward. "You'll sleep now," she whispered. Her thumbs stroked his eyelids closed, and she kissed them.

She left the room quietly, the taste of salt on her lips from the tears that were caught in his lashes.

Chapter Forty-five

How will he be today? Ginevra woke with the question in her mind. What will he say? What should I say, how should I act, now that everything has changed?

She danced with happiness when she got out of bed, hummed while she washed, laughed to herself when she rubbed her skin with the perfume that had sat unopened for more than a year.

Then she stood in front of her wardrobe, and her gaiety fled.

What should I wear? A lucco, to tell him that I'm still his companion? We might go riding, to the farms, maybe, or one of the villas. Or my patched gamurra costume that I wear for a disguise? I'd look like a real contadina. He might like that. Or he might want me to dress up, in celebration of last night.

She held her hands against her breasts where Lorenzo's head had rested and rocked her body from side to side, as she had rocked him.

She lifted the rose-sewn cioppa from its shelf and shook it, held it up to the light to enjoy the shimmering colors of the silk.

No, she decided abruptly. I'll dress as I usually do, in the lucco. No one else need know that today is a special day. It can be our secret. But I'd look prettier in women's clothes.

"Clarice," she said aloud. The sound of her voice made her jump. She put her hand over her mouth.

She had never liked Clarice, rarely thought about her or even saw her. Clarice lived a separate life. She was content in a world of women friends and talk about

315

childbirth and lazy servants and new clothes, Ginevra imagined, and she had always dismissed Clarice and her world as frivolous and unimportant.

But Clarice was Lorenzo's wife. She had a right to be considered; her pride should be protected.

Ginevra threw the festive cioppa on the bed and grabbed a lucco from the wardrobe. Everything must seem to be the same. She and Lorenzo were friends, nothing more.

Before dressing, she washed off the perfume.

'I don't believe it,'' Ginevra said.

''But yes, donna, he left early, with Piero and his tutor. They were going to visit the cousins at Castello, I think he said.''

Ginevra dismissed the steward and stared down at her breakfast plate. Wrong. She was wrong. Wrong in thinking what she thought, wrong in doing what she had done.

You've been through this before, she told herself. Wanting what you cannot have, letting yourself believe that wanting will make things be the way you wish they would be. You'll get over this. You have to. And you did before.

She left the food untouched. She'd eat later. Her own food, from La Vacchia. And after she satisfied herself that everything was being properly handled at the villa, she'd go to Morba, learn what her responsibilities were going to be.

After that enough time would have passed and she could be with Lorenzo again, a friend.

Chapter Forty-six

"Why don't you have the Academy meet at your villa in Fiesole?" Ginevra asked Lorenzo once. "Marsilio never leaves his little house, and a change would do him good."

"He'll never change," Lorenzo replied. "None of them will. My grandfather started the Academy, and he gave the house to Ficino to live in while he worked on his translation of Plato. They were meeting there when I was still a boy; it's the home of the Academy. Nothing less than an explosion would make them alter the pattern."

The explosion came in May.

His name was Pico della Mirandola.

"It was an omen," Marsilio Ficino said. He had just completed the translation that he had been working on for more than twenty years when his servant told him that a young scholar was at the door asking to see him.

Pico was a phenomenon; to the tenets of Neoplatonism, which he understood in all their complexity, he added new, extended, elaborated theories based on his studies of Eastern religions, the occult, and the Hebrew Cabbala. He had taught himself Hebrew, one of the twenty-two languages he commanded.

"I must paint him," said Sandro Botticelli. And all of the other artists in Florence.

Pico was the ideal embodiment of young manhood. His flowing hair was the color of gold, his eyes the blue of the Tuscan sky. He had a lithe, perfectly proportioned body and a beautiful, symmetric face made radiant by the blazing intellectual excitement that ruled his nature.

"He is a saint," said the people of Florence. In spite of his virile athleticism and his beauty, Pico was celibate. He did not condemn the libertine life around him, but he did not take part. Not in the popular pursuit of women, nor in the prevalent relaxed practice of homosexuality.

"He's like a comet," Lorenzo said, "filling the world with light and excitement." He was fascinated by Pico's genius and gave him rooms at the Medici palace at once.

He's my fantastic new friend, thought Ginevra. Pico's mind fascinated her, too, as it did everyone. But what she liked best was that he was only nineteen, several months younger than she. For the first time in her life, she had a companion her own age.

Pico was interested in everything; his intelligence had no boundaries. Ginevra took him to meet Leonardo da Vinci, and Pico matched her enthusiasm for Leonardo's inventions and ideas. His parachute, Pico declared, would make travel through mountains infinitely more practical, and Leonardo's plan for straightening the Arno should be carried out at once. It would make the city more geometrically pleasing, and it would require the destruction of the ugliest buildings in Florence.

Even with Pico's support, everyone, including Lorenzo, continued to laugh at da Vinci's inventions. But Pico was able to succeed where Ginevra had failed: he persuaded Lorenzo to extend a limited patronage to the artist. Lodovico Sforza had asked Lorenzo to send him some of Florence's wealth of talent. Lorenzo commissioned Leonardo to make another lute in the shape of a horse's head, this time in silver.

"I cannot say that this inventor is an artist, but I know for myself that he is a master musician. The Duke of Milan can decide on his talents as an artist when he sees the lute that will be my gift to him. I'll send it with a letter praising da Vinci's music; Leonardo can deliver both to him.''

The lute and the musician were only two of the many gifts that Lorenzo sent to Milan. The alliance with Sforza was more vital than ever. The Pope's nephew, Girolamo Riario, with Venice's backing, attacked Ferrara in late April.

In May he declared war on the small city-state in the name of the alliance between Venice, Genoa, Siena and his own state of Imola, with Rome an implicit partner through his relationship with Pope Sixtus.

Lorenzo had been preparing for the danger. He constructed an opposition to Riario with Florence, Milan and Naples as allies. To represent Florence, he hired an army led by Costanza Sforza, a relative of the Duke of Milan.

There was nothing more he could do, except keep up a steady flow of dispatches between the allies and the armies fighting in the north. And calm the worries of the Signoria and the Republic's citizens.

He traveled a great deal that summer, in spite of recurring attacks of gout. In each of the Republic's subject cities, he gave banquets for the local government officials and businessmen and took part in the celebrations and public entertainments of the ordinary citizens.

''You'll have to take care of the Carnival preparations,'' he told Ginevra. She was happy to agree. She'd have Pico's assistance, and she had a special project of her own.

Pico was as dazzled by Florence as the city was dazzled by him. What impressed him most was the diversity and richness of the art. He had spent the previous ten years in universities, graduating from Bologna with a degree in law when he was fifteen, then going from one institution to another in search of more knowledge. His education was in language, poetry, history, philosophy, theology. Now he was able to educate his sight and his touch.

Ginevra took him from one studio to another, introducing him to all the painters, sculptors, craftsmen in gold and silver, wood, and pottery. She also showed him Florence's treasures in churches and chapels, on streets and piazzas, in the Medici palace and at La Vacchia. Pico's enthusiasm and curiosity were endless.

"May the angels save me," groaned Andrea del Verrocchio, "your friend is as tiring as you are, Ginevra. 'How do you do this?' and 'Why do you do that?' and 'Let me try.' He's like having you around when you were younger."

But Andrea was delighted to be admired and annoyed by the young genius who was the idol of Florence. He agreed immediately to work with them on the Carnival float.

Lorenzo returned from a visit to Pisa just in time for Carnival. "Is the float finished?" he wanted to know, and "What theme did you two finally decide on? According to Andrea, you were changing your minds every hour when I left."

Ginevra and Pico exchanged conspiratorial grins. "Just enjoy the celebrations, Lorenzo," Ginevra said. "You'll be surprised."

The surprise came hours before the float was unveiled. Morello, Lorenzo's racehorse, won the Palio, with Ginevra riding, dressed as a page.

It was the first time in the history of Florence that a winner was disqualified. Even with a new haircut and disguise, she was too well-known in the city to pass for a man, and it was unthinkable for a woman to be in the Palio.

Lorenzo did not even pretend to be angry with her. "You have disgraced me and the house of Medici," he said, smiling, "with the greatest triumph of my life. Morello shall have all the sugar he wants for the rest of his days, and you, my devilish contadina, shall have anything you name. What will it be?"

"I already have everything I want," Ginevra said. It was very nearly true.

Pico's design for the float was so elaborate and learnedly metaphorical that no one in Florence could understand its meaning. Therefore it was widely acclaimed as the finest of them all.

"I'll tell you in confidence," Lorenzo murmured to Ginevra, "I don't know what it represents."

"I don't either," Ginevra laughed, "and I was there, nodding vehemently, when Pico explained it all to Andrea."

Of all the artists, Sandro Botticelli became Pico's closest friend. Sandro was an ardent Neoplatonist, and he came closer to understanding Pico's rapid speech and leaps of thought than any of the others.

"He's like fireworks," Sandro said. "Pow, pow, pow, pow, words one after another, one on top another, with ideas shooting off in all directions at once in explosions of brilliance . . . I wonder that beautiful head doesn't burst."

Botticelli was just beginning to work on a large painting that Lorenzo commissioned for his young cousin's villa. The subject was the Birth of Venus. Pico announced that he would serve as Sandro's assistant. "I'll tell you about the Venus-worship cults, and of course the more interesting worship of Aphrodite, while you paint. It will help you."

Sandro chuckled. "I'll show you how to separate eggs and which pigments to mix with the whites and which ones are fixed in the yolks. Then we can both work while you talk."

Pico also served as the model for one of the zephyrs that were blowing to shore the shell that carried the figure of Venus.

Ginevra mixed the paints. "Geniuses," she said with a laugh, "seem to have little skill with their fingers. Pico was so busy talking that he kept crushing the eggs in his hand."

She was glad to have an engrossing and amusing project like the painting. Lorenzo was preoccupied with a new love affair. He violated all the laws of the curfew and of good sense by riding out to the villa of Bartolommea dei Nasi every night and returning at dawn. His guards grumbled more and more as the weather got colder. They had to wait outside while he had his amorous adventure.

1483

Chapter Forty-seven

The Birth of Venus was hung in its place at Castello soon after the first of the year. The weather was cold enough to freeze the road surface, and Lorenzo arranged a gala procession to accompany the cart built especially to transport the nine-foot-long painting.

The manes and tails of the horses were plaited with ribbons, and rosettes of ribbons fluttered on the cart and on the sleeves of all the riders. Pico led, carrying a banner Sandro had painted with a scene of a procession like the one he was leading.

Lorenzo and Sandro were next, one on each side of the cart, with anxious eyes watching the packing that held the painting steady. The most skilled and most cautious drayman in Tuscany was the driver of the cart.

Poliziano and Ginevra were in the rear, with equally anxious eyes on the children. All of them were included. Even Giuliano, who was not yet four, was seated in front of one of Lorenzo's guards on a little saddle arrangement.

When Lorenzo rebuilt the Villa Castello for Pierfrancesco's sons, he included many more chimneys than usual, and the boys spent almost the year round at the villa instead of the darker, less comfortable house in the city. There were warm fires in all the rooms when the chilled procession arrived.

"What a luxury!" Ginevra said when she saw the fire in the entrance hall. She immediately began to calculate how many barrels of wine and oil La Vacchia would have to produce for her to earn enough money to add chimneys there.

Lorenzo's namesake offered to show her the other

luxuries of Castello. He was very proud to be master of such a fine house.

Ginevra and Pico accepted his offer eagerly. Neither of them had been to the villa before. Their exclamations of surprise and admiration made young Lorenzo grin with pleasure.

How strange, Ginevra thought, I might have been living in this house and married to this boy if there had been no conspiracy to assassinate Giuliano and Lorenzo. How strange and how awful. He's only a child. My age, but a child. It would have been a miserable life, no matter how many fireplaces and other elegancies the house has.

She had seen young Lorenzo only at big family parties; this was the first time she had talked to him at all. She decided that she liked him, as long as she didn't have to marry him.

As the day went on, she liked him even more. Even though he had a host's good manners, it was obvious to Ginevra that he did not like Piero, Lorenzo's oldest son. Neither did Ginevra.

She tried, but she couldn't find anything about Piero to like. He was not particularly intelligent. Giovanni, not yet seven, was already more advanced in his studies than Piero, who was almost five years older. Worse, Piero had no charm. Ginevra couldn't understand how any child of Lorenzo's could be so lacking in a quality that Lorenzo had in such ample measure.

The other children were charming, each in his or her own way. Ginevra loved Giulio best of all, but she admitted that she was biased in his favor. He was the first baby she had ever held; she felt protective, too. He was old enough now to know that he wasn't really one of Lorenzo's children, even though Lorenzo called him son. Ginevra would have bet that it was Piero who told Giulio he was a bastard. It was the kind of thing Piero would do.

Young Lorenzo's brother Giovanni didn't care for Piero either, Ginevra saw. She smiled at him, thinking how glad she was that he was betrothed to Luisa. Of all the girls, Luisa was her favorite.

Once the painting was hung and toasted and Sandro was congratulated and Pico was complimented for making a superb zephyr, the customary rowdy games began. Within minutes the children had all the adults acting just like Lorenzo, wrestling or playing tag or serving as horses to be ridden. Even Pierfrancesco's sons gave up their dignity as hosts and became horses for the joust that Lorenzo organized between the two teams he selected with a careful balance of ages and stamina.

Botticelli, with Contessina kicking him and screeching orders to go faster, finally declared that he could play no more. "Another five minutes of this, and I'll have so much sympathy for horses that I'll be condemned to walk for the rest of my life."

In spite of the children's protests, Lorenzo said that it was time for them to leave.

Without the cart, the ride back to the city was much easier and faster. When they stopped at the San Gallo gate, Lorenzo, who was talking with the guards about their work and their children, turned in his saddle and grinned. "How would you ill-behaved young demons like to have an adventure?"

The cheers made the people around them smile at the big happy family.

"Well then," Lorenzo said. "We will not go home yet. We'll all have an early dinner at the trattoria."

The children were ecstatic. None of them had ever been to a restaurant.

The hospice of San Gallo was a long two-storied building attached to the monastery just outside the gate. Originally it was a simple shelter for travelers who reached the city after the gates closed at sundown. But when Lorenzo rebuilt it in his mother's memory, it was enlarged and improved, with comfortable rooms instead of dormitory spaces and with a dining room that served meals to any needy citizen of Florence in the daytime as well as meals for the travelers staying overnight.

The complex had opened only a few months earlier, but already the news had spread that the food there was the best of any trattoria in Florence. Many Florentines came and bought their dinner.

The restaurant was operated by a family that shared in the profit it made. Lorenzo, who had given them the job, was welcomed as if he were Zeus himself.

In less than a minute, the long tables were pushed to new positions so that one was left in the center of the room with ample space setting it apart from the others. A white cloth was spread over it, cushions put on the benches, and flasks of wine at the four corners.

"The rumors are true, for a change," said Sandro an hour later. "The food is superb."

"I think it's better here than it is at home," Maddalena said. "Can we come here every day, Father?"

"No, we cannot," Lorenzo said, "and you'd better not tell the cooks what you just said, or you'll be given nothing but bread and water for weeks . . . Now, all of you, wipe your hands and faces and go tell the *padrone* how much you enjoyed your meal. It's near dark and time to hurry."

While the children were crowded around the proprietor and his wife, Lorenzo poured himself a cup of wine. "Agnolo . . . Ginevra . . . will you take the children home? I'm going to stay a while and find out how the hospice is doing. Sandro . . . Pico . . . you can go or stay, as you wish."

Sandro reached for the wine. "I could be persuaded to eat some more."

Pico said that he would go. He had some writing to do. Country air always gave him fresh ideas.

The serving girl brought more *osso buco* for Sandro; Lorenzo waved the ladle away from his bowl. His fingers turned his cup, but he did not drink. He was watching the girl as she walked away.

Sandro grinned. "A new interest, Lorenzo? What has become of the intriguing Bartolommea, then?"

Lorenzo grimaced. "Don't mock me, Sandro. The ache in my bones was punishment enough for that folly.

I wonder sometimes if the gout affects my head as well
as my legs."

Botticelli chewed slowly, his eyes thoughtful.

The girl brought more food, but he shook his head.
"Magnificent?" she said. She stood behind Lorenzo,
her breast barely touching his shoulder. Sandro turned
his head to look at her, and she stepped back hurriedly.

"Later, perhaps," he said. The girl blushed and went
away.

Lorenzo turned on the bench to face his friend. His
face was angry. "You assume too much, Sandro."

Botticelli laughed. "A safe assumption, I thought."

His joke didn't lighten the tension between them. He
shrugged, swung legs over the bench, stood. "I have
the feeling I should go home." He started to adjust his
cloak, then stopped, threw it across the bench.

"Listen to me, Lorenzo." He sat again, lowered his
voice to speak for Lorenzo's ears only. "Put your anger
aside and know that I love you like a brother. I have
something to show you. I've been waiting long
enough."

Lorenzo's curiosity outweighed his temper. "It had
better be very interesting, you meddling loudmouth."

Sandro nodded. "We'll see." He got up and walked
quickly to the fireplace. He raked out a half-burnt stick;
three hearty puffs, and the flame was out. He sat down
again and began to draw on the white tablecloth with
the smouldering charcoal, shoving the dishes to one side.

The conflict was forgotten at once. Lorenzo moved
closer to his side.

"Now, my friend, tell me who this is." Botticelli's
hand moved with broad, sure strokes. A face looked up
from the table.

"It's the maid," Lorenzo said. "Bravo, Sandro. I'll
have the cloth mounted and framed. It will make a good
gift." He reached for the portrait, but Botticelli stopped
his arm with the stick.

"Wait, my friend," he said, "the artist is at work."
He made eight lines, and a second portrait was magi-
cally before him. "The illustrious Bartolommea." His
left hand shoved the tableware onto the floor. While the

clatter still sounded, he drew another face on the cloth he had cleared. "Madonna Luisa Felceroccia," he said.

Standing now, Botticelli made room for three more faces sketching so rapidly that Lorenzo's eyes could not follow his movements.

"The peasant's widow when we went hunting last summer; the whore you visit so often; the wife of your latest appointment to the finance committee." The stick tapped each portrait as Sandro identified them. "You remember, do you not?" He grinned at Lorenzo. "You've been busy these last months, Magnificent."

Lorenzo shrugged. He was frowning, but his wide thin mouth quivered with suppressed laughter. "I am but a man like any other," he said blandly. "Luckily you do not accompany me more often on my travels. We'd need a bigger cloth."

Botticelli held up a hand and demanded attention. "Now look at this, Lorenzo," he said. He was not laughing.

His thumb touched the portrait of the prostitute, smudging the outline of the chin, adding a shadow beside the nose. Then it moved to the next face, softening, contouring, adding dimension. And to the one next to it, and the next, and the next. Lorenzo made a deep growling sound in his throat. Botticelli's hand hovered over the face of Luisa Felceroccia.

"Stop!" Lorenzo commanded. He grabbed Sandro's wrist.

"I have finished," Sandro said quietly. "You see, my friend. It would be the same with this last one." The portraits on the tablecloth were transformed by the tiny alterations the artist's thumb had made. Now they were all different aspects of the same woman. It was Ginevra's face, repeated six times over.

"I don't understand." Lorenzo shook his head from side to side. "It's some kind of trick."

"No trick. Just your blindness. You have not the artist's eye. The wonder is that you, a poet, have been so deaf to your own heart."

Chapter Forty-eight

"Why are you looking at me like that, Lorenzo? You make me nervous." Ginevra combed her fingers through her hair. "Do I have a spot on my face? Spinach between my teeth?"

Lorenzo forced a laugh. "No, nothing. I was thinking of something else, not really seeing where my gaze was fixed. Forgive me, please."

Botticelli's revelation had made him uncomfortable. It couldn't be true, he told himself, that he was in love with Ginevra. A man knows if he wants a woman. And all of Sandro's nonsensical talk about loving as different from wanting was just that . . . nonsense. As for the business of searching for Ginevra in the arms of those other women . . . he had never heard anything so absurd in all his life. It was just the kind of medieval overblown romantic notion one could expect from a man who had nearly destroyed himself over the death of a woman he had never even met.

The troublesome thing was that, in some way he couldn't understand, Ginevra now seemed different. It was as if a stranger had moved into her place. She didn't even look quite the same. She was older. Not the child he remembered, with her prankishness and ignorant recklessness. She was a woman, and her mannish clothes were not really an adequate disguise. Her skin was tanned, like a man's, but it lay over the bones of her face in gentle contours, covering firm, soft flesh . . .

"Stop that, Lorenzo. Stare at the wall when your mind wanders, not at me."

* * *

After several weeks Ginevra was so edgy that she turned to Gigi Pulci for help.

"I can't understand what's wrong with Lorenzo, Gigi, and it's driving me crazy. Do you know? Is he worried about something? Does he have some sickness? It's not the gout, I know that. He's had no trouble lately, I thank God."

Pulci rubbed his chin, a habit of his when he wanted to delay an answer to a question.

"Ha! You do know. What is it?" Ginevra snatched his massaging hand away from his face.

Gigi laughed. "You notice too much . . . In truth, I don't know. I've seen the way he's been acting to you at dinner. I thought you must have had a colossal argument, and I was hoping you'd give it away . . . Did you, Ginevra? Fight? About what?"

She shook her head. "If we did, I don't remember. Surely I'd remember a quarrel. One day, for no reason, he was different; that's all I remember. He started looking at me as if I were a statue he was examining for the collection at Bertoldo's garden. And then he began to avoid me. He's even having breakfast in his rooms now. I don't know what to do, Gigi. Should I say I'm sorry for whatever I did that I don't know I did?"

"Are you sorry?"

Ginevra's temper flared. "Most certainly not. I'm not the one who's at fault. I haven't done anything to apologize for . . . But I'm ready to jump out of my skin. I wish it would get warmer. Then I could go to La Vacchia and work my nervousness out in the fields. I'd really like to get away from this house."

"Let me see what I can find out," said Pulci. "I'll take Lorenzo on a tour of the taverns to loosen his tongue."

"And then you'll tell me?"

"Word of honor."

Ginevra hugged him. "You are a good friend, Gigi. I love you dearly."

And I'll make do with that, Gigi thought. He no longer made elaborate protestations of love to Ginevra. The humor of his adoration had been as short-lived as all good comedy must be. But his affection for her was a permanent part of his life. The only truly decent part, he admitted to himself.

There was no opportunity for Gigi to learn anything from Lorenzo. He left to take the baths on the same day that Ginevra asked for Gigi's help.

From Bagno a Ripoli, he sent word two weeks later that he was going to Pisa for meetings at the University. He also sent an invitation for Pico to join him.

Ginevra was furious. She and Pico had been enjoying themselves, she more than ever, without the tension that Lorenzo's mood had caused. They were helping Domenico Ghirlandaio with the ambitious fresco he was doing in the small old church of Santa Trinità.

The Sassetti had commissioned it as a votive offering for their child's recovery from sickness, so of course the parents would be portrayed. But many other Florentines were going to be in the groups of people witnessing the miraculous resuscitation by St. Francis. Pico had succeeded in doing the impossible. All the scholars of the Platonic Academy were actually coming to Ghirlandaio's studio to be drawn.

Pico kept them occupied while Domenico sketched, arguing the finer points of his most recent theory on the true nature of witches.

Ginevra translated Ghirlandaio's requests for posing into Latin so that the Academy did not have to break their train of thought with a shift into Tuscan.

Now that Pico will be leaving I suppose I'll be expected to do both, she grumbled, dispute the origin of evil and move Ficino's arm back to where Ghirlandaio wants it. I won't do it. I'll send word to them not to come. I'm not fit company for anybody, not even myself.

She scrawled a letter to Ficino, then grabbed it back from the messenger she told to deliver it. "Wait," she said. "I'll bring it back in an hour."

Her irritability was not sufficient justification for the blotted, nearly illegible letter. She climbed the stairs to the third floor of the palace.

It was an area that she almost never had cause to visit. The priest had his room here, and the astrologer, and the servants, men-at-arms, guards. Also the dozen scribes that Lorenzo employed to make copies of books from his library. He gave the copies away. To the library at San Marco or to rulers of city-states or to the scholars of the Academy or to the Universities. He had been building a collection for Poliziano ever since Agnolo came to live at the palace. Four books had already been made for Pico. A bookbinder had a room on the third floor and a workshop, next to the many-windowed scriptorium where the books were copied.

Ginevra barged into the scriptorium. "Good morning," she said. "Would someone please make a handsome letter for me? My writing is out of control today."

All heads turned to look at the newest, youngest scribe. Ginevra smiled at him and gave him the paper in her hand. "Lucky you," she said. "Just paper, please, no parchment. And no decorated letters, no gold, no flowering vines, nothing elaborate. I'll be back for it in a half-hour."

Before he could argue, she left.

She wandered through the maze of intersecting hallways, mildly curious if any ambassadors might be living in the suites that were always ready for official visitors to Florence. It was usually interesting to talk to people from a different city.

"Good day," said a rasping voice.

Ginevra looked around the edge of a half-open door. It was the astrologer's room. She tried to back away, but he urged her to come in, and he sounded so lonely that she relented.

She stayed for more than an hour.

When she left, she was so preoccupied that she turned in the wrong direction and found herself walking into one of the third-floor dining rooms instead of the scriptorium.

"I'll run into the Minotaur next," she muttered as she retraced her route.

The young scribe was sprinkling sand on the letter when she found the right door.

"All finished, Madonna," he said, exhibiting his work.

"Thank you," Ginevra said. She did not even notice the splendid red and gold letter A that began the letter. Nor did she pay any attention to the marked annoyance of the impatiently waiting messenger. Her thoughts were chaotic, spinning uncontrolled in her mind.

She walked automatically, as if in a dream, to the one place in the great house that had been her refuge from confusion in the past, the sitting room that had belonged to Lucrezia de' Medici.

Nothing had been changed in the comfortable sunlit room. There was even a faint echo of the rose-scented perfume that Lucrezia always wore; it came from the simple straw basket filled with the potpourri Lucrezia had blended from her garden. Her maid stirred it every day in memory of the mistress she had so loved.

Ginevra moved erratically, touching the tables, cassone, Lucrezia's desk, the bench beneath the window that overlooked the garden, and lastly, the chair at the desk where Lucrezia sat to write her poetry. The chair faced a wall hung with green silk brocade. The portrait of Giuliano was in the center of the wall. Below the painting were two fluted terra-cotta pedestals, holding the busts of Lucrezia's two sons.

Ginevra went slowly toward Lorenzo. "Why?" she said to him. "I don't understand anything that's happening." She touched his face with tentative fingertips, then sobbed once only and pressed her hands against his cheeks, holding his head between them. Her fingers explored the bone beneath his brow, the indented crease above his eye, the irregular contours of his nose and the straight thin line of his mouth. Just so had she longed to touch him.

The sculpture was hard. And cold, although she willed it to draw warmth from her hands.

Ginevra backed away from it, her fingers still reaching toward it. She drew in a long, ragged breath and turned. "Madonna Lucrezia," she cried, "I need you so much." She knelt by Lucrezia's chair as she had so often done and buried her face in the cushioned seat. Then she wept, as she had wept in Lucrezia's lap.

"I'm so bewildered, and there's no one I can talk to, no one to help me see reason in anything that has happened. Lorenzo shuns me. I'm hateful in his eyes. And I don't know why.

"I don't know him anymore. He's so cold and far away. He's no longer Lorenzo.

"He's been visiting the astrologer, Madonna. You know that's not his way. I don't mean for ordinary things like choosing the best day to begin a voyage or sign a treaty or open the ground for a new building. He always did that, like everyone else. But this is different. I'm frightened. He ordered my charts done. For my whole life and my future. Why? What's he looking for? Have I become all Pazzi to him, someone to guard against?"

Ginevra sat up on her knees and pivoted to look at the bust. "You had no right," she cried, and she shook her fist at him. "If you wanted to know something about me, you had only to ask. I would have told you anything . . . except my heart's secret, and that is something you wouldn't want to know. Why did you go behind my back, set that horrible old man to spying in my stars?"

Tears poured down her face, and she rubbed them away with her fists, venting her anger on herself. When she had no tears left, she leaned back against Lucrezia's chair and stretched her legs out on the floor. "I'm so unhappy, Madonna," she said quietly.

She looked at the sunlight slanting through the window onto the painted songbirds of the tiled floor. After a long time, the colors began to fade with the dying day. I should wash and change my clothes before dinner, she thought, but she didn't stir. She felt too tired to move.

The curtains billowed, and she turned quickly toward the door that was opening in the shadowy wall, scrambling to her feet, forming an apology for intruding into Lucrezia's room.

"Ginevra?" It was Lorenzo. "What are you doing here?"

"Forgive me. I'm sorry. I know I shouldn't be. I'm going right now, and I won't ever . . ."

But Ginevra stood where she was. His dark outline was in front of the door, blocking her way.

"Don't go," Lorenzo said. "Please." He walked toward her, into the dim light, his hand held out.

Ginevra stared at it, then looked at his face.

"Will you stay with me, Contadina?"

She put her hand in his.

"Your hand is cold," he said.

"Yours is warm."

Lorenzo's eyes traveled from place to place in the room. "Mamina," he murmured.

"I'm glad nothing has been changed," he said to Ginevra. "I can almost feel her presence. Do you feel it too? Is that why you're here?"

"No," Ginevra said. She couldn't lie to him. "I came looking for her, but I didn't find her."

"You found me instead." Lorenzo squeezed her hand.

Did I? Ginevra wondered. Why? Why are you holding my hand, why are you changed, another different Lorenzo that I don't know?

"I thought you'd gone to Pisa," she said. It was an accusation.

Lorenzo released her hand, walked away from her. "I was going to, but I changed my mind. I met Pico on the road and turned him back." He looked out the window, unfolded a shutter, then folded it back again.

"Ginevra." He turned as he spoke. "Contadina, help me." The light was behind him, and Ginevra could not see his face. His voice was rough with need.

She ran to him, but he called out to her to stop. "Let me speak from a distance," he said. "I came to say what I have to say to Mamina first, as I would have done when she was here. I thought . . . I hoped . . . it's so hard to explain. If I could tell her, then in the telling it might all come clear to me . . . That used to happen, when I talked to her. Do you understand?"

"I think I do. Maybe."

Lorenzo laughed. It was a harsh, short sound. "Of course you don't. How could you? I'm talking like a fool, making no sense at all. Ginevra, will you turn your back, for God's sake? I can't say these things when you're looking at me, when the light is on your face, when I can see you."

"I'll go, then."

"No!" It was a roar of anger. "This is bad enough. I could not go through it a second time. Ginevra, you're not helping me."

"What do you want me to do?" Her shout equaled his.

His voice rose to a bellow. "I want you to tell me that you love me, and then I won't feel so much a fool when I tell you that I love you . . . What are you staring at, Ginevra? . . . Are you laughing at me? By all that's holy, I'll kill you if you're laughing."

Ginevra put her hands over her mouth, but she couldn't stop the sound of laughter. She dropped them, palms outward, beseeching, begging his forgiveness. "I love you more than my life," she said through the laughter. "I do, I swear it."

Lorenzo stalked across the floor, grabbed her shoulders, shook her. "Stop that! You find me so comic?"

Ginevra sobered in an instant. She put her hands over his and pressed. "Lorenzo," she said, and he stopped shaking her. Her fingers curled around his, and her eyes sought his face. Through their linked hands he could feel her trembling, and when she spoke, her voice vibrated with emotion.

"Hear me, my most dear beloved," she said. "I have longed for you to want my love. It was always yours, though you didn't know it. It is yours now and will be yours for as long as I live. Do you understand what I'm saying? Do you believe me?" She looked into his eyes, hers speaking more than her words could say.

Lorenzo read her heart through them. Astonishment, relief, gratitude, joy were clear in his face. Then its harsh angles melted into the radiant gentleness that is the portrait of love.

Ginevra touched her fingertips to her lips. "Don't say anything," she whispered. "Let me . . ." She lifted her hands to his face and felt its textures, its powerful structure, and it was all she had dreamed it would be, a possessing she had never dared hope for.

She asked no questions about the gift of this exquisite happiness. Not to Lorenzo, to herself, to the heavens. Her desperate "why?" was in the past. She accepted and was suffused with transcendent joy.

Lorenzo held her palms to his lips and kissed them. Then he spoke through her fingers.

"Why did you laugh?" A frown of worry creased the ridge between his eyes.

"My Magnificent, not at you," Ginevra replied. Her mouth quivered, and her eyes were merry. "I had imagined, daydreamed, invented so many ways to hear you say you loved me. But never in a shout. Never in a rage. Not the most musical poet since Dante. It's why I knew it must be true."

It was Lorenzo's turn to laugh. But just as he began, Ginevra raised her lips to his, and they lost themselves in the solemn mystery of their first embrace.

BOOK THREE

Careggi
1483–1492

Chapter Forty-nine

Lorenzo and Ginevra went in together to dinner that night. They walked side by side, not touching, not with hands clasped, behaving in no way different from any other evening when the friends gathered around Lorenzo's table. It was customary for the first arrived guests to take the places on each side of Lorenzo's chair, with every later arrival filling the empty spots from the head of the table downward. Ginevra went to the next available place, as if it were a day like any day.

But it was not. And the moment they entered the room the fourteen men at table knew at once that something remarkable had occurred. There was a current of emotion between the two that charged the air with excitement, and a radiant happiness illuminated their faces to such a degree that every one of their friends looked away from them, feeling himself a trespasser.

Lorenzo took his place and slapped the table with the flat of his hand. When all eyes were on his widely smiling face, he said, "I feel good tonight and fortunate to be back with my friends. Let's have a round of *rispetti*. I'll begin."

He tapped the rhythm with a spoon and sang in his tuneless voice.

> "A salute now to Sandro
> His drawings are unmatched.
> But if you want to hang them
> You'll have linens torn and patched."

Everyone pounded on the table and laughed. Botticelli's habit of drawing on whatever was closest to hand was a trait that they often teased him about.

Filippino Lippi was at Lorenzo's right. He added his verse to the theme.

> "I suffer as his helper
>   From women on the street,
>   Who admire me through the window
>   When I sleep without a sheet."

The table rocked with the pounding of approval. Everyone knew the story about Sandro pulling Filippino's sheet off when he ran out of the tremendous pieces of paper he used for life-size sketches.

They looked toward Pico, seated next to Filippino. Rispetti were an import from Sicily, a childish game of wit that went back further than anyone knew. The impromptu verses had to be sung one right after another, going around the table and back to the initiator of the subject. To falter, to break the rhythm, was to earn loud criticisms and insults from all the other players.

Pico's mind was occupied with an elusive idea that had just come to him about a connection between mathematics and the hierarchy of the angels. He didn't realize it was his turn until too late. Chunks of bread pelted him from all sides, and Agnolo Poliziano, next to him, took up the game with an altered focus.

> "Beware the profound thinker
>   His is a woeful lot.
>   He says he's not a drinker
>   Yet has less wit than a sot."

The rispetti went on, taunting Pico's appearance, his verbosity, his perpetual tardiness, his hot temper. Gigi Pulci's verse was the most applauded of all. He emptied his wine cup and gargled as he sang.

> "I drink a toast to Pico
>   With hair of fairest gold.
>   I hope you shed your virginity
>   Before you get too old."

The young philosopher's face flushed, and he started to rise from his seat. Ginevra, next to Pulci, sang so loudly that her off-key notes made the others groan.

> "I have these thoughts for Pico.
> Don't let Gigi make you mad
> For you can say in twenty tongues
> Pulci, your joke is bad."

Pico settled down, with a smile for Ginevra, and the rispetti took up the new theme of attacks on Gigi's humor.

He relished the challenge and replied to each singer with a verse of his own, doubling the pace and the raucousness of the game.

When the stewards brought in the food the game ended. Pico offered up his new theory for discussion, and the disputation was intense.

Without losing the tangled thread of the argument raging over the table, Lorenzo caught Botticelli's eye. He said nothing; there was no need to. His opening verse of rispetti was his acknowledgment that Sandro had shown him the way to the happiness he now knew, and the oblique expression of his gratitude.

At the end of the evening, Lorenzo ordered torchbearers and an escort of guards to take his friends to their homes. It was the way the dinners always ended in the months when darkness and curfew came too early.

Ginevra said her good-nights with no visible indication of the turmoil she was feeling. How could she tell Lorenzo that her love knew no limits, that she wanted to express it in every way, that she yearned to make love with him—but not yet?

Not in this house, with his wife and his children by that wife sleeping quietly under the same roof that sheltered the union of her body with his.

For there were no qualifications to Ginevra's love. There had been a terror of submission in her deepest soul ever since she was raped, but it had no place in her emotions now. She wanted to be a part of him, with him a part of her, no matter how great the pain to her body.

But her heart begged for more than an invitation to Lorenzo's rooms or a visit by him to hers. Secrecy and hypocrisy would tarnish the beauty of the most important moment of her life, the fulfillment of all her dreams.

How could she make Lorenzo understand that her reluctance did not mean that her love was less than entire?

The guests were gone, but Pico showed no signs of going to his room. He began immediately to defend the thesis he had proposed earlier.

Lorenzo held up his hands. "Pax," he said, laughing.

"I'll happily argue with you all night, philosopher. But Ginevra doesn't deserve such a punishment. Hold your arguments until I come back."

He walked toward Ginevra, his eyes speaking love. "Come with me, Contadina."

She rose from the bench to meet him, her head whirling with the conflict between her longing to be with him and her aversion to the circumstances.

Lorenzo's arm was strong around her waist when he walked her into the hallway. At the top of the stairs he stopped, turned her to face him. "Good night, my love. Will you meet me for breakfast?"

Ginevra's heart hammered with joy. How foolish she had been. Of course Lorenzo understood, without the need for words.

"I'll see you in the morning," she said.

"Do you love me?"

"With my whole self."

"As I love you."

He kissed her hand, and it was all that she required for ecstasy, a promise of caresses to come.

She did not know that Lorenzo had no plans to take her into his bed that night. Or any night.

As days and then weeks went by, Ginevra grew convinced that the love Lorenzo professed to her was of a kind different from what she felt for him.

His looks and his words and his kisses and his hands holding hers were a feast for her heart. But a feast was not enough. Her love was gluttonous. She spent dejected hours tormenting herself for her failings. If she were more intelligent he'd love her more, she told herself, and she studied through the night. If she were talented . . . she practiced for hours on the lute. Again and again she looked into the polished silver mirror in her room and wept. She was too ugly.

Finally she went to a house on the *via delle Belle Donne,* the street of the Beautiful Women. She felt people staring when she turned into the street; it was lined on both sides with houses of prostitution. Ginevra stuck her chin out and knocked at the biggest house.

"I want to see the patroness," she told the servant who opened the door. "I have money."

She chinked the bulging purse at her belt when she was ushered into the madam's studio. "I will pay well to be made beautiful," she said.

And a day of torture began.

First she was stripped and scrubbed from head to toe with pumice stones. Then, while she soaked in a bath of nettle juice to whiten her skin, the patroness plucked her eyebrows. The whores worked in relays to pluck the hair from the front of her head to give her the exaggerated tall forehead that was the ultimate of ideal beauty.

"Now there's a strip of white scalp over that brown face, you stupids," the madam hissed when they were finished. "Quick, go to the markets and get the ingredients for the strongest complexion potion."

To Ginevra, she said, "Already, donna, you are the rival of any beauty in Florence. By the end of the day, you will be the queen."

Ginevra had nothing to say. The nettle juice was a fire on her raw-rubbed skin, and her head felt as if it had a thousand wounds.

She submitted dumbly to being dried with rough toweling and coated with a foul-smelling black paste, then wrapped like a mummy in strips of linen soaked with egg white. This is worse than when I was bandaged over my broken bones, she thought, but I will bear it.

Her hair was washed in vinegar, then pulled through the open crown of a wide-brimmed hat and covered with a white ointment.

"Now we go on the roof to let the sun work for a while," said the whores cheerfully. While Ginevra baked and itched and sweated, they played dice and shouted down to any man who entered the street, "Go home and surprise your wife with her lover. We're closed today."

Strong odors rising from the open door of the house made Ginevra's nose twitch and her stomach rumble. How can I be hungry when I'm suffering so much? she wondered. But she was, and she ate the bread and the cabbage soup the madam brought her with a healthy appetite. "What else are you cooking?" she asked. "It smells delicious."

The patroness laughed extravagantly; all the oiled rolls of rosy fat on her body shook with delight. It wasn't food, she explained, although some might think it was. It was a cosmetic lotion better than any apothecary could make. Proud of her expertise, she gave Ginevra the recipe: a white dove, purest white, killed and plucked, beheaded, disemboweled, wings and feet removed. Washed a hundred times with equal amounts of grape juice and sweet almond oil, a handful of ground pepperwort added. And afterward the washing solution boiled and strained to distill the dove's whiteness. "It is a lotion of my own design, donna, and every other house on the street is desperate to learn its manufacture."

Ginevra took a solemn oath not to reveal the secret.

When she was wondering if she could endure one more minute on the hot tiles of the roof, her beauticians took her back into the house for more treatments. She lost count of the number of times her head and body were washed and rubbed with secret distillations.

Finally she was dressed in a chemise and seated next to a table that held a greater assortment of rock crystal jars and gold pomade boxes than she had ever seen, even on the street of the goldsmiths. What a profitable business prostitution must be, she thought. I'll ask Lorenzo what it costs to visit a house like this.

For the first time since she had arrived that morning, Ginevra remembered why she was there. "Will I be beautiful?" she asked. Her voice quavered with hope.

"But most assuredly," said the madam. "I know my business. Now close your eyes so that nothing will get in them." Ginevra obeyed.

The sensation of practiced fingers at work on her face and shoulders and hair was thrilling. She *would* be beautiful, and Lorenzo would say that not even Lucrezia Donati had ever been so desirable.

"*Ecco,* Madonna," the patroness said triumphantly. Ginevra opened her eyes.

One of the prostitutes was holding a mirror up for her to look in. It was one of the fabulously valuable Venetian mirrors made of silvered glass that even the Medici palace did not have. It gave the most accurate reflection that she had ever seen.

Her face was her own and yet not her own. It was covered with a white paste and brightly rouged and it extended far up onto the top of her head. Black lines surrounded her eyes and made thin arcs above them; a black velvet heart was at the corner of her mouth.

All this, and still there, prominent, was her long nose, made longer and more visible by its whiteness between the red on her cheeks.

Black velvet hearts dotted her hair, too. But her hair was not the light brown braid that she knew. It was paler and redder and nearly invisible in the intricate constructions of shiny yellow silk false hair.

A red velvet heart was nested in the hollow of her white-painted throat.

She was a grotesque. Lorenzo would be repelled when he saw her.

Ginevra looked in the mirror with despair. Beyond her painted, powdered shoulders she saw the pride-filled faces of the madam and the whores.

"A transformation," said the youngest of them. "You must be very happy, donna."

"Oh, yes," Ginevra said. "You've worked a miracle." Why should she make them as miserable as she was?

"You have something fitting to wear? A red silk, perhaps, or an amethyst velvet? And jewels?"

Ginevra promised that she did. She put on her secondhand gamurra and cioppa and handed the patroness the bulging purse.

"I'll take two florins, Madonna," the woman said eagerly. "You understand, the cost of doves these days is a scandal, and my girls could have been earning . . ."

"Yes," Ginevra said, "I understand. Keep the purse, all the money. You've been so kind, all of you. I must run . . . someone waiting."

As soon as she was out of sight of the women waving goodbye, she did run. She kept her face down, looking at the pavement, so that no one could see it. When she crossed the river she slowed to catch her breath.

Then she climbed the hill that led to La Vacchia, leaving bright streamers of false golden hair at the sides of the road as she walked and tore it off her head.

Chapter Fifty

Ginevra dug out the stubborn weed with the buffed, shiny fingernails the whores had been so proud of the day before. She wanted to obliterate every trace of her foolish attempt to change what she was. Then maybe she could erase the memory of it.

"Where is she?" It was Lorenzo's voice; he was in the house. Ginevra pulled her kerchief farther down on her forehead to cover the loathsome white plucked skin, bent closer to the flower bed, wishing she could burrow into it. She tried not to hear his footsteps on the gravel path, forbade herself to look around at him, no matter that she yearned for the sight.

"Ginevra!" He sounded angry. She hunched her shoulders. "Ginevra, look at me."

She could not do otherwise.

Lorenzo's arms were full of flowering branches. Above the soft pink blossoms his glowering face looked like a thundercloud. "Why didn't you come home last night?" he growled. "I had the guards out on the streets until dawn, looking for your dead body."

"You did?"

"Of course I did, fool. And this morning, what was I supposed to do with all these? The Careggi cart was first through the gates when they opened, with Ginevra's May Day bouquet. But where was Ginevra? Playing at mud pies at her villa."

Ginevra's whole body felt as if it were filled with bubbles, as if she could float up into the air in weightless cartwheels of exuberant happiness. He did love her. He worried about her. He gave her May Day flowers.

In Florence, on May Day, a suitor fastened a bouquet to the door of the house where his beloved lived.

Lorenzo glared at her, then he exclaimed, threw the flowers to one side and fell on his knees near her. "My heart," he said, "forgive my temper. Let me hold you." One arm pulled her close to him. "What happened? How did you get hurt?" His hand touched her brow, pushed the slipping kerchief back some more.

Ginevra struggled to pull it forward. "I don't want you to see. Stop. Stop, Lorenzo, I beg you."

"What is it? I have to know. I'll kill whoever did this to you."

Ginevra folded her arms over her head. "I did it." She began to cry.

Lorenzo held her to his chest, rocking her as she had once rocked him. "Hush," he said in a tender voice, "hush little one, hush my sweet, silly contadina. Nothing is worth your tears."

"I look like a clown," she wailed.

"No you don't. You look like a grubby peasant girl who had something go wrong with her hair. Hair grows, Contadina. And I love peasant girls above every other kind."

"I was such a fool." She was blubbering now, enjoying her misery because the comfort was so precious.

"Yes you were . . . Now we're both fools to be sitting here on the muddy ground when the May Day celebration has started in the village. Stop your crying and let's go join it."

Ginevra sat up, eager to go. She loved the village festivals, but she had never been to one. Then she clapped her hands to her head. "Somebody will see me," she moaned.

"I'll tie your kerchief tight. And pin a flower on it."

May Day in the country villages was a much livelier affair than the respectful, quiet city tradition of leaving flowers. There was always music: sometimes bagpipers from the hills, often a tethered donkey with cymbals tied to his back and a thistle tied under his tail to make him move constantly and produce a resonant clanging.

And the age-old tradition of the Maypole had survived away from the cities, so there was dancing to the music. Village maidens, wearing garlands and girdles of flowers, leapt and danced and displayed their charms while they wove bright ribbons down the pole.

The music had already started when Lorenzo and Ginevra reached the village. They joined the group of peasants laughing at the donkey and clapping in counterpoint to the cymbals.

"The Maypole, let's have the Maypole," the crowd shouted. The men's eyes were bright with anticipation of seeing the young girls; the women's were dreamy with memories of their youth; the children capered with high spirits.

A breeze tugged at the ribbons fastened tight at the top but looped in a loose knot at the base of the pole; it pulled them free. They flew upward, swirling out from the pole like a rippling tent of colorful stripes, and the crowd ran laughing to catch them, work-roughened hands reaching high to try and capture the elusive brightness. Lorenzo held his hands around Ginevra's waist and lifted her up among the fluttering colors. "I've got one," she cried, "no, two . . . three . . . oh, one got away . . ."

The maidens ran out from their waiting place in the chapel. They, too, were lifted by strong hands to capture ribbons of their own.

"Dance," the people demanded, "dance." They fell back to the edges of the tiny village square and clapped, stamped, whistled, shouted.

"May I?" Ginevra asked the girls around her.

"With pleasure," one replied, then another and another.

"Begin," said one of the girls. Ginevra faced her and threw up her arms in imitation of the girl's stance. Then, following the pattern of the other dancers, she dipped under a bridge of ribbon, passed her streamer over the dipping flowered head bobbing toward her, under, over, leaping, laughing, over, under, faster, faster, under, over, closer and closer to the pole until her arms were around it, mingled with the arms of the maidens, embracing the interwoven colors around the pole.

Above their heads, the ribbons that had had no dancers danced wildly in the wind.

"Again," the villagers cried, and the young men ran to hold the maidens high.

Lorenzo took Ginevra's hand and drew her away. "We must leave," he said in an undertone. "Someone recognized me. It will ruin everything."

"Over the wall," Ginevra said. "I'll show you where."

La Vacchia's lands bordered the south end of the village; Ginevra had sat on the wall hundreds of times when she was young to watch the contained busy life of the square. She led Lorenzo to the spot where a tree's roots had weakened the stones' balance and tumbled half the wall down.

The grasses in the hayfield were only inches high. Yellow and red and white wild flowers were blooming thickly above them. Ginevra ran in a spiral through the vivid colors and ended at his side, swaying and giddy.

"It's wonderful, Lorenzo, how I could have been so dispirited and now I'm so happy. I'm dizzy with happiness."

"I am, too," he said. He was intoxicated with her freedom, her abandonment to life and its music and color.

Her kerchief was askew, and the white streak of forehead was a dreadful vulnerability on her brown pink-cheeked face. Lorenzo steadied her with firm hands on her shoulders. Then he pulled with hesitant fingers at the edge of the kerchief. Ginevra flinched and pushed his hands away, shifting the cloth with rough shoving motions to cover the baldness.

"Don't," Lorenzo said. "Not like that. You'll hurt yourself. Why did you pluck your hair that way, Contadina? And your lovely brows?"

Ginevra looked at the flower-studded ground. "I wanted to be beautiful. I was a fool." She swallowed her fears and looked up at him. She had to know, had to ask, although the answer might destroy her. "Is it my ugliness that you cannot bear, or is it something else, something I can alter? I'd do anything, anything at all, Lorenzo."

His face twisted with bewilderment. "I don't know what you're saying, what you mean. I love you, Contadina. I love everything about you. I love to look at you, to hear you speak, to watch you move. What are you saying?"

"You don't make love to me."

Lorenzo was stunned. He shook his head, trying to clear it, to think, to make sense of her words and her wide, questioning, apprehensive eyes.

Then "Ginevra," he said, "sit here beside me." His fingers circled her wrist and pulled her down with him onto the young grass. He looked into her searching eyes and spoke slowly, trying to explain to her all that was still a mystery to him.

"I am thirty-four years old, Ginevra, and I am like a child with this love I feel for you. I thought I knew what love was; I loved often and strongly. But this . . . I knew nothing of this.

"What you're talking about, 'making love,' was what I used to call love. Not always. A man can have a woman sometimes for no reason more complicated than the pleasure of it. But when I thought I loved, it was the taking, the possessing that I wanted.

"With you, my love, everything is different. I feel that you are mine and have been mine forever; before the world began you were mine, just as I was and am yours. You are part of me and I of you.

"And yet I love you in a way that has nothing to do with me . . . or rather, I love you by means of ignoring and eradicating myself. When my body rises and my hands ache to caress you, my heart controls them. I love you too much; I can't let you know again the agony of a man's lustfulness . . . I remember your scars and think of your suffering, and my very soul recoils."

Ginevra took his hands in hers. Her eyes glistened with tenderness. "I've been a bigger fool than I knew. I promise you that I'll never let my worries fester anymore. And you must promise me that you won't hide anything from me. Not your basest thoughts and not your noblest ones. If we're both going to be fools, at least let's be fools together.

"I want you, Lorenzo. I want you to touch my breasts, like this." And she held his hands to her breasts. "Ah, I've wanted this for so long."

Under his palms her breasts stiffened and thrust against his hands. Lorenzo cried out, held them, pressed his lips to her heart, felt it leaping at his touch.

They loved each other on a bed of flowers, slowly yet urgently, exploring their separatenesses with gentleness that became strength and then burst into power that swept them into a melting of hearts and souls and bodies that made them one.

After, they looked deep into one another's eyes, eyes heavy with the languor of spent passion and love. Lorenzo kissed the curved scars on Ginevra's breasts. And Ginevra kissed the thin straight scar on Lorenzo's neck. And the tragedy of the Pazzi murders was healed.

Chapter Fifty-one

"I want to show you my work," Ginevra said after they dressed, and she led him through all the fields and vine-yards and olive groves of La Vacchia.

When they came across one of the farmers, the man's awed reaction to Lorenzo made her understand why they had left the village so quickly. To these people, Lorenzo was the Magnificent, and they were semiparalyzed in his presence.

"Is it always like this for you?" she asked him.

"Except with my friends. Sometimes even with them, if they want something."

"How sad and lonely." She held his arm close to her.

Lorenzo smiled. "Don't romanticize, Contadina. I had a choice when I was young, and I chose to have power. I've never considered the price too high."

But she still thought his isolation was sad, and she vowed silently that she would so envelop him in love that he would never know loneliness again.

At midday they took bread and cheese and wine back to the flowered field and ate there, then made love again.

"I'll never cut this grass," Ginevra sighed. "I want it to stay untouched forever, as a shrine to this day."

Lorenzo laughed. "I'll remind you of that when September comes and you look at the fine hay to be made." He dodged the pretend blows of her fists.

In the afternoon they rode to Careggi. "This will be our home," Lorenzo said. "I've always been happiest here; it's the right place for us to be lovers."

* * *

A little more than two weeks later, Lorenzo rushed into the garden at Careggi in search of Ginevra. She was transplanting her favorite iris from La Vacchia to the newly dug beds by the table under the trees.

He picked her up and swung her in a circle. "I told you that you were my luck," he cried. "What I most wanted is beginning to happen." He set her on the table and kissed her.

Ginevra was too breathless to ask what he meant. Lorenzo needed no prompting. He walked back and forth in front of her, telling the good news.

The King of France had finally responded to the letters written by other heads of state and ambassadors and noblemen at Lorenzo's urging. He had presented the Abbey of Font Doulce to Lorenzo's son Giovanni. That meant that the boy now had a position in the Church. He was an Abbot.

Or he would be as soon as the Pope confirmed the grant.

"My son will be a Cardinal one of these days," Lorenzo declared. "This is only the beginning."

Ginevra frowned. "I don't see how you can expect Sixtus to do you any kindness when the war has begun again at Ferrara. Rome is Florence's enemy, I thought."

Lorenzo chuckled. "But France is my friend and more powerful than Rome. Sixtus cannot offend King Louis. That's why all the letters were written to him."

Ginevra grinned. "I see, you fox. It's the fleur-de-lis neck chain you wore to Naples all over again. No wonder you're such a good chess player."

Lorenzo's grin was even wider than hers. "The reason I'm such a good player is that you always concede halfway through the game so that we can go to bed. Wanton." He kissed the soft stubble on her forehead.

In the short time since they became lovers, they had created a life together that ideally suited them both. The city was still the center of their lives, and their separate lives were still busy. But Careggi was only a short ride from the city gate, and they easily found occasions to retire to its tranquil privacy.

Sometimes they stayed the night, sometimes met for

a midday meal under the trees, sometimes went separately to carry out the changes they planned together, changes that would make the villa specifically theirs. Careggi was retreat and sanctuary, the place where they were most truly themselves, where they could give their hearts and minds and love to one another without reservation. Careggi made it easy to live in the city the way they had always done, as friends. There was no deceit, but they never displayed their love. It was a private treasure, too new to be shared with anyone else.

On May 31, a message arrived from Rome. The Vatican had approved King Louis's benefice to Giovanni.

It was what Lorenzo had expected, and the next step was all arranged. The following day his old tutor, Gentile de' Becchi came to the palace in his role of bishop of Arezzo. The family gathered in the tiny chapel to watch as he confirmed Giovanni and then clipped his hair at the crown to make a tonsure.

During the celebration that followed, Lorenzo toasted his son, using Giovanni's clerical title *Messire*. Pico was standing next to Ginevra. "Curious system this Republic of Florence," he said, "where a child can be titled while his father, the ruler, is not."

"I don't understand this whole thing," Ginevra admitted. "How can a seven-year-old boy be the Abbot of a monastery? Even if it is a French abbey."

Pico's beautiful smile lit his face. "Ginevra, you delight me. Do you really believe the Church is as simple as a priest bringing God to the people? The Church is politics and diplomacy and power . . . and behind all that, the repository of truth and the guardian of heaven. Anything is possible in the Church."

Ginevra remembered his words a week later when word arrived that Giovanni was also now the Archbishop of Aix-en-Provence.

"I thought our opponents must be just about ready to start fighting among themselves," Lorenzo said in the middle of July. "Now I'm sure of it. Venice is going to leave the Pope's nephew to dig his own grave."

He had just come up from the city, and he was hot and dusty from the ride. Ginevra poured water into a bowl and dampened a cloth for him to wipe his face and neck.

"Thank you, my love."

When the grime was removed, Lorenzo's lips showed the telltale rim of paleness that meant he was in pain. Ginevra silently cursed the war that demanded his daily rides to the city for work at his desk and in conferences with the government. This latest attack of gout was not as severe as some earlier ones, but it had lasted for more than a week. The war was shadowing their summer at Careggi.

It affected Florence hardly at all, she knew. All the fighting was well to the north, and there was no danger to the Republic. Florence's only role was to support Milan, which might be at risk if Venice's ambitions extended beyond the small city-state of Ferrara, the announced objective. But even that limited participation called for Lorenzo's careful attention to the reports from his informers that came to the palace every day and for interminable meetings with various committees and officials.

"If Venice breaks with Riario, how soon will the war end?" she asked.

"The fighting, probably not until the winter truce. The division of the spoils could take years. We'll need to set up a series of negotiations."

Ginevra's expression was glum.

"Cheer up, Contadina," said Lorenzo. "Even a war can bring unforeseen benefits. Don't you want to know why I'm certain that Venice is abandoning Riario?"

"Why?"

"Because the Doges have asked Andrea if he will accept a commission. They want a Florentine artist, even though Riario is the enemy of all things to do with the Republic. Clearly they don't care whether he likes it or not. Ergo, that alliance is not as firm as it once was."

Now Ginevra was genuinely interested. "What did Andrea say? Is he going to take it?"

Lorenzo laughed. "You know him. Verrocchio is always interested if the fee is big enough. But he's a man who loves his comforts. I don't know if even the wealth of Venice can lure him from his studio and his home.

"He must be in a real quandary. I got the news from a man in Venice, not from him. I guess he can't make up his mind. I sent word to him that we miss his noisiness at table; I hope he'll come for dinner. I want to see him stew."

Careggi had replaced the palace as the regular gathering place for their friends. The long days made it possible for them to return to Florence before the gates closed. And the union between Ginevra and Lorenzo was so complete now that they did not need to shelter it from intrusion.

"You guessed wrong," Ginevra teased. "Andrea's was the most made-up mind I've ever seen. I've never known him so excited about anything."

Venice wanted Verrocchio to make a statue commemorating the general who had led their army in earlier wars. Not just a statue, an equestrian statue in bronze. And life-size or larger. Padua, a small city in the Venetian State, owned the only statue of that kind that had been successfully executed since the days of the Roman Empire. It, too, was a memorial to a Venetian general, a bronze figure on horseback. It was one of the wonders of the age. It had been made by the great Donatello.

Andrea's voice had been unnaturally hushed when he talked about it. "To think that I'll have a chance to match the master. It's the most daring work I'll ever be called on to attempt. And if I succeed, I will have done something that no other man living could possibly do. It will bring me immortality."

He left a month later. At the farewell dinner Lorenzo and Ginevra gave for him, everyone had too much to drink and many people cried. Andrea would be gone for years.

Ginevra's tears had already been shed that afternoon when Andrea arrived at Careggi before Lorenzo was back from the city.

"I wanted to see you alone first," Andrea said, "and to give you a present. It's a different kind of memorial. I couldn't say these things if I weren't going away, Ginevra, but I am so I can. I've been fond of you ever since you were a little girl, but this summer I've come to love you. For the happiness that you give my friend Lorenzo and for the lesson you've taught this cynical old heart. You two are proof that a perfect love can exist. I never thought I'd believe such a thing."

"Andrea . . . thank you."

"Stop sniveling, Ginevra, or I'll have to blow my nose. You haven't even seen the gift yet. It's one of the best things I've ever done, a happy thing for this oasis of happiness you've created."

Andrea unrolled the bundle he had taken from his baggage, and Ginevra saw the enchanting playful smile of a bronze cherub. He was very young, with the chubby feet, creased wrists and ankles, round cheeks, round stomach that make little children so delectable. Small wings suitable for his age held him balanced on one foot while he clasped a large gracefully twisting fish that was trying to escape his hands.

"Andrea, I love him. And you. He's a masterpiece, and . . ."

"Enough, Ginevra. It's a fountain for the garden you're making here. Water will spout from the mouth of the fish. I would hate to learn that you had done something tritc like St. Francis and the birds."

1484–1486

Chapter Fifty-two

"We must be crazy," Lorenzo said.

Ginevra laughed. "You do look just a little bizarre," she said, "but definitely magnificent." The rain coursed down his nude athlete's body and plastered his hair to his beautifully shaped head. Rivulets spattered onto his thick chest from the wreath of vines that was askew across his brow.

"You're like a water nymph who fell into the river." Lorenzo grinned, flicked a drop off the end of her nose. She, too, was nude, her wreath a sodden circlet of wild flowers. Lorenzo had picked them and plaited the wreath with his long, supple fingers before the rain began. They were in the field at La Vacchia where they had first made love three years before. Every year on May Day they came back to recreate the joy of that discovery. This was the first time it rained.

Ginevra reached up and adjusted his wreath; Lorenzo's hands touched hers, then slid down her wet arms to her sides and pulled her close to him. She clasped him around the neck, their eyes met, exchanged wordless vows, and their laughter ceased. As their lips met, the rain stopped as suddenly as it had begun and a warm breeze brushed the chill from their wet bodies.

Ginevra held one hand above Lorenzo's face to shield his eyes from the sun while he slept. With her other hand she moved his wet hair from his forehead. She was always happy when he took his short naps; they restored the strength that so often deserted him as his illness became more and more debilitating. And they gave her the opportunity to look at him, gloating over the treasure

361

of his love the way a miser gloated over his hoard of gold. She only did it when he was asleep. It made him uncomfortable if she feasted on the sight of him this way, made him feel, he said, like one of the casks of olive oil that she counted with such glee every year after the pressing of La Vacchia's harvest.

She had told him about the gloating, of course, the way she told him everything in her heart and in her mind. As he told her everything. The intimacy they shared was complete, the union of their bodies only a part of it.

Ginevra brushed an insect from Lorenzo's shoulder and inhaled the sweetness of the grass and flowers drying under the sun. She alone knew that Lorenzo was at bottom a sentimentalist. The anniversary ceremonial was his idea, as was the celebration of their birthday every year. There were never guests for dinner that night. Just the two of them, at Careggi. While they ate, they celebrated all the good things that had happened since the previous birthday, and then, after dinner, they drank a toast to one another and said "I make a gift to thee of my heart" before they made love.

She smiled, remembering the first year. They had nearly frozen to death. Careggi was designed for summer living, not for naked romps on the first day of January. Lorenzo built the loggia that spring. It extended to the rear of the house, to the south, and the arches were filled with panes of glass. Everyone they knew was shocked by the heresy. A loggia wasn't a loggia if it was enclosed.

They all ate their words, though, when winter arrived and they came to have the midday meal in the sun-warmed room edged with lemon trees covered with premature blossoming.

"Doesn't your arm get tired making a parasol that way?" Lorenzo was awake.

Ginevra flexed her arm. "Now that you mention it, it does. I didn't notice. I was remembering that first birthday at Careggi."

Lorenzo smiled. "We were even more crazy that time than we were today. You were blue with cold."

"Ha! You were green."

"Nonsense, woman. I'm a hot-blooded Italian male. Come here and I'll prove it to you."

Ginevra nestled against him; her head found the hollow near his throat where she loved to rest, and her hands began their slow exploration of the body they knew so well.

"That feels good. Over to the left a little, then scratch. Something bit me."

"How's that?"

"Perfect. That's enough; you can move on now."

"With pleasure, if you're willing to let Pico cool his heels."

Lorenzo made a growling, grumbling sound. "I'd forgotten. We'll have to go." He turned to his side, and Ginevra's head slid off his chest and onto the ground.

"Brute," she said. "Just for that, you'll have to go alone. I'm going to go look at the vineyards while the farmers are busy in the village getting drunk."

"Coward," Lorenzo said. He laughed at her vehement nodding. "Don't think you'll escape that easily," he warned. "Tonight I'll tell you everything he tells me."

"I don't mind that. You don't insist that I agree with every word."

Ginevra was annoyed with Pico. She was doubly annoyed that Lorenzo thought her irritation was funny. She grudgingly admitted that the Platonic Academy was more exciting with Pico as a member. More agreeable, too. Invigorated and prodded by him, the scholars had become more flexible and more human. They actually came to Careggi now, where the meetings were more comfortable. And when Ghirlandaio's fresco was finished, they went to Santa Trinità day after day, just to be sure that the thousands who came to see the painting would recognize them as the same men who were in the group on the left side.

But, she insisted, Pico's self-esteem had exceeded all decency. Two years before he had gone to Rome and presented the Curia with a monumental list of nine hundred questions. "I am able to give answers to all of them," he boasted, "and I will debate them publicly with anyone who dares."

The questions covered every subject from mathematics to theology, based on texts he had studied in Hebrew, Arabic and Chaldean, including his favorite, the Cabbala. There was no debate. The Cardinals examined the list and declared that thirteen of the questions were heretical.

Pico escaped from Rome before he could be arrested and fled to France. But the Vatican's influence easily crossed the border, and he was taken prisoner in Vincennes. It took almost a year and all of Lorenzo's influence to have him released from the dungeon there.

Ginevra believed that Pico would be grateful to be free. In Spain heretics were going to the stake.

But Pico, when he returned to Florence, announced at once that he was right and the Church was wrong.

Now he wanted to show Lorenzo the treatise he had written "to prove it," as he said.

Lorenzo tied the laces of Ginevra's gamurra and patted her bottom. "There," he said, "all done. I like you in wet clothes, Contadina. They emphasize your charms."

"I like you in wet no-clothes," Ginevra replied with an exaggerated leer. "Too bad you have to go listen to absolute proof that a word with seven letters and no vowels means that Pico della Mirandola is the smartest man in the world."

Lorenzo smiled. "Cruel. Waspish and cruel. Why is it that I love such a nasty woman so much?" He took her hand in his. "Walk with me to get my horse, harpy. Are you sure you won't come?"

"I'd better not. I might crease Pico's beautiful scalp with a heavy object."

Before he mounted his horse, Lorenzo held Ginevra close. "Happy anniversary, my love."

"Very happy," Ginevra whispered. "Always."

She waited until Lorenzo would be well on his way to the city and then she rode to Careggi. She didn't really want to examine the grapes; it was too early in the year. And this villa was no longer her chief interest. She kept close watch on La Vacchia, just as she did on the baths at Morba that Lucrezia had willed to her. But Careggi was home; they were only businesses.

Both of them produced money that she squirreled away in a lockbox designed for jewels. Lorenzo tried to convince her to put it in the bank, to invest it. Ginevra just replied that she had the heart of a peasant and wanted her gold coins where she could look at them.

"I'd sew them in my mattress, but I know you'd complain about the lumps."

Lorenzo seldom slept in his own bedroom at Careggi.

When she arrived at home, Ginevra turned her horse over to one of the grooms and had a long talk with Emilio, the tyrannical old man who was in charge of the stables. Lorenzo's racehorses were now known all over Europe, thanks to Emilio. He was both breeder and trainer.

It took all of Ginevra's patience and charm to listen to his angry complaints and soothe his offended pride. Lorenzo had sold the horse that Emilio was sure would win the Palio this year.

As she left the stables, she stopped at the pasture fence and whistled for Morello. It was always a thrill for her to watch the handsome stallion running like the wind in response to her signal.

"Ho, beauty," she said, stroking his mane. "I stole some sugar from Emilio for you." She held out her palm and smiled at the precision of Morello's bite when he took the wedge of loaf sugar. "That will have to comfort you, my champion. Lorenzo won't be here until tomorrow." She was certain that he'd stay in the city for the night. He hadn't seen the children for three days, a long time for him.

Morello nuzzled her arm, asking for more. "Sorry, friend, that's all I have," Ginevra said. She put her mouth near Morello's ear and murmured to him. "Emilio has lost his Palio winner, and he's mad at the world. But we don't care, do we? When we had our turn, we won."

Before she went into the villa, Ginevra walked through the olive grove to the pig house. The pigs were the newest addition to Careggi, a breed that Lorenzo had imported from south of Naples. They were reputed to make a prosciutto worthy of the gods.

She scratched a sow's back with a stick while the keeper reported on the feed he was trying out and how much weight his charges had gained.

When she got to her room Ginevra wrote the figures in her journal. She kept a record of everything that happened at Careggi, the dates of planting and harvest, the yields, the weather, the results of the experiments Lorenzo was making in search of the perfect cheese.

She made notes of events in her life, too. Even the sad ones. A page with a thick, inked-black border marked the February day when Gigi Pulci died. But there were blessedly few sorrows to enter in the book. And many joys. At the end of the information on the pigs, she wrote, "May Day. Rain."

She'd need no more than that to bring the whole experience back to her mind.

Her lips twitched with laughter. Lorenzo was right; they must be crazy.

That night when she knelt for her prayers, she thanked God for the craziness.

Chapter Fifty-three

"Your friend Pico is really insane," said Lorenzo when he came home the next day. He was laughing so much that he could hardly get the words out.

Ginevra braced herself.

"He's written a brilliant defense of his supposed heresy," Lorenzo continued, "with an introduction that says that it really should be unnecessary to defend himself at all because it's apparent to any educated man that the Curia's pronouncement is so badly written that all the cardinals must be too ignorant to understand his thesis. Therefore . . . q.e.d . . . they condemned him because his conclusions were too difficult for them, not because they were in error."

Ginevra was horrified. "How can you find that funny, Lorenzo? If he sends that thing to the Vatican, they'll do much worse than put him in prison." She was angry with Pico herself, but she didn't want him to come to harm.

Her solicitude disappeared when Lorenzo finished the story. "Furthermore, the fool has dedicated the defense to me. In gratitude for my support."

"Oh, no! That's too much. I can't believe Pico's such an idiot that he doesn't know what that will do to you. You should put him in a dungeon yourself, Lorenzo. And wall up the door. He'll destroy everything you've worked so hard for. The Pope will turn against you."

The Pope was Innocent VIII, successor to Lorenzo's old foe Sixtus, who had died two years earlier. Innocent was well-named. He was an amiable man, interested primarily in the comforts and pleasures that his position provided for him and for his illegitimate children.

Lorenzo was one of the main sources of those comforts, and his influence over Innocent was already strong.

He hoped to make it much stronger. Very soon. Ginevra's rage against Pico wasn't baseless. The next few months were crucial to Lorenzo's success with the Pope.

"Calm down, Contadina, I'm not going to let Pico take me into the lion's mouth. I persuaded him to leave the defense with me so that my calligraphers can make a suitably impressive copy. He'll probably have some new passion by the time he gets back, and we can all forget this one."

"Where is he going? To China, I hope."

"Next best thing. To Mirandola to see his family. His father cut off his money when he was arrested. Even Pico will need time to regain the Prince's favor."

Ginevra decided to change the subject. Pico was giving her a headache. "I think the pigs are going to be a big success. They're on a new mix for food . . ."

The philosophers of the Academy came to Careggi that evening. Ginevra concentrated on drawing out the young men Lorenzo had invited as guest participants. She sympathized with their shyness because she remembered vividly how she had felt when she was first included. And she liked them because they weren't Pico.

She couldn't help noticing, however, that without him the discussions were predictable and just a little bit dull.

The Academy stayed overnight. The next day the School of Harmony was giving a recital at Careggi. Ginevra watched the sky nervously most of the day, then decided it was safe to arrange to have everyone outdoors in the garden.

The music mingled with the rich perfume of magnolia blossoms, and the sky became rose-tinted. Ginevra sighed inaudibly at the perfection of the moment.

"It was perfect, wasn't it?" she said aloud when everyone went home and she was alone with Lorenzo.

"Perfect," he agreed.

"You're responsible, you realize. You started the School."

Lorenzo kissed her hand. "You remind me after every recital."

"Do I? I didn't realize. I'll stop."

"No need. I like it. I like everything you do."

He held her hand and they were quiet, sharing the tranquility of their home and the beauty of the starlit magnolias, like a hundred pale moons in the trees around them. Verrocchio's fountain splashed gently in the stillness.

With Pico gone, Lorenzo's relationship with Pope Innocent was secure, at least for the time being. In midsummer, he decided that it was time to offer the Pope the alliance that would cement his influence.

Ginevra was away, at Morba, when Innocent's response arrived in Florence. When she got home to Careggi, one look at Lorenzo's face told her that the offer had been accepted.

"God bless those dear little birds," she exclaimed. For two years Lorenzo had included a bag of fattened ortolans with every letter to Rome. Innocent was extremely fond of their delicate flavor. "He said yes, didn't he?"

Lorenzo nodded. "Yes to everything. My problems are all solved."

Innocent's son Franceschetto Cibo was betrothed to Lorenzo's daughter Maddalena. And the papal account was returned to the Medici bank.

"Hurrah!" Ginevra cried. She whirled in a dance of celebration. No one but she knew how desperate Lorenzo had been about money. When his oldest daughter, Lucrezia, was married, he had to sell the great palace that housed the Medici bank in Milan to Lodovico Sforza to raise the funds for her dowry. And when his young cousin Lorenzo came of age, he had to give him the villa at Cafaggiolo and the farms in the Mugello to settle the loan he had made to himself years before.

"Hurrah! Come dance with me, Magnificent!" Ginevra grabbed Lorenzo's hand and pulled him into her wild leaping circling.

"Contadina, no." He stumbled and fell against her.

Ginevra stopped at once, threw her arms around his waist to support him.

She smiled, as if nothing were wrong. "I've got a good idea. We'll go take the baths as a celebration. Morba is beautiful and it's cool up in the mountains."

Lorenzo stroked her cheek. "You never have been able to tell a lie convincingly, my love. There's no celebration to it. You want me to have a treatment for the gout."

"Yes, I do. Last year it did you a world of good. You had no pain at all for months. And I really should have stayed longer at Morba. I'm building a new set of rooms, and I should see them finished. If we leave tomorrow . . ."

Lorenzo put his finger over her lips. "That's enough. I'll go to the baths. I've been planning to, as soon as Innocent's reply arrived." He removed his finger and kissed her.

"But I won't go to Morba with you. I don't like being 'the friend of the owner.' I prefer a place where I can complain and be disagreeable like all the other gouty old men. I'll try Spedaletto this time. You can finish your buildings while I'm there, and we'll both get home at the same time."

"No, I'll go to Spedaletto with you. I like to know what the competition is doing. I hear there's a splendid new masseur there, and I might just hire him away."

She had, in fact, heard about the masseur. She intended to take lessons from him. Lorenzo's legs stiffened in the winter, and her massages no longer seemed to help.

Chapter Fifty-four

There was snow on the terrace outside the glassed-in loggia. Ginevra and Lorenzo scattered bread crumbs over it so that the birds could share their birthday celebration.

"What was your favorite thing of the whole year?" Ginevra began the ceremony.

Lorenzo answered immediately. "May Day in the rain. What was yours?"

"That's what I was going to say. Now I'll have to find something else . . . I think I'll choose the song you wrote for Carnival. It was so funny that the boys singing it kept stopping to laugh . . . And do you remember the one with the curly red hair? He was so dense that even after all the rehearsals he didn't realize what it was all about."

Lorenzo laughed. "And then one of the others explained, and his face got as red as his hair . . . get the instruments, Contadina, and let's sing."

". . . Look, Lorenzo, we've driven the birds away." Ginevra stuck another chord, and Lorenzo began another song. They sat on benches facing each other, Lorenzo with the lute, Ginevra with the mandolin. And they laughed at their own tuneless voices and at the marvel of being with the one other person in the world who didn't mind the cacophony.

They often made music together, because both of them loved music and both were good instrumentalists. When they weren't singing, the pleasure was more serious. On their birthday, the pleasure came from sharing everything, even their common weakness.

* * *

The rule was that only happy subjects would be allowed on their birthday, so Lorenzo waited until the following day to tell Ginevra about the problem that had developed with Pope Innocent.

"I never thought that lazy old man would be in a hurry about anything," he grumbled, "but there were four letters from him yesterday. Four. All dictated on the same day. That's in addition to the five that came last week. He says that his son is impatient, but that can't possibly be true. Cibo is even more indolent than Innocent."

The Pope wanted the marriage between his son and Maddalena to take place in the spring, as soon as the weather permitted Maddalena's travel to Rome.

Lorenzo needed to wait until the bank's income from the papal account accumulated enough money for the tremendous dowry he had promised to give with his daughter.

"All my financial problems are solved, I said. Remember? Now lack of money is about to ruin the very alliance that was supposed to do the solving. I can't tell Innocent why he'll have to wait, that's obvious. I have to find a plausible excuse."

"Her age?"

"She's almost fourteen; that won't do. I'll have to try something that's at least reasonably believable. I could say that Clarice doesn't want to let her go. That's true enough, but I don't know if it's plausible. Still, Clarice is an Orsini, and in Rome that means a lot, even to a Pope.

"That's it, Ginevra. It's worth a try, anyhow. I'll tell Innocent, with all the heartbreaking eloquence I can manage, that I want the wedding as much as he does, but that I must ask for a postponement. Ask on Clarice's behalf. She cannot bear to part with her favorite daughter just yet. She begs to keep Maddalena with her a bit longer, because she's not well, and her favorite is such a comfort to her.

"That's true, too. Innocent's spies can tell him that. Clarice hasn't been really well for weeks. She has severe indigestion . . ."

Ginevra stared at him. He had just violated their other rule. He had talked about Clarice.

It was allowable to talk about her as an element of diplomacy. But not as a real woman who could feel pain. Ginevra always had, at the back of her mind, the knowledge that she was an adulterer, that Lorenzo was a husband as well as a father. But she managed to keep it at the back of her mind by avoiding Clarice in person and in conversation.

"I'm jealous," she had told Lorenzo. And when he tried to convince her that jealousy was uncalled for and unworthy, Ginevra was adamant. "I don't care about any of that, Lorenzo. The fact is, I'm jealous, and I don't want to talk about Clarice. Ever. You'll have to respect my feelings, whether they're reasonable or not."

Until now, he had remembered. And when he saw Ginevra's expression, he remembered again.

Pope Innocent accepted Lorenzo's excuses and agreed to delay all preparations for the wedding until Clarice's health improved. He also sent a gift for her, a crucifix that he had blessed and a vial of water from the River Jordan to sprinkle around her room.

Lorenzo told Ginevra only that the delay was accepted.

She hugged him with ferocious affection. "There's never been a diplomat to match you," she said.

She said it again a few days later when Lodovico Sforza sent a gift to Lorenzo. It was a deck of cards, each card intricately painted with scenes, symbols, figures against a patterned gilt background. Cards were something new in Europe; even Lorenzo did not own any.

"Sforza's letter says that they can be used to tell the future or to gamble," he said. "Which do you prefer? I could send to the gypsies for a teller."

"I prefer the present to the future. We can figure for ourselves how to use them for wagering. We'll play after dinner. Everyone can help invent the game."

The cards were an immediate sensation with their friends. Botticelli tried to persuade Lorenzo to commission him to paint a set. Lorenzo refused with a laugh.

"I already have this set, Sandro, and I can't afford to buy another one."

Everyone laughed at that.

The gift Lorenzo received in the spring was a sensation for all Tuscany. The Soldan of Egypt sent him a giraffe.

The Florentines fell in love with the fabulous, graceful creature. They lined the streets when it was led in procession around the city and flocked to see it in the special tall stable that was built for it near the church of Santa Maria Novella. As word of the marvelous animal spread, people began to come in from the countryside, then from nearby towns, then from towns and cities at distances up to a hundred miles away.

The guild of goldsmiths made a chain to tether it; silk painted in the pattern of its hide appeared in the clothes of both men and women; streetwalkers copied its swaying movements when they walked and glued on stiffened dark hairs to copy its fanlike eyelashes; every artist in the city sketched it, painted it, modeled it in clay, sculpted it in marble; elegant women of all ages wore their hair dressed in a style that had knobby twists of hair in front like the giraffe's soft horns.

For May Day, Lorenzo introduced the country Maypole to the city. It had long been the custom for the nuns of Santa Trinità to feed the poor in the small piazza in front of the church on May first. Lorenzo had the Maypole erected in the center of the piazza. He convinced the families of a dozen young maidens that it was perfectly respectable for their daughters to perform the Maypole dance. "My own Maddalena will be one of the maidens," he said.

Ginevra was given the task of teaching the girls how to dance; Agnolo Poliziano wrote the poem for the music Lorenzo composed; a singer and a lute player learned the song.

"Personally, I think the donkey with the cymbals is more fun," Ginevra said that afternoon, "but it was lovely, and everyone thought it was perfect."

"We'll talk about it later," said Lorenzo. "After our anniversary celebration." He unlaced her gown and drew her down onto the carpet of flowers in the field.

They went to a new spa that year. It was at Filetta, near Siena, and it was the newest thing in luxury. Ginevra barely had time to take the baths because she was so busy making sketches and notes of improvements for Morba.

Lorenzo delighted in teasing her by saying that the marble-columned building for the hot sulfur spring was irrelevant. Filetta's waters were better than Morba's; he felt better than he had in years.

But then a courier arrived, and his high spirits disappeared.

"Ginevra!" He was distraught. "I thought I'd never find you. We're leaving at once. Hurry. I'm leaving a man to bring our things. We can't be slowed by a pack-horse." His healthy color was gone; he looked drawn and ill.

"Clarice is dead." His voice was full of pain and sorrow.

On the racing, punishing ride to Florence, Lorenzo said scarcely a word. At the palace, he went straight to his children.

Ginevra went to her room and waited to be told what to do. She felt very isolated and lonely.

Chapter Fifty-five

"Contadina, I'm sorry that I can find so few chances to see you. I must be with the children, and there are all the letters to all the Orsini about the burial and the other letters about Piero's betrothal to Alfonsina Orsini and the arrangements for Maddalena's wedding and . . ."

"It's all right, Lorenzo. I understand. I don't mind, really I don't."

In truth she did understand. And she didn't mind being alone at Careggi. What she minded was that Lorenzo worried about her as if she were one more of his responsibilities, like the children or the government. She minded even more that he was so tired and that the white rim of pain was circling his lips. Most of all she minded her own uselessness to him at a time when he should be helped and comforted.

If her hidden heart cared that he was so stricken by Clarice's death, she didn't allow herself to recognize it. She was very busy. Although she stayed away from the city and her friends there to avoid gossip from the Florentines and uncomfortable sympathy from them, she had plenty of work to fill her days at La Vacchia and Careggi. At harvest time there is always something to do on a farm.

And as the days grew shorter, there was plenty of time to think during the long evenings.

About Lorenzo. About herself. About the two of them together. And separately.

There wasn't enough of her without him, she decided. If Ginevra were truly separate and self-reliant, Lorenzo wouldn't feel responsible for her, wouldn't feel the need to apologize when she had to fend for herself.

But I'm a part of him, just as he's a part of me, her heart protested. We can't be separated. He's my love and my life.

You will be separated, her mind said. Lorenzo is fourteen years older than you are.

Ginevra covered her ears with her hands, refusing to listen.

And her thoughts continued, loud and cruel inside her head: he's ill and will get worse; you have the strength of a peasant.

She struggled against her mind, but it caught her off guard when she was least prepared to shut out its insistent voice.

When she took out her journal to enter the number of new olive trees started, it fell open to the note she had made so many years before when Gigi Pulci died on the floor of his favorite tavern in a puddle of wine.

And she woke in the dark night, terrified of what she saw in her dreams.

Until at last she knew what she had to do.

"My heart, I'm so glad to be home." Lorenzo's arms were strong around her. "Leave your gardening and let's go inside. I want some food and some wine and the haven of our loggia. There's so much to tell you."

The plans for Maddalena's marriage were complete at last. She would leave for Rome immediately after Christmas, with Piero heading the escort. He would have ample opportunity to talk to Innocent about making Giovanni a Cardinal during the weeks he'd stay in Rome before the wedding on January 20.

Lorenzo was talking very fast and eating very little. Ginevra waited for him to tell her why he was nervous.

"There's not enough money yet to make up the dowry, Contadina," he said. "I'm giving them the Pazzi palace and villa at Montughi to complete it."

Ginevra smiled. "Did you think I'd mind? I never knew those places. La Vacchia was my home."

Lorenzo tore a piece of bread and dipped it into the

sauce on his plate. "This is exactly what I wanted, I'm ravenous."

Between mouthfuls, he told her about Piero's wedding. It would be in May, on the twenty-second. Alfonsina's party was scheduled to arrive around the first. "But I wrote the Orsini that anything earlier than the second of May would not do." His glance was mischievous. "I always strip to the skin and do pagan things in hayfields on May Day, I told them."

Ginevra giggled. She felt girlish, a little shy after so many weeks apart, and tingling with excitement.

Lorenzo looked rather shy, too, and his smile was like a boy's. He took her hand and said, "After we suffer through Piero's ceremonies, we can get our strength back. Then we'll get married here, with only our friends for guests. It will be a joyful occasion instead of a circus."

Ginevra held the smile on her face. "You must be teasing," she said. "You know very well, my love, that I don't ever intend to marry. Not even you. I need my freedom to be happy."

It was the first lie she had told him since the day they became lovers. It was a lie demanded by the love she felt for him. She could not let him die without peace, thinking about her, worrying about her, feeling responsible for her. There would have to be many more lies in the years ahead, until he was satisfied that she would be able to have a full life without him.

Lorenzo had always said that she was incapable of lying, but love gave her the skill in the hours of argument that followed her blithe rejection of what she wanted most in the world.

She imagined that she saw a flicker of unconscious relief in his eyes when she convinced him that she would love him forever but would not be his wife. I'm doing the right thing, she thought.

Later, she became certain. After the rapturous release of their lovemaking, Lorenzo wept in her arms. "I should have been with Clarice when she died," he cried. "I owed her that. She always did her duty, and it would have meant so much to her to know that I realized it. I wasn't there to tell her. A man is responsible for his wife's comfort, and I failed to give her what she was entitled to have.''

After his uncontrolled outburst, Lorenzo slept. Ginevra looked at him, as she always did, greedy for the sight of his beloved face and body.

An icy vise squeezed her heart. His beautiful, long-fingered hands were scarred across their enlarged knuckles. And the little finger of the left hand was bent and stiffened forever at the tip.

Not so soon, she begged silently. Oh, please, dear God, not so soon. I'm not ready. I know I have to lose him one day, but don't let it begin so soon.

Chapter Fifty-six

A rustling of anticipation moved through the crowds on the piazza. "It's coming. It's coming." Ginevra craned her neck, like the people around her. She knew it was premature, and so did they. But they all stretched to see anyhow, as they always did. It was the contagious excitement of holiday and spectacle.

A brisk wind made the colorful banners on the Palazzo della Signoria billow and wave so vigorously that they made sharp cracking sounds. On the broad platform below the banners, priors held their brilliant red robes to their sides to control the pull of the wind in the folds. The gold stars of the Gonfaloniere's robe flashed in the sunlight. Everything was in readiness to welcome the new ambassador from Bologna.

And then the procession entered the piazza. The crowds joined their cheers to the cheering that still rang in the streets along which the procession had passed. Between shouts, people exclaimed and laughed and commented about the ambassador's retinue.

It was led by a horseman carrying a gold-fringed and tasseled banner with the bright embroidered seal of Bologna. When he met the wind in the wide space of the piazza, it tried to tear the banner from his grip, and his gold-caparisoned horse sidestepped with dangerous nervous jerks. The watching crowds made eager bets on the battle between pomp and the elements.

But then the gusts abated. A sigh of disappointment from the crowds made a soft, breezelike noise.

The ambassador was wearing a plumed jeweled cap, the plume tattered by the wind. His richly decorated costume won a murmur of approval, and when he made his horse curvet in front of the Signoria, the crowd cheered again.

And continued cheering his mounted attendants with their striped silk uniforms and gilded breastplates. And his forty foot soldiers with ribbon-streamered shining lances.

The ambassador dismounted and faced the governors of Florence. His bow was flourished. The Palazzo's trumpeters saluted him, and the great tower bell rang when he mounted the stairs to be welcomed by the Gonfaloniere.

Then the crowd burst out in a roar of cheering that dwarfed the bell's mighty booming.

Three horsemen were riding across the piazza. Two outriders on sleek, burnished black horses wore red and white gameboard squares of silk, the Medici livery. Between them on a huge white stallion was Lorenzo, in the plain black wool lucco of a simple citizen of the Republic. With the priceless, gigantic Medici diamond pinned casually to his black velvet cap.

"Magnificent! Magnificent! Magnificent!" The words rebounded from the stones of Florence, like thunder in the air.

Like power, Ginevra thought, her heart thrilling with the hearts of everyone around her.

Lorenzo reined in at the steps and jumped easily from the saddle. Then he made a courtly obeisance to the ambassador, a respectful bow to the Signoria. His concentration on the guest and the government seemed to make him unaware of the loud frenzied approval of his people, the tribute of their wild cheering.

His black unembellished scholar's garb eclipsed the brightness of the priors and made the ambassador's finery suddenly garish.

Oh, you master politician, Ginevra thought. And she shouted with the others. "Magnificent!"

When the speeches were over and the doors of the Palazzo closed behind the official party, the crowd dispersed. People talked excitedly about the fireworks to come, the rumor that Bologna had sent a gift of wine to be given free to everyone who visited the park along the river near the Porta al Prato. And they boasted to one another that Bologna was nothing, no more was Venice or Milan or Rome, France, Spain, Burgundy. Florence was superior to them all. Florence was Lorenzo the Magnificent.

Ginevra walked among them, smiling to herself. Lorenzo would be like a child with a basket of sweets when she told him about the crowd's remarks. How he loved these fickle Florentines and basked in their love for him.

She wouldn't tell him that they were already wondering when the next embassy would come, with the holiday and fireworks for them. She, too, wondered. There were so many now. Bologna was the third this year, and it was only April.

There had always been emissaries, of course; every city-state kept a representative in every other, unless they were actively at war. But usually they were businessmen, their function the promotion of trade. Plus their role as spies. These latest ambassadors were genuine diplomats, empowered to speak for their governments.

They were proof of Lorenzo's growing power throughout all Italy. He was the peacemaker. The masterful coup of his visit to Naples had established his reputation as a daring and persuasive negotiator; the common belief that the Turks had invaded at his instigation had added to it. But it was the peace treaty that ended the war over Ferrara that made all the world take notice. He was not negotiating for Florence alone in that settlement. His was the voice that persuaded all the combatants to accept the peaceful settlement that his mind had devised. Lodovico Sforza spoke the words and took the credit, but everyone recognized the author of the agreement. "The needle of the Italian compass," Lorenzo was called in the capitals of Europe.

Now Bologna wanted his help. Lorenzo, with the papacy effectively ruled by his advice, was now able to do more than settle a war. He could prevent one. After centuries of fighting among themselves, the bellicose city-states of Italy were learning that it was wiser to arbitrate than fight. Provided that Lorenzo was the arbitrator. If they accepted his guidance, they didn't have to worry that he might metaphorically flex his muscles, use the combined strength of the Republic and the Church against one or more of them.

Not since the Caesars had a man been so respected.

Ginevra let herself be carried along by the crowd, enjoying the festive spirit and the bright sunshine. It had been a cold, wet spring this year. A cluster of peasants near her was talking loudly about going to see the giraffe, and she pushed between two corpulent women to join them. They were heading in the direction she wanted to go.

She stayed with them for a few minutes outside the stable where the giraffe was kept. "Poor thing," crooned one of the women. Ginevra agreed. The giraffe was swathed in blankets, and it looked bewildered by the constriction. The climate of Florence was too harsh for the fragile creature bred under the sun of Africa. Men had been on watch day and night all winter, keeping torches burning in the stable to warm it.

Ginevra looked at the shadow the stable cast on the street. It was time to meet Agnolo Poliziano. She headed for the Via de' Fossi and Ghirlandaio's studio.

She and Agnolo were in charge of Lorenzo's carnival float this year; he was too busy with embassies and Piero's wedding arrangements. Domenico Ghirlandaio had agreed to make and decorate it. Agnolo was extremely pleased; Domenico's narrative style of painting was perfectly suited to Agnolo's themes from classic mythology.

Ginevra threw herself wholeheartedly into the project, as she always did, and she enjoyed the meticulous planning. But, for her the preparation of the float had never been the same after Andrea del Verrocchio left. She missed the hearty laughter and the ribald jesting and the huge happy voice of the big artist. This year she thought of him more than ever. Andrea had died in February. Still in Venice, his equestrian bronze not yet finished.

Ginevra had wept for hours, huddled and shivering

on the rim of the laughing cherub fountain he had made
for Careggi.

Agnolo was approaching the studio from the opposite
direction when Ginevra reached the door. She waved to
him and waited.

He had never been a favorite of hers, but in the past
few months they had finally become friends. Ginevra
believed that Poliziano was different now that he was
no longer tutor to Lorenzo's sons. Agnolo was more
relaxed, less didactic. He even laughed once in a while.

It made sense to her. Getting rid of Piero, she was
sure, would make life an infinitely better thing for anyone.

Except Lorenzo. He remained blind to his son's de-
fects, even when Piero was involved in street brawls
and his guards did terrible damage to Piero's real or
supposed enemies. Probably Lorenzo is hoping that
being married will make Piero grow up, Ginevra
thought. Sixteen was very young for a man to wed.

His sons were his future, Lorenzo told her, and the
future of the Medici. He was relentless in his pressure
on the Pope to make Giovanni a cardinal.

"Hello, Ginevra, what good timing. Did you see the
Bolognese?" Agnolo was smiling.

Ginevra returned his smile. "I saw his best moment.
His horse did a dance for the Signoria."

"I saw his worst. I was on the bridge he crossed, and
the wind from the river tore his pretty plume to pieces."

They were laughing together when they entered the
studio.

"I'm glad somebody's happy," Ghirlandaio said. "I
hate these holidays. My apprentices think they're entitled to a day of play."

Ginevra looked around the big studio. It was deserted, except for a youth on his knees scrubbing the
floor. Ghirlandaio stepped close to her and spoke quietly. "He's the newest, and he shouldn't be here at all.
I want to talk to you about him."

He raised his voice. "Buonarotti, you might as well

take a holiday too. Run along. The dirt will wait until you get back.''

The boy stood up, bobbed a sort of bow and ran out through the rear door. There was just time for Ginevra to see that he was a sturdy youth with a strong, handsome face that looked older than his years.

The boy was thirteen, Domenico told her. His name was Michelangelo Buonarotti. ''He wants to be a sculptor, a marble cutter, but his father apprenticed him to me because he thinks that painting is more respectable.'' Ghirlandaio smiled. ''Because it's cleaner, he said. I took his money and put the boy to work . . . Then yesterday I found this.''

Domenico opened a small cassone and took out a crumpled paper. He smoothed it as best he could on the table in front of them. ''This is the boy's. He doesn't know I have it; he thought it was thrown away. It changes everything. This is a strong talent.''

The paper was covered with charcoal sketches of arms, feet, legs, backs, shoulders. All of them rapidly done, all of them showing the shaded contours of bone and flesh beneath the skin.

''Agnolo,'' said Ginevra urgently, ''come here and look at this. What does it look like to you?''

Poliziano scrutinized the drawings. ''Someone's been sketching bits of statues. What about it?''

Ghirlandaio nodded. So did Ginevra. ''The boy knows his strength,'' Domenico said. ''He is a sculptor. Possibly a great one. There were no models for these drawings except inside his heart.

''I want you to ask Lorenzo if he'll accept the boy in Bertoldo's school. I'll give up his apprentice fee.''

''We can speak for Lorenzo,'' Ginevra said decisively. ''Send him to the sculpture garden tomorrow. I'll talk to Bertoldo today.''

Ginevra didn't tell Lorenzo anything about Michelangelo until Piero's wedding extravaganza was over, six weeks later. Then she was playfully mysterious. ''I have a surprise for you,'' she said. ''You must come with me without any questions.''

She took him through the entrance to the sculpture garden and stepped away from him. "It's someplace in here. You have to find it."

"Ginevra. That's absurd."

"Don't worry. It's not a tiny cameo or anything like that. It's quite large. And remarkable. Go on."

Lorenzo grimaced. Bertoldo was hurrying toward him, already complaining that Lorenzo had not visited him for months. He took Lorenzo's arm and led him through the garden, talking ceaselessly about the handicaps under which he was forced to work, the stupidity and laziness of his students, the sorry state of art in the current day.

Ginevra tagged along behind them, close enough to watch Lorenzo and far enough away to escape Bertoldo.

Michelangelo was crouched down by the side of the path, polishing a small marble. Lorenzo stopped, looked at the statue, spoke to the boy.

Ginevra grinned. Then Lorenzo walked on, his head cocked to hear Bertoldo's lament. Ginevra was appalled. Her surprise hadn't worked. She looked at Michelangelo. Then she gasped. The boy had picked up a chisel and, as she watched, he drove a fierce blow into the smooth marble.

She ran to him. "Stop, stop that, don't destroy it."

Michelangelo looked up at her. "I'm not hurting it," he said, "just making it better."

Ginevra gasped a second time. The startlingly handsome youth was gone. In his place was this boy with a grotesquely misshapen nose.

"What happened to you?" she asked.

Michelangelo's smile was sweet and boyish. He touched the flattened bridge of his nose. "I got in a fight with him." His thumb pointed over his shoulder to a richly dressed student. "He broke my nose, but I made him admit he was wrong."

"About what?"

"About art. He thought a nothing painter was good and didn't know Masaccio was great. So I taught him."

Ginevra laughed. "I admire people with strong con-

victions . . . What are you doing to your statue? May I
see?"

The boy showed her his work without shyness. He
knew it was good. He had carved a satyr of impressive
age and villainy. Its mouth shaped a loathsome evil leer
in its lined, sagging face.

"It's quite marvelously disgusting," said Ginevra
with admiration. "How do you know about such evil?"

"I look at faces in the streets," said the young sculptor calmly. He looked at the face he had made. "It
wasn't this awful before. But the Magnificent made it
better. 'Anyone that old,' he said, 'couldn't have a smile
like that. Your satyr has all his teeth, like a youth,' "
Michelangelo rubbed his finger across the statue's
mouth. "So I knocked out some of the teeth. Now it's
old and nasty."

"What else did he say?"

The boy's face was luminous with joy. "He said I
should go home and send my father to him. He said
I should come live in his palace where I could study the
art there."

Ginevra stood up, her hands on her hips in a classic
pose of frustrated anger. "He did, did he? And not a
word to me." She glared at Lorenzo's back at the far
end of the garden with Bertoldo.

Then she began to laugh. "I guess two people can be
surprised as easily as one," she explained to the boy,
who didn't understand at all.

Michelangelo joined the dozens of residents on the
palace's third floor. Unlike most of them, he was invited by Lorenzo to join his table of artists and philos
ophers.

When he learned the informal rule about seating, the
boy was overcome. He could be next to Lorenzo if he
was the first to arrive at table. Every evening he was
there, waiting, when the stewards came to open the door
and prepare the room.

If Lorenzo dined at the palace, Michelangelo drank
in his words and his presence as if he were at a banquet
of the gods. When Lorenzo was away, the boy sat

closer to Lorenzo's chair; from time to time he touched it with reverent fingers. Lorenzo was his hero and his benefactor and his god. Ginevra loved the boy for his worship.

Chapter Fifty-seven

A terrible scream woke Ginevra from deep sleep. She sat up in her bed and it came again. From beside her. From Lorenzo.

"What is it? My love, what?" She reached out, fumbling for him in the darkness.

"No!" he cried. "Leave me . . . oh, sweet Christ, don't touch me, don't make the bed move . . . God! God, help me in this agony . . . ah, the pain . . ." He screamed again, in torture.

Ginevra rolled as quickly as she could, falling off the bed onto the floor. She crawled to the table, found a candle and tinderbox, lit the light.

Lorenzo was rigid with pain. His neck was corded, his mouth stretched in ghastly rictus, his eyes wide and white with fear.

"Sheet," he groaned, "get it off . . . easy . . ." Ginevra lifted it as gently as possible, knowing from his screams that she was hurting him.

His right knee was the size of a child's head, the reddened skin stretched until it looked ready to burst.

Lorenzo was panting, his face bloodless. "Better . . . no weight . . . sorry . . . frighten you . . ."

Ginevra sobbed. "My own beloved, hush. There's no need to talk, to be sorry for me. If only I could do something for you, ease the pain." Her hands twisted together, helpless.

Lorenzo looked at her, and his pain-twisted mouth made a shaking attempt to smile.

"Sing . . . to . . . me . . ."

Ginevra's hands flew to her lips, held back the whimpering cries until she could control herself.

Then she sang, her voice strong and tuneless, the voice of their singing together. She sang all she knew, carnival songs and hymns, folk songs and lullabies. Her mouth grew dry and then her throat, and she sang them again. Then again hoarsely, again through cracked lips croaking. The candle guttered and died, the window grew gray, then rose, then the porcelain blue of the summer sky. And still she sang.

Until Lorenzo's ragged pain-filled breathing slowed and eased and finally became a sigh and he slept.

She was sitting by the side of the bed when he woke, her anxious eyes watching the peaceful rise and fall of his chest.

"It's past," he said. "Don't worry, Contadina."

Ginevra smiled. "Shall I bring you a cup of cool water? A cloth for your forehead?" She kept her eyes fixed on his, away from the sight of his cruelly swollen knee.

"Some lemon and water. Very sweet."

He was able to hold the cup and drink. Later, he ate some bread. The pain was manageable, as long as nothing touched the knee or moved it.

The swelling began to subside that night. Two days later he was able to hobble on the leg. The following day he could walk.

"We'll go to the baths," Ginevra said.

"Soon," Lorenzo agreed. "When I can ride."

He waited until the baths had restored him to his full strength before he told her what it was necessary for her to know.

"I love you, my contadina." Lorenzo kissed the top of her head, and Ginevra nestled closer into his shoulder. She was warm with the afterglow of making love.

"I adore you, my Magnificent," she mumbled.

Lorenzo's arm tightened around her, and his even voice was soothing. "I remember hearing my grandfather's screams, and my father's. It will happen again. Then again and again, each time a little sooner than the time before . . . no, don't move, you must listen. Now, when I'm well and can speak with calm reason.

"I don't know why I'm afflicted so early, when I have so much yet to do. I thought it would be a gradual thing, and the pain would be no worse than I could bear. The unbearable should not have come so soon." He held her closer, forestalling her protest. "I'm not yet near the end, my love, but it will come, and you can't stop it by saying it's not true.

"I'm going to become crotchety and demanding and self-involved. I saw it happen to Cosimo and Piero. I'll be lame, and then I'll be crippled.

"You don't have to see it, Ginevra. You don't have to stay."

This time, all his strength could not keep her still. She rose from his embrace and struck him on the chest with her fists. "I'll kill you," she said, "I'll kill you if you try to send me away. Who do you think you are to insult me so? To insult the love I have for you and you for me? How dare you take pity on me as if I were some kind of weak, pale gutless girl. I can stand your tempers when they come, and I'll carry you across my back when you can no longer walk. But I won't leave you, and if you try to make me, I'll put a knife in this hand and tear out your heart."

Lorenzo caught her wrists. He was laughing. "Stop. Stop beating an old man. I think your cure for gout is too drastic for me. I'd rather be lame with you than murdered by you. Stay, then. Stay and be the sunlight in my life. Stay and love me. But less forcefully."

Ginevra's hands went limp in his grasp. She looked at him and grinned. "You make me extremely angry sometimes, Lorenzo. You really shouldn't do that; it's dangerous . . . Did I ever tell you about how I almost killed you when we went to Naples? No? Well, then, give me a kiss, and I'll tell you a bedtime story . . ."

"You are a terrifying woman," Lorenzo said when she finished her tale of deception. "Why didn't you do it?"

"I realized that I loved you too much . . . I think it was your pure tenor perfect pitch that won my heart."

"Witch. I'll be afraid to go to sleep tonight. I'll have to pass the time by ravishing you."

Ginevra stretched like a cat. "Ravish away, then."

The long, happiness-filled summer days went on, and she learned not to anticipate tragedy, to live in the joy of the present moment.

She never imagined that tragedy could come from anything unrelated to Lorenzo's illness. Then, in October, Lorenzo's daughter Luisa came down with a sore throat. Twenty-two hours later she was dead.

She was only eleven years old.

Lorenzo's grief was terrible and silent. Ginevra, suffering for the loss of the child she had loved, suffered even more for her inability to help him. She could not share the anguish of a father because she had never been a mother. The only thing she could share was his quiet. She sat with him, walked with him, rode with him and always without a sound.

After ten days, Lorenzo broke the silence. "Thank you," he said, and he took her hand in his.

The weather grew colder, and Lorenzo moved from Careggi to the palace. "Will you come too?" he asked. "I'd like to have you with me."

"Of course I will," Ginevra replied. She understood what he had left unsaid. The gout was always worse in the winter. There would be no more laughing rides to the villa, no more long dinners in the sun-warmed loggia. The home he had chosen for their love was once again only a summer villa. And their birthday celebrations were over. They must try to stop time, not toast its passing.

Ginevra had a different room at the palace, a bedroom next to Lorenzo's.

The newest addition to the household had a room on the other side of him. His name was Piero Leoni, and he was a doctor.

Ginevra begged Lorenzo to send him away. "He'll kill you, my dearest. Your mother knew. She saw the doctors torment your father with their nostrums and hasten his death. The baths, and extracts of herbs to soothe and strengthen, they are what you need. We'll move to Morba for the winter. To Filetta, if you prefer. To Bagno a Ripoli; the government can come to you there. Anywhere you want. I'll follow you anywhere, and I'll take care of you." She fell to her knees, pleading with him.

Lorenzo put his hand on her bent head. "Hush, my love. It will do no good; I need a doctor near me. Doctors know medicines that aren't found in the herb garden."

She persisted until Lorenzo lost his temper and told her to leave him alone. "I'll go," she said, "but I'm not done. I'll keep after you until you see reason."

That night she woke in the darkness. She could hear her heart pounding. And then, through the thick stone walls, she heard Lorenzo's screams.

She knelt by her bed and prayed and listened. And soon the screaming stopped.

She ran to his room, so desperate that she didn't even stop to wrap a blanket around her. The doctor looked up in alarm at the shouting nude virago that threw open Lorenzo's door.

"You've killed him! I knew this would happen."

She threw herself at him, hands like claws, reaching to tear his eyes, his face. Leoni swung his arm and knocked her to the floor.

"Quiet, woman! He's sleeping and you'll wake him. Go back to your room and cover your shameless nakedness."

Ginevra got to her hands and knees, shaking her dizzied head. She heard Lorenzo's harsh, regular breathing. "Sleeping," she whispered. "Oh, thank you, Heavenly Father." She struggled to her feet, saw the vial of medicine near the candle.

"Thank you, Doctor," she said before she stumbled

into the hallway. She would thank Satan himself if he could ease Lorenzo's pain.

There was no more rest for her that night. She prayed and cried and tried to quell the riotous disorder of her thoughts and emotions. Lucrezia de' Medici was the only mother she had ever had; she had loved and admired Lucrezia, trusted her absolutely, hoped to become a woman like her.

Lucrezia had brought her back to life, to health when her body and spirit were broken. She had done it without doctors. The only anger that Lucrezia's gentle heart ever knew was her rage, even hatred, for doctors.

Lucrezia was so wise; surely she must have been right.

And yet . . . and yet . . . Lorenzo was sleeping. But the drug might kill him. Murderers, doctors were, Lucrezia said.

Ginevra wanted to believe what she knew was impossible. She wanted to believe that Lorenzo would never die, that he would get well, that they would be together forever.

She could not. She had a nature too honest to lie, even to herself.

But honesty did not preclude hope. And the doctor had stopped the pain. Perhaps . . . Almost twenty years had passed since Lorenzo's father died. Perhaps new things had been found, new knowledge, new plants.

In the morning Ginevra dressed and went to the doctor's room. She humbly begged Leoni's pardon.

The chair that Cosimo had used, and Piero, and Ginevra, was brought out again. The gout was concentrated in Lorenzo's left foot, and the swelling would not go down. Lorenzo would not give up his work or his pleasure. Like his father and grandfather before him, he was carried from room to room in the palace so that he could eat, read, write, receive visitors, entertain guests, see his children.

He tried to make light of the disability. "This is an

excellent system," he said. "I save so much energy that I can do twice as many things."

But Ginevra saw the opaque fear in his eyes. And shared it. Suppose he was never to walk again? She went to his room in the night, when he could not sleep and was alone with the fear. She massaged his body, save the foot, and sang to him until he was able to forget the fear and laugh and beg her to stop damaging his ears.

When Christmas drew near, Ginevra ordered the servants to carry the Neapolitan cassone from her old room to Lorenzo's bedroom. "Let's remember Naples," she said with a smile. She took out some of the costumed terra-cotta figures of the manger scene that Lorenzo had given her.

"Take those shabby souvenirs out of here," Lorenzo said harshly. "I'm not a sick child to be amused with toys. It's no diversion for me to relive the times when I had the use of my own body and could be a real man. Leave me alone, Ginevra. I can't stand to look at your healthy face and brave little smile."

The boy Michelangelo helped her arrange the creche in the palace's loggia. He examined every figure with an enthusiasm that rekindled her own.

"In Naples there is a Nativity that moves," Ginevra said, "and it's like a miracle to watch it. I went over and over again to see it."

Michelangelo's marred young face was bright with excitement. "Tell me, Madonna Ginevra, please tell me."

Lorenzo, his face free of pain, spoke from the entrance to the house. "Tell him about the holy fool who spied for me."

Ginevra held the tiny pottery Christ Child to her breast and sent silent prayers of gratitude into the heavens. Lorenzo was on his feet.

"We have a guest," he said; his voice was bright with happiness and laughter. "He says he hasn't had a decent meal in months."

Sandro Botticelli had returned from the work he had been doing in Pisa.

"Sandro? Where is he?" Ginevra lay the figure on the table and ran to the door.

"He's in the dining room. What do you expect? The blessing of Botticelli is that he never changes."

Ginevra looked behind her as she left. "Michelangelo, put those back in their box. We'll do them later. Come up and meet my most favorite painter in the whole world."

Michelangelo arranged the figures with shaking fingers. He crossed himself, breathing a prayer of thanks. Sandro Botticelli. Here. And he was going to share a meal with him.

Chapter Fifty-eight

Beginning on Christmas Day, the weather was as warm as spring. An omen, people said. Some saw it as a good omen, the warmth of God's love. Others read a warning in the unnaturalness of prematurely blossoming flowers.

To Ginevra it meant only that the ride to Careggi was possible and that she and Lorenzo were able to have their birthday celebration. When she caressed his body, she kissed the ridges of scar tissue that the gout had left and told him that they were very small, really insignificant. He pretended to believe her. "No matter," he laughed, "the joint that men care most about is never attacked by gout." He was as sexually vigorous as a youth, and he was proud of his virility. "You'd never know I was an old man of forty, would you? Now, as for you, Contadina, you're holding up quite well for a crone."

Later that month winter returned, and the city's cherished giraffe died. All Florence sorrowed, and messages of condolence came to the Signoria from all the towns of the Republic.

Lucrezia Donati met death, too. Lorenzo cried briefly. "Two beautiful, gentle creatures are gone," he said.

But another beautiful creature reappeared. Pico della Mirandola dashed into the palace one day, as vivid and enthusiastic as ever. It made Lorenzo so happy to see him that Ginevra forgave Pico all his earlier follies and embraced him wholeheartedly. On the evening he arrived, she could almost believe that time had run backward. He dominated the table, fascinating Michelangelo and the other recent additions to the group, stimulating

Agnolo to earnest expostulations, making Lorenzo laugh and setting Sandro's fingers flying as he sketched Pico's changeable vibrant face on the tablecloth.

"I swear to you," Pico exclaimed, "this is the greatest preacher the world has ever known. I've been following him from Brescia to Padua to Bologna. Everywhere he goes, he sets the congregations afire with his sermons and his visions. He has second sight. He can tell the future. Lorenzo, you must bring him to Florence. He will fill the Duomo, and the piazza before it will be jammed with people clamoring to get in. There's never been a preacher like him."

Lorenzo smiled. "I seem to remember those exact words from you, Pico, when you first heard Fra Mariano. We'll go tomorrow to San Gallo and you can fall in love with his eloquence all over again."

"Gladly, Lorenzo. I thirst for the friar's wisdom. But this new man is different. Fra Mariano speaks to our minds and through our minds to our souls. He's an Aristotelian, a man of exquisite reason. The Dominican's words fly straight to the soul. His congregations are the common people who know nothing of the intellect."

Lorenzo was interested. The Church was the primary source of entertainment for the people. A dramatic preacher pleased them even more than the sacred plays on feast days.

"I'll do it," he said. "For you, my young firebrand, and for Florence. I'll ask the prior of San Marco to invite him to visit and preach in San Lorenzo. What is your visionary's name?"

"Fra Girolamo Savonarola. You'll see, Lorenzo. He's a magician. You'll never regret bringing him here."

All winter Lorenzo was busy with peacemaking. And with the fruits of his labors: an ambassador came from Naples with a richly decorated scroll of vellum, the official document by which King Ferrante conferred the abbey of Monte Cassino on Giovanni; two weeks later, Lodovico Sforza, Duke of Milan, awarded the boy the abbey of Miramondo; smaller city-states gave him smaller benefices, and Pope Innocent surpassed them all with the gift of Passignano, the richest abbey in all of Tuscany.

"My dreams are coming true," Lorenzo confided to Ginevra. "Giovanni will be Cardinal, and then Florence and the house of Medici will be forever protected." He redoubled his efforts to persuade Innocent to confer the red hat on Giovanni, and couriers left daily for Rome with letters to the Orsini, to cardinals friendly to Lorenzo's cause and to the Pope. He sent men north to the mountain passes to net more ortolans for fattening and added casks of Tuscany's best wine to the packages of birds that the couriers took to Innocent.

In March, the Pope made a partial surrender. He would make Lorenzo's thirteen-year-old son a cardinal, but there were conditions.

The appointment must be kept a secret on pain of excommunication. No one so young had ever been given the red hat. And the boy must go to the University at Pisa to study theology. When he graduated at sixteen, the appointment would be made public.

"Kiss me, Contadina," Lorenzo said. "There. Not every peasant girl gets to kiss the father of a cardinal."

His mood was soaring. When word arrived that Pico's preaching friar was on his way to Florence, Lorenzo arranged a formal welcome for him at the San Gallo gate. "We'll let Pico be the center of attention," he said with a laugh. "He can make the speech for me."

Ginevra laughed with him. "I'd like to see you try and stop Pico from being the focus of all eyes. It would be easier to stop thunder in a storm than to quiet Pico."

The friar was riding on a white donkey. His face was invisible, deep inside the black hood of the Dominican habit, and his hands were hidden in the white sleeves. He was accompanied by a band of followers, some of them peasants, many of them richly dressed men and women with bare feet. One of the peasants was leading the mule; everyone else walked behind singing a hymn.

Ginevra whispered to Lorenzo. "Why didn't he wait a few days? Then it will be Palm Sunday."

"Bad, blasphemous woman," he said under his breath, "don't make me laugh. Pico would never forgive me."

Pico walked forward, his hand held up as a signal for the friar's procession to halt. Then he went down on one knee and swept his hat off with a flourish.

"I beg your blessing, most holy man of God," he cried, bending his head.

Lorenzo smiled. A crowd was gathering at the gate to watch the drama. Pico would entertain them, even if his friar remained invisible, he thought.

At that moment a woman in Savonarola's train began to scream. She whirled in a mad dance, her arms reaching toward the sky, into the center of the road. Then she stopped turning and stopped screaming. Her arms descended, her quivering fingers pointing at Pico. "Such beauty," she said in a sepulchral voice. Her eyes rolled up in her head. "He will depart this earth in the time of the lilies."

Ginevra clutched Lorenzo's arm. "What does she mean?"

"Shhh." Pico was on his feet, his face red with anger.

"Get that woman away from me," he shouted. "I have some words to speak to Fra Savonarola."

But no one was listening to Pico. The people near the gate were backing away, and Savonarola's followers were on their knees in a huddled group, crossing themselves and murmuring prayers. The prophetess had fallen in a faint and looked lifeless in the dust of the road.

Lorenzo's gesture brought two of his guards forward. "Carry her into the hospice," he said. He smiled at the group of welcomers he had arranged. "Come, let's meet our guest," he said, and he went to Pico.

"Another time, Fra Savonarola will appreciate your words even more than today, Pico. Present us, if you please, and we'll let the friar go. He must be weary from his journey."

Savonarola didn't move or speak when Pico introduced Lorenzo and Lorenzo presented the government officials who were representing the city. After the last name was announced, he pulled one hand free and made the sign of the cross, then gestured with it to the man holding the donkey's bridle. He returned it to its hiding place while he rode away.

The officials looked nervously at Lorenzo. Never had there been such an insult to the head of the Republic. Lorenzo grinned at them. "This is the monk," he said, "that the Count of Mirandola tells us is the most eloquent man in Italy."

Everyone laughed. Except Pico. He walked away from them, muttering to himself.

And except Ginevra.

She had watched Savonarola ride away. Just before he entered the city gate his donkey jolted him and his hood slid back. Ginevra shuddered when the sunlight touched his face. The monk was disgustingly ugly, with a huge hooked nose and purplish, thick lips. He had heavy, scowling black eyebrows above inhuman green eyes with red lashes. A shaft of light slanted into his eyes, and he blinked. But before his lids fell, Ginevra saw that the light made his eyes flash red.

She felt as if her backbone had turned to ice. The nape of her neck was stiff, and she knew that the hairs at the base of her skull were standing upright. For the first time in her life she was truly terrified. She crossed herself, unaware that the fingers on her other hand had formed the primitive gesture of protection against evil.

For the rest of her life Ginevra believed that Savonarola was the devil and that she had seen it in his eyes.

She tried to convince Lorenzo, but he laughed at her. "You just recoiled at his ugliness, my love. You're no customed to handsome men like me."

"No, Lorenzo, don't make a joke of this. What about that woman who cursed Pico? She was a witch, a disciple of the devil."

"She was Camilla Rucellai, the crazy cousin of my brother-in-law Bernardo Rucellai. She's been crazy all her life . . . And so for what you call a curse, it was only an imbecile's prophecy. People are saying that it means Pico will die in his youth, like the fragile lilies that fade so quickly. But Pico's youth is past. He may look like a beautiful boy, but he's twenty-six, your age, Contadina, hardly a child.''

Ginevra took her fears to Fra Mariano next. He didn't laugh, but he pointed out the errors of her thinking. ''Fra Girolamo is a man of God, Ginevra. He preaches the word of God, words that are the weapons we use against Satan.''

She shook he head. ''No, Fra Mariano, I've been to San Lorenzo when he was preaching. He doesn't preach from the gospels, he denounces with his own words. He tells the people that they're wicked and sinful, that Florence is a sink of iniquity. He preaches against Lorenzo.''

Fra Mariano took her hand. ''My dear child, you mustn't worry about Lorenzo. There's nothing that can be said against him. He is the most Christian layman I know, more spiritual than most clerics . . .

''You're surprised? And you know him so well. But not in every way. You see, Lorenzo comes often to me. We talk about Aristotle and about Christ. I think it's a pleasant change for him after all the years of Marsilio Ficino's unremitting emphasis on Plato.''

''But Plato . . .''

''Yes, yes, my child, I know my Plato, too. You needn't explain him to me or defend him. I spend many hours at Fiesole with the Academy . . . You do too, Ginevra. You know that the essence of Neoplatonism is to form a synthesis between the wisdom of the ancients and the greater wisdom of the teachings of our Saviour, who came to this world after their time. The true emphasis is on Christ, not Plato. That's where Lorenzo places it. Have you read his poetry?''

Ginevra nodded.

''Then you know that many of his poems are *laudi*, hymns of praise to our Lord. His love of God is profound, also his search for spirituality. Lorenzo cannot be harmed by words, no matter whose. His soul is safe.''

''But . . .'' She shook her head, unable to say what she was thinking.

The monk patted her hand. ''We religious know more

about the world than you realize, Ginevra. Are you worried about Lorenzo's adultery? His wife is dead. About his fornication, and yours? God created our flesh as well as our souls. He knows our weaknesses and forgives them.''

Ginevra smiled at the gentle, scholarly friar. His elegant bearing was altogether different, but he reminded her at that moment of the gentle Fra Marco, the monk at La Vacchia, who had given her her earliest religious education.

''I'm grateful for your kindness, Fra Mariano,'' she said, ''and for your understanding. But I respectfully believe that you're wrong about Savonarola. He means to destroy Lorenzo. He's saying that Lorenzo is a tyrant, that he has led Florence to sin, that God will punish him . . . He's prophesying Lorenzo's death. Soon.''

Fra Mariano looked at the fear in Ginevra's eyes. ''My daughter,'' he said quietly, ''every man must die before he can find salvation.''

The friar's words were a comfort to Ginevra, a comfort for Lorenzo. She had seen that he was increasingly preoccupied with spiritual questions and she knew that he was having mass said daily in the palace's chapel, often for himself alone. Fra Mariano's certainty about Lorenzo's relationship with God was convincing to her; it must be a support for Lorenzo.

But the friar had not shaken her conviction about Savonarola. She saw the tiny congregation for his sermons getting larger, and she became frantic.

Lorenzo's friends would not listen. She didn't try to talk to Pico, but she thought Sandro would understand her worries.

He told her she was blaspheming.

Agnolo Poliziano said that she was mad.

The devil is taking them away from Lorenzo, she thought. He's trying to make Lorenzo defenseless, alone, vulnerable. But he can't. I will never leave him.

On May Day, Lorenzo and Ginevra were trying not to laugh at the maiden who was out of rhythm in the dance around the Maypole when disaster struck. Ginevra heard Lorenzo's sharp gasp, felt his hand grasp her shoulder with convulsive strength.

She looked at his guards, but they were watching the dancers. There was no time, Lorenzo's fingers were pressing harder.

"The pole," she shouted with all her strength, "it's falling!" And she screamed.

The piazza was so crowded that no one could move. At Ginevra's cry, people tried to run away from the towering pole and when they found themselves trapped, their screams joined hers in a cacophony of terror.

"Guards!" Ginevra called them to protect Lorenzo from the milling, thrusting people. And to him she said, "Now, my love, now. No one will know." She threw her head back and screamed and screamed and screamed, covering the sound of his agonized cries of pain when the guards carried him away from the oblivious, panicked crowd.

When she reached the palace, Lorenzo was already in the deep semicoma sleep that Leoni's drug produced. "Go away, Madonna," the doctor said. "He'll be this way for many hours."

Ginevra held her tears inside while she rode to La Vacchia. She released them in the grasses of their anniversary bed of love.

Then she picked wildflowers and packed them in leaves she dampened in a stream and carried them home to Lorenzo. Even though she knew that she'd never give them to him, that they'd be dead before he woke from his artificial sleep.

Chapter Fifty-nine

"Contadina, are you still here?"

"I'm here. Go back to sleep."

"I've done nothing but sleep. For how long?"

"Three days. But those weren't good rests. Now you're sleeping naturally. Sleep, my love. It's healing."

"I woke up before . . ."

"Yes, and fell asleep again. It's good for you. Don't try to stay awake . . . Do you want a drink? Do you want me to sing?"

"Not yet. I want to talk. After, you can sing your nightingale song." Lorenzo chuckled. "I wonder if the School of Harmony will let us join."

"We'd teach them a new kind of music."

"Contadina . . ."

"I'm here, Lorenzo."

"I want to tell you something important . . . No, don't tell me to rest. I need to tell you."

"All right. I'm here by your side. I'm listening."

"I love you, my Ginevra. And I know that you love me. I don't believe you know how rare it is to be what we are to one another . . . I used to look at my mother and father together, and I knew that I was seeing a miracle . . . You're my miracle, Ginevra. I never thought miracles could happen to me, but I was wrong. I wanted you to know . . ."

"I do know. It gives me the greatest happiness in the world to hear you say it, my love, but I've known from the beginning. You've told me in a million ways."

". . . I'll sleep now. Sing to me."

She sang to him, long after he was asleep. Tears welled from her eyes and she let them fall. While she sang words of love undying.

Chapter Sixty

Doctor Leoni went with them to the sulfur baths at Spedaletto and then to Careggi for the summer; Lorenzo was afraid to be separated from him and the relief he carried in his apothecary chest. The attacks were less intense, but more frequent.

When they returned to the city in October, Lorenzo said he wanted to go hear Savonarola preach.

Ginevra was horrified. "You mustn't," she protested, "he's a horrible, vicious devil."

Lorenzo laughed. "I'm told that my name is mentioned more than God's. I'd like to hear what makes me so important."

He looked thoughtful when they left the church. "I can't see why people like to be told they're sinners and certain to be damned. But there was a big congregation."

"Much bigger than before," Ginevra said. She was sick with anger and apprehension.

Lorenzo declared that he was going to devote himself for a while to domestic diplomacy. Italy was at peace; he could concentrate on conditions in Florence.

"You should get rid of Savonarola," Ginevra insisted. "Your gifts support the monastery of San Marco. The prior will send him away if you ask."

"I'm not worried about a fanatic monk. And he's popular with the people. What I care about is making the city government secure for Piero. He hasn't enough sense to manage on his own."

407

Ginevra was astonished. She had believed him blind to Piero's deficiencies.

Lorenzo smiled, reading her thoughts. "I have three sons, Contadina. One is foolish, one clever, one good. If I had to choose which should govern Florence, I would still have to make Piero the one. The cardinalate can do the family and the city the most real benefit, so it's right that the clever son should be cardinal.

"And Giuliano's sweet nature would make him the prey of every patronage seeker in Tuscany.

"That leaves the fool. I can compensate in advance for his foolishness."

The courtyard of the palace became a hubbub of people visiting Lorenzo, waiting to visit Lorenzo, leaving after having visited Lorenzo. He had his finger in every government pie. He even convinced the Signoria to enact a law making his approval necessary before a betrothal could be ceremonialized.

"I know which men and which families would like to seize power when I'm gone. There'll be no alliances between them."

Ginevra looked at his shaking hands and glittering eyes. He was driving himself to exhaustion, working day and night, enduring pain as long as he could, relying on Leoni's drugs when he could bear no more.

She begged him to rest.

"I can't, Contadina. I don't know how much time is left."

She had no response to that. Everyone close to him could see how ill he was.

The wonder was that he did not kill himself with work. Instead, after the winter he seemed to become stronger, to need less rest and less food than ever and to have regained the energy that illness had stolen from him.

He presided over the dinner table with all the laughter and wit and penetrating philosophical disputation of the past. He argued with Pico and Agnolo on levels so far beyond the understanding of the others that they begged for freedom from profundity.

He moved the arena for philosophy to Fra Mariano's study at San Gallo in the mornings and reinstituted the rispetti at the palace dinners in the evening.

Day after day he talked to committees and commissions, businessmen and merchants, giving attention and influence, preferment and privilege, gaining support for his policies and his son.

He visited Piero in his part of the palace, charmed Piero's wife Alfonsina, talked eagerly to his foolish son about the art of diplomacy and the challenge of government.

He had conferences with the younger children's tutors and ordered books for them from the scriptorium. And he invented new games to play with Contessina and Giulio and Giuliano because he could no longer roughhouse and become a child's steed.

On New Year's Day he set the spark to the fireworks he gave to the city, and on Easter he led the procession of his bankers' guild for the ceremonial presentation of candles to the Duomo.

He worked on the Carnival float himself, overseeing details with such care that Ghirlandaio threatened to destroy it rather than finish it. Lorenzo charmed him into forgiveness by writing a sonnet to his decorations. And he wrote four songs for Carnival.

"Lorenzo, I beg you to stop," Ginevra said a hundred times, but he only smiled and kissed her and told her to get the lutes for a duet or the cards or dice for a game.

More and more often she heard him screaming in the night. Then she dressed hurriedly. Often he sent Leoni to bring her to him when the cries stopped. He liked for her to sing him to sleep, he said. He was sure that his heart could hear, even if he was unconscious.

The gout was worse, Ginevra was certain. The knots of scarring were more pronounced, and the swelling subsided more slowly each time.

Lorenzo refused to give in to the disease. When his feet and legs would not carry him, he rode in "Cosimo's chair" until they were better. Then he ordered horses from the stables and took Ginevra and the children hawking in the woods near the villa at Fiesole.

"Leoni and I have defeated the curse of the Medici," he boasted.

But then in November a severe attack left his hands too swollen to write. Lorenzo was distraught. "I must send letters and gifts to people for Epiphany. Messengers are so slow in winter that they must be sent soon. Innocent is sick; he may be dying. I have to convince him to announce Giovanni's red hat, to make the appointment official. And I'm uneasy about France. This King Charles is only nineteen, and young men are ambitious for glory. I wish that King Louis had lived longer. He was a trustworthy friend. Ferrante is ill, too, and Alfonso has no love for me. I must make him our friend before his father dies and he takes the throne."

Ginevra swallowed tears. All this talk of death and dying. Could he think of nothing else? It seemed to her that Lorenzo was racing toward his own end, rushing forward to meet what he feared. He slept scarcely at all unless he was drugged. Even on the rare nights that he came to her bed the release of climax gave him little escape from his tightened nervousness. His naps, and her eyes' possession of him, were things of the past.

On the night before Advent began Ginevra heard Lorenzo scream. She dressed herself quickly and waited for Leoni's knock.

But Lorenzo's cries did not stop.

"Help him," she said when she ran into Lorenzo's room. "For the love of God, Doctor, give him the medicine."

Leoni was weeping. "If he has any more, Madonna, he will die. He has needed larger doses every time, and now the maximum is not enough to kill the pain without killing him."

The following day, when all the bells of Florence's churches were ringing, a secretive group left the Medici palace. The litter bearers were clumsy from nervousness, and their uneven progress brought moans from the blanket-swaddled figure inside.

Ginevra della Vacchia walked beside the litter, talking earnestly in a crooning tone. "We're going to the baths at Bagno a Ripoli, my beloved. It's not too far. We can walk it easily in two days. You'll get better there. You always feel better with the hot baths. The guards are with us, with horses and packhorses. We have everything we need, and when you're well, we'll ride home together. We'll race, the way we always do. There is the Magnificent, they'll say in the villages when we pass through them.

"Everything will be the way it used to be again."

Chapter Sixty·one

"The baths always cure me," Lorenzo said.

"I was sure they would," Ginevra agreed.

Both were lying, and both knew it.

Lorenzo was emaciated. His saddle was padded to soften the impact on his bony seat, and it had a built-up back to support his spine. They held the horses to a walk and stopped every few miles to dismount and rest by the side of the road.

The distance that Ginevra had covered on foot in two days took them three on horseback.

When they arrived at the palace, Cosimo's chair was ready. Stewards carried Lorenzo to his room and prepared him for bed.

Ginevra stayed in the courtyard. Lorenzo had made her promise to wait until he sent for her.

She walked slowly toward the garden, her steps as leaden as her heart. The sound of stifled weeping stopped her. The young sculptor Michelangelo was trying to hide behind an antique column in the corner.

Ginevra hurried to him.

He raised his tear-stained face from his arms. "I saw him, Madonna. He's dying. I love him. Why does he have to die?"

"I can't answer you," she said. Her pent-up tears burst from her eyes.

Michelangelo held out his callused workman's hands to her in sympathy. Ginevra clasped them. Together they mourned the approaching death of Lorenzo the Magnificent.

* * *

Lorenzo fought death. The disease was also inside his body now, a fever that never left him, and the killer gout wracked and twisted one joint after another. But he continued to work. When he could no longer stand, he sat at his desk. When he could not pull his misshapen spine erect, he dictated from his bed.

Leoni gave him ineffectual drugs.

Ginevra massaged him when he could stand to be touched.

Neither helped.

Lorenzo fought alone.

On their birthday, Ginevra dressed herself in the monk's disguise she had worn in Naples and walked beside the curtained litter that carried Lorenzo to the tomb of his grandfather.

The bearers withdrew, closing the great doors of the church behind them. They would wait until summoned, as Ginevra had ordered.

She opened the curtains that hid Lorenzo's deformity from the people of Florence.

"Was the pain too bad?" she asked.

"The bearers are skillful," Lorenzo said. His voice was unchanged, and his smile. Ginevra kissed his lips with a gossamer pressure.

"Call him for me," Lorenzo said. She knelt on the floor in front of the marble plaque that marked Cosimo's resting place and traced the letters of his epitaph with her fingers.

Pater Patriae

Lorenzo watched from his pallet. When she finished he spoke.

"Cosimo, here is your grandson Lorenzo. If you can hear me, then know this. I have carried out the tasks life gave me with honor. I have cared for the State. I have given the family six living children, one of my sons a Cardinal in the Church of Rome. I have preserved the peace you gave to the Republic, and I have brought peace to every corner of Italy as well. When we meet at the foot of the throne of God, I will be able to face you with pride. I made a vow to you when I became a man on this day twenty-two years ago. I have kept that vow.''

Lorenzo closed his eyes and breathed a deep sigh of exhaustion and completion. His pilgrimage was done.

''Well done, Lauro,'' said Ginevra.

Chapter Sixty-two

"Is this what you give me when I call for red? Fool!"

Ginevra heard Lorenzo's voice as soon as she entered the hallway. She smiled and hastened her steps. He sounded angry, and he sounded strong. A good day. She hurried to his room.

He was propped up on a mound of pillows. His freshly shaven face was flushed, and his eyes were blazing. A length of red silk made a vibrant slash across the bed. Lorenzo's crippled hands held crumpled wads of it.

The silk merchant was bent over, bobbing and bowing, making incoherent apologetic, frightened noises. Lorenzo's rage was magnificent.

"Red is the color of power and strength," he shouted. "It's a man's color. And you bring me this woman's boudoir rose. You must be blind, or expect me to be." He pushed the silk from him with the heels of his hands. "Take this gauze away, and bring me a thick silk. IN RED."

Ginevra ran to the bed, disentangled the fabric from his twisted fingers. She balled it up and thrust it into the merchant's arms. "Don't be slow in returning," she said with a smile. The man scurried away, still bowing and mumbling.

"Do you have them?" said Lorenzo. His words were an accusation.

Ginevra imitated his nasal voice, adding a dripping sweetness to it. "Good morning, Ginevra," she said, "how happy I am to see you. Were you able to get the drawings of the decorations from Sandro? You did? How very kind of you. I'm extremely grateful."

Lorenzo glared at her.

Ginevra raised her eyebrows for a moment, resumed her normal speech. "I have them. They're very beautiful. The stewards are mounting them on easels and bringing them up for you to study."

"I am happy to see you," Lorenzo said.

"As I am to see you, my love. You look very well and choleric. Are you able to take a massage?"

"No. I have work to do. Come sit by me and listen to my idea for the music."

She put a stool near the bed and sat beside him. With great gentleness she slid her fingers into his clubbed hand. Lorenzo's deformed thumb bent across them.

The ceremony for Giovanni's elevation to the cardinalate was scheduled for March sixth, little more than a month away. Lorenzo was organizing a celebration that would surpass anything ever seen in Florence. The project invigorated him, but he paid heavily for the bursts of energy. He had periods of excruciating pain and on some days he was too weak to open his eyes. He was a dying man determined to live to see the culmination of his ambitions.

On the day of Giovanni's honors, observers raced from the ceremony at the ancient Badia in Fiesole and horsemen stationed at every point of the procession sped to the palace as soon as it passed to report to Lorenzo.

Botticelli's arch of triumph was an explosion of color in silk hung above the Porta San Gallo, and twenty trumpeters atop the gate saluted the new cardinal when he entered the city.

Windows along the route displayed banners, flags and tapestries, and flowers carpeted the streets to the Duomo. The cathedral was so crowded that the procession could scarcely enter. All Florence wanted to see and pay tribute to their own Cardinal, son of their Magnificent.

Lorenzo could hear the cheering through his open window. Joyful tears spilled from his eyes. Ginevra caught them with a soft cloth before they could reach his velvet doublet. He was dressed in jewel-sewn splendor, a testimony that he was Lorenzo the Magnificent in his proudest role, father to the Cardinal Giovanni de' Medici.

When the mass ended the procession reformed. Followed by all the dignitaries of Florence it moved at a stately pace through the cheering crowds to the Medici palace and a banquet that lasted throughout the rest of the day.

Lorenzo was carried into the grand salone on a litter to see his son.

"He was at the center of the table on the elevated platform," Lorenzo told Ginevra when he was back in his bed, "wearing his red hat . . ." His voice was faint. "Sing me to sleep, Contadina. I can rest now."

From the walls of the great banquet room the Medici coat of arms glowed in embroidered stitches of spun gold thread on the background of thick red silk.

And that night all the rooftops of Florence blazed with torches that lit the city's streets for the bands of musicians that played and sang the music that Lorenzo had written for his son's celebration.

"Contadina?"
"I'm here."
"I want to go home to Careggi."

Chapter Sixty-three

The whole world knew now that Lorenzo de' Medici was dying. Couriers brought letters from every city in Europe to Careggi. Lorenzo's secretary, with a phalanx of scribes, answered them from the scriptorium set up in the glassed loggia.

Officials of the city government and ambassadors from Florence's allies walked around the garden and the courtyard in small, conspiratorial groups. They talked in hushed voices until they herded to the foot of the stairs whenever Lorenzo's doctor appeared with a report on his condition.

From the pulpit of San Lorenzo, Savonarola's denunciations rolled like thunder over the heads of wailing, terrified throngs of people. "God's punishment is on the tyrant Lorenzo! He is dying, stained by the sins that will bring down the wrath of Heaven on all lovers of luxury and vain display. Repent, before the sword of Judgment falls!"

Lorenzo's bedroom at Careggi was small and plain. It had only one window, and the walls and floor were bare of decoration. His bed was in the center of the room; four lemon trees from the loggia filled the corners. The sharp sweetness of their blossoms refreshed the heavy air of the room; the window was closed because the pressure of the light spring breeze caused him great pain.

Two nursing brothers from the monastery at Camaldoli sat on stools at the head of the bed. They prayed silently, moving only if the doctor asked for their help.

Leoni paced from window to door to the bed and back to the window again in a ceaseless triangle. His small gold spurs clicked against the polished clay tiles of the floor. His plump shiny hands rubbed each other in synchronization with his steps, and his shoulders sagged with despair. He had believed until now that in the end Lorenzo would somehow recover.

Ginevra observed the little man's anguish and found it in her heart to pity him. Then her eyes returned to Lorenzo.

He was like an olive tree, she thought, his legs and arms gnarled and bent, his color a luminescent gray. She wondered if she should tell him her thoughts. The olive tree was the essence of the Tuscan countryside that he loved so much; many of his poems were attempts to fix in words the beauty of its silver and green leaves and the grace of its lifting branches.

She'd wait and see if he wanted her to talk. More and more he wanted only that she be there when he opened his eyes. Listening tired him, and he needed his waning strength for his farewells.

He had sent for Piero first. "You must be like a father to Contessina and Giuliano," he said. "And tell Giovanni that I put Giulio in his care. He is the son of my beloved brother and deserving of the family's protection. Soon he will be fourteen, and he should enter the Church, where Giovanni can obtain preferment for him . . . You will do these things, Piero?"

"I will, Father."

Lorenzo smiled at his foolish son. Then, for the final time, he tried to explain to Piero his role as head of the Republic.

Ginevra could read on Lorenzo's face that he knew his words were wasted, but he had to try.

Later, when he regained the power to speak, he saw the old men of the Platonic Academy one by one, talking to them in the fluent, beautifully musical Latin that was his alone.

Agnolo Poliziano saw each of them to the door, his arm across the philosophers' bent sorrowing shoulders.

"Let me stay with you, Lorenzo," Agnolo had said, and Lorenzo had granted him his wish.

It was the fifth of April.

Ginevra heard voices outside the door and started toward it, but Agnolo was ahead of her. He opened it gently and stepped outside, closing it behind him.

Lorenzo opened his eyes. "What is it, Contadina?"

"I don't know. Agnolo will tell us . . ."

As she spoke, Poliziano returned, accompanied by a tall white-haired man wearing costly fur-trimmed robes. "Lorenzo," said Agnolo, "the Duke of Milan has sent his personal physician. This is Lazaro di Pavia."

The doctor strode to the bed. His elaborate griffin-carved gold spurs crashed against the tiles. He looked at Lorenzo's face. Then his eyes moved slowly down Lorenzo's body, his jeweled hand tossing aside the cloth that lay across Lorenzo's hips.

Ginevra rose from her seat to drag him away.

"I can cure this sickness," he said loudly.

Lorenzo's pain-dulled eyes opened wide, and desperate hope shined through them. Ginevra's hand flew to her heart as if to feel it breaking. She looked away, to hide her expressive face from Lorenzo, and she saw in Agnolo's eyes the same despairing compassion she was feeling. Then he willed himself to smile. "I'll leave you, then," he said to Lorenzo, "while Messer Lazaro begins his treatment." He left the room quickly.

He will be able to cry, Ginevra thought. I envy him the release of it. She smiled at Lorenzo. "Lodovico must love you very much," she said.

Lazaro ordered the ingredients for the medicine he declared would effect the cure: pearls, rubies, emeralds. He had, he said, brought everything else with him.

He supervised Leoni when he ground the jewels to powder in a silver mortar. Then he insisted that everyone turn his back while he added ingredients from his sandalwood apothecary chest.

Then he mixed the medicine with wine in a gold cup and gave it to Lorenzo to drink.

Ginevra stared with horror at the terrible efforts he made before he succeeded in swallowing.

The next day the treatment was repeated. It was raining, and Ginevra fled to the open windows of her own room to breathe in the clean wet air and wash her mind clear of the murderous anger she felt for Lazaro.

Lorenzo was talking to Agnolo when she returned. "Why hasn't Pico come?"

"He didn't want to disturb you."

"Send for him, Agnolo. Tell him to come after the storm passes." Lorenzo's voice was very weak.

Pico was an explosion of energy into the stagnant air of the room. He talked rapidly, as he always did, with his customary crackling enthusiasm. He acted as if Lorenzo were not ill, as if death were not nearby. Ginevra soundlessly blessed him for it.

He and Agnolo argued about iconography, Pico maintaining that the widespread symbolism of the lion as the Christ-figure was inappropriate for the speaker of the Beatitudes, Agnolo supporting the validity of the King of Beasts as symbol of the Second Coming. Lorenzo looked from one to the other as each spoke; he had more vitality than Ginevra had seen for weeks.

"The lion is overused," Pico declared. "Any meaning it might have is diluted by the using. It's the symbol of too many rulers, too many states. Florence is not the only one to have adopted the lion. Besides, it's a volatile, undependable creature. Yesterday in the storm, lightning struck the Duomo and broke off a piece of marble from the lantern. When it fell, the lions went crazy in their pen and started to fight. Two of them were killed."

"Where did the marble fall?" Lorenzo's voice was cracked; his eyes were dark with apprehension.

"It did no harm," Pico said. "It didn't even break any tiles on the dome. It shattered on the piazza, near the Via Ricasoli, but no one was there because of the rain."

Lorenzo's exhaled breath was a moan. "The direction

of the Medici palace,'' he whispered. ''I am going to
die . . . Agnolo, bring Fra Mariano to me.'' His eyes
closed; his face was stark and bloodless.

Fra Mariano administered the last rites and said the
prayers for the dead.
But Lorenzo's suffering was not yet done.

The following day the door flew open, sending a swirl
of air across the room. Ginevra turned toward it in protest.
Savonarola stood in the doorway. His hood was
thrown back, and his eyes were green sparks above his
massive predatory nose. His fleshy lips parted. Spittle
flew from them. ''Strumpet,'' he shouted, pointing and
staring at her. ''Will you take a dying man to the eternal
pit of fire with you? Leave this place.''
She looked at Lorenzo. His eyes were open, gazing
at his fanatic enemy. They were calm. Alarm entered
them when Savonarola rushed toward Ginevra, his fist
raised like a club.
She faced him, her arms outstretched, shielding Lorenzo from the devil. Her body shook uncontrollably,
cold with dread.''Go,'' said Lorenzo.
Ginevra rocked from the blow of his rejection. Her
arms closed across her body to contain the agony of it.
She bent and stumbled, under Savonarola's arm, to the
door.

Poliziano found her on the floor in her room, her head
covered by her arms, her knees drawn up to warm her
shivering body.
''Ginevra, come quickly. He's near the end.''
''The devil?''
''Gone.''
''He didn't hurt . . .''
''Of course not. He asked Lorenzo if he was at peace
with God, and when he said yes, the friar gave him his
blessing . . . Come, now. Lorenzo's asking for you.''
The anguish left her, and she ran to him.
Lorenzo's eyes were closed; his lips were moving,

the sounds too faint to hear. Ginevra put her ear close to his mouth.

"Con . . . tadina . . ."

Her heart leapt in her breast. "I'm here," she said quietly. "Here I am, my beloved."

"Sing . . . to sleep." Lorenzo's eyelids quivered, but could not open. His hand shifted a fraction of space.

Ginevra slid her fingers inside his. Love made her voice strong and free of sorrow while she sang the simple ancient songs of the countryside.

ALEXANDRA RIPLEY grew up in Charleston, South Carolina, the setting for her bestselling novels *Charleston* and *On Leaving Charleston*.

When she was in her twenties, she lived for a number of years in the Villa Pazzi, on a hill outside Florence. There, she developed a lifelong interest in the Pazzi family and an enduring love for Florence. In this novel, the Villa Pazzi is called La Vacchia, the name that was used when it was built by the Pazzi in the fifteenth century.